The Fall of Tyr:
Book Four of
The Circle of Ceridwen Saga

Also by Octavia Randolph

The Circle of Ceridwen

Ceridwen of Kilton

The Claiming

Tindr

Light, Descending

The Tale of Melkorka: A Novella

Ride: A Novella

The Hall of Tyr

Octavia Randolph

The Hall of Tyr is the fourth book in The Circle of Ceridwen
Saga by Octavia Randolph
Copyright 2014 Octavia Randolph This print version 2014

ISBN 978-0-9854582-8-7

Pyewacket Press

Bookcover design: DesignForBooks.com

Photo credits: Viking ship, iStockphoto©Sylphe_7;
Landscape/Limestone stacks, iStockphoto©Bildvision_AB.
Textures, graphics, photo manipulation, and map by Michael
Rohani.

The Circle of Ceridwen Saga employs British
spellings, alternate spellings, archaic words, and
oftentimes unusual verb to subject placement. This
is intentional. A Glossary of Terms will be found at
the end of the novel.

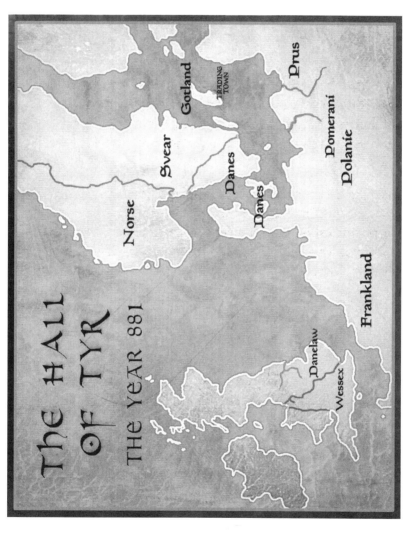

Contents

The Hall of Tyr

Chapter the First: The Hall of Tyr

Island of Gotland

Late Summer 881

I opened my eyes and saw that day was upon us. A thin beam of Sun streamed through the casement in the stone wall, lighting my red gown where it had dropped on the wooden floor. I lay on my belly next to Sidroc, who still slept. I kissed his ear and whispered, "We need food."

He stirred, and rolled his shoulders, and then lifted himself on his elbows and looked across the floor boards. He smiled at me, and turned his head to the other end of the hall.

"We need everything," was what he said. I laughed too, for now in daylight we saw that save the fire pit and us, our new home was utterly empty. There was no table, no bench, not a single rush stand for fire light. We would have to buy or build everything we needed. But I welcomed even that, that everything in our lives together should be new.

It was the second time we had awakened and not arisen, and I felt the blush upon my cheek as he lay back and looked at me. To hide my face I reached for the pack that held my shift, found it, and pulled it on over my head. "I will bring water from the well," I told him, and began to rise. But he shook his head, and reached out and took hold of the hem of my shift and pulled me back down to him.

When we finally arose I took up my red gown, and began folding it so I might lay it away. Sidroc came up behind

1

me and wrapped his arm about my neck. "Do not put it too far; I want you to wear it tonight," he whispered. I lowered my chin and kissed his wrist in answer.

Now I pulled on my russet gown, glad to think that soon I could wash the dried salt water from all my clothes, and choosing this as it was much the cleanest. I put the thick necklace of braided silver around my neck, and draped my green wool mantle over my shoulders, for tho' the Sun shone bright I knew the day might cool quickly.

When we had dressed we stood within the hall in which we had just passed our first night, and looked around us. It had three doors, the broad front door of oak which looked out to the sea and which sat in a narrow end of the hall, another at the opposite end, which I could guess must go out to the kitchen yard, and one in the long side. The grey-white stone walls at each narrow end reached up solid and strong, and the timber of the long walls was well fitted and tight. The steeply-pitched timber roof rose above us like hands with pressed fingertips, and where the narrow stone walls met the roof at the ends there was a small opening at the gable-peak to carry off smoke.

The few little alcoves were empty but could easily be made welcoming, and the plank floor beneath our feet was smooth and firm. The whole place gave out a dry and pleasant smell of old wood and hard stone. A door led to the separate room in which I had changed my gown last night, and we stepped through it together. It was not large, but had the same smooth plank floor, and a window high in the wall for light.

"This will be our treasure room," Sidroc said. When we had stood outside the night before I had felt my heart move with longing to the small wood and stone hall, and now Sidroc gladdened me the more by saying, "I will buy this house from the brewster; whatever she asks for it I will give."

The Hall of Tyr

We made ready to leave the hall and looked at our packs ranged about the floor. Sidroc's shield and two spears were there too, and for the first time he felt safe in leaving them behind. I saw him hesitate a moment after he buckled on his seax, and then reach for and put on his sword as well. "Until we are known," he told me, and I nodded.

Until we were known here in Gotland he thought it best to show his weapons, but from all he had told me of the place I did not think he would for long feel the need to carry the heavy sword. He opened the broad wood door to the bright morning outside, and after he turned the key in the iron box-lock we looked out over the trading town, and then out over the wide blue sea behind it. We held nothing in our hands, nothing, and to feel this freedom of walking unencumbered after so many days of shouldering heavy packs made the lightness in my heart the sweeter.

We walked down the hill, passing the few small crofts that lined the narrow road. In the yard of one a man was at work with an adze smoothing a long wood plank, and he lifted his head and nodded at us as we passed. The brew-house was before us, the awnings once again partially furled, but the door was ajar and we stepped within. It would be hours before it opened, but it was not quite deserted, for at the same trestle at which had sat a few folk the night before now sat the brewster, wiping the pottery cups in which she served her ales.

We walked towards her and she raised her head and spoke. "Goþr morgun," she said in her Norse tongue, and nodded at both of us in turn. Sidroc returned the greeting, for his tongue was the Norse of the land of the Danes; and I did as well, for if this was to be my new home, I must learn its speech and so be able to speak to its people.

The brewster said a few things to Sidroc, at which he answered and nodded, and then she gestured with her hand that we sit at her table. She rose, her ring of brass and iron keys tinkling softly at her waist, and went out through two hanging curtains. She soon returned with a wooden platter on which sat two cups of warm meat broth, a pile of small loaves, a lump of butter more yellow than ever I had seen, and a small pot of a light brown paste. She also brought two pottery bowls, from which wooden spoons peeked out, resting in something creamy white. She placed a little pot of honey between us.

"How rich a land this is, that honey is given out in brew-houses," I said to Sidroc. I dipped my spoon into the bowl, and found it held something thick and cool and tangy. The brewster called out something to Sidroc, and he answered and turned to me.

"It is cow's milk, thickened from standing," he explained. "She says to put the honey on it."

Only when I began to eat and drink did I know how hungry I was. The tangy cow's milk I liked very much, and the honey was of the best, mild and almost as fragrant as the flowers themselves. The loaves were tender and fresh, and the yellow butter as rich as the finest cheese.

"What grass they must have, to make such butter as this," I told Sidroc after our first pangs had been stilled. The little pot held a kind of cold pounded fish; spread on the bread with some of the golden butter it was savoury and much to my liking. I ate, and drank, and Sidroc too ate so that the brewster smiled and brought us more of all.

When at last we were full she sat across from us and stopped in her wiping tasks. She had a whole range of cups behind her, ready on a table for the afternoon's trade. But now she looked at us and spoke again.

"Mitt nafr ir Rannveig," she said, touching her chest where rested ten or more strands of bright glass bead necklaces. "Rannveig" she repeated, looking at me.

Sidroc spoke, and said his name and a few words more, and then looked to me. I smiled and touched my own chest, and tried to repeat what Rannveig had said. "Mitt nafr ir Ceridwen," I told her, and her smile let me know I was not too far off.

Sidroc and she spoke a while, and while it was clear they did not understand all of what the other said, their speech was near enough.

"She will feed us here until we have set up our household; and tells me who to see to buy what we need," he told me.

"I want to tell her, thank you," I answered. I knew the sound was close to my own word, "thank". "Is it "Þakk", as it is in your tongue?"

They both smiled at me. "Þakk," I told Rannveig, and Sidroc said, "Good."

I looked with gratitude to the brewster. She was past middle-age, but with a vigour unslowed by her bulk and years. Her long hair had paled to grey where it showed under her head-wrap, and I thought it must have been reddish when she was young, for her skin, tho' lined now, was fair with rosy cheeks and a dusting of freckles upon her small nose. Her pale blue eyes were steady, sharp, yet not unkind, and she held me in her gaze now. She was our first friend in this place, and had welcomed us with food and drink and her snug hall at the top of the hill.

As we rose to leave a young man entered through the split curtains. He paused when he saw us, but Rannveig waved him over. He was fairly tall but slightly built, with light brown hair resting on his shoulders. His blue eyes were so light as to be blue-white, like that of a rare dog or wolf. Those eyes lingered now on Rannveig before once again looking to us. "Tindr," she said, touching his arm, and I took this to be both his name and her son.

She said more, gesturing to her own ear, and then making quick motions to her son with her hands.

"Her son is deaf," Sidroc said, "but he is a good worker, and will come and serve us if we like."

"Já, já," I quickly said with a nod, using the word I knew was Yes. I wanted to repay her trust in this way, and accept her offer of her son's service. Tindr had been looking at me, and now a shy smile broke across his face, and he nodded too. Then I looked to Sidroc, abashed I had agreed without asking him. But he gladdened me with his answer. "The hall will be yours to run as you like," he told me, with a nod.

He looked back to Rannveig and her son, and spoke a few words more. As we turned to go he told me, "Only I asked the boy not to come for two days," which made me hide my smile behind my hand.

We stepped out into the smooth clay road and looked at the range of buildings fronting the water. They were mostly tall and narrow, built of long staves of fir timber set upright, and some had end walls of blocks of grey-white stone, as ours did. The timber walls on most were weathered to a light silvery grey, but some had walls stained a rich and dark red. I had seen the insides of great halls and churches lime-washed for lightness, and even with bright designs of vines or animals worked in coloured paints, as at Kilton, but never before had I seen the outside of walls with any colour, and these red wooden buildings much pleased me. The steep roofs were neither of woven thatch nor sheets of lead, but broad planks of wood, often spotted over with small clumps of bright green moss.

Sidroc too looked at the red timber walls, and asked a man about them. "They are stained with a paint made from copper," he told me. "Like rust," he thought aloud, and indeed the walls looked a bit like bright new rust.

Some of the buildings were store-houses where merchants and tradesmen must keep their goods, but others were clearly shops and stalls where goods of all kinds could be had. We looked to the sea, now at full tide, for the shingle beach was narrow, and saw that our little boat was still high and dry amongst the pebbles where Sidroc had hauled it. Perhaps it was the golden Sun, and our nearness to the water, but the air itself seemed wonderfully clear, with a crisp freshness to it when I drew breath. Mewling sea birds dipped and rose above us, their hinged wings dark and then white as they turned in the sky.

First we just walked the length of the road, enjoying our full bellies and the sunshine that fell upon our faces. We passed shops where iron goods such as cauldrons and basins sat upon tables or hung from overhead supports; and stalls selling bolts of wools and linen, the wools dyed blue, red, or green, and others which held barrels of plump red apples, white turnips, and the furling heads of green cabbages. Inside doorways we could see men and women bent at work over leathern hides, where shoes and pack bags were crafted. A man was striking together short wood staves to make drawing-buckets in one stall, while next to him two women, young and old, carved hair combs from flat pieces of veined ox horn.

Almost opposite the long pier there was a tar-seller, with pots of the gooey black stuff giving up their smoky scent. "With so much pine it would be easy to burn it into tar," said Sidroc, lifting his head to the forests that ringed the edges of the road. He had told me it was a rich land, and indeed it seemed that all needs could be met here on the trading road. "And here he is closest to the ships which come in, in need of fixing their leaks."

In the middle of the settlement we came across those who handle precious goods, for there we saw a worker cutting beads out of a small store of yellow chunks of amber heaped up before him, and next to him, a shop which had arrayed on long tables all manner of silver goods, beads and necklets, and necklaces of braided silver chain such as I wore as gift from Sidroc.

The folk working, and walking too amongst us, were a good-looking lot, fair and on the tall side, with open welcoming faces that glanced our way and nodded in greeting as we passed. The women had mostly yellow hair, and many of the men as well, and the women wore the large paired bronze brooches on their over-gowns as did the women of the Danes, and their head-wraps tied behind their heads, in the way of the Danes. Their brooches tho' were not of simple ovals dressed with bosses, but instead were cast into shapes of animals' heads, cats or cows or other beasts. Many of them wore amber beads at their throats, or strung from brooch to brooch, and some too silver necklaces or bracelets. The men wore the same tunic and leggings of Saxon or Dane, and hanging at the waist a long knife like that Sidroc once had carried. Some of the men passing us let drop their eyes, and we saw they took in the bright hilted seax Sidroc wore across his belly, which told them he had fought and won in far Angle-land.

It was a trading place, where merchants came from many parts. The Gotland folk would be used to strangers, and we answered their greetings in kind. In the past weeks when we walked amongst strangers Sidroc was the one on whom eyes fell, and returned to. If I was looked at but briefly it was because of him I stood by. He had always been heavily armed, and that was part of it; but I thought the set of his face when we moved in crowds the greater cause; alert, watchful, but not wary. His height, the scar upon his face, his eyes, so dark a blue they flashed like flint; those we passed saw and took note.

As the buildings thinned we walked on, still following the shoreline. We saw before us a cleared area across the road from the shingle beach, from which a tree trunk arose, of a girth too wide for a man to encircle with his arms. We stopped when we saw it, for it was a carving of a God. It had wide staring eyes, a peaked cap like that which hunters wear upon its head, and a long and braided beard which shot forward from its chin. It was painted in colours of green and yellow and brown, and was not the rotting and abandoned images of the Gods I had seen in Wessex or even at Four Stones; this was firm and solid and cared-for. It was almost twice as tall as me and I stood looking up at it in wonder.

"Freyr," breathed Sidroc at my side. The images of the Old Gods I had seen were all of one-eyed Woden, All-Father, who Sidroc called Odin, the God of wisdom and rune-making; this was Freyr, the God of bounty and increase in animals and crops and folk as well, just as his sister Freyja was the Goddess of these things. Behind him were set many shorter poles into the ground, some topped with small platforms or projecting tines upon which animals had been Offered, for fur and feathers were stuck on bits of bone caught there. I thought of the piglet, a beast sacred to Freyja, that Sidroc had killed and stuck upon such an offering pole at Four Stones for me.

The face of Freyr was not fierce, the wide and staring eyes looked out, I knew, in protection for the things the God loved; and tho' it filled me with awe I had no fear of it.

"It is for merchants and sea-men, that they might ask for profit in their dealings when they leave, and give thanks for their safe arrival when they return," said Sidroc. He looked to me and smiled. "Where Freyr is so honoured, so is his sister; she has led you to the right place, shield-maiden."

We stood some little time looking at it, and turned our heads so that we saw what the God did. He faced East, and so saw each rising Sun, promise of increase, and saw too each ship as it left and sailed in. I recalled my long-dead kinsman telling me of Freyr's magic ship, which only met favourable winds; so great that it could ferry all the Gods, and yet so small the God could fold it up and carry it in a pouch at his belt when not needed. The riches of Gotland came and went across the sea, and here Freyr was God of Increase, and Lord of Ships.

Then we were at the end of the road, for it dwindled to a track. Beyond it were sheep pens, holding sheep with curling horns and long springy fleece; and a few pens too for cattle. These were smaller than the cattle of Angle-land, and had long horns, shaggy red or spotted brown coats, and lively tails that slapped at a few late Summer flies on their flanks. Then we neared tall wooden frameworks where flayed fish dried in the sun, racks of them; and our noses too told us of these drying fish.

"They will sell much of this," Sidroc thought aloud, and I knew that dried and salted fish was valued, and not only by sea-men on voyages, for it gave nourishment to all in deep winter, long after fishing boats could be launched.

He looked along the beach beyond the long drying racks to where stout-hulled fishing boats were heaved up. There were two-score or more boats there, broad-beamed for both fish and to carry cargo. "Fishing is almost done for the year; I will easily find men to help me build the tables and benches we need."

Now that we had passed through the whole of the settlement we could walk back and begin to buy what we most needed. Nearly all of our wealth I wore, for about my shoulders was my wool mantle with the gold pieces sewn into the hem.

"Do we need gold now?" I asked, lifting the hem of the mantle and wondering why I had not cut out at least one piece before we had left the hall.

Sidroc considered a moment before answering. "We need to buy more than we can carry. I will have the goods we seek brought to us, and we can pay then."

But first he had me take his seax tip and snip the threads from one of the tight channels that Burginde had stitched, and free one shining piece of gold. I placed it in his hand and smiled, and he smiled too as he placed his other hand over mine.

To see him thus, free of care and smiling, and to know I was at the heart of it brought a flush of joy to my own heart. We had won our way out of danger, yes; but there was an added ease about him, and it was this: Fate and the Gods had brought us to a land like unto his own, with a speech close unto his own speech, and folk who held the same beliefs and customs. After ten years of living in a strange land he would feel at home again. His voice when he had said the name of Freyr told me this.

We headed back to the workshops and stalls. Our first stop was to the silver-smith, which puzzled me until I saw Sidroc lay the coin upon the man's wooden chopping block. The silver smith swiftly chopped it into eighths with his sharp hatchet, and Sidroc placed the precious gold pieces in his belt with our dwindling silver.

We went then from stall to stall, choosing cooking pots and toasting forks and basins and buckets, wooden and crockery bowls and cups and some of bronze too, carved stone cressets for oil light, and small iron cressets on stands as well, jars of whale oil to fuel them, a spool of braided linen wick, tallow tapers, lengths of linen for sheets and towels, bags of cooking grains of oats and barley and rye, great clusters of purple grapes, and small baskets of apples, medlars and pears. I thought we were done when Sidroc paused a moment in the road.

"Ah –" he said. "I promised you a comb." We turned back a few stalls, to where the two women sat at their work-bench, sawing and polishing. They had an array of finished combs set out before them, small and large, fine toothed and widely spaced, all carved from the veined horns of oxen. I chose one of the longer, wider-spaced ones, a good fit for my thick and wavy hair. The cool smoothness of the horn made it a pleasure in the hand, and as I carried it away I looked forward to using it for the first time.

We headed back then, and as we passed the brew house waved at Rannveig as she stood pulling up the awnings to signal she was open for the day.

As we began up the hill I turned to look back. I could not see the huge carving of Freyr, but I was thinking of it, and then thinking something more. "There is no preaching-cross," I thought aloud; for a place so small would not likely have a church or chapel, even if some of the folk were Christian.

Sidroc gave a laugh. "Then we are safe from their bells and their chanting," he said. He looked across the settlement to its boundaries, and then out to the endless expanse of sea.

"Yes," he ended, "I think here we will be safe." The note of his voice told me it was not priests he thought of.

Then from the side yard of one of the crofts an iron cooper's hoop came rolling in front of us, chased by a gang of six or seven children, laughing and waving their turning-sticks in their hands. One boy had bright coppery curls. He turned his head to call back to his fellows, and tho' his face was so different from my own Ceric's, my heart of a sudden clenched as he ran by.

I know a little sound escaped my throat at this, and Sidroc too had seen the boy. He said nothing, but touched my hand.

That night we went down to Rannveig once more, and she fed us a meal of smoked pig and boiled barley and lately made ewe's cheeses and much of her good and strong ale. It was clear her business was a good one. Local folk used her brew-house as a gathering place to visit and to drink, and she fed those merchants and other travellers passing through. Men and women from the trading road sat about her tables, drinking of her ale and talking, or gaming with dice or bones. They looked over at us, and Rannveig spoke to them, and they nodded their heads to us in acceptance. Back at the hall our new goods sat ranged about the floor, and the tradesmen and workers who had carried them in that day were now home with their silver, and some with thin slices of gold.

We walked up the hill to the hall waiting there for us. As Sidroc turned the key in the lock to let us in he looked up at the peaked roof. "I will call it Tyrsborg," he said. I knew this meant the hall of Tyr, the God to whom he had given himself, the one to whom he credited the strength in his arm in winning our way to safety at last.

It was almost dark, and we used the rush torch Rannveig had given us to light the fire in the fire pit. I had poured oil into the cressets before we had left, so we had both the light of our wood fire and oil light to see by. The cressets were shallow bowls carved of the same grey-white stone as the walls of our house, and as I handled them for the first time they already had a familiar and welcome feel. I set the cressets near the fire pit, where our bedrolls lay, and our shadows were cast against the bare walls as we moved about. I was grateful for the light, and yet it made me for a moment feel almost shy, too.

Sidroc had asked me to again wear the red gown with the coloured thread-work he had bought me at the first trading post at which we had landed. Again I went into the room – the room which would be our treasure room – and stripped off my clothing. I put the gown on over my naked skin. I tipped the tiny pottery vessel of rose oil to my throat and placed a drop of its precious scent in the hollow there.

Again I came out to find him waiting by the bedroll. But this time the silver disk bracelet was on my own wrist, where he had fastened it last night before we gave ourselves, one to the other. I went to him and he took my hands and enfolded them to his chest, and kissed my fingertips. His lips went from my fingers to my chin and then to my own lips, and as he grasped my hands in his own we kissed. He broke from my lips and breathed in my ear, "Now I will take the gown off you."

When he had done so last night I felt almost a maid again; his ten years of wanting me took me back to the day when he had held me, a girl of fifteen, hard against him by the fire pit at Four Stones, and held himself back from doing more. Fate had divided us, but Fate and his desire had brought us back together once again.

Tonight I felt fully a woman, a woman who loved, and one who would give and receive full measure as proof of that love, as I had not done in over two years. In the last two years I had known great loss, suffering, despair; and then fear unto death as a captive, or from drowning.

This hardship and pain had been mine, but now I lived and was safe, and stood with a man who had fought hard to win both me and our safety. All we had lived through, alone and together, had brought us here; it was the web of Fate which brought me to this moment in which I not only was desired, but could feel the heat of animal desire rising within me once again.

His hands reached to pull at my gown, but I gave a little shake of my head and stayed them with my own. He wore his tunic and leggings and I pulled at the hem of his tunic. He let me pull it off, and I pressed my hands onto his bare chest. The outline of the blue dragon was faint, but I could just trace it in the flickering light, and I did so with my fingertip. Then I leaned forward and kissed his chest, and ran my fingers up the sides of his waist into his armpits, and curled them in the hair there as my lips travelled up to his throat. He let out a soft sound, and his head fell back, and I reached up on tiptoe to kiss his face and lips.

He drew his arms about me and pressed me to him, and we kissed deep and long. He reached for my skirts but again I stopped him, holding his hands back and forcing him to just kiss me. When we drew breath I placed my hands on his leggings and pulled at the fastener at the waist. The toggle opened. I knelt and gently pulled down the leggings, freeing him.

He pulled me up and now I let him draw off my gown. He looked at my face and my body as he had the first night, with burning eyes, and now he spoke to me.

"You are magnificent, like Freyja herself."

For answer I reached down and took his prick in my hand and raised myself on tiptoe to straddle it in the damp fur between my thighs. He made a soft groan and pulled me against him and we dropped together to our knees on my plush weaving.

His desire for me was as great this second night as it had been the first; perhaps the greater as he now knew I welcomed and returned that desire. His strength as he lifted and moved me thrilled me, and the surety of his hands and mouth as they caressed me made me pant. But he did not rush to feel me beneath him, but spent long kissing my face and breasts and belly, and stroking my arms and legs, feeling and knowing each part of me. By the greater glow of the cressets he gazed upon my body, and to see the light in his eyes as he did so gave me a flush of pride. Then his mouth followed where his stroking fingers had been, and he used his lips and tongue to explore and tease me until I cried out in supremest pleasure. Still panting I reached for him, wanting to give to him that bliss he had given me, and with an urgency to feel him within me, to surrender every part of my woman's body to him, and feel the power of his prick filling my wet and waiting woman's hollow. I pulled his hips to mine, longing to receive and shelter his man's body in my own womanly one. Even then, hanging above me, he took his time, giving and receiving such pleasure that I wished each moment to be endless, and yet yearned for every new way in which he touched and possessed me. One moment I would be pinned beneath him as he held my arms over my head as he filled me with deep and urgent thrusts, and the next he would pull me atop him so I might ride him freely at my own will. Through it all he kept his gaze upon me as we entwined and clung together in passion's dance. When we finally lay still he spoke to me.

"Ten years I waited for you. It will take ten years of this, of touching you like this, of having you like this, to satisfy me."

Tears were in my eyes at his tenderness, and his long wanting of me.

"It is you I love," he went on. "It is you I have only loved, shield-maiden."

I kissed his eyes, his lips, the long scar beneath his left eye, and whispered back. "And I love you, Sidroc. A part of me always has, and now, all of me."

We lay hard by the cressets, and in their dancing light I saw the scar that curved against his ribs under his left arm. My fingers went to it, and traced it, and then my lips too touched it. I raised my head and saw his eyes were closed, but a faint smile was upon his lips.

"Yes," he said. "That night in the hall. From that night came everything."

It was the night I had searched and dressed this wound, and he had first given me the silver disk bracelet that was once again circling my wrist.

He went on, "I had already marked you for my own. But it was that night I knew you would be mine. When you spat in my wound we were mingled, forever." He shook his head. "I thought soon you would be my wife. Then the Gods moved us, like game-pieces, far apart from the other."

He reached for the hand that still lay upon his scar. "But all is restored. One night like this is worth ten years of nights, waiting."

I awoke later in the dark, and reached my hand out past my plush weaving to touch the solid planks of the floor boards. I pressed my palm against it, feeling that it did not move. I was not aboard a ship; I was safe and on dry land. It was not that I rode the night-mare, but that sense that I had roused myself just before I had found myself carried away, bridle-less, upon her back, to fearful sights I could not stop.

Sidroc's hand moved and he touched me. "Shield-maiden," he whispered.

The Hall of Tyr

I turned to him. "You are awake," I answered.

"Yes," he said, and wrapped his arm about me. "Did you dream?" he asked.

I shook my head. "I feared I would ride the night-mare, but woke up." I felt him nod, and then I went on, "But you yourself are awake."

"Yes," he said, and breathed out a long breath. "Was it of the ship?" he asked me.

"Yes; of the ships, all of them," I answered, squeezing my eyes closed to block the memories that began to rise up. The Idrisid ship in which I had been marked a flesh-slave, the ship of the Danes from which I had leapt into the cold Baltic during the bloody battle, and the little boat which Sidroc had claimed as plunder and in which we nearly had sunk in the storm.

"I will never take you on a ship again," he promised, and tried to jest by adding, "Nor will I throw you from one."

I buried my head in his chest. My gratitude at our safety was beyond speech, and I just lay still, my face pressed to his bare skin. At length he began to speak again. His words were quiet in the still night.

"I too awoke thinking of the ships. When I fought on Red-beard's ship, to aid Ulf who was attacking..."

He paused such a long time that I knew he did not like to follow the end of his thoughts. I recalled what he had said just before he turned to fight. It was said more to himself or to the Gods than to me, and was not a challenge, but a vow. "I will not die; not like this," he had said, before he lunged, sword drawn, into the fray.

"Few battles I have been in were bloodier. Dane against Dane. Ulf's men were good warriors all, and Red-beard was defending his own ship and kin; it was bound to be bad. And on a ship…"

I gave my head a little shake. The desperate men crammed into narrow quarters, the streams of hot gore pouring from hacked limbs, the smell of blood as I clawed my way to the side of the ship to free myself from the terror: It was all too near.

"So many men dead," he went on. "The sounds of their screams. The moment when your eyes meet as you drive home your spear or sword. These were men I had eaten and gamed with. That young whelp – Red-beard's nephew – he was just a boy.

"And for what," he went on. "Red-beard had little on his ship; Ulf won it, but little else.

"But worse for me was the red-sailed ship of the Idrisids. I was captive, and could not fight. All my words could do nothing to free us. All my wealth meant nothing. I could not think of how I could help us; I could not know where they took us, only that we would at last sail South and there I would be made to fight, and you be taken from me."

I felt him shake his head before he drew breath and went on. "Then everything changed. Ulf and his partner attacked the Idrisids. I had a chance. I could fight – we both could – and we won our freedom. Tyr guided my arm, and Freyja guarded my shield-maiden."

He was stroking my hair with his hand when I spoke my wish.

"I do not want you to fight again, Sidroc. Ever."

"I do not want to kill another man," he allowed. "There have been many. Now thanks to your gold I can set up in trade, and so win treasure that way, and not by blood. But I will fight again, and kill, too, to keep all I have."

When we awoke in the daylight we sat up and looked about at the stacks of goods that filled the alcoves and lay upon the floor around us. We had bought much, but much remained to be bought, to outfit the hall and help us provide for ourselves.

"The man in the croft below," said Sidroc, and I remembered the one we had seen working at long planks yesterday. "I will see if he can come today and help me build.

"First we need a table and benches," he went on. "And a bed," he smiled, patting the weaving on which we had slept. "We will sleep in the treasure room. This can go on the floor there, as we saw at the spice-merchant's house. What did that priest call it?"

"Carpet," I remembered. "And Eardwulf said wars were fought over shipments of them."

"Good. We should have everything costly and fine."

This mention of the Mercian priest made me think back to our days at the trading post at which we had met him.

"Sidroc," I said of a sudden. "Where are we?"

He began to laugh until he realized what I truly asked. He had carried the chart I had copied from the great one of Eardwulf, and now rose and went to his pack and drew it forth and unrolled it. I had drawn it out on a long scrap of the precious vellum that the priest had a store of. Sidroc pressed it to the floor and we bent over it.

"Here is the trading post where we met Eardwulf," I remembered as I pointed, "and here, the small trading post he told me we would pass, and then the great river called Vistula. And here," I said, touching a point I had inked far to the North, "is the settlement of the Prus he told me we should go to." Our eyes followed my finger as I traced the route.

"But where are we now – where is Gotland?" My tracing showed nothing at all to the West of the Baltic shoreline.

"Ah…it is here," said Sidroc, placing his hand down to the left of the trading post of the Prus. "In the middle of the Baltic Sea. It is long and narrow and runs North to South."

We had seen this ourselves, for when we had sailed here we approached it from one narrow tip, and sailed a long way up the coast. "On the other side of the Baltic lies the land of the Svear." He put his left hand down, a distance from the other. "And under the land of the Svear, and to the West of it, is Dane-mark, my homeland." He looked at me and I nodded my head in understanding. "Then if you keep travelling West, you reach Frankland below to the South, and then the island of Angle-land, far to the West."

I closed my eyes and tried to remember the chart Father Eardwulf had showed me. "I do not know if Gotland was on the chart the priest showed me; I cannot recall." It seemed at that moment important to me to recall if this place was yet known to the far-travelling priest.

Sidroc seemed to read my unease, and just said, "We are safe here, shield-maiden. Whether we are on his chart or not. The priest is far from us now, and thinks we went to the town of the Prus, anyway." He lifted his eyes up to the timber roof for a moment. "We are safe from all, here."

He rolled up the chart and laid it aside. It would be a full day, and first we must dress and walk down the hill so we might eat and so be ready for all that lay before. But before we stood Sidroc turned to me and made a little sound to clear his throat.

"You have been my wife for two nights now," he began, "and I have given you no morning-gift, as befits a bride."

He spoke here of the morgen-gyfu, the morning-gift given to all brides of Angle-land by their new husbands on the day after they were wed. I do not know if I blushed, but I know I looked down, and not at him. Such a thing seemed fitting once, and long ago; but not now.

Sidroc did not agree with me. "I am lucky that your kinsman the war chief is in the Halls of the Slain, or else he would be staring at me and tapping his foot."

He was smiling when he said it and trying to make me smile too. "I do not want to give you just jewels, tho' I hope to give you many; or sheep or pigs, but I will give those things too.

"What I give to you is twelve pieces of your gold."

On the little boat I had given him my hidden gold coinage, all twenty pieces of it, and told him it was my bridal-goods. It was meant to spare him from having to sell his weapons, and to give us a rich start in our new lives, and I gave it fully and freely as part of my pledge to him. Now he wished to give the greater portion of it back.

"The gold is yours," I told him again, "all of it, so we might live without hardship."

"I need only eight pieces to make my way," he countered. "With eight pieces I can equip the hall, buy us horses and a cow, and hire a ship and crew for next Summer's trading season. Also buy the goods I wish to sell."

"But what of Tyrsborg," I asked, looking up at the steep roof above us. "That is not enough to buy it from Rannveig; it will be costly."

"Yes. But I will earn silver, and gold too, from trading, and so buy the hall from the brewster. She will not sell it to anyone else; she knows I want it. I have already spoken for it."

I was moved by what he said, and the thought behind it. Yet after so much hardship I wanted all to be made smooth, and little in life smooths the way as well as coin does.

"But – " I began, but he spoke again, and his words revealed his deeper meaning.

"With twelve pieces of gold you will still be rich, if anything happens to me."

"Nothing will happen to you," I said, as if I could order Fate. I could not bear even to think of this. "You said you will not fight again unless you must."

"True. But there is accident, and sickness; or Odin might envy me and cast a lightning-bolt from the sky and kill me – "

I knew he was trying to make me laugh, and now I had to smile. He got up and brought my mantle from where it lay folded upon the floor, and brought too my work-basket with its fine Idrisid shears.

I snipped away at every tight channel Burginde had sewn, freeing the gold from my hem. We spread them out upon the floor, nineteen bright golden faces. He picked up seven, and lay them aside, then picked up the remaining twelve and turned to me.

"I give you your morning-gift, shield-maiden," he told me, pressing the cool disks into my palm. "It is to be yours and only yours, to do as you see fit. Tyrsborg will be our hall, and after I am dead it will be yours and our children's. But this pure gold is yours alone."

Chapter the Second: Thread Broken and Unbroken

Four Stones in South Lindisse, Angle-land

BURGINDE stood looking out through the open window of the weaving room, a thick strand of wool roving thrown over her left shoulder, her right hand steadily pulling thread to the spindle that dropped at her knee. Its spinning slowed and she drew it up again, winding the new thread on the worn shaft before feeding another tuft of carded wool between her fingers. I stood at my loom, pulled at the heddle bar to make way for my yarn-charged shuttle, then stopped. I let the heddle fall back, unable to do more than place my hands upon the warp threads. I glanced down to the clay warp weights hanging near the floor. If I had been working they would be moving with the action of my shuttle, sometimes hitting each other with a dull and comfortable thud. Today they hung still.

I raised my eyes to the wooden cross nailed upon the wall above my loom, and crossed myself and breathed yet another prayer. I had hoped hand work would calm me, but each time I took the shuttle in my hand found I laid it down again. I gave up trying and sat down on a stool, my back to my loom. It was watching Burginde in the simple act of spinning that gave me most comfort.

"Burginde," I said. "Please to – to stay near me."

She looked over at me as she wound up her spun thread, and nodded. "Ach, my sweet, I'll not move from your side 'til you yourself shoo me away."

The Hall of Tyr

Godwin, Lord of Kilton, would arrive at Four Stones sometime today. Over two weeks had passed since Sidroc's men had ridden back on lathered horses, telling of how Sidroc and my dear Ceridwen had vanished. The two of them, along with two of Sidroc's men, had ridden away a short distance from the pier at Saltfleet from which the merchant ship to carry Ceridwen back to Kilton was to land. The ship arrived on a swelling tide and they had not returned, and the other men of the escort soon found the bodies of two of their brethren at the foot of a bluff.

This sudden news stunned me, but not so much to shield me from pain and fear. My grief at this double loss took my breath away; I recall gasping as I wept, my prayers a shriek. Asberg, trusted by Sidroc and wed to my sister Æthelthryth, sent men that very hour to scour the coastline. Ashild, my eldest daughter, Hrald, my son, and Ceric, Ceridwen's boy, all clung to me, as I tried to comfort them with assurances that I could not myself believe in. As I kissed Ceric's brow all I could do was to thank God that Ceridwen had allowed him to stay here with us at Four Stones, and that he was not lost too.

I knew Godwin would come himself; his land was at peace, and the disappearance of his sister in law, a cherished part of the fabric of Kilton, would be a major blow to all there. I knew he would come, and welcomed it, for he would be an ally to me in my distress. He was a man of great ability; his deeds over the years as war-chief and ealderman had proved it. He would help me, I knew. Yet, as his arrival grew near, I did not know how I could look upon his face and remain composed. Ceridwen had been a guest on my lands, and had vanished in the keeping of its lord. Marauders or worse were loose here in Lindisse, and had seemingly brought calamity upon the folk of two lands.

Everything that awe-ful first day of their loss was a jumble. When Burginde had taken the children I met again with Asberg in the hall. It was not yet time for the evening meal, and with the household in an uproar and many men away I knew the meal would be late. Æthelthryth was in the kitchen yard, and would, I know, do her best to marshal the serving folk. Just then I needed to hear again from Asberg what the returning men had told him.

The two dead men were Ernmund and Gudrick, both young and thankfully not wed. I recalled their faces just three days ago, laughing in the hall, at the farewell feast we held for Ceridwen on the eve of her departure.

"But their bodies were not touched – their weapons still there with them," I repeated. "What robber would leave such treasure behind?"

"They wanted their silence, not their swords," is what Asberg answered.

"Why? Why?" I asked, my hands on my face. All I could think of was ransom; it was all I wished to think of, for then Sidroc and Ceridwen would be well treated. "Where are they, who took them?"

For answer Asberg only shook his head. The silver cross he wore about his neck moved on his tunic, and his rough hand closed briefly upon it. Asberg had pale yellow hair, and mild blue eyes in a broad brow, now creased in worry. He was good hearted, slow of speech, more thoughtful than he looked; and he had been a good husband to my sister Æthelthryth, gladly embracing the True Faith so that she would wed him; and been as well a good father to their two little boys. Most of all I knew him to be utterly loyal to his war-lord Sidroc. Never was this more important, for Asberg was himself now placed in command of the defence of Four Stones. He was my kinsman and I trusted him.

We spoke longer, and he told me he had sent men to Saltfleet, both to the new pier and to a small cove at the base of the bluff where the dead men were found. These men took white pennants with them, large enough to be seen from a ship, as signal that a ransom demand would be met and the marauders could land unafraid. The thegns Godwin had sent upon the ship to collect Ceridwen had, after their own quick search, borrowed horses from us and ridden overland to Kilton to deliver the news. This was all Asberg could tell me. He left me then, and the trouble on his own brow told me how he feared quietly, and within himself.

I went to the treasure room with Burginde. The waning Summer sun was coming through the high window, casting all in a yellow glow that mocked the darkness in my heart. My eyes moved around the room. Sidroc's shelf, and its flanking pegs, on which he kept many of his belongings. His big clothes chest, and mine. Our bed, laid with the wolf-skin spread my mother had sent me long ago. The large iron-bound chests that held the extra weapons, and the small caskets holding silver and gold. I stood to leave; I did not want to see these things, but to go up to my weaving room and be away from all of it.

Æthelthryth came in and placed her arms about me, and told me that soon the meal would be ready. I began to weep again, my throat too tight to cry out that our mother, now a professed nun at Oundle, could not be with us. I thought of her and the great abbess of Oundle, the holy Sigewif, and wished to the depths of my soul that they could be here with me now; or far better, I with them.

"I cannot, cannot, sit at table in the hall tonight," I sobbed out, at last.

"Ah, Ælfie," my sister said, using my childhood name. I saw in her face she was tired, and frightened, too.

"I think you should, Ælfie," she said, "I do." She looked back to Burginde.

The Hall of Tyr

"I cannot," I sobbed again. "Not tonight."

She drew a breath and hesitated. "If you do not sit at table in the hall, then there is only Asberg and me to act as heads…"

Æthelthryth was right; I was Lady of Four Stones, and if I abandoned my role this first night, I would be showing weakness and not strength to all the folk of Four Stones.

"Would you have the wee ones there in the hall, looking for their mother?" added Burginde.

She too was right. I could not think only of myself. I had Sidroc's son and heir to think of.

I straightened myself in Æthelthryth's arms, and smoothed my rumpled head-wrap. "Thank you, Æthelthryth," I told her. "And let us have Hrald, and Ceric both, come and sit with me at the high table. It is where Hrald was always meant to sit when grown; that day has come quicker than we thought."

Then I looked from Æthelthryth's face to Burginde's, and said with all the force I could, "They are alive, alive and whole. By blessed St Mary, they are alive."

I went into the hall that night arrayed as I would always be of an evening. The men and women of the hall were still coming in, and by their hushed voices I knew they spoke of nothing but of the vanishing of their chief. Burginde sat at the children's table with Ashild, with my second daughter, Ealhswith, now two, and also with my youngest sister Eanflad, and around them sat the children of the hall old enough to eat here. Looking at them gave me some measure of strength. I saw Hrald sitting at the high table, perched on the edge of a bench, waiting for me. He sat near, but not quite at, the place his father sat; and he looked so small and young as he peered at me. Ceric was there too, and as I moved to take my chair by them I saw Asberg approach. He held in his hands Sidroc's round painted shield, and without a word he laid it down on the table where Sidroc would have sat, marking his place. The eyes of the hall were on him as he did so, and my heart was moved with gratitude that he would stand before all and place this reminder of Sidroc, Jarl.

In the days that followed we hoped each dawn that some message would come by land or sea, demanding gold. But none came, only word that Godwin of Kilton had taken ship and would arrive soon with his picked men.

Now in the weaving room I heard the shrill whistles from the palisade that told me Godwin must be near. It was well past noon. Burginde put down her spindle and I rose from my loom and walked wordlessly down the stair and out into the hall yard to greet our guest. Asberg stood near me, and many of Sidroc's men, but I had sent the children to the bower-house and ordered them to stay until Burginde fetched them.

A small troop of horsemen was riding to the gate, and I saw Godwin from afar. His coppery hair stood out, and I fixed my eyes upon him as they rode nearer. He was as richly dressed as a king, in blue leggings and a tunic of bright yellow linen, his mantle trimmed in brown fur, and its borders picked out in spirals of silver wire; but other than his sword and seax carried no weaponry. A young thegn at his side led a riderless horse which bore a blackened ring-shirt and helmet, and a spear of darkened wood, and these I understood to be Godwin's own. No colour or bright metal-work adorned any of this, quite unlike the weaponry of other chieftains of wealth and prowess. The plainness, severity even of his warrior's kit struck me. The contrast between his rich dress made me feel I was seeing one man with the weapons of another. The man himself sat rigidly upright in his saddle, and as he neared I could not move my eyes from him.

I was not alone in my gaze. Everyone looked to him. He was a man of high good looks, yes, but it was more. He had about him that native sense of command that makes other men pause in what they do and watch. His erectness in the saddle, the way he held his head, the manner in which his eyes fixed on each of us in turn, made us all watch him and wonder what were the thoughts behind that short but piercing stare.

The day at Kilton when I had first seen Godwin came back in memory; and today his likeness to my own lost Gyric would have made my heart fall if it had not been so numb. Even in my dulled state I felt an odd and sore excitement in his coming nearer. It could be Gyric, riding in state with Ælfred, the morning they arrived at Cirenceaster and I first beheld him. I could feel my heart swell within my breast.

The man on horseback glanced at me. But his eyes, a honey-green, so like his brother's as I still recalled them, did not rest on mine, but flicked amongst us, from man to man, to palisade, to rooftops within. He had held the reins with both hands, as Ceridwen told me he could do with his weakened shoulder, but when he went to swing down from his horse he rather jumped, using only his good right hand on the pommel.

Now down from his horse, he looked at me again. For one mad moment I did not understand why he did not know me, did not see me for who I was. He looked at me as if I were any other woman. Madness. He was not Gyric, he had not loved me. I shook myself from this folly and readied myself to greet him.

He came closer and I saw how wrong I was in thinking him like Gyric. The likeness which had been heart-turning to me once seemed now a bitter jest. How hard you are, I

31

thought; everything has marked you. Although the face was so similar he was nothing like his brother. As he inclined his head to me I had to drop my eyes to avoid meeting his.

"My lady," he said, and nothing more.

"Lord Godwin, this is Asberg, my brother in law," I answered, and Asberg bent his head a moment before returning Godwin's fixed stare. I made a weak gesture of welcome, lifting my hands silently to the hall door.

The gathered men dispersed, and Godwin and the young man with him followed Asberg and me inside. Three-fingered Jari, another trusted man of Sidroc's, came too and joined us. The high table sat ready, and as we approached it Wilgot, our priest, came forward from where he had waited. Burginde too stepped out of the shadows and sat upon a stool not far away, spindle in hand.

As we crossed the stone floor I saw the tilt of Godwin's chin as he took in the stronghold of Four Stones. His eye swept the length of the hall and I thought he read much in what he saw. He marked first the passage to the kitchen yard, the dim flight of stairs to the upper rooms, the treasure room door at the far end; places of entry and departure, from which could come surprises good or ill. And he judged too, I was certain, whether this hall be run well or poorly; its men content or quarrelsome, its women good managers or wastrels. A war chieftain could not lead without being a good judge of men and conditions, and in these things Godwin had long experience. He could not have been more unlike Sidroc, yet this thing I knew was common to both.

We had nearly reached the table when Ceric and Hrald darted in from the kitchen yard passage. "Uncle!" cried Ceric, and now I saw some tenderness in Godwin, for he wrapped his arms about the boy's back as Ceric hugged his waist.

Godwin bent over the boy. The colour of their hair was almost the same, and I wondered if he saw the ghost of his younger brother in him. But Ceric was not very like either Gyric or Godwin; he had much of his mother in him, and favoured her. Godwin kissed his cheek, and as he straightened up Ceric clung to his leg. It lasted but a moment longer, then Godwin sent the boys away with a promise to see Ceric later.

A serving man brought basin and linen, and we washed our hands as would be done in any fine hall in Wessex. I would not let any courtesy be forgotten in our distress. Ale, in our best silver ewer, was waiting for us on the table.

We sat at one end, so that we might see and hear each other better. I had had my own chair placed at the head; it took courage to place myself thus, but I would assert myself as Lady of Four Stones. On the flanking benches Godwin would sit on my left, with his young warrior, whose name was Worr; and Asberg on my right, then Jari, and Wilgot. The priest would listen, and remember; and tho' I might not think him the wisest of men, I knew his counsel would ever cleave to mercy and clemency.

We lifted our cups in silence, and I saw the huge bracelet of braided red-gold on Godwin's right wrist. He put down his cup and turned his head to Asberg.

"Were you with them, at the pier?" he asked.

Asberg shook his head, his regret clear upon his face. "When Sidroc goes overnight, here I stay," he answered.

"You are his chief man?" Godwin wanted to know. Asberg paused, then said, "I command when Sidroc is gone."

"The two men killed – how did they die?"

"One was hit on the head with a rock, one stabbed in the back."

"Both killed from behind, then?" He considered a moment. "Where in the back was the stab wound? High in the back, centre, by his waist?"

"Ah...high. The right side of his body."

"As if he was turning to look?"

Asberg nodded, and then spoke. "They stood together; their bodies fell – " he folded his hands one over the other.

Godwin considered this a moment. "Who were the last to see them?"

"The men they rode with, and left at the pier. Jari was one," he said, and Jari lifted his maimed hand in assent.

Godwin turned to him. "The ship was not there, so they rode a short distance to the bluff."

Jari nodded, Yes. "There are places where one can see a long way up the coast. I think they walked the bluff to spot the coming ship from there."

"What did they carry with them when they rode off?" Godwin asked.

The men looked at each other.

"Nothing," said Jari. "The lady's packs and goods were all still in the waggon."

"She carried nothing in her hands?"

"Nothing."

"How was she dressed?"

Here Jari looked to me helplessly.

"Very simply; for travel," I told him. "Ceridwen feared being sea-sick again; all her finery was packed away. She wore a rather plain gown, russet. Her fine wool mantle, of course, the one trimmed with otter fur, and a large bronze pin to close it. A simple silver pin, a circle – one I had given her – upon her gown."

Jari nodded. "She wore her mantle."

"So she had nothing, save the clothes she wore, nothing of real value with her, other than the silver pin?"

Here I saw Burginde lift her head in a quick movement. I looked to her, but she did not speak, just lowered her head to her spindle.

"All her jewels and other goods were in her leathern bags," I told him.

"And Sidroc?" he asked. "What weapons did he have? Was there anything on his horse that was missing?"

"His horse was untouched," Jari said. "The bridle and saddle he used each day, nothing more. He wore his sword and knife."

"No spear, no ring shirt, no helmet?"

"No," Jari answered. "We had ridden with the lady fully armed, but the day was warm, and he left everything but his two blades at the pier."

Now Godwin turned to me. "How much silver did he carry that day?"

"I – I do not know," I began, startled by the question. "No more than usual when on his own lands; quite little in fact." I grew more sure of this, recalling that I had found nothing amiss amongst his things in the treasure room. "There were a few more coins in a pouch left on his shelf in the treasure room." I thought of all the ready treasure there at hand. "All the silver – coins, and jewels, were untouched. His arm cuffs of twisted silver, and one of gold. All were left behind in the treasure room, where he keeps them."

Godwin looked from Asberg to Jari. "You know these parts well. Are there caves where men could hide?"

"Do you mean, brigands?" I asked, and began to shake my head, for Lindisse under Sidroc's care was well patrolled and guarded.

"Anyone," answered Godwin.

"Two or three small ones. We have checked them," said Asberg.

"We will check them again," said Godwin, and nodded as if he need hear no more. He looked from me to Asberg as he spoke. "I have thirty men. If you can horse us, we can ride in pairs across Lindisse, until we find something."

Strange men from Wessex ranging over the countryside – Sidroc would never allow it. I looked to Asberg, who had shifted in his seat.

"Our men know the countryside, and its people," I began.

Asberg picked up for me. "We will go together," he nodded. "One man for one man."

Godwin looked Asberg in the eyes. "You and I will ride together," he agreed.

All seemed at an end. "We will start at dawn. I will see to the horses," said Asberg, as he and Jari rose.

After a moment Godwin went after them. Jari had already gone out, but I saw Godwin stop Asberg at the foot of the steps to the main door. The two men moved in close to each other. I heard the low tones of Godwin's voice, and saw rather than heard Asberg's reply. Asberg was not quick to anger, one of the traits Sidroc valued in him. But now I saw the man's shoulders square, and his head jerk back. It lasted but a moment, and the two parted.

As we were gathering for the evening meal I saw Asberg in the side passage. "What did Godwin say to you?"

His mouth twisted and I thought he would not answer, but I urged him on with my eyes.

"He asked if Sidroc would kill his own men."

I took a slow breath to recover myself, and reached for Asberg's arm. "Asberg," I asked, "do not ride alone with Godwin. Please to take another man with you, your young cousin or whoever you will." His eyes widened, and I knew I had injured his pride as a warrior. But now I feared Godwin, and did not want Asberg to be alone with him. "If you find anything together, you will have a rider to send back with word," I urged.

But Asberg did not need my excuse. "I have seen him fight," he said; for he had been with Yrling when Godwin had killed him. "I will take another man," he ended.

That night at table Godwin sat as honoured guest to the left of Sidroc's empty chair. Sidroc's red and black painted shield lay upon the table, marking his place, just as it had every night since he had vanished. The table was an old and thick slab of oak, scarred from many years' use, and darkened with waxing. As I saw Godwin look at the shield I thought of what that table had witnessed, going back many years before the long-dead Merewala's day. The ten years I had sat at that table were nothing to it. I had first sat there next to Yrling, the man who would be my husband, Ceridwen at my side to give me courage and calmness. It was Yrling who had killed Merewala. Now Godwin who had killed Yrling sat there, a mere shield's breadth away from me. To stop myself from these thoughts I turned to Hrald and Ceric. They had played and ridden during the day but now at table their eyes too rested on Sidroc's shield, and both were quiet.

It was a mild night, but I ordered a good fire in the fire pit to give us more light and cheer, and had every cresset filled with oil and burning. The stone floor of red and black blocks was swept, and its waving pattern caught the eye by firelight. On the high table I had placed three thick wax tapers, now aglow with their costly clear light, and on the treasure room wall behind us was draped a large woollen hanging of a raven, wings outstretched in a blue sky, aloft over green hills and fields, all stitched in coloured thread-work by Burginde and me over a span of three years. The men's massed spears were clustered in iron holders at the ends of this hanging, and the alcoves around the long walls of the hall were hung with bright weavings. Four Stones was nothing so grand as Kilton, but it was become a fine and strong hall, and I would take pride in showing it at its best to our guest.

We ate a meal of particular richness, for we had slaughtered and roasted an ox. Our best ale was poured, and Godwin ate from a salver of silver, and the cup he lifted was one of silver with a golden rim.

I closed my eyes a moment as I took a sip of ale. When I had first come to Four Stones, the floor was so littered that I could not know it was of stone; and the raven was one drawn in charcoal on the wooden boards by one of the men. It was a hall of men, all warriors, all young, who had destroyed the lives of Merewala and his family. The serving folk had been reduced to slavery and the remaining folk of the village to misery. Tonight I looked over a hall filled with men and their wives and children; men and women who farmed and raised sheep and cattle and lived in peace with the folk of Lindisse.

With the day-to-day cares of the hall, it was easy for me to forget this. It was easy for me to forget that a land at peace, with men who farmed and raised horses rather than raided and killed had been a dream to me ten years back, one that at times I did not think I would live to see. My own home in Cirenceaster had been reduced to ashes and my father killed, but here at Four Stones a ruined hall and village had been lifted to peace and even bounty. My mother and sisters, so cruelly ravished, knew contentment and safety, living useful and valued lives.

Sidroc and I had done this; and as I looked out amongst my people I allowed myself to feel a swelling satisfaction that ten years of effort had not proved fruitless. Even greater than the peace and plenty to me was the fact that the True Word of God now was heard and known in Lindisse. This was the prize that I clung to; the gain I would not relinquish for any other. Wilgot the priest had baptised nearly everyone here at Four Stones, and my silver had done much to build up the foundation at Oundle that the holy Sigewif ran. Oundle was a refuge to all, a shelter and fortress to men and women who released themselves from earthly bonds and gave themselves up to quiet work and contemplation. My own devout mother was there, and the time I had spent there, alone or with my children, counted as the hours in which I had felt most at peace, and most content. I had been lax in my prayers as a girl, but sorrow and loss, coupled with the sparing of my mother and sisters, had taught me to trust and believe in Christ's promise, and the love of his own dear Mother, St Mary.

The food was being cleared away, and now a ewer of mead brought to me. I rose and poured the golden liquid into Godwin's cup, as befit my role as lady of the hall to her guest. Glancing at Godwin I wondered what he thought as he turned his head and took the measure of the hall and its people.

Wilgot stood, and spoke. My priest could not know why I lowered my head over my silver cup when he began his tale, nor did he even see me, so wrapped in his own story-prowess was he. But he had chosen to relate the story of how Christ had cured the blind men at the Fort of Jericho by touching their eyes. Unbidden I thought again of my past, and he whom I had loved.

The evening ended early, as the men would ride upon the dawn. Godwin had spoken little during the meal, mostly to Asberg sitting next him, but now as I rose I gestured to him to follow me. Asberg rose too, and began the tasks of breaking down the hall for the night, and Ceric bid his uncle goodnight. Godwin followed me to the door of the treasure room. I stepped within but left the door open.

Before me on one of the large clothes chests sat a long and slender box. The freshness of the wood proclaimed it newly made, and I gestured Godwin to come near it.

"I wish to show you something," I told him, and placed my hand on the box. "When Sidroc left for Saltfleet, he showed to us these gifts he had prepared for Ceridwen to take to you."

I lifted the lid, and then parted the fleecy sheepskin covering inside. There lay the sword with its hilt of horn wrapped in silver wire, resting in the dark leathern sheath. A small square box next to it held the broad armlet of hammered gold, and a third, the silver cup with garnet and lapis stones on its base. "He meant to send these things to

40

you in friendship," I told him, and remembered his words. "Also in trust for Ceric staying with us for the year."

I studied Godwin's face as he looked down upon these treasures. His eyes had narrowed, but I could not read the set of his mouth. I swallowed and told him the rest. "He also said that he would send you our own son, Hrald, to foster, when he was older."

He said nothing, so that I began to be impatient with him. "This was not an act of craft, or cunning," I ended.

Again he was silent, and I knew he would not make things easy for me. If he would not offer, then I would ask.

"My lord, when we spoke today, some of your questions – troubled me." He said nothing, and I began again. "You asked what they carried…"

I went ahead and said it. "You think Sidroc has stolen Ceridwen away."

The sharpness of his answer surprised me. "I think nothing," he said. His green eyes were now upon me, hard and bright.

You lie, I said within myself; you lie. Here was a man, a guest in my hall, who had killed with his own hand my first husband, and would I think, now kill my second if given the chance. I could assume no less after what he had asked Asberg in private. Yet I had bowed my head to him in welcome. I could near taste the bitterness of it in my mouth. I was a woman of Wessex, twice wed to Danes, and now I feared more bloodshed and hurt from a man of my own kind. I felt a wash of anger mixing with my fear; the satisfactions I had felt in the hall were swept away by it. It was war that caused such ugliness and confusion. How many peace-weaving maids had been sent – as I had – into danger, only to find, despite all their skill and sacrifice, they were unable to weave a lasting bond?

What I said aloud to challenge him was, "If Sidroc planned to kidnap Ceridwen, why did he leave all his treasure behind? He would want as much as he could carry to ease his way."

"I have no answer for that," he admitted. His voice had softened but slightly, and the pause that followed was long and awkward. I was the one to break it.

"You are surprised to hear me speak thus, but let us both speak plainly, my lord. I have known for these ten years, ever since I first came here, that Sidroc desired Ceridwen. He had chosen her from the first; she could have wed him anytime. I myself urged her to do so, to keep her here with me, against my loneliness."

He said nothing, and I went on.

"When Gyric was brought here –" here I paused, knowing that I should have said 'your brother' – "and she rode away with him to save his life, Sidroc went after her, but could not find her. When Yrling – died, Sidroc won Four Stones away from his cousin, and in doing so likely saved my life. That he has been a good and just lord of Lindisse you can see for yourself. That he has been a good husband you shall have to accept from me, for it is the truth."

"You know I killed Yrling," is how he answered this. It was not a boast, nor was it a plea for forgiveness. It was a simple and quiet statement of fact. His eyes rested steadily upon me; even this admission could not make him look down in discomfort.

I nodded. "Yes. Ceridwen told me, long ago. It was not just, but I understand why. Even though he was innocent of Gyric's maiming, you needed someone more to punish for the act. And as a Dane, he was your enemy."

"This cursed place," he said, looking around to the walls that surrounded us. He spoke almost as if he was alone. "Merewala died here. Gyric was dragged here to die. Now this."

The baldness, even the injustice of this, stirred me.

"Four Stones has seen its share of sorrow, and more," I told him. "That is true. Merewala died here for his hall and his folk. It was an honourable death. I was sent here much against my will to wed Yrling. The peace I sought then was not lasting, but it is now. Today the folk of Lindisse know peace and plenty. Sidroc, Yrling's nephew, has brought them that; given me a free hand in every dealing with the village and hall to raise it up once more. And Gyric – you should thank God that it was to Four Stones he was brought – for it was here that Ceridwen found him, and risked her own life to save his."

I saw he listened, and I went on. "Four Stones has given you much. Without Ceridwen, Kilton might have had no heir."

He looked at me so sharply that I quailed a moment, and I said, "I mean that she gave you her own son."

"Yes," he said. "She gave me a son."

He stared at my face so long that I was forced to look away. If I had felt fear of Godwin earlier in the day, it was doubled now, and I knew not why.

I wanted to turn from the past, and took breath and went on. "I do not know what happened on the hillside. But not one bone in my body believes for one moment that

Ceridwen or Sidroc planned any part of it. I would go through trial by fire proclaiming their innocence."

I was fighting rising tears now, and worked to control my voice. "All I can do is care for my family and folk as best I can. That, and pray they be alive, safe, and free."

He made a short laugh. "Yes; you can pray. And she is no Christian."

"I know that," I said. "But I believe Lady St. Mary and Her Blessed Son love her all the same. Ceridwen is the best friend, best mother, and best wife that woman can be."

He did not challenge this with words, but with his face. I felt a sort of rage against him at that instant, and let it show in my words.

"You do not know her. No man can know her as I do, just as no man can know me as she does!" I was afraid he might speak, and went on, to block his coming words. "Even if she has kept secrets, I know it would be only to protect others from hurt."

I wanted to end this now, to hear and say no more, save one thing. I cleared my throat.

"I have spoken freely to you and beg you to do the same. Tell me the truth: Do you think they still live?"

He looked me full in the face. "I do not know. But if they do, I will find them."

Chapter the Third: An Awakening

Four Stones in South Lindisse, Angle-land

SIXTY men rode off at cock crow, thirty from Kilton and thirty from Four Stones. I rose with all the hall and bid them fare-well, Hrald and Ceric at my side. They had wanted to ride with them, and only my telling them how important it was that they remain at Four Stones, lest any word come directly from Saltfleet, made them give up their goal of going. The men were headed in all directions across Lindisse, riding by twos; and although all were to return within seven days, the uncertainty of their seeking made it feel they might be gone for weeks. Asberg had left Jari here in command, and had taken his young cousin with him as I had asked.

I had lain unsleeping in the treasure room as I heard the men gather in the darkness. I could not help but think back to the day when Sidroc had stormed off in pursuit of Ceridwen after she had set off with Gyric, and of how I both wished and feared that he would catch them. I had wanted Ceridwen back with me, and safe, and none other to find her but Sidroc, who would I thought, do her no harm; yet knew that if he had found them he would have killed Gyric. I did not believe Gyric would want to live maimed, and yet the thought of his death after we had schemed and risked to free him was equal torment to contemplate. These were the unquiet thoughts I had dealt with in that long night before the men rode. Now I pushed this memory from my mind and went to bid my fare-well to Asberg and Godwin. With the jangle of the bridle rings still sounding in the yard I turned and forced myself to start my day.

The Hall of Tyr

My sister Æthelthryth and I, along with Inga, Jari's wife, worked at putting all to rights after the feast, numbering and locking away all the extra cups, bronze and some of silver, that had been brought out to serve our guests, taking care that all the bronze and silver salvers were cleaned and safely locked in their chests. The kitchen folk were still busy with their own clearing away, for they had arisen before dawn to fill the saddle-bags of the men before they rode off. After that I went with Inga down to the nearest sheep-folds, where some of our best ewes had been gathered by our shepherds so that we might together judge which should be bred up to which rams. Inga loved our sheep almost as much as me, and had a quick eye for a deep fleece and a thrifty keeper. Walking amongst our noisy ewes, petting their bony faces, and testing the oily curl of their fleece between my fingers gave me a sense of calmness and purpose.

We returned to the hall to see all had been swept and the cressets refilled for the night. Wilgot had the older children at his little house, as he did every morning, teaching them their letters and sums. After noon I let Hrald and Ceric take their ponies to the valley of horses by the flax fields. It was a safe and known place, as many of Sidroc's men lived there with their families. I had let the boys ride there by themselves before; but today I sent Mul the stable man with them just the same, lest any raiders be near, seeking more prey.

When I went up to the weaving room Burginde was fast at work with her spindle. My silent sister Eanflad stood at her loom, her slender form upright and gently swaying as she cast the shuttle back through the woollen warp, still only when she beat the weft up, packing it with her weaving sword. She had now almost twenty years and had not spoken since our hall was taken and our father killed when she was ten. We all spoke kindly to her, but she listened to no one but Burginde, who had taught her to weave and with whom she would stand hour upon hour at her work. Little Ealhswith sat at play on the floor by Eanflad's loom, pulling at a coil of wool roving with her plump fingers. Ashild stood on tiptoe, peering out the window, her spindle lying at her feet. I kissed the girls and had to smile at Ashild's lumpy thread as she held it pinched between her fingers; but perhaps mine was no more even at nine years. I reminded her to wind it up evenly along the length of the spindle shaft. I went to my own loom to continue the length of heavy wool fabric I was slowly adding to. The yarn was a deep dark blue, for our dyers had had a fine woad crop, and the thick weft beat easily between the warp. I had meant it for new mantles for Eanflad and Ashild, and would have to apply myself each day for it to be ready by Winter.

We worked steadily as the afternoon light grew brightest and then began to wane. I was grateful for the rhythmic work of building the soft weft between the warp threads, seeing it grow as I pushed up line after line of it towards the loom head, and grateful for Burginde's chatter with Ashild and little Ealhswith. Even hearing the shuttle move and heddle shift of silent Eanflad as she worked next me seemed a comfort. She was always with us, and yet I thought, knew nothing of our recent grief and worry; her eyes, so fixed and blank, never revealed to me if she truly saw the things she looked at. Burginde oftentimes told me that she did understand, but locked in her silence, could not let us know. As we lost the light I sent the girls down to play in the kitchen yard, where I thought Hrald and Ceric might already be. The kitchen folk would be working on our evening meal, and have buttered bread or other treat for small and hungry mouths.

I stepped from my loom and went to the dimming window where Burginde stood drawing her thread, for spinning wants little light, and one can spin good thread even in the dark. We still kept the three narrow beds in the weaving room, reminder of our first days at Four Stones when Ceridwen and Burginde and I had slept here, awaiting the arrival of Yrling. Burginde and the girls slept now in the bower house, and I of course in the treasure room; but I had never removed our first beds, for sometimes we liked to nap there. Now I looked at the nearest to the door, which had been mine. Burginde's eyes followed my own.

"I do not want to sleep in the treasure room," I told her. "I would rather be here, in my old bed, than alone down there. Help me bring my things up, Burginde."

We went down to the treasure room, and I unlocked the door and we both took armfuls of my clothing, and carried them up the creaking stairs to the weaving room. I went back and gathered up my bottles of scent and oils, and my comb and silver mirror, and took also these things up with me. We went back for more, and I saw Ceridwen's leathern packs sitting on top a chest in the treasure room, untouched since Asberg had carried them in. "Let us take her things, too," I said. "I will feel closer to her to have them near me."

When we climbed again to the weaving room I lay Ceridwen's packs down upon her old bed next mine. One of the packs was her green-dyed one, the one she had made herself when still a girl at the priory, and I fingered the soft and creased leather as I sat next to it.

Burginde sat down on the bed as well, then clapped her hands upon her lap, and leaned forward. "Lady," she said, and I knew she meant to speak of something important, for otherwise she would have called me her Lamb or Sweet. "If she has her mantle, she has gold."

"What?" I could not understand how one led to the other; Ceridwen had no golden pin with her.

She looked down at the packs.

"The Lady had a small pouch in her jewel casket. It was filled with gold coins, a fine fortune of them. I chided her for carrying them with her jewels, especially while she travelled. She let me stitch them up in the hem of her mantle. I had forgotten it until Jari said she wore her mantle, and then forgotten it again until just now."

My hand lifted to my forehead as I blessed myself.

"Holy St Mary, how you have provided," I praised. I leaned forward and took Burginde by the shoulders and kissed her cheek. "Burginde, you are the best of women, the wisest of women!"

My thoughts raced on. "If they have gold, they may be able to buy their freedom...or to ease their path, in any way they can..."

"Lady, we are not sure they yet live," Burginde warned.

"I know they do – they live; I would feel it if they did not." This did not make sense but I felt it all the same and would say it aloud to all who would listen.

"How much gold?" I asked.

"Twenty coins of it," she said. "I sewed them up one by one so they would not touch and make any noise."

"Twenty!" I clapped my hands, realizing what this could mean to them. "Now I will not mourn that Sidroc had so little with him."

I jumped up, feeling more alive than I had in days. I must do something, and I began folding my clothing and laying it away in my big weaving chest, and setting out my scent bottles and comb on the small wall shelf. I was tucking down the blanket on my bed when I had a sudden thought and turned to where Burginde was folding some towelling.

"Lord Godwin must never know about the gold," I said.

"'Tis why I did not speak up in the hall when he asked," she answered. She straightened up and put her hands on her hips as she so often did. "'Tis the lady's gold; none other than hers; and 'tis her matter and hers alone that she has both nothing and a fortune with her."

I kissed her again for that, and she headed down the stairs to bring up my copper wash tub.

Eanflad stood alone and silent, her back to us, weaving all this time, not turning at our trips up and down, or our speech, whether glad or sombre. I looked to Ceridwen's packs, and again sat next them. I drew open the smallest pack, the green-dyed one, and saw the little casket of carved wood that held the few jewels she had travelled with. I lifted it out and set it on my lap, and opened it. The first thing I saw was the linen pouch that held her great pearl. I pulled open the drawstring and let the pearl and its silver chain flow into my open palm. Almost four months had passed since Ceridwen had showed me this pearl, and told me that she meant for me to have it after her death. I had waved this off, telling her that the egg-like pearl was the emblem of new life, of new beginnings, and that she was sure to find such for herself.

Now as I closed my hand over it I began to weep. I did feel in my heart that she and Sidroc lived, but where and in what danger they might be filled me with the fear I felt she must be feeling. Even knowing she had gold with her did not help; it could have been taken from her already. I longed for that which I could not have, to know that they not only lived, but were safe. The helplessness of this longing rent my heart. My tears ran down my cheeks and dripped from my nose over my clenched hand. Those tears awakened a hundred more, all shed in this same room, for then I was weeping for Gyric, laying blinded in the cellars of Four Stones, and for Ceridwen, resolute in her desire to run off with him into dangers we could only imagine. I let my head drop over my lap as I cried, and pushed my thoughts from what had been, and what might be now, to the future that had awaited her. If she had returned to Kilton it would have been a union with a man she did not love, a life away from Kilton and its sea; a life of duty. Anger was mingled in those tears, anger at what she had suffered and what she might be suffering now; and I fairly choked on my tears as I sobbed.

Then I felt a gentle touch at either shoulder, as a woman's hands pressed down upon my upper arms from behind me. I lifted my head, and was aware that I no longer heard the rhythmic slide of Eanflad's shuttle as she drove it cross her warp threads. A face lowered near mine, and a soft voice, almost a whisper, said, "Ælfwyn."

I turned my head. It was Eanflad, and the face which had been blank for so long now had a brow pinched in worry and eyes tender with love. She seemed to see me for the first time, but I was too surprised to speak back to her.

"Do not cry, Ælfwyn," she said. "Burginde is here, and Æthelthryth, and me. All will be well."

She had awakened at last, whether from my anguished tears, or as kind benison from St Mary, as proof of Her love. It is said some beauty always comes from sorrow.

Chapter the Fourth: Tyrsborg

Island of Gotland

ON the morning of our third day in Gotland Sidroc
brought a small bench he had found in the stable and set it
against the outside of the front door of the hall. He jumped
up on it, pulled his seax, and above the door carved a bind-
rune, one upon the other: the rune Tyr for the hall, and the
rune Sigel for Sidroc. ᛏ It was as long as his hand, and like
his hand, straight and bold. As his blade dug into the plank it
turned back the brighter fibre of wood un-weathered by Sun
or wind, revealing something new of the old hall. It was the
same bind-rune he had drawn on the inside of his shield, a
mark of power and dedication, both.

He did many such things as this, large and small, and
each of them gave me pleasure to see. The pleasure he took
in me was the greatest of these; not only the pleasures of our
bodies, but also the times when I saw his sureness in his
happiness. That same afternoon I had stayed at Tyrsborg
while he went down to the trading road for something. As he
walked back up the hill to me he began to smile, and then to
laugh, a full and deep laughter, with his head thrown back. I
had never seen him thus. I was smiling, and laughing too,
feeling but not understanding his joy; and he caught me up in
his arms and lifted me from the ground.

"It is everything," he told me. "To see you, and walk
towards you, knowing you are mine. To know we live here
untroubled, and have this hall. That we had last night, and
then this night to look forward to. That after Winter there
will be Spring, and sailing, and the silver I will earn."

He set me down, still laughing. Then he craned his neck and looked over his shoulder and behind him.

"My hamingja is strong today, even bigger than me," he said.

I had never heard this word, but looked too. Not even his shadow was there, it fell on his other side.

"My luck-spirit," he told me. "We each of us are born with one."

I saw he was teasing me about seeing it, but that the spirit itself was real. That night in bed I asked him more.

"The luck-spirit," I began. "Do I have one too?"

"Yes. All are born with one. Yours has stayed close to you, most times. When you rode away from Four Stones into the forests of Lindisse your hamingja was strong with you; other times too. Your luck-spirit is there even if the Gods look away."

"Hamingja," I said, after him. The sound of it was gentle, almost a hum, something low and soft. "Is it then a part of your Fate?"

He gave a single shake of his head. "Only if you listen to it, and many will not. When you feel it moving strongly within you every venture you undertake will succeed; you must listen and take your risks. When that happens the luck-spirit will build within you. Luck can bring more luck."

I had seen that many times, just playing bones or watching Sidroc at dice.

"Does your hamingja stay with you until you die?" I asked next. I wondered if it was like the soul to the Christians.

He did not answer at once. "It can desert you. When it does you are almost always doomed."

"Desert you?"

"Your hamingja can run out of you. Your luck will vanish, never to return. It is close to a doom."

His voice was low and near to halting. I felt he was telling me deep things, things which were rarely or never spoken of. Only one cresset was alight in the treasure room. His eyes were looking up into the dusk of the ceiling beams. I put my face down upon his chest so that if he wished to speak more he could do so only to the darkness.

"Twice in battle when I feared death I felt it loosen, and begin to flee. But I called it back in time."

"How did you…call it?"

"I…summoned it. I cannot say. I did not believe, believe utterly, it was my time to die."

Sidroc was a warrior so skilled that I knew these times must have been dire indeed. Then I recalled him telling me, years ago at Kilton, of watching Godwin kill Yrling, and that he felt if Godwin had turned his hand to him he too would have died. I closed my eyes in the dark and tightened my hands where they lay on his chest.

His hand slid up across my back and rested there. "The shield-maiden was not before me, was not pointing to me."

"And you called your hamingja, your luck, back. And lived."

For answer he nodded.

So like one's place in the web of Fate, it was an active thing, something to be listened to, heeded, and even worked, as Sidroc did when he called it back.

"Are there other spirits who can help us?" I whispered.

"Just as important is the family-spirit, our fylgja, who follows us. She comes in dreams, gives you visions, guides you when you need her aid."

"She?"

"Yes," he said. "Your fylgja is always a woman-spirit, whether you are man or woman."

"What…has she told you?"

"Many things. To make Offering to white-armed Freyja when I was young. To travel certain ways, to turn or not to turn if danger was nearby. And – she told me you still lived, when you had run from Four Stones."

I knew I had felt something akin to this myself, a voice within giving warning or counsel.

"Do all Danes know of these things?" I asked.

"All people of the North do."

I knew Yrling had never told Ælfwyn of this; such things would be hard to share with anyone who did not hold the same beliefs.

I thought of my own past. My father and kinsman had worshipped the same Gods. I wondered if they too knew of, and honoured, their hamingja and fylgja. If they had lived they might have told me of my own.

The Hall of Tyr

Rannveig's son Tindr came to live with us next day. He was a good-natured young man, and good-looking as well with his straight nose and smooth brow. He kept his light brown hair smoothly combed to his shoulders, or, as I was to see, sometimes in two braids. Tindr had, I thought, no more than twenty Summers. He had a shy but ready smile, and a way of looking straight at you and watching which must be rooted in his deafness; he learnt of people and the world through his eyes. Those eyes of piercing blue-grey – almost blue-white – might be startling to look back into; and I could not help but think back to my first thought of them, that they were the eyes of a wolf.

His mother told us he had gone deaf following a fever he had had when about two, and just beginning to speak. Because of this he sometimes tried to speak, but as no one, even his mother, knew what he meant, he kept silent unless his news was urgent. He laughed, tho'; a sound like the honking of a young goose, which I did not find unpleasant. He used his slender hands to gesture his meaning, and to ask questions. To those he knew he could tell many things, quickly and well; and Rannveig showed us how we might tell him things too.

Tindr had a sign for all he knew. He seemed to choose quickly, based on how he first saw the person. If he meant Sidroc, he would tap his left cheek under the eye, where Sidroc bore his long scar. His sign for me was touching the ends of his hair, and then flicking his fingers open; Sidroc watched it and said it meant "bright hair". Rannveig he signed by touching his waist and rubbing his fingers, in token of the great ring of keys which hung at his mother's waist. His sign for himself was a touch at his ear, a reminder of his deafness. He carried too a little bone whistle, hung from a cord about his neck, and with it could summon who he wished when they were out of sight.

The Hall of Tyr

Rannveig told us Tindr prized all animals, and had a way with them, but we had as yet not so much as a hen, tho' we wished to buy fowl, a milk-cow, and at least one horse, all of which he would care for. But Tindr came with his own beasts, tiny ones to be sure, for he kept bees in a woven hive, and was the source of the golden honey we had tasted at his mother's brew-house. He had hives behind his mother's house, in the garden there where she grew her brewing herbs, and hives already up at Tyrsborg, with honey made from forest flowers. His skeps he kept in tree hollows and on simple platforms of wood he built on the edges of glades and clearings, and he cared for these creatures almost as a shepherd cares for his flock. He took us to one of his forest hives, and we watched while he gently lifted the skep and turned it to us so we might see the mass of dark bees crawling about the yellow honey-comb; and saw him smile without flinching as the bees buzzed drowsily about his head or landed on his arms without stinging him.

But Tindr was also a hunter of skill. He used a bow shorter than that of the men of Angle-land, for the land behind the trading post was heavy timber, where a long bow could not be carried with the ease of one more compact. He made and feathered his own arrows, and with them took the red deer that ran leaping in the white birch woods. He made and set snares and so caught the large blue-grey hares that thumped through the undergrowth. Rannveig told us all this, and with pride. They had always lived together in the little house behind her brew-house near the shore, but as Tindr was now a man and she did not often need heavy work done about the place, was glad to see him come and live with us and so make his start.

Our hall had been her girl-hood home, but when she wed years ago she had moved down the hill with her husband to a house nearer the pier. He fished in the Summers and they raised grain and animals in their upcountry farm, and so the hall sat empty after the death of her people. From a young woman she was known for her fine ale, and began to sell her excess and so earn more silver. Tindr was her sole child who had lived beyond childhood, and their small house was more than room enough. After the death of her husband she had remained at her brewing work, and had sometimes let the hall out as a store-room, but it had not been lived in for years.

Now Tindr lived for the first time in his mother's old hall, and chose the alcove closest to the yard door for his own. Outside this door was the kitchen yard with its outbuildings and cooking rings, and the stable, as large as the hall itself, in which we would house our animals. Behind this were some scattered and dark spruce trees, as tall as Tyrsborg's peak and hung with great shaggy boughs, and beyond them woods of oak, elm and ash, lightened with patches of hazel and bright birches. Tindr knew the forest well; that part behind the hall ran all the way to Rannveig's upland farm, now deserted, but with active farms near to it.

Sidroc and I were both outside when Tindr came up the hill to us, driving a small cart pulled by a single spotted ox. His mother walked with him, and his belongings, clothing and tools mostly, lay heaped in the centre of the floor boards of the cart. He wore his bow on his back, to save it I thought from any jostling, and lifted his hand to us in greeting as he smiled.

"Goþr dagr", said Rannveig, and as I knew she bid me a good day, I returned her greeting. Sidroc had been helping me learn the Norse names of things, and I was eager for any practice in my new tongue.

Tindr looked at where Sidroc stood, standing over the planks of a table he was building. He pointed to Sidroc, and then lifted his bone whistle to his lips and let out a sharp, single, and long note. Rannveig spoke to Sidroc, and he nodded at both she and Tindr. Then Tindr turned to me and blew out two shorter, deeper notes.

"It is how he will call us, when we are out of sight," Sidroc explained.

Tindr took his things from the cart while Rannveig came and stood near me. The strings of coloured glass beads about her neck shone as the Sun struck them, and the small and many- toothed brass and iron keys knotted at her waist gave off a merry tinkle as they jostled together. We turned and faced the sea, and as she smiled I thought she recalled her days here, looking out over the few roofs below to the waters beyond.

Of a sudden she pointed to the sea and said, "Sjo."

"Sio," I repeated.

"Nai," she corrected. "Sjo."

I tried again, shortening the sound, and was rewarded with, "Já."

Now she turned and pointed to the well. "Sauþ," she told me.

"Sauth," I answered, and then said it again, more slowly, "Sauþ."

"Já." Now she pulled at the well-cover, and pointed at the water glistening darkly below. "Vatn."

"Vatn," I said.

"Sol," she said, pointing straight out at the Sun above us, and then "Himl," opening her arms to the expanse of sky. She turned and pointed at Tyrsborg. "Hus," – a house.

So we went about the hall and yard, as she pointed at or touched things, and I learned their names in Norse. Some were so close to those of Angle-land, just said aslant, with only a slight change in the way they were spoken that I

59

wondered at them, and at myself too for not having listened
better whenever I had heard the speech of the Danes; but
others were sounds that were so hard for me to make that she
laughed as I tried. But I had made a start, and before she left
Rannveig took me by both hands and gave them a little
squeeze, as if she were proud of my trying.

The next few days were as happy as they were busy.
Sidroc was fast at work outside the front door of the hall with
Alrik, the man who lived on the road below, building that
which we would need for life at Tyrsborg. Alrik walked up
the hill with a barrow full of axes, adzes, and hammers, and a
big oxen-drawn waggon lumbered behind him, filled with split
timber ready to be worked. Together they made a long table
with paired trestles, enough for ten or more to sit at, two
smaller tables, six benches of varying lengths, and our bed.
This last was not a simple framework, for Alrik had skill at
joinery. It had four thick posts which rose into the air above
the level of the bed, and between the posts at head and foot
he placed flat boards which bridged the span. It was large and
solid and the rising posts would give, I thought, a sense of
shelter when one lay within.

As they were finishing I came and praised it. They had
worked on it three days and their grins told me they were
both proud of it. Now they were kneeling on a ground
covered with sawdust and curled wood shavings, their brows
glowing with sweat under the warm Sun. Sidroc arose and
disappeared into the hall for a moment. He came out with a
long fragment of charcoal from the fire pit, which he held in
one hand. With the other he lifted my left wrist, that which
bore the silver disk bracelet.

"Draw a knot, one like this which we both have
worn," he told me, and looked to the interlaced design
adorning the disk of the bracelet. "There," he said, nodding

to the boards bridging the area at the head of the bed. "Draw it as big as you can."

I looked down at the small silver many-armed knot, twisting in upon itself. Now he wished this same design to embellish our bed. I stepped in within the empty framework of the bed and knelt down before the wood, and judged the centre of the piece, and then made a mark to begin. I drew a circle, as wide across as the length of my hand and forearm, and then stroked in the twisting curves of the knot as they folded in and over each other. It took me some little time, looking back at my bracelet and then to my drawing, but the men sat back from their labour and drank Rannveig's good ale from the crock we filled each morning, and were content to watch.

When I had done I stood and brushed the crumbling charcoal from my hands. Both hands were filthy and I had a feeling some had gotten smudged across my nose as well, but Sidroc as he looked at me only smiled.

"I will carve it in," he said, "this knot that cannot be broken, which we both made."

Tindr was much away these first few days, for to him we entrusted the task of buying us fowl and a milk cow. He went to the upland farms of his cousins, going by a forest path behind Tyrsborg, and came back next day leading a brown cow with a dainty head and huge eyes. Her calf had just been weaned from her, her first, so she was young and we could hope for many years of good milk. Butter could only be made when cows were on grass and their milk at its richest, and soon she would have to be kept on Winter fodder; but for now she could still crop the long grasses which grew outside the front door, and those which fringed the forest behind the hall. The Gotlandic butter was the finest I had ever tasted, and I knew that it would not be long before this treat we must do without. But even in Winter she would still give milk to us, and next Spring when the new grass came we should have our own butter again too.

Tindr brought us also twelve hens, white-feathered, speckled with brown; and a rooster who flew up, crowing, into the rafters of the stable as soon as Tindr released him from his withy cage. These he had bought from folk in town, for all kept their own fowl, as townsfolk nearly always do. He surprised me by buying us six geese too, grey-feathered, already plump and swaying as they waddled about; but as we meant to keep horses he knew we would have grain with which to keep them, and fatted goose is a dish all look forward to at mid-Winter feasts.

It was Winter and its coming I often thought of, tho' still the days were warm enough at their height to go about without a mantle, and the Sun shone, it seemed to me, every day in the clearest of blue skies. But each day the Sun sunk lower quicker, and each morning, I knew, rose later, and the growing chill in the air when he hid his face in the dark reminded me that soon I would see a Winter unlike any I had known.

My work these first days was almost all towards this end. Down on the trading-road I bought bolt after bolt of heavy woven woollen goods, which they called wadmal, to make us warm clothing, and many more bolts of costly linen to furnish our bed, to sew into shifts for me and tunics for Sidroc, and to make into towels. Parting with so much silver for this made me bite my lip, but there was no help for it. Alrik was building me two looms, but I had as of yet no spun thread, of either wool or flax, and the spinning of thread enough to weave was the work of more than one woman, work that took many weeks. I bought bags of carded fleece, for over the Winter I could spin and so build up my store of woollen thread.

Rannveig had sent to her nephew's farm and got me sacks and sacks of fowl feathers, and with them at my feet I sat in the afternoon Sun and stuffed up the feather-bed casing I had sewn from linen. She told me too to make another featherbed, with half as much of the down within, to use as blanket, for this was the warmest coverlet against the coming cold. I did this, and seamed up blankets of wool as well, and hoped that with the new brass brazier we had bought the treasure room would be warm enough in the long nights.

Then I would look up at Sidroc where he stood with Alrik as they bent over the wood they smoothed, and know I would be kept safe.

Each day for Sidroc and Alrik was spent at the building of our tables, benches, and bed; and they took time as well to add shelves to the treasure room walls, and a rank of shelves also near the door to the kitchen yard. Around the hall they pounded in many new pegs, useful to hang things upon, and before he was done Alrik even built a ladder for the stable loft.

I had never seen so much new furniture, and its smooth and unmarked surfaces, its cleanness and brightness, almost dazzled me when I looked upon it. Tindr had his own part in this, for with a piece of tanned hide he rubbed a thick and fragrant paste of golden beeswax into the raw new wood, and then burnished it with a piece of shearling until it gleamed.

Sidroc had used a special knife of Alrik's, one with two edges joined, to carve in the great knot design I had drawn at the head of our bed. When it was finished they took it apart and carried it into the treasure room in pieces, and then re-pegged it there. Alrik did not string the bottom with a netting of hempen rope on which to lay the feather-bed, as was done in Angle-land, but instead, to keep the cold from rising from the floor, laid solid planks of wood from side to side across the bottom. This made a platform for the thick feather-bed I had sewed and stuffed, just like the wooden box-beds within the sleeping alcoves in the hall.

The first night we were to sleep on it I unrolled my plush weaving and laid it at the side of the new bed. It was growing chillier each night, and I had already filled our brazier with chunks of burning charcoal from the fire and carried it in. It glowed softly, and I had lit a stone oil cresset where it sat on its new shelf on the wall, so we had light as well as some warmth. The door opened behind me and Sidroc stepped in. The bed was heaped high from the loft of the featherbed and the down-filled coverlet I had made.

"It will be soft as a snow-bank," Sidroc said; and at that I hugged myself and laughed, "I hope it will be warmer than a snow-bank."

"You will be warm," he answered, and grinned. We looked at the huge knot I had drawn and he had carved. In the little light the grooves he had dug to outline its twisting arms looked deep, and they seemed to fold in on each other in endless embrace. We stood silently, looking on it, and then Sidroc pulled from off his neck a small tuft of long dark fur tied at the end of a leathern cord. It was cut from the mane of the great bull aurochs which had nearly trampled me. He hung it now on the wall over the bed, on a tack I had not seen. He had no need of a talisman of male strength, but I knew he honoured the might and potency of that beast which he had slain by taking, and keeping, this small trophy. Now he placed it above our bed in silent invocation of increase for those who would sleep below.

One morning we awoke and Tindr was not in the hall or stable. His alcove was empty, and the pail of milk he took from our cow each morning was waiting for me, but we ate our toasted loaves and barley browis without him. I was out in the kitchen yard rolling the milk in the churn when he appeared at the edge of the trees. He was leaning forward, dragging something heavy on the ground behind him, which was fastened to a sling bound round his waist. He wore his hair in two braids, which I had not seen him do before. As he neared I saw his bow upon his back, and his leathern arrow-quiver at his elbow.

Sidroc came through the door of the hall, and Tindr raised his face and nodded to us both, his tiny bone whistle moving in the air as it dangled from its cord. Tindr's face was oddly grave, and I too stood as he dragged the heavy sling to the edge of the larger fire-ring. Now we saw the red deer he had taken, a young stag. He untied the ends of the sling from round his waist, and as the flaps fell open I saw that he had already gutted it. He knelt down by the body and placed his hands upon it, and they rested there a moment.

There was reverence in how he did this, which I had never seen in a hunter before.

Then I noticed his hands. On the backs of his hands were drawn runes in charcoal, one large rune on each, but I could not make out what they were. Now he grasped the beast by its slender legs and braced himself on one knee and with a grunt swung it up upon the kitchen work table. We were now near him, and as he took his hands from the stag I saw two more runes, one each drawn on the inside of his palms.

Sidroc watched, and nodded to me. Then Tindr turned to us, and gave his shy smile. He opened his hand to the stag, and we again saw the rune drawn there, smudged but still visible. I made the gesture his mother had taught us

65

to thank him, a quick touch at the heart and the hand turning back towards the one you were grateful to. He smiled again, and nodded with a movement of his head to the forest behind us.

Sidroc stepped forward and pointed to Tindr's left hand, which he raised in response. The rune upon it was ᚠ, Feoh. It was the first letter in the names of both Freyr and Freyja. The rune itself meant animal wealth, such as cattle; and I thought he brought us the wealth of the forest that ran under the protection of the Lady of the Beasts, Freyja.

Sidroc took a cooking-poker from the fire-ring stones and drew the point in the hard earth of the ground. He drew Feoh, and then pointed to me. Tindr looked at the rune, then at me, then smiled and nodded his head at me.

"He knows now that you share the same fulltrúi, that one you have given yourselves to. On the backs of his hands he calls to Freyja, and on the inside, on his palms, I think he asks her to open her sacred pen and let loose a beast she has chosen for him to kill."

I was greatly moved by this, both the devotion Tindr showed, and the trust behind that devotion.

Tindr opened a pouch at his belt and pulled from it a stout cord, and set to work tying the hind legs of the deer. Together the men lifted it and moved to one of the kitchen sheds, and Sidroc slung the cord over one of the high pegs hanging at the roof beam within.

We had as yet still no serving man nor woman who cooked for us, but the stag would need to hang for several days to grow tender. I saw now that with Tindr in our household we should not want for fresh meat. Indeed, the next morning he dragged another stag, a true hart, into the kitchen yard from the forest, only to slide the leathern sling from out it and vanish once again up the path. He returned shortly with a second hart; he must have shot them both in quick succession. All were shot cleanly, a single arrow at the heart, a fast and merciful death; and each he touched with the same reverence with his rune-drawn hands. It was early Fall and the woods ran with game, yet I knew he possessed special skill, and greater still I thought was his favour with the Lady of the Woods, Freyja.

That night was cool, a true sense of frost coming on, and when Tindr came in from shutting the fowl in the stable I saw he wore his mantle. It was fastened now with a silver pin. I had not seen it before. It was large, round, and with incised designs in both the circular part and the stabbing pin itself. It was a handsome piece, a pin such as a lord would wear, and my face must have shown this as I pointed to where it lay fastened on his rough brown woollen cloak.

He grinned at me, and his hand went to the pin, and then he touched his left cheek with his hand. Sidroc. Sidroc had gone to the silver-smith on the trading road, and bought this fine pin as reward for Tindr's hunting prowess. He had ever been open-handed with his men at Four Stones, and now here at Tyrsborg he gave his first gift in like manner. Tindr wore the pin thenceforth, and it became, I think, after his bow, his most prized possession.

Despite the gladness I felt in each new day I would sometimes awake in the dark, trying to keep myself from riding the night-mare. Sometimes she carried me off, and I awoke with a start, or even a muffled cry. If Sidroc slept I calmed myself by curling up to him and burying my face in his chest. The solidness of him, his steady breathing, his smell of man and leather, all gave comfort, and in a while I would sleep again. Sometimes when I woke he too was wakeful, and he would stroke my hair as he tried to lull me back to sleep. One night when he himself awoke with a start we spoke of it.

"In the day I feel happy, with no fear," I told him in the darkness that surrounded us. "Then when I sleep…" There was no need to tell him of my night-horrors; he had lived them with me.

"It will pass," he told me. "It is soon yet. They will lessen with time."

I thought of this, and then reminded him, "You too awake when the night-mare snatches you away, as you did just now."

I felt him nod. "Yes," he allowed.

If I suffered thus, how much the greater it might be for him. The more you have killed, the more blood you have drawn, the more danger you have seen – all these things could, at night, rise up to surround you.

I thought back to the danger I had known at Kilton, the great slaughter that had taken place in the hall in the surprise attack of the Danes at Yule-tide. I had been in desperate fear of my life, and those of all who I loved. When it was over I had felt sick at it, and numb, and had fearful dreams a few nights, but they had passed. I was with child then; perhaps my need to look forward to the coming babe, fraught with remorse as I was over it, kept me from the kind of dreams I suffered from now. I thought all this, and said none of it, and Sidroc spoke again.

"It is bad this time, for there was not one battle, but many; not one fear for your life you felt, but almost always; danger every day, sometimes great danger." He could have been speaking for us both. He paused a moment and then went on, "And you feared me too."

I lowered my face again to his chest. He spoke the truth; at times I had feared him. Yet if I had been alone when I was taken by the Idrisids, I could not have borne it. I think I would have cast myself over the ship rail and into the sea. It was knowing Sidroc was there with me, even tho' I could not see him, that gave me what hope I had in those dark days.

I thought back to an earlier fear, one bland and commonplace next to this, but one that had been much on my mind as I had said my farewells to Ælfwyn and Ceric. I felt I must go to Sceaftesburh and make a new life there, and this I did not want. I found it hard to accept that the web of Fate held this for me. As a girl I had not wanted the life the Prior had cast for me, and I left. I had left the new and good life I had found with Ælfwyn, left it only to save Gyric's life, but I had left. I had ever been active in the weaving of my Fate. Yet I could not see a way to re-work the destiny seemingly in store for me as I rode away from Four Stones a few weeks ago.

When we were captured and the web of Fate suddenly restrung that fear fell away, as did any others in the goal of escaping the ship. Then as Sidroc took us further from Angle-land and the lives we had lived there, I felt the loss of the good that still remained in my life at home, and suffered too from their fears for us.

"I did fear you, yes," I whispered to him. "I could not see Fate, our lives together, as you did, as you always have. Now I know you were right. I am living it each day."

"Freyja sent this to you," he told me. "This new life. To come to this place we had to go through fearful things. The night-mare is a relic of that. Time will drive her away."

"I want to believe you," I whispered. I wanted to feel my life, and the goodness I knew now, as the gift of the Goddess. It was part of the web we had to build together, strands pulled from loss and from fear, of which we would make a new pattern. I knew she gave life to men through fields of growing grain, and in wool-giving sheep and milk-giving cattle. I knew she gave the hunt with its blood and death and life-giving gift of the beasts she protects to the men she loves.

"Ask Freyja," he returned. "You are her daughter. She will help you. And – she is feeding you now, through Tindr, more than me."

I knew he meant to make me smile at that, but my question to him was as grave as I felt. "Do you ask Tyr to help with the night-mare who takes you? You are his son, will he not help you with that?"

His pause was a long one. "Tyr gave me the sureness of my right arm, so that I still live. But Tyr is also the Law-giver. He sees and gives justice, even when it is not pleasant. The night-mare is the price I must pay for the men I have killed."

"Some you killed to protect me, or to keep yourself alive; does that not matter to him?"

"Yes, he sees and knows a just killing, from needless slaughter," he said. He drew breath before he went on. "I killed my own kin – Toki. I had to; he gave me no choice. But blood is blood. I have watered the Earth with the blood of men, left much for the carrion birds to fight over. And I have done both; killed to stay alive, and killed, many times, for treasure only, even when I got little."

There was no answer for this; it was the way of the raiding warrior, the path he had been called to, and he did not excuse himself from his deeds.

"But I have never killed a woman," he went on, across the darkness. "And I have never forced a woman. Even when all about me were. I saw there was no pleasure in it. And to do so enrages Freyja, whose favour I sought. Even when I was young I would look for a woman to come to me willingly, even if I need press silver into her hand."

He made a soft sound, as if laughing at himself. "I tell you everything, shield-maiden," he murmured. "Every warrior's secret now you know. At least those given to one who has lived to see three and thirty years." He breathed out a long breath. "There is a price for all."

"Perhaps Freyja wishes me to pay a price too," I said.

His answer was swift and sure. "No. From you she will exact no such toll. She made you to follow her in courage, and in love. She made you beautiful too. To be like her, but live here among mortal women. And to be mine. You need do nothing more."

Chapter the Fifth: A Chance at Happiness

EACH day I walked down the hill to see Rannveig, to ask her counsel, to fill our crock with ale, or merely for the gladness it gave me for a few minutes' visit. She worked each morning over her ales, sprinkling the ever-sprouting barley with water, toasting that which was of the right size in her small malting-oven, grinding this dried malt in her stone quern, plucking and pounding mugwort, borage, and other flavouring herbs from her garden. She had a serving girl who came to help her in late morning with the endless tasks of cleaning and readying the scores of pottery cups in which she served her wares, and another woman, Gudfrid, nearly her own age, who had been with her for years, who cooked and helped with all else.

Sometimes we took time to sit in Rannveig's snug house beyond the brewing yard, a place filled with odd and colourful things, bought here on the trading road but come from distant places, or carried back long ago from voyages her husband had made. She had game pieces for dice and for bones, of the purest white, and carved from walrus ivory; and she told me of those huge sea beasts, brought back from the hunts of the men who lived on the Baltic coast and far to the North. She had many cushions of bright fabric of yellow and red woollen stuff and adorned with clever thread-work of prancing horses and laden waggons, and these too were the work of the far North, of the women thereof. There were candle-holders of hammered brass filled with honey-scented beeswax candles she made herself, so many that to step inside her house and take a deep breath was a joy to me.

When I came to Gotland I owned nothing of value save the carpet and work-box Sidroc had claimed for me from the slave women on the Idrisid ship, and when I had shown the box to Rannveig she had marvelled over the ivory comb, long and sharp steel needles, balls of strong silk thread, and most of all the gold-washed bird-shaped shears. Here in her house I saw many such costly stuffs, small precious things made far away and in a manner strange to me, her gain from a lifetime lived in a trading town visited by merchants from across the sea.

She was my first and so far sole woman-friend on Gotland, and she had liked us enough to offer us not only her hall to live in, but her son to serve us. She was good-humoured in teaching me the tongue of Gotland, and I think my eagerness to learn pleased her. And she asked us no questions. She did not, as most women would, ask me who we were, or where we came from, or why. Like the good woman of business she was, she let our silver and our actions to her speak for themselves. She knew Sidroc was a Dane; that she could tell; but tho' she knew I was not, she never asked from which land I had come.

Today I found her hovering over the last crock in a long line of them, a wooden spoon dripping with Tindr's golden honey poised above it. She glanced up at me and nodded her head, then with her practised eye tipped the spoon and let it dribble in until she judged how much was needed. She took up a wooden paddle and stirred the honey in, the last step in her ale-making before letting it rest. Her ale was the best I had tasted, as good I thought as the Lady Modwynn's at Kilton, but so different it was hard to compare. I had had to stop myself once from telling her of it, and of her, a woman I admired so well, a good woman too, but so unlike Rannveig.

She finished her stirring and looked along the line of crocks. They were tall, thick-walled, as deep as my arm, of dark brown pottery, their outsides so heavily glazed that light glinted off their curved sides when the Sun raked in under the shed roof. She shook out a light linen cloth and laid it over the top lip of the crock she had just added the honey to, then lifted the cloth off the next crock and bent low to take a sniff, checking I knew, for any hint of sourness. She nodded her head in a satisfied way and turned back to me.

"Tindr's honey has been good this year; I am happy with my ale, and I will make a lot of mead," she told me. She lifted her hand to the edge of the garden, where two of her son's hives were set. We had already tasted her mead, and I smiled to hear that she would have a ready supply soon.

"You must miss him," I said by way of answer. I knew he saw his mother every day, but he was no longer about the brew-house and garden, and no longer did he sleep in her snug house.

"Já," was all she said with a sigh. "But you give him a start, and that is good. Tindr cannot be a brewer; he must make his way as he can, and with you he can care for your animals and keep you in meat." She dipped her head to the shed nearest the malt-oven; it was a smoke-house, and inside were hanging several haunches of the deer Tindr had brought us, curing.

I had already such affection for Tindr that he was almost a younger brother in my heart. I think Rannveig knew this, and was grateful for all who were kind to this shy young man who could not hear and was more at home in the forest glades than along the bustling trading road.

This morning it was the trading road Rannveig and I were headed to, and she pulled off her stained brewing apron and looped a small hand basket over her wrist. Thus prepared, we set out across the brewing yard and through the empty brew-house. Rannveig had hoped to find us a serving-woman from amongst her upland nieces, or the daughters of friends, but it had proven more difficult than she had thought. The niece she had her eye on declared she would wed her sweetheart before the onset of Winter, and as soon as she found another who might suit the girl would be needed at her farm to help with the last grain harvests, or apple-picking; or illness or misfortune at home meant she was needed there. Today we were going to one of the woollen-seller's stalls, who Rannveig knew had a likely daughter.

There was enjoyment in walking along the busy trading road and its quieter side ways with her; folk knew and respected Rannveig, and her head over her plump neck was kept bobbing up and down in returning the greetings she received as they passed us. But all the women of Gotland had a forthrightness I admired; none feared looking at a man directly and dealing with him as equals, even strange men. It was a trading-town where folk from all over and with many differing customs came to buy and to sell, and the women of Gotland who made and sold their works of leathern goods or fabric or cheese raised their faces quietly and without boldness or guardedness to do their business with all who came and bought.

I had before visited the woollen-seller's stall that we stopped at, for it was there I had bought lengths of the heavy and brightly-dyed wadmal to make curtains for Tindr's alcove and blankets for our beds. Today I saw the same young women I had seen before, three who I judged to be sisters, and another woman, their sister in law perhaps, all at work, two at their looms in the rear of the stall, weaving the same heavy wool that they sold, and two spinning in calm and steady motion. The eldest of them stood up front to greet customers, drawing thread onto her hand spindle from a length of fluffy roving thrown over her left shoulder. Before her sat a narrow counter stacked with bolts of wadmal dyed in blues and greens. A babe of several months slept in a basket near her feet, and two little boys of three and four years tumbled around the feet of the women in the weaving room. I thought the eldest sister to be no older than me, and the youngest to have sixteen or seventeen years.

The sister at the counter smiled at us and made her greeting, and I too returned her "Goþr morgun" with one of my own. She turned her head and called, and one of the weavers slid her shuttle between her warp and came out to us. She was the youngest of the four, a pretty thing, plump and with curling yellow hair that peeked out from her blue head-wrap. She had bright blue eyes and high colour in her round cheeks, and would have been a happy sight to look upon if she had smiled. As it was her small lips turned up for just a moment as she curtsied to us. It was clear she knew that we looked for a serving woman, but I could not tell if she was unwilling, or saddened by something.

Rannveig and the older sister spoke at length, and while I understood some of what they said, they spoke so quickly that I could not hear all. Rannveig knew the family, of course; in a place so small it was not possible she did not. During this time the girl, whose name was Sigvor, looked mostly at the floor, sometimes raising her eyes to glance at Rannveig or at me.

"Do you want to ask her anything?" Rannveig said, turning to me of a sudden. Without waiting for my answer she went on, and slowly enough for me to understand. "With Winter coming on and trading season over, they do not need her at her loom; she could come at least until Spring. Sigrid says she's a handy girl, good-tempered and quick to learn. She was to have wed this month, but her sweetheart went out to fish at Mid-Summer and never returned."

My mouth opened at this, and Sigvor shot a look at me. I thought her eyes welled, and she lowered them again.

"The family is a good one;" Rannveig went on, "their farm lies past the end of this cross-road, where the rest of their people raise the sheep the girls spin and weave from."

Both Rannveig and the older sister Sigrid were now looking to me for my answer.

76

"Sigvor," I began, and the girl again looked up at me, "do you want to come? I have need of you if you do." I spoke slowly, for in my new tongue I must, but I saw she understood.

Sigvor nodded her head, and Rannveig clapped her hands together.

"Can you come tomorrow," I asked the girl, for I was eager to have help as soon as I might. With a quiet "Já," and a nod of her head she said she would, and after thanking Sigrid and bidding all four women good morning, we left the woollen stall and headed back up the trading road.

I took Rannveig's hand in gratitude for all she had done to help me. She laughed and waved away my thanks, but I saw that she welcomed being of service in this way, and welcomed the fact that I recognized her importance in the town, and asked her aid.

As we neared the main pier we slowed, for a fishing boat was unloading its cargo of fat silvery fish, laying gleaming and heaped to the brim in dripping baskets. Rannveig wanted fish for her dinner, and as she knew the boat-owner well she went up to the nearest basket, and sorting through with her hands, pulled a few silver-scaled herring out and dropped them in her hand-basket.

"I will come tonight and drink my catch's worth and more of ale," he joked to her, for indeed, many folk paid for Rannveig's ale and mead not in coin, but in goods.

I smiled too and looked at him, a man of about thirty years who looked as strongly built as his stout boat. He fished the waters round Gotland, but Rannveig had told me his brother was a trader who sailed the Baltic coast. Of a sudden I thought to speak to him, and so I tried.

"Your brother – does he sail to Frankland?" I asked.

I do not know what made me think of this then, other than the man being before me, but I could not help my question. My heart began to beat faster thinking of what I would write in a letter to Ælfwyn.

He tilted his head to me, and I repeated my question, looking to Rannveig for help. She nodded and spoke to him herself.

"Nai, nai," he told me. He looked over his shoulder at the sea behind him. "Frankland is far. Far."

I nodded and turned, but not before I read in Rannveig's eyes her question. She and I turned to leave the pier. There I saw Sidroc standing at the foot of it, looking at me.

That afternoon I stood at one of my new looms, working. I had warped it two days before, and made a fair start on a length of linen I had begun, drawing thread from costly balls of fine thread I had bought along the trading road. Both looms rested against the wall, one on either side of the door in the long wooden wall which gave out to the grassy court before the stable, so that I might have the best light with which to work.

When we had returned to Tyrsborg late in the morning it had begun to rain, the first we had had in the weeks since we had come to Gotland, where, unlike Wessex or Lindisse, the Sun was glad to show his face every day. It fell gently enough that we could have the hall doors open, and between that and the two windows I had light to weave. The linen thread was smooth between my fingertips as I lay it down, and I could not help wonder but from whence it had come, and then think further of Ælfwyn and her fields of flax.

From there my thoughts moved quickly to remembering Ceric standing at her side, her arm across his shoulder, as I turned one last time in the waggon seat to hold my hand up to them in fare-well. I shook my head to rid this thought; suddenly I felt close to tears.

I heard bounding steps coming from the kitchen yard door, and Sidroc came through it, shaking the rain from his arms and tossing his head. He came to me, but I did not turn my head to him; I did not want him to see the tears filling my eyes.

He knew when I thought of them; he could not help but do so, for it was the only time in our long and full days I was sad. Yet I had never once uttered their names since we had come here. Now he sat down on the bench near me, and waited.

I drew breath and spoke.

"There is one thing I do not feel I can speak to you of. Ceric – and Ælfwyn."

He straightened up, but did not speak.

"It is hard to be happy when I know they suffer, grieving us." He still was silent, so I made bold to speak again. "If we could send a letter to Ælfwyn, let her know we live –"

He jumped up. "What have you done?" he broke in, looking over my head almost as if he expected to see someone there. "Do you ask for something you have already done?"

I shook my head, but he went on. "Did you ask the man at the pier if he would carry a letter for you? To Lindisse? Did you?"

Now I was almost trembling.

"I asked only, that is all. And not to Lindisse, nor even Angle-land. I asked if his brother, a trader, went to Frankland, that is all. I did not say why. I thought if he went so far as that, he might find another man to carry a letter to Ælfwyn."

His silence and his staring eyes were worse than if he had screamed in anger at me.

In my panic I went on, my words tumbling out. "But he said no; it was 'far, far'. I think no Gotlandic man sails as far as Frankland."

He spoke now, and his voice was low.

"When we are in danger, you must obey me," he said. "Why can I not make you see the danger in this wish of yours." He looked at me and nothing else, and I felt that his eyes burned through me.

He shook his head at me. "You were a full partner to me. Now I cannot trust you." He sunk down upon the bench, and held his head in his hands.

Little he could have said would wound me as much as this, and I fell upon my knees before him. I wanted to cling to him, beg his pardon, but something in the quietness of his words stayed me, and I sat back on my heels in the misery I had brought upon us both.

He lifted his head to look at me. "We cannot have everything; we cannot have all. I cannot have Four Stones and my children, and you. You cannot have me and our new life here, and your son and Kilton too."

My eyes widened, and he added, "I mean, your treasure and folk at Kilton, not the man. Him I know you do not want."

He drew breath, ran his hand through his hair, looked up. "I made the choice for us, yes. It was not your choice. I saw a chance, at last, to live with you, and took it. I fought and killed to keep you safe and bring us both here alive. Now we are here, and the Gods smile on us. I did not want you for one night, but every night. All my life. Now you ask to risk all. We can send no message without fear of losing all we have built here, all we are building."

"But Ælfwyn – her not knowing if we live…sometimes I cannot bear it."

He paused a moment. On the small table by my loom were a pile of short threads I had snipped. He took up two and held them in his fingers, side by side.

"You and she are like this," he told me, moving two free ends. "You did not start together, nor will you end together –" He moved the other two free ends. Now he twisted the two threads together so they crossed tightly in the middle. "But here, in the middle, you are bound. You are tied tight together here, even though at either end you run free."

Yes. Ælfwyn and I were bound; first through our love of the other, and then through Gyric, and now Sidroc.

I looked at him wordlessly.

"The Gods made it so, we cannot know why," he went on. "Her path must run on; yours is here at my side."

I heaved a sigh. "But one letter, telling her that we live –"

His eyes were fixed on me, but I went on. "She reads now; no one else need know, not even her priest."

"You think she could keep such a letter secret?" His voice spoke his disbelief. "And beyond this, she could keep from telling your son you live?"

I had not thought that far; of course she would in pity send to Ceric and tell him too, and even should she implore him not to speak, he was a boy; others there at Kilton would surely find out.

"Why do you wish disaster upon us? It is better that they grieve for us, and go on with their living. Only evil will come if they know we are alive. A letter, a token sent; these things will cause Kilton to hunt for us. Is this what you want, always to be fought over?"

"No, no," I choked out, stung at the thought behind this claim. "I only want Ceric and Ælfwyn to know we are well."

"And you cannot see beyond that. You cannot see disaster."

He braced his hands on his knees and lifted his head. "If we leave things as they are, we all have a chance at happiness. And what happened to us happens often. My father went out sailing one morning and never came back. Folk leave all the time on journeys, to trade, to settle in new places, and never are seen or heard from again. Raiders grab folk as slaves. That happened to us! Yet we live, and this is not enough for you."

I made a little gesture to him, trying to let him know I heard, and understood. But he went on, his voice now so quiet that I must strain to hear.

"I know I do not mean to you what you mean to me; this I know. But the way you give your body to me made me feel you…had regard for me."

Now I could not stay my tears, and I threw myself at him. He let me place my arms about him, but did not hold me in return. "Sidroc, I love you. I love you. You are my husband. You are my man. It is you I want."

He pushed me gently away. "Then why do you call for my death?"

The shock of this made me rock forward, and I placed my hands upon the floor boards and then hid my face in them. Over the racing of my heart I felt the blood pulsing in my temples, almost deafening me. He had risked his life over and over for us, done nothing but his best to keep us safe and alive. Yet my wish to send word would place him at more, and greater risk. He had given me his whole trust, and I had shaken it. Now he even doubted my love for him.

I stood on my knees to face him. He sat before me, but his head was turned away. I did not try to touch him.

"I beg of you to forgive me," I began. I spoke slowly, drawing breath often. My eyes were dry, and beyond tears. "It was selfish of me, only selfish, to act so; to try to make myself feel better about them. I will never do so again. It was not our fault we were captured. You are right, we must let them grieve, and then let them go on to live."

He did not turn his head, and I would not stop until he would once again look at me.

"When we were finally free and I realized you meant for us to go on together, I felt a captive once again. Then the night you won me this necklace –" I touched the thick chain of braided silver – "you made me see that we could never go back. Even if we survived the sea-voyage, we would have to face Godwin and his wrath towards us both.

"What you do not know is how much, even then, I cared for you." He turned his head back to me now. "You do not know that even then I began to – want you.

"I would rather die myself than see you fight again. This is what you mean to me. I want to deserve your full trust, to be your partner in all things. 'Regard for you' – if this is all you feel I have for you after our nights and mornings of love – if you feel I do not trust you, honour you, cherish you with my whole being – that is my fault. I have shaken your faith in me."

I reached for his hand and he let me have it. "You are right, we cannot have everything. What I want most is life with you." I placed his hand over my breast. "To be your wife."

His other hand lifted and reached behind me, and swept me in between his legs. Our faces were close now, and my words low. "'Regard for you' – I give you my body as I do because I love you. I give you my body because I want yours, want to feel your hands on my skin, your strength as you lift and move me, and then to feel you moving within me as you make me yours over and over again. Freyja did mark me for you; I know you were right, for she fires me with passion and yearning for you. I want to delight you, and accept the delight you so freely give me."

He pressed me against him, and began pulling me off the floor and into his lap. I hooked my hand into his belt and made him stand. Behind us was the treasure room door; I made to pull him towards it as I said, "If you do not think I love you as you love me, then let me take you to our bed and show you now that you are wrong."

Chapter the Sixth: The Red-Sailed Ship

Four Stones in Lindisse, Angle-land

EANFLAD'S return to us gave us unlooked-for joy. She moved and spoke as one just arising from a long sleep, yet was at last more of us, and with us, than she had been since girlhood. I promised to take her to Oundle as soon as I could, so that our mother could behold her, whole again in mind, and so that Abbess Sigewif might bless her.

Four Stones itself was quiet with so many men gone. It had been well over three weeks since the disappearance, and I had near given up hope that any message might come from the men left at Saltfleet, waiting there for a ransom demand. But with thirty pairs of men combing Lindisse I hoped some might return within a few days with word. And three days after they left, one pair did return, with news that some fisher-folk up the coast had told them a tale of a strange ship seen last month. The men they had told it to had ridden and found Godwin and Asberg, who had gone to search the caves Asberg had told him of. Two days later Asberg's cousin rode to me, saying that Godwin and Asberg would themselves return on the morrow, after they had spoken to the fisher-folk.

I met them in the hall, Burginde and Æthelthryth at my side. I knew little about the ship-sighting, and tried to read the men's faces as we offered them ale. There was no look of expectancy on either of them; and Asberg looked so grim that I steadied my hand with difficulty as I tipped the ewer over our cups.

"You have news," I said.

"We have some," Godwin answered.

"Tell me, please, of the ship we have heard of," I asked first.

Asberg nodded. "We spoke to an old woman, of a fisher-family. We went ourselves to question her; she lives a day's ride from here, up the coast. She was out whelking at low tide. She knew it was just on, or about, St Mary's Day; she could not be sure, but she was gathering whelks for their feast-meal from the sea-rocks with her grandchildren. They saw a ship, sailing North up the coast, one they had not seen before. Large, high, and broad. Red sails."

"Red sails," I repeated, looking at them and wondering what sort of sea-men sailed so close to our shores. "Who would sail such a ship?"

But Godwin took up without answering me. "The caves we searched were empty, with no sign of recent use. But we rode back to Saltfleet to check the bluff again. We went over every path that led to a view of the sea below." He stopped and took something from his belt. "We found this," he ended, and passed a small object into my palm.

It was a tiny and bright silver coin, stamped with a seax on one side, and flowing marks like embroidery on the other.

"It is a seax," I offered, gesturing to the angle-bladed knife. "But these are no letters of a king's name we know." I handed it back to Godwin.

Godwin turned the coin between his fingers, then glanced to me.

"It is not a seax, but a long curved sword." He studied the flowing marks on the other side. "They are letters, but of a speech so different from our own no one can read them."

86

He looked to Asberg and said, "Tell her what you told me."

Asberg paused. "The curved sword tells me they are of the South. Maybe Abbasid or Khazar."

My face must have shown I had never heard of them. "The red-sailed ship was theirs? Who are these folk? What do you know of them?"

"They are from beyond Cadiz. They are great slavers."

My heart fell. Then there would indeed be no call for ransom.

It was hard to form my next question. "And it was found on the bluff?" The same bluff that they had been upon.

"Up on the bluff, in a clearing, in trampled brush," Asberg said. "Trampled by men," he added. "No hoof prints. There were men, only a few."

"If they came, and went, by ship…" Godwin shook his head. "Still, the coin alone cannot point to Abbasids or any other tribe; any trader who sails may have had such silver. But it has not been there long; it is still bright."

I forced my thoughts forward, until my throat eased enough to speak again. "Whether for ransom or by slavers, if they were stolen away I thank God they are together. Sidroc will die before he lets harm come to her."

Godwin looked at me a long time. "That I believe," he answered.

Our words hung in the air. I have rarely regretted speaking the truth, yet I knew Asberg shifted in his place. I addressed them both. "What now?"

Asberg shook his head and answered. "We wait."

But Godwin said, "I return to Kilton, as soon as a ship can be found to take us. There is nothing more to be done here. If word is sent, or ransom demand made, you will send to me, and I to you." He had been holding the silver coin, and now passed it once more to me as he moved away.

I asked Æthelthryth to see to the evening meal, and went up to the weaving room with Burginde. The coin was still clutched in my hand, and I opened it only when we gained the room and I sat down upon my bed. It was so small, smaller than any of the coins of Wessex or Lindisse, but the silver must be very pure, for it was bright and the stamping sharp and clear. It, and the tale of the red-sailed ship, was all that remained to speak for those who had vanished. The men had done what they could, and found only this. Now Godwin would set off for Kilton, and life at Four Stones would need to go on. I felt a hollowness, sere and dry, within me.

"Do you want him back?"

It had been so long since we had spoken that Burginde's voice startled me. She stood, looking down at her dropping spindle, then drawing it up and winding the newly spun thread upon the shaft. It took a moment for me to realise what she had asked.

"I care for him, of course. You know that."

"'Tis not what I asked."

"He has always been kind to me."

"Do you want him back?"

"He has been a good and loving father; the children miss him so."

"'Tis not what I asked."

"He has built up much here; done everything he could to make, and keep, peace. No man could have done more."

"And do you want him back? He has been stolen away with the Lady, that we know. If they still live, would you want him back?" She had stopped in her spinning and was staring at me.

I closed my eyes. "I want – I want what the Holy Mother of God and our Lord Christ wants for them. These things I cannot know."

I knew this alone would not satisfy her, and I paused a moment and thought what I wanted. All I could say was what I had always said. "I want them to be safe. And happy."

"And for yourself? Do you want him back?"

I did not answer, and she went on, "His Fate, and the Fate of the Lady Ceridwen, are tangled together; that we have seen from years long passed. He cannot help that."

I nodded, and had to sigh. "He has won everything he wanted in life, but her. If they can free themselves from their captors, he would not come back."

I had kept myself from thinking much on this, for my greatest desire was that Sidroc and Ceridwen still lived. My second wish beyond that was that they be safe, and free. If this could be granted I would have to think of what they would do with that safety and freedom.

The work of building, of amassing treasure, of assuring peace, was over at Four Stones and throughout Lindisse. Those excitements and dangers had been replaced by the cares and concerns of running the hall and its lands, of keeping many men in good order, of ensuring a rule of law and the carrying out of justice. He had been restless at times, yes; but I knew too he had taken pleasure in what he had won, and we had built. I knew he took pleasure in our children; even Ashild, Yrling's daughter, he treated as his own, as he had promised. Yet I felt deep within me that he would relinquish his treasure, sacrifice those things he cared for, risk even his very life, for the one he loved, the one he felt – as Burginde had said – Fated to love. I knew this because of my love for Gyric, and my eagerness ten years ago to risk everything, even my own life and the lives of others, for a chance at happiness with him.

I had still not answered her first question.

"I let him go," I finally said.

I rose from my bed and reached up and placed the coin on the base of the wooden cross above my loom, as an offering.

That night, after we had eaten, Godwin came to me. We stood by the locked door of the treasure room and spoke there; I did not want to invite him within. Men moved about the hall, lifting the trestles from the tables and stacking them along one wall. Serving folk still carried ewers and salvers and cups from the high table before us, while others trimmed the linen wicks on the oil cressets. Hrald and Ceric were darting about the hall, chasing a few other boys as they hid behind carried tables, and Ashild was right at their heels.

"My men told me that Ceric had stayed behind at Four Stones with his mother's consent," he began. "He will, of course, come back to Kilton with me."

I knew Ceric must return, but was not willing to surrender him, or his mother's wishes, without reminding Godwin of Ceridwen's rights to her own son.

"It was my idea that Ceric stay the year with us, so that Ceridwen would return next Summer for him, and we might see the other again. Ceric greatly desired this, and as his mother, Ceridwen had every right to allow him to do so. And I am sure you thank God, as I have, and undoubtedly she has, that he was not with them, and so exposed to the dangers they face."

I knew my tone was cool, and he stood a little straighter at my speech.

"He and Hrald have a rare, and real closeness, one that Ceridwen and I both hoped would bring a deeper peace between our lands." The two were now trying to clamber up one of the timber posts leading to the nearest roof-support, with Ashild jumping up and down and laughing as she tried to reach it from the floor. I could not help but smile at them, and did not look forward to their being parted.

"But yes," I went on, "I agree that now his place is back at Kilton. His aunt and grandmother must long for him."

I did not think many women, or men either, stood their ground with Godwin; he was well used to having his way in all things. If he was relieved that I surrendered his nephew to him so readily he hid it now.

"I will tell him tonight that he will leave with me when a ship is found," he answered. He paused a moment. "And you – what will you do now?"

I did not answer at first, and he added, "How will you go ahead?"

That I could answer. "As I always have. Pray. Wait, and hope. And there is always the work of the hall."

"But beyond that?"

"If hope is lost?" I shook my head against the spectre of that day. "I shall not wed again," I said.

"That would be a sad waste," he said.

If any wife or husband were gone for five years, the marriage could be declared void, and the remaining spouse might wed again.

I let my eyes lift to him. Ceridwen had told me of his own wife, Edgyth, that she was an admirable woman, loving mother, and skilled healer; but when I had visited Kilton they had been living apart, so I had never seen her. I recalled Ceridwen sitting in my garden on High Summer's Day and telling me, "He must use me as he can" when she explained that she felt she must make a marriage away from Kilton for the good of all. Now he seemed to be judging my own worth as marriage-goods. It was that, or empty flattery.

You men always speak thus, I thought, as if our value in life was nothing more than what you choose to see in us – to wed us, and bed us, use us as you need us to forge peace or wage war, give you sons to send into battle, and daughters to barter in marriage.

"I have wed twice," I said, "and have three children. Hrald will rule Four Stones soon. I need not wed again."

I have loved once, was what I said within myself; I wonder if you ever have.

Chapter the Seventh: The Counting Stone

The Island of Gotland

NOW that Sigvor had come to live with us our days began to settle into the rhythm of a great hall. There was nothing grand about Tyrsborg, but it was a fine and solid house, and with Sigvor here I could spend more time at my loom and thus make quicker progress on the lengths of linen we would need. Both Tindr and Sigvor were now in our keeping, and I must provide clothing for them both, as well as food and drink. We could buy much on the trading road, and buy it we did, for we had need of everything to start our lives together; but linen fabric was dear, and by weaving our own I could save much precious coin.

Sigvor was an expert weaver, as I had reason to expect, and just as good a spinner. She worked at the second loom, weaving the same heavy woollen fabric I had earlier bought from her sisters, and her work was as careful as if it was for sale at their stall. Together we did the household tasks of sweeping and washing up, and she helped me with the simple cooking I was able to do, for we had not yet found a man or woman who would take over the kitchen yard. We had two cauldrons of carved soap-stone, and one large one of riveted iron, and irons and frames and roasting spits and toasting forks. Only a few were those Sidroc and I had used upon the road in our journeying, for now with a household we needed everything in a greater size.

The hens Tindr had brought us were still laying, and I roasted their eggs, whole and in their speckled shells, in the ashes of the cooking-fire; made browis from the deer meat, boiled up with barley and oats and shredded parsnips, beets, and onions; and made in our big cooking pot stews of savoury fish. Each day Sigvor went and bought bread from the trading road, tho' we had covered iron pots in which to bake bread upon the coals in the cooking-ring; but the baking of bread must begin with the grinding of grain, and Sigvor and I could not do all. The bread she bought was better, I knew, than I could make, and we ate this with butter, both that we bought and that which we drew from the milk of our cow. I attempted no brewing, with Rannveig's fine ale a short walk away, and we replenished our crock at her brew-house nearly every day. To cook and eat well with Summer's abundance is easy, but to do so in the depths of Winter on short rations would be beyond my skill. I did not want to expand our household too quickly, with no way to earn silver until the coming of the sailing season, but with four of us we must have a cook if we wished to eat better, and cheaper.

Save for the weeks we had been on the road I had lived for years without doing any heavy work. Spinning and weaving and child-minding, and the tasks of numbering and caring for the fine plate and silver cups for the table, had been all that had been expected or needed from me, and I had had help with even that. Now with Sigvor's aid I swept and scrubbed, hauled water and laundered. This was our morning work, and past noon we spun and wove. Yet it was easy to take pleasure even in this. The great gratitude I felt for freedom and safety was still full upon me, and the hall I laboured in was my own, in a land which had welcomed me. I had lost flesh on the ship of the Idrisids, and then more while on the road, and now even with my modest cooking I gained it back, and felt strong and fresh and more like myself than I had in years.

Beyond all of this was the fact that I was in love.

It was Gyric who had taught me love, when I was yet a maid of fifteen. Fleeing with him, working to keep him alive, feeling that deep sorrow and grief for his blinding, coming to

94

know him as we faced danger together, being so much alone as we travelled over many weeks in the hope of reaching his home at Kilton; these things worked on my maiden heart and mind so that I felt a desperate need to be and stay near him. When he declared me his wife on the wooded pathway to Cadmar's hermitage I thought I should know no greater moment of joy. He had taught me too the sublime pleasures of my woman's body; taught me to give and receive that bliss a man and woman partake of in the fullest sharing of their bodies when they love. I knew Fate had favoured me, that this should be my experience of the giving of my body to a man; I had only to contrast it, when I could bear to recall it, to the way in which Godwin had used me.

Yet as devoted as Gyric was, I knew his love for me was rooted in his need of me. He believed I had saved his life, and because I had not known him before his maiming I stood on a different footing than any other in that life. The woman he had loved and hoped to wed had been Ælfwyn, but Fate had parted them. Each had had to find happiness in what was left to them. For Ælfwyn it was the fulfilment of her duty as a peace-weaver, the comfort of her sisters and mother, and her love for her children. In these later years she took much succour in her growing faith, as I had seen.

But lost with Gyric's eyes was much of his sense of value to his kin and king. He had loved me, and our children, truly; but his feeling that he was so much less than he had been led him to distrait and brooding sadness, and fearing he had already lost my love, to his finally yielding me to Godwin.

I took solace that our last few months together had been nearly as joyful as our first few weeks. The bond between us, so tried and challenged, was repaired. Little Ninnoc, our daughter, was a source of joy, a new beginning for us and a happy return to life for the folk of Kilton. When the fever took them both I had wished to die as well.

But I did not die. Ceric remained to me, and little
Edwin, no longer mine but destined to one day rule Kilton;
and these sons of mine, the elder born from love from my
dear Gyric, the younger out of my pride and Godwin's lust,
remained to call me to live again, as children ever will.

On the day Sidroc and I were captured I was separated
from all my possessions, rendered nameless to my captors, left
struggling for freedom and perhaps even life. That fearful
time had served as violent re-birth for me, one I did not think
I could have survived without knowing Sidroc was near. His
courage and calmness, his faith in himself and his Gods had
directed his actions and kept us alive. Even when I feared his
goals I knew he valued me above himself. His abiding love
and desire for me had guided him. Now, after all these years
of his waiting for and wanting me, I found myself anew in
that love.

I had come to love this man who had loved me deeply;
and did believe we had been led to Gotland that we might
start our lives in peace. Everything here was new, and in the
newness of my love for him there was much sudden joy. It felt
between us like some keen but quiet power of self-renewing,
and rising, strength. And Sidroc too was the source of the
deep pleasure of the re-awakening of my womanly passion.
Walking out into the kitchen yard and seeing him, stripped to
the waist, chopping into lengths an endless pile of seasoned
timber to add to our wood supply; his strong and sure hand
closing over mine as he reached to help me haul the heavy
pail up from the depths of our well; feeling the length of our
thighs touch as I sat next him at Rannveig's brew house of an
evening as we savoured her faintly bitter ale. All this gave me
joy, and such moments came every day.

Sidroc showed not one sign of regret or loss. He who
had been for years a powerful and rich jarl commanding a
hundred men was now content to chop wood with Tindr, to
plan for our comfort during Winter, and scheme for the far-

distant trading season. He had won what he wanted. In doing so he offered his happiness to me, and I grasped it with both hands, and an open heart.

One afternoon when I went to my loom I saw something small and yellow sitting upon the little table there. I grew nearer and lifted the piece in my hand. It was the bloom of a flower, a rose, all formed of beeswax, its petals so thin that light shone through them. It was a lovely thing, and I knew Tindr had made it, and this made me smile. When I saw him later I thanked him, my hand touching my heart and turning out to him. A flush came over his cheek as he smiled and looked down.

Sigvor was a good worker, and knowing she mourned I tried to be as kind to her as I could. I let her go home as often as she wished, and sometimes she stayed the night at the family farm. It had been her choice to come to us; perhaps being away from her family and her weaving work on the trading road gave her respite from the pain she must feel at the death of her sweetheart. With her plump prettiness and high colour I thought she was by nature a quick, gay, and talkative creature; but at Tyrsborg she spoke little and smiled almost never. But then we were strange to her, and I was yet learning to speak her tongue. Tindr of course she had seen many times in her life, but at first she only nodded to him, and did not return his simple gestures of question or of greeting, tho' I prompted her to do so. In the evenings after we had eaten she did the washing up, and Tindr made haste to draw the heavy bucket from the well for her, but she did not thank him with a touch at her heart.

If her sweetheart still lived, she would be wed now, living in her own croft, as humble as it might be, but with her own man and her own future to look forward to. There were many young men on Gotland, and all I could hope was that when her pain faded she would find another, and be able in time to go on with her life.

I had lost count of the days since we had been taken captive. I was hauling water from the well when I realized this, and my hands tightened as they gripped the rope.

I took a swift intake of air. I had kept careful count, numbering each while we were on the road, and inwardly noting each dawning since we had come to Gotland. Now I no longer knew. It had been two and thirty when I had last been sure. The days came quickly, were full; and I had lost count. When I become Sidroc's wife I told myself, There is no going back; let the days pass. And now I no longer knew how long we had been gone.

I had lost more than just the number. At the root of those days was the first day, that last day on which I had beheld Ceric and Ælfwyn. I knew I could do nothing, yet the thought of what they were going through each day shadowed me. By numbering the days I had kept a secret link to them, tho' they could know it not. By losing count I had let the bond grow thinner.

This was what I had pledged Sidroc to do, to keep them in my heart and yet leave them free to grieve and then go on. Shock, grief, and fear – I had known what they would feel. I had felt it all myself. Now another thought struck me: I had not thought about what they would do.

Godwin. A hand of ice reached forth and clutched my heart. The thegns from Kilton who had come for me would have swiftly gone to Godwin. I could picture him in the great hall, in one of the many work yards, or astride a horse when breathless men told him the news. I could see the gold-green eyes flash, the beautiful mouth twist, the head with its copper-gold hair toss back. He would go to Lindisse, ride I thought, almost on the instant, to find us. He could be there now. I could not know how tense this meeting might be, but I shuddered for Ælfwyn. What had Sidroc's men told him of our vanishing; had they seen the Idrisid ship from afar? Would he be angry at Ælfwyn, somehow blaming her for my loss? What would he say to her, what might he tell to her...? He would take Ceric back to Kilton with him, and raise him as his son; he would direct and colour Ceric's thoughts of me...

I hauled the bucket up in one final jerk, but found myself hanging still over the dark water below. As I stared at it I thought I glimpsed Godwin's face in the receding ripples. I had seen him in his hot rages, and I too had seen him cold, steely, and sure, and knew that this was just as deadly.

I pushed myself back and came face to face with Tindr and his ready smile. Tindr, part of the new life Sidroc and I forged here at Tyrsborg, come to take the heavy burden from my hands.

"We will take a walk today, and see if we can ride back," Sidroc said to me one morning as we broke our fast.

We had been waiting to hear when we could go to the upland farm of Tindr's cousin Ragnfast and select one or two horses from those he had brought in from Summer pasturage. Rannveig must have told Sidroc at the brew-house the night before that they were ready for us. I was glad to hear it. I felt hungry for the freshness of the forest walk, and eager to see more of the land that lay beyond the trading town. I looked forward, as well, to the meeting of new folk; and I knew that Sidroc wanted to find horses before the snow came. Tindr had come to table with us wearing his mantle, and now I knew why he ate his broth and bread so quickly; he too was glad of this small adventure. I glanced at Sigvor, quietly spooning her browis into mouth. She might not welcome being alone all the day. Tindr had already watered and fed our animals, and there was no pressing work she must do.

"Would you like to come?" I asked her. I knew the walk to the farm might take half the morning, and so was not surprised when she shook her head, No.

The three of us set off along the path that began by the spruce trees in the kitchen yard, Tindr leading, me in the middle, and Sidroc last. The path was narrow in some places and wide in others, and took us past stands of straight elms, broadly spreading oaks, and here and there a massive and solitary ash tree, arms raised to the blue sky around her. Tindr had left his bow and arrows hanging by his alcove back at the hall, for today he was not hunting, and wore his knife at his side, and Sidroc wore his seax, as he did each day. We carried water flasks should we grow thirsty, and I had brought too a few loaves to eat, in a little satchel. I wore my yellow gown, a shade much like the clusters of drying leaves that lay amongst the still-green ferns and ringed lichens.

Not far into the woods we crossed another track, leading left. We had been told it led to the farm of Ketil the rope-maker from the trading road, from whom we should buy our Winter barley, but we had not yet visited him at his upland farm. Beyond his farm lay that of Rannveig's, empty many years, and I glanced down the path as we left it behind, hopeful that soon we should be able to visit that as well.

We passed an open glade where Tindr kept some of his bee hives, the rush-work skeps shading into the pale golden hue of the ripening leaves of the undergrowth. I had been no deeper into the woods than this, and each new step brought pleasure. Damp and rounded rocks sat at the base of arching hazels, and where there were no taller trees above, the Sun sent brilliant shafts of light upon the moss that capped the rocks, a green more vivid than any other. Some trees still held their leaves; the oak of course, who does not surrender them, russet-curled and dried as they are, until Spring; but many others had begun to drop their leafy coverings, so that sudden Sunlight pierced the forest dimness as we followed the path, twisting over stony ground and spongy mats of fallen fir needles. It was quiet; few birds sang, unlike in Spring when the forest must ring with their calls, and as I watched Tindr go before me up the path thought how sad that he who loved the woods and spent so much time in them could not hear the song of birds.

I was still thinking this when a group of white birch trees to the left of the path caught and held my eye. There were six or seven of them, both tall and straight, their white bark flecked with black, dazzling against the dark background behind them, for it seemed they stood in a small glade or clearing of their own. Then, before the birches, I saw the top of a tall rock, crowned with a many-pronged rack of stag horn. Someone had set the antlers there, high above the forest floor. The shrubby bushes rimming the path had dropped most of their leaves; in Summer one would not know the stone was there.

Tindr was walking steadily before me, head slightly lowered, and I reached forward and touched his arm. He stopped and turned to me. I pointed to the place, wanting to go there, and Tindr's eyes followed my hand. Sidroc stopped and looked where I was pointing.

Tindr paused, and looked back at me with his blue-white eyes. He did not smile, and I thought he was unwilling to go there. But I cupped my hands together like a bowl and extended them to him in the gesture he used when he wanted something.

"Please," I said aloud, and repeated the gesture to him. He looked at us both, then nodded his head and led us to the clearing.

The stone was nearly as tall as me and rose up out of the soil before the bright birches. It was almost level at the top, and a slender flat rock, tapered at one end, had been set upon it, to give a true level surface. Atop this was set the rack of deer horns, and my eyes rested on them until I saw the face of the stone. It was all but flat, and scratched into its surface were scores of small drawings of deer, and some too of boar. The figures reached almost a third of the way up the height of the tall stone. Whoever had made them had used a sharp point, and had spent some little time on each, for the deer had antlers of varying sizes, and the boar-drawings shown the ridged backs and sharp tusks of these fierce creatures. The figures started at the bottom of the stone, and went up in rows and ranks, a deer, a deer, a deer, a boar, a deer. Those at the bottom were not as sharp as those at the top.

Now I saw it was a sacred place, and looking at how Tindr stood before it, sacred to Tindr.

It was so quiet that I almost feared to speak, but speak I must. "What –" I began to ask.

Sidroc stood staring at the stone. He pointed to Tindr, and then at the stone with its etchings. Tindr nodded.

"It is a tally of all the game he has killed," Sidroc answered.

I turned to Tindr and made the gesture for What? – a fingertip tapping the temple. In answer he reached back with his right hand as if to pull an arrow from his quiver, and then pulled back a bow-string I could not see. Sidroc was right.

I looked at the figures on the stone again, scores of them, and then asked Sidroc, "He numbers them all?"

"No," he said, still looking himself at the sacred stone. "He draws them so they will return. By remembering them they do not truly die; they will live again to run the forest."

The five last drawings were of deer, two with the small knobs of a young stag, the other three with full antlers. They were the five deer that Tindr had so far dragged to Tyrsborg, that we might all eat; their haunches were being smoked in Rannveig's smokehouse, so that the bounty continue in Winter, but I had eaten already of the shoulders of these beasts. Yet here their tiny images remained, not to be numbered as a boast of a hunter's skill, but to be remembered for the lives they gave.

I knew I should not touch it, but I drew closer, for there was about it an air that pulled me in. The single stone, erect before the graceful birches, the cap stone carefully chosen and just as carefully set, the great rack of bleached antlers, all made to frame and shelter this wild herd of forest beasts; it struck me with awe.

"They are all stags and harts, no hinds," I said, my eyes fixed on the etchings. I looked to Sidroc, who asked the question for me. He lifted his hands to his head, fingers spread like antlers, and pointed to the stone, then made a milking gesture with his hands and pointed back to it again.

Tindr shook his head fast and hard, made fists and crossed his wrists together, one over the other – Do not do.

"He takes only the males; he will not take any hinds." He looked around the clearing at the bright birches. "Freyja herself sometimes comes as a white hind. She is known too as Syr, sow, for her love of the boar; it is her animal. It is all for her; it all comes from her."

I looked again at Tindr, standing reverently before the stone, and thought of him coming here after each kill, a sharpened point held fast in his fist, to carve its likeness into the hard grey face. Each beast ran forever though his act.

We left the place, thanking Tindr for showing it us, and again took up the track to Ragnfast's farm. A path branched out from it, and this I thought must lead to other farms, as it showed wheel-ruts. After some little time we came upon a tiny rivulet with a sandy bottom in which pebbles glistened, and we followed alongside it. As the stream grew in breadth the trees thinned, so that we could see the Sun standing in the sky above us. We were come out to a grassland, the grasses so tall and golden that I must blink as they swayed in the breeze that swept them.

Tindr led us on along the stream edge which cut through this pasturage, until before us stood a tall stone, set upright at the water's edge. It was not like Tindr's numbering stone, but it had been made with similar care. The stone itself had been shaped so that it looked like the keyhole in the box-lock on Tyrsborg's door, with a rounded top and slightly flaring bottom, and its edges outlined with a border of curving interlaced lines. The stone was flat front and back, and the face we neared had been scored and painted with men and animals and ships. The carving was crisp and skilful, and the painting done in red and black and russet, wonderful to see.

As on Tindr's stone, the patterns rose up in ranks and rows, tho' these pictures were few and large. At the very bottom, the yellowing grass waved over a great carving of a ship in full sail, a ship full of men with their shields hung at the ship-rail. Above this two men holding spears aloft faced a giant stag, one on either side of the beast; and above this I saw Odin's horse Sleipnir, for he had eight legs, as befit the fastest horse that ever ran. A small figure was upon his back, and another, with long and streaming hair, was flying aloft above Sleipnir's running body.

"A shield-maiden," I said aloud, for this warrior's companion I knew without ever before beholding her.

My delight in seeing her was matched only by the deep and sudden impress of doing so. As a girl my kinsman had told me of the shield-maidens, and of course Sidroc had used this as my name for these ten years past. In between the Prior had marked them as part of the error I had been first taught. But here one flew, hurrying to the battle-field to choose those men who would in glory die to join either Odin or Freyja in their halls. To see her here incised in the rock and then painted with such care made her as real to me as the saints remembered in any statue in any church.

I turned to Sidroc, my mouth still open, and he smiled and nodded to me. I thought he had not seen such a stone before, for he looked at it almost as I did.

My eyes rose to the top picture in the head of the keystone, and saw a man kneeling in front of a stallion. Something came from his hand and touched the horse's shoulder; a spear perhaps, of sacrifice. Horses were sacred to Freyr; this could be the God or his devotee.

We both looked to Tindr, and he pointed from the stone to five or six broad flat rocks set into the stream, from one bank to the other. The water had not carried them there, they were evenly spaced to make walking easy.

"Those who set the picture-stone set the bridge-stones," thought Sidroc aloud.

Tindr was now stepping from rock to rock, and we followed. Almost as soon as we were over I saw Ragnfast's farm, for across the grasses browsed a herd of twenty or more horses. There was no fence or paddock to enclose them, but as we grew closer I saw they all wore hobbles upon their front legs to keep them from straying. Buildings stood in the near distance. First was the timber house, steep-roofed to shed the coming snow; an equally steep-roofed and even larger barn, and several small wooden outbuildings, roofed in the dried sedges of the fenlands, like unto the thatching used in Angle-land. The timber of the buildings was not set upright for the walls, but set in long planks one on top of the next, like the strakes of a ship; and tucked into any gaps was stuffed a dark tarry mixture to stop the draughts, which when I neared gave off its peculiar smell in the Sun's heat. To one side of the buildings raised rows bore the mark of the grains that had grown there, now harvested. A smaller area bristled with the tops of as-yet-ungathered skirrets, turnips, and radishes, and the rounded white shoulders of fat onions. Next these great whorls of green cabbages spilled over their hills and touched each other.

Now two children, a boy and a girl of about five and seven years, came around from the kitchen yard of the house and with joyous cries began to run to Tindr. He squatted down and closed them up in his arms, and in excitement began to make the braying sounds he sometimes did in place of speech. It did not frighten the little ones; they hung on their uncle as if he truly spoke to them.

A young man now came out to us from the barn, followed by a woman with a babe in a sling at her hip. This was Ragnfast and his wife, Estrid. It was easy to see the likeness between Tindr and his cousin. They both had the same light brown hair, and straight and fine noses. Ragnfast was broader in the chest and not quite so tall, and his eyes were a mild blue, not the sharp blue-white of Tindr; but they could have been brothers. As they greeted each other and Estrid kissed her husband's cousin, I too felt their affection, and was glad that he had such friends in his life. She took a moment and touched the large silver pin fastening Tindr's mantle, and he grinned and inclined his head to us.

We greeted them with our "Goþr morgun," and told them our names, tho' they were expecting us. Estrid lifted her babe for me to see and coo over, a sweet and twinkling-eyed girl, and then she led us all to the bench before the front door. She laid the babe in a basket in the grass and stepped inside, returning with ale and cups. I brought forth the loaves from my satchel, and we sat as we took our rest after the long walk. Estrid tore off pieces of the soft bread for her boy and girl, but they barely let their uncle sit, for their pulling him off to the barn or to the fowl house to show him something, which he met with good humour.

Estrid was almost as tall as her husband, willow-slender, grey-eyed, her hair the colour of Tindr's darkest honey. The bronze doubled brooches which clasped her over-gown were of particular size and fineness, and the amber necklace round her neck was not rough chunks, but carefully smoothed beads. I thought her from prosperous people, and it was clear she and Ragnfast, with their herd of horses, were flourishing. The ring of keys at her sash told me she had several chests of valuables to lock. Her agile hands never rested, like that of all young mothers, and she took a bit of sewing from a basket to hem. She sat next me with a smile, happy I think for another woman's company, and happy to meet those who now lived in Rannveig's old hall.

Then it was time to look at the horses. We turned first to the barn, where the few stallions were stabled, for the horses in the pasture were mares and geldings. Estrid and Ragnfast kept three red-haired cows, for she made butter and cheeses, and these were kneeling in the grasses aside the barn, their flat jaws working. We stepped through the wide doors into the dim coolness, hearing the horses rustling in their stalls in the back, turning in the straw and likely eager to be out again in the open air.

Ragnfast brought out one after the other, leading them into the yard so that Sidroc might see them. These were almost our first looks at the Gotland horses, for we had seen few on the trading road, where folk used waggons drawn by oxen to transport their goods from ship to ware-house, or off to upcountry farms. They were not the large and splendid mounts of Angle-land, but were fine-looking in their own right. They were little bigger than the hardy ponies of the Polonie, but their coats were finer, and their necks more arched, with a small head, held high. Their eyes were darkly lustrous and fringed with long black lashes, and they seemed to look at and take note at all that came in view, their pointed ears moving atop their heads. Their hooves were small and hard enough that they needed no shoes, only trimming. The stallions were bay, chestnut, and black, tho' I had seen a dun and a grey amongst the horses in the grassland.

Because Sidroc was so tall, he looked for the largest horse he could buy, and he chose between the two biggest. He opened their mouths and looked at their long teeth, ran his hands along their legs and flanks, and had Tindr lead them while he stood with Ragnfast and watched the animals move. One was chestnut and one was black, and it was the black he asked to ride. Ragnfast brought out saddle and bridle, and Sidroc took them and himself put them on, so he might see how the beast handled. Then he was up and with a touch of his heels had the stallion walk and then trot as they headed to the herd. He spent some time circling the horses there, for they gathered as the stallion approached, and then he came back to us.

He swung down and told Ragnfast, "There is a dun mare, and the chestnut with the blazed face," and Ragnfast and Tindr went and brought these two mares to us. I knew by the way that Sidroc kept his hand on the black that he liked it, and as he waited he again lifted its hooves. It was a handsome creature, a true black with no brown in it, even in the bright Sun which shone above us. The mane and tail were not overly long, but were both thick, and had the same high gloss as the coat.

The dun and the chestnut were brought, and after Sidroc looked them over he rode them both. The chestnut was pretty, a golden hue with matching mane and tail; but the dun mare was almost like a pale bay, reddish and with mane and tail so dark as to be striking. Like all duns she had a dark stripe on the ridge of her back from withers to rump, and dusky, almost black legs. I had rarely seen a horse that caught and held my eye as much, and tho' she was a bit smaller than the chestnut she was a perfect size for me.

Sidroc was watching my face as he checked her teeth one more time, and he nodded at me.

Ragnfast had been standing quietly, answering Sidroc's questions, offering to bring more or different horses, and now seeing that a bargain would be struck. His horses were glossy-coated, fat on the rich Gotland grass, well-cared for and unafraid, and I was glad that we could buy from him.

"The black, and the dun, with saddles and bridles," said Sidroc to the waiting Ragnfast.

He took from his belt a few coins of silver and one of gold, too; in whole rounds, half pieces, and quarter pieces, ready with earnest money. He opened his palm and let Ragnfast see the size and quality of what he held.

"How much for both?" he then asked, for Sidroc, a good bargainer like all Danes, believed the seller should always name the first price.

Ragnfast eyed the gold piece. "For that young stallion, and that rare dun mare, half of this coin," he pointed.

Sidroc paused. Horses were always dear, but not quite as dear here in Gotland as they were in lands where warriors needed them to ride to battle, or to raid. Still, I knew he meant to save our coin, while being just.

The Hall of Tyr

"I cannot part with so much gold. I can give a third piece of this pure and new gold."

Ragnfast's face began to fall, but Sidroc was not finished with his offer. "But I will breed them, and you will have the second foal they produce. Gold now, and a horse later."

It did not take Ragnfast long to consider and nod his agreement. We began to take our leave.

"I hope you will come to Tyrsborg soon, and visit with us," I told our hosts. I gestured to Tindr, pointing at Estrid and Ragnfast, and then pressed my fingertips together, the sign for Tyrsborg.

Tindr grinned and nodded, and Ragnfast said, "Já, before the snow. We are many now and travel less in Winter for it," he said, opening his hand to the children. "But we will come and see you, and Rannveig, before the deep snow comes."

Tindr boosted me up on the black stallion behind Sidroc, and himself rode the dun mare, and we turned their heads back to the path home. We splashed through the stream not far from the painted standing stone, but Tindr led us back a different way from there. The track was broader and smoother, and I thought he chose it because we rode horses, but there was another reason as well, for before long a farm came into view. The buildings were not so large as that as Ragnfast and Estrid's farm, and as we neared we saw that the big barn had lost half its roof. But Tindr rode ahead at a canter on the dun mare and stopped before the house. No folk were about, and the fields were unplanted and overrun with grass, but the aspect was a lovely one, for there was a stand of apple trees, now laden with fruit, before the front door, and a big oak which gave shelter in the kitchen yard.

Tindr jumped down from the mare and waved to us to come down too. He was smiling, and put his fingers to his waist as if he was numbering keys, his sign for his mother. Then he pointed to us.

"Is this then Rannveig's farm?" I asked.

It was to be ours, with Tyrsborg, for farm and hall were both in her mother's family, and we would need a farm to provide our grain and vegetables. Sidroc had given Rannveig one whole gold piece as partial payment for Tyrsborg, and in return she had told him that the upcountry farm was ours as well. Few folk lived in the trading town without an upland farm to provide their wants, and many folk left the trading road and spent the Winter at their farms. Rannveig was one of the few who both remained in town and had no need of a working farm, for her wants could be met from goods folk traded her for her ale.

We walked about the place. The door to the house was locked, but the walls and roof looked sound. It was all of timber, and tho' half the barn roof had fallen in, the walls were not rotting. "A new roof," Sidroc said, and I thought he considered the labour. "We will need someone to farm it," he went on.

"A young couple, starting out," I thought aloud. "Ragnfast and Estrid may know of one." We could do nothing this late in the season but plan for the coming Spring.

We saw that Tindr was glad at the prospect that soon the old farm would be made productive, for tho' he had never lived there, he walked about with familiar ease. Our new horses had moved under the apple trees, and were now biting and chewing at the drops they found in the long grasses beneath. Tindr took the satchel from me and filled it with those which still hung, and we went on our way.

Each day grew cooler, and shorter. The sky was just as blue above, and the Sun shone as brilliantly, but it rose less high and set much earlier. The pile of wood which Sidroc and Tindr had chopped grew to touch the eaves of the stable roof. Tindr had brought in sacks of grain and much hay, roll after roll of it, as Winter fodder for the cow and our horses. This filled the tall hay-loft within the stable to its very peak. He began fattening a few of our geese on the spillage from the oats, for which the geese flew at each other, squawking, their strong grey wings beating at the air.

He brought as well two half-grown kittens from his mother's brew-house sheds, one black-and-white and one yellow-and-white, and with their long fur and thick paws the largest cats I had ever seen, young as they were. We had noticed cats like them on the trading road, twice as big as those of Angle-land, and with fur and tails like foxes. Rannveig called them skogkatt, said that they came long ago from the forests, and that their coats were such that they shed water, and could withstand the bitterest cold. Our two kittens were great climbers, scampering up the posts of the stable in an instant, and such avid hunters that we need not fear losing any but a few kernels of grain to mice. Hardy as they were, they were gentle and liked warmth well enough, and would curl up, one each, on the broad backs of the horses to sleep. They ran to Tindr when they saw him, and he gave them warm milk from the cow in a wooden bowl each day.

He sang to them as he did to the cow and fowl and horses, a kind of sing-song braying hum, which he only used with animals and children, as I think he knew it did not fall lightly on the ears of grown folk. Yet I thought he had real need to speak to these beasts, and somehow knew they answered him with their own voices, for I often heard the cow low back to him when he sang to her.

Our horses proved their usefulness at once, and Sidroc and Tindr used them for trips to the trading road when they need not carry back anything greater than would fit inside the saddle-bags. They cleared a space on the South side of the stable and built a paddock for them, and I liked seeing them so close.

Sidroc and I rode out too for the sheer enjoyment being on horseback brings. My dun mare went well and easily, with a soft mouth, and her furry ears always in motion, waiting for cues from me. Her odd beauty I found striking, and I liked to run my hand down the black stripe which led from her dark-maned withers and over her strong back to her rump. She was happy to canter when I asked her, but of a more settled nature than my spirited bay mare had been.

One day when we had ridden out beyond the tall carving of Freyr I thought of this earlier gift of horse-flesh from Sidroc, and thought too of the great bay stallion he so valued who he had bred to her. I did not want to ask if he missed that horse; I knew he must. For answer I reminded myself that Sidroc did not dwell on those things he could not have, and then caught myself in this thought. What had I been but just that in his life; a thing he greatly desired and could not have? Long desiring could end in the satisfying of that desire, if the Gods were kind.

Perhaps I had been quiet too long, for he asked me, "Of what do you think?"

We had passed the tall racks of drying stockfish, and were now on a path through a place of burial; Rannveig had told us of it. Round-topped stones, some carved with runes, marked the places of the dead. Off to one side was the pyre mound, where some of the dead were burnt with honour before being buried.

"I thought of your bay stallion, and that you must miss him," I said.

It was his horse I had been thinking of, so that is what I said. I did not mention that which he valued far more than the bay. I did not speak of his three children, of Ælfwyn, of the men at Four Stones, a few of whom who he regarded almost as brothers; nor of the vast treasure he had left behind in lands, silver, gold, and horses. But I would not lie to him, so I spoke of a thing which I knew he had taken pleasure in for years, and had relinquished, like all the rest.

"I will not have so fine a horse again," he allowed. "But this one I ride with you."

As Fall came on Tindr was much at the hunt. He would arise long before us and make his way along forest tracks, to return in late morning. More often than not he dragged home a red deer stag. The first day he brought home a boar we all gathered to see it. I knew men hunted boars with hounds and with spears, and that many dogs and men too were killed doing so. As a girl I had seen the grievous wounds the tusks could drive. But Tindr with his slender bow and an arrow fitted with a longer head brought down these beasts revered and feared by others. It took two and even three arrows to do so, for we saw the puncture wounds on the beasts' bristly mane; but the boar had been spared the harrying of hounds in a frantic run through the underbrush. I felt that Tindr was guided to the place where the boar would appear to him, and knew Sidroc believed this too. With his bow he brought the bounty of the woods to feed himself, his mother, and now us at Tyrsborg.

Of the many deer he took he made good use of the hides. The wooden floor boards of the treasure room were now covered with them, so that along with my plush weaving, the wood itself was hard to see. Likewise he used the hides, tanned and scraped of their fur, to make leathern bags and to cut into tying cords.

The boar skins, tho', he made into boots for himself, and I felt this too was part of his veneration, that he should use the skin of the beast sacred to Freyja upon his feet. When he trod the forest he returned that power and strength into the very soil which had nourished the boar he stalked. He returned all to her.

Chapter the Eighth: Flare-up

ONE morning as we all sat at table together, I noticed Sigvor smile at Tindr. She rarely smiled, and had, I thought, never done so at him. She carried in the eggs seethed in butter I had made, and the loaves and baked apples to the table, but after she laid a salver before Sidroc and me she did not set the rest of the food in the centre of the table as she had before. She had made up a plate for Tindr, and now set it before him, and smiled.

The day before she had gone home to see her family, and I wondered if being with her sisters had heartened her. If so I was glad, for her sake as well as Tindr's, for she paid him so little mind that I thought she must hurt him without knowing it. Tho' he tried to make himself known to her, she often came to me asking what he wanted, and if she needed him to do something, she would ask me to tell him rather than attempt to gesture her wants. Now, and in the days that followed, this was behind her, for she not only smiled at him, she worked to learn the simple signs he used to speak with us.

I thought Tindr unused to the attentions of a pretty maiden, and saw how he began to look for ways to help Sigvor in her chores. One afternoon just before dusk she went to draw more water from the well for our cooking. I would not have seen her do so save that I need borrow some salt from Rannveig, and came through the front door to start down the hill. Tindr had helped her haul the pail up, and now had it in both his hands. Their backs were to me as I saw Sigvor extend her hand and lay it over one of his.

I stepped back into the hall. A young woman should never touch a man not kin, nor a man a woman. For an unwed maid to do so was no less than a declaration of courtship.

I went through the hall and came out the door to the kitchen yard; when I reached the well by the front door both Tindr and Sigvor were gone.

Rannveig was already busy at the brew-house, and so I took the salt with little more than my thanks. I did not know to feel troubled or glad for them; Sigvor was of good family and seemed a good girl, yet I wondered for Tindr.

The next day I went to Rannveig's with the gift of some eggs, for I knew her hens were not laying. It was a short while before the brew-house would open, and so she led me to her house so we might visit. Gudfrid, her cook, was busy in the small kitchen yard, and we passed the eggs into her keeping and went into the house. Rannveig knew we had bought horses from Ragnfast, but had not yet been up to Tyrsborg to see them.

"Tindr will be glad with horses to care for," she said, and this was true, for we had seen how he delighted in them. "It has been years since we kept one."

This mention of her son and his bond with animals led me to say the next.

"While we were in the woods, Tindr took us to his – memory-stone," I told her.

She cocked her head, and I went on, "The stone on which he draws the beasts he hunts."

Now she nodded, her eyebrows rising for just a moment; I thought she was surprised that he had done so.

"For Freyja, his fulltrúi," she said. "She loves him very much."

Tindr had given himself to the Goddess, and in return had found great favour in her eyes.

"He has marked that stone since his fourteenth Summer," she said, remembering.

"How many Summers has he now?" I asked in return.

She thought a moment. "Three and twenty," she said.

"He is almost as old as I am. I thought him of no more than nineteen or twenty years."

"Já," she answered, with a little sigh. "Tindr will always be young."

"How does he know to do this?" I wanted to know.

"His father. But he was a fisherman and offered to Njord," she told me, naming the God of the sea. "And Njord took him in the end," she went on.

"His ship was lost?"

"Nai. The God was kind," she said, and a smile bowed her mouth. "When he did not come back, other men went out looking. They found his boat, drifting. My husband was dead, aboard. No violence, just dead." She touched her heart here. "They sailed his ship back so I had both it and his body. The ship I sold, and it brought me good silver. He provided well for me, in life and in death. He is buried out by the farm he was born on; I have raised a stone for him there."

"I hope you will take me one day to see it," I told her, and meant it truly, for the stone at Ragnfast's farm was wondrous; and I felt certain his too would be so.

Now I asked a question about her son. "Tindr – does he have a sweetheart?"

Her hands lifted and fell back into her lap, and her lips pursed. She shook her head. "Never," she told me, without hiding her sadness. "None will have him. There are more men than women on Gotland; any maid can choose between three or four men."

I felt a pang as she said this; Tindr was unlike any man I had met. Deaf, yes; but good and true, and with deep reserves which sprang from his devotion to his Goddess and the creatures she sent him to care for and to cull. I did not wish to say now what I had seen with Sigvor; it might raise false hopes in both son and mother and nothing might come of it.

I saw Rannveig feared for him, that he would live his life alone and unwed; and she would have no grandchildren to gladden them both. I said the only thing I could.

"He will always have a home with us," I promised. "And surely one day a woman will see his worth and love him for it."

Sidroc had spent much time walking along the trading road, looking at the goods for sale, and especially at those made there. If he was to hire a ship next year and send it to distant ports he wanted to fill it with those goods which would return the greatest yield, and for this reason he thought long and hard about what he would buy, and to what land he would send it. We had bought so many things in so many of the stalls that we were both known and liked by the folk there, but today he wanted me to go with him to a stall at which we had only stopped once, and that our first full day in Gotland.

"I will send amber to Frankland," he told me, as we headed down the hill from Tyrsborg. We spoke in Norse, so that I might more quickly learn the tongue.

I turned to him, surprised. Had he in fact found a ship-master who would sail that far to the West? We knew most of the Gotlander traders visited the trading posts East and South around the Baltic coastline, and sailed as well to the ports of the Svear and further West to Dane-mark. I need not ask him my question, as he went on, as if thinking aloud.

"The amber here is good, but amber is found all through the Baltic, and many folk collect and work it. It is prized in Dane-mark, but along the coast easily found if one is willing to pay the price.

"But in Frankland," he went on, "amber is precious. Few women will have necklaces of amber. Fewer still will be the number of other ornaments made from amber."

"But to Frankland – ?" I began.

"Já. To Frankland. I will find a ship to go that far, on promise of the greater gain to be found there."

We were on the trading road now, and could not help but see that the pier was empty of any ship. A few of the stalls had already closed for the Winter, their folk retreating indoors to their workshops or to their upland farms.

The stall of the silver-smith was just before that of the amber-worker, and amongst all the other glitter my eye was caught by a pile of silver beads on his counter. Their surfaces were not smooth, but had been worked in swirling spiral designs, so they seemed even more perfectly round than they were, and looked like they were moving even when I held one still in my palm. The smith, seeing my interest, hastened to come forward, but I smiled and shook my head to excuse myself as I placed the bead back in the bowl.

Sidroc gave a little laugh at this. "That is what I want you here for," he said. "To show me what a woman will most want."

The amber-worker rose as we walked in; a man and a woman coming in together must signal a sale for him. But Sidroc gestured that he sit back down at his work-bench, and he and I began to look about at his wares. He had many strands of necklaces, some of irregular but smoothed chunks of amber, and others in which each bead had been carefully rounded and polished until it gleamed. The chunks of smoothed amber were opaque, like honey which has been chilled; but the beads were all clear enough to see into. Many of them held tiny seeds or leaf-bits, and a few even held small insects prisoned in their golden depths.

I thought of the necklace I had given Ælfwyn. The amber chunks had been rounded into oblongs, sawn into flat pieces, then pierced and joined by gold wire. He had nothing like that, but did have necklaces made of small flat pieces, chips really, drilled through the middle and strung together.

"Which do we send to Frankland?" Sidroc asked me quietly.

I considered. Frankland was the place from whence came rare wines. It was the place where many of the priests I had met or heard of had made pilgrimage to, for there were great churches there. Fine silks came to Angle-land through there. I knew it must be a rich land.

"The clear and polished beads," I told him. "And – some too I think of these small chips; a mother might with gladness give one to her daughter."

Sidroc reached onto the table that held them and drew up a large fistful of the polished bead necklaces. He turned and laid them down on the amber-worker's bench. The man raised round eyes to him.

"All?" he asked.

"Nai," said Sidroc, turning to gather up the remaining necklaces. "These too."

I took up a handful of the amber-chip necklaces; thirty perhaps, and laid them next to those which Sidroc had piled before the man. "And these," I added, smiling.

There were baskets of varying sizes on the man's bench, some filled with unworked amber, others with smoothed or polished beads. Sidroc gestured to one nearly empty, and the man lifted the few pieces from it and handed it to him. With both hands he clutched the golden mass we had chosen and laid it within. The necklaces came almost to the brim.

"How much silver?" asked Sidroc.

It was clear the man, even set up as he was in a trading post, had never sold so much of his wares at one time. He made a gesture at the table behind us, now nearly empty, and then looked back at us. He was a small man of more than forty years, his fair hair now fading to grey, his back a bit bent from years at his workbench. His eyes were a watered blue, and looked us over carefully.

Sidroc said nothing, just made a slight gesture to the mounded treasure in the basket. The man shook himself and turned for his scale and weights. He laid the basket on one end of the balance beam, and kept adding small squares of lead to the other until they balanced. It would be a great amount of silver, but because the sale was so large and trading season at an end, he removed one lead weight. He then looked up at Sidroc.

Sidroc nodded, and pulled from his belt a whole handful of silver. Most of it was not in coins, for here in Gotland folk often used hack-silver, broken jewellery; or lengths cut from thick coils of plain rolled silver, just as the Danes did. The amber-worker removed the basket, leaving the lead weights in place, and Sidroc dropped the silver piece by piece upon the other end of the balancing beam.

When they were level the man picked up the basket and set it before us, and swept the silver into a small chest. He looked dazzled, but bowed his head to us and smiled in way of thanks.

But Sidroc was not done. He placed his hands upon the filled basket we had just bought and spoke.

"If you will fill me another basket by Spring, in Fall I will pay you a quarter more silver than I did these."

"A quarter more," the man repeated. He glanced at the basket, then said, "Holmgeir the amber-man is happy to say yes."

Sidroc grinned, and again spoke. "And can you make a few ornaments from your largest pieces," he wanted to know. "Tiny cups, and figures of deer or horses."

Holmgeir nodded. "I can do that," he agreed.

"And," I made bold to ask, "can you string some of the necklaces with silver beads also?"

Both men looked at me, and I said, "The carved silver beads next door – think how they will look mixed with the amber."

Now Sidroc laughed. He held his hand up to Holmgeir, and left with me. We came back with the bowl of carved beads, the puzzled silver-smith following in our wake.

We left the trading road having bought all the beads from the silver-smith, and left them in Holmgeir's keeping. We carried with us a whole small basket of amber necklaces. I felt almost giddy at having spent so much silver, but trusted Sidroc's judgement that the amber would bring a good profit. And I knew we would send two tradesmen home that night, happy in their day's work.

Once at Tyrsborg we went into the treasure room with the basket, pulled my plush weaving away, and knelt down on the floor. A few days earlier Sidroc had lifted a few floor boards there, dug out the earth beneath them, and sawn the boards so they fitted tightly over the hole in the shape of a square. Sidroc slipped his seax blade into one of the sawn ends and lifted it up. My twelve gold pieces were there, in a little clay pot topped with wood and sealed with beeswax, along with a second pot, holding much which remained of the eight other pieces. Sidroc lowered the basket in for safe-keeping. He stopped himself and looked up to me.

"Choose one," he said. "There are many; you should have one now for yourself."

I began to reach my hand to the bead necklaces as they sat, softly gleaming, in their basket. Then I thought: This was to go to Frankland, and give Sidroc his start in trading. One less sent would mean that much less silver in return.

"Nai," I said, and had to laugh a little. "Every one must go to Frankland. When the silver comes back you can buy me my Brisingamen."

He laughed too. "You forget none of my promises. You will deserve white-armed Freyja's jewelled necklace, and I will get one for you."

Sigvor and I were sweeping out the hall next morning, doors open to the light to guide the small clouds of dust our birch brooms made. Ash from the fire pit was always being scattered on the floor, even tho' Sidroc had built up the ring of rock around it, for if the fire was low the wind at times blew in through the open gable end, carrying the finest of the ash with it.

I neared Sigvor's sleeping alcove, and the light coming in through the open door shone on something barely tucked behind her drawn-back curtain. She always smoothed the blankets on her box-bed, and her few things hung neatly on pegs within, her wool night-shoes placed side by side on the lower platform. What I saw was near them, and it was this: a small flower, made of beeswax, such as Tindr had made for me. I looked up. My rose still sat on the little table by my loom; he had made this one for her.

When he had made it for me it was a sweet gesture to the mistress of the hall he now lived in, and in whose service he worked. I had shown it to Sidroc without fear that he would think amiss of another man giving his wife such a gift. Now he had made one for Sigvor, and she had accepted it. I looked over at her where she stood, broom in hand at the other end of the hall, her face intent on her sweeping. A maid would not accept a man's gift, even one so slight as this, without knowing that she gave him hope.

I did not know if I should speak to her or not. She had been broken-hearted at the loss of her sweetheart, and I feared she might in loneliness reach out to the first man who was kind to her. I feared the more for Tindr; that she might choose him in haste, and later, with a healing heart, regret that choice.

I said nothing. If she could love him, I would be happy for them both, and resolved to hold that hope along with my silence.

The Hall of Tyr

Two nights later Sidroc and I were at the brew-house. Tindr had come with us, and disappeared behind the curtains leading to the brewing yard to perform some task for his mother, but we took our places at the long benches set before the tables. The Sun had been down for hours, and Rannveig had the awnings rolled down for warmth, and had braziers filled with glowing charcoal set upon the floor amongst the tables. It would not be long until the evenings were too cold for folk to gather here. Instead they would come by day to her brewing yard, and fill their crocks to take home with them. But now it was pleasant to sit with other men and women, to practice my growing skill at their tongue, to watch the men at dice and for me to play bones with the women. We had met many of the trading road folk here, and several of the upland farm families, come into town for final provisions before the cold set in. It was a chance for Sidroc and me to know and be known, vital when making a home in a new land. I hoped to meet more women who might be my friends, and I knew Sidroc looked for a seasoned ship master to whom he could entrust his goods for the long sail to Frankland next Summer.

We usually sat together, but Sidroc had gotten up, lured by a game of dice, while I sat with the rope-maker and his wife. Ketil wove strong rope from hemp, and even stronger did he make from the spiral-cut hides of the great walrus beasts, whose ivory tusks I had seen at Rannveig's. In a sailing port this was good business, and he dealt with merchants from all around the Baltic, for rope was needed not only as line in the handling of sails, but to tie and secure goods on the pitching decks of ships. He sold too to town and farm folk, for few things are as useful as good rope.

His wife made a sort of open weave netting that cushioned and made fast such things as wooden casks of salted fish or pottery wine jars, and she and I had been speaking of this. As we paused in our speech I saw Ketil's eyes as they rested on Sidroc. Sidroc stood before a table, holding the dice in his fist, then casting them down on the table face. Sidroc grinned, and the men flanking him gave a hoot of praise, while others wore the good-natured grimace of the loser.

"Who is he?" Ketil said.

He startled me; Ketil knew Sidroc's name, and I knew he asked the deeper question.

"He is a Dane," I answered, telling him nothing he did not already know.

"He wears the knife of the men of Angle-land," he pointed out.

"You have been there?" I asked, trying to quell the sudden racing of my heart.

But he shook his head No.

"He has fought there," he finally said, keeping me from having to say more. He kept his eyes on Sidroc. "And I would say that he has won there."

He looked to me, and I feared he would ask if I were part of what he had won. Even if he asked if I were from Angle-land I did not wish to answer. No one on Gotland had been so far as Angle-land, and I knew I should have no fear to tell folk if I must; but neither Sidroc or I had told anyone here from whence we came. Like many who earn their silver from strangers through trade, the Gotlanders were not a prying folk; and I valued the fact that they judged us only as we behaved to them.

The serving woman who worked for Rannveig came by the table just then to refill our pottery cups, saving me from needing to speak. I took a sip and the long moment passed. The door leading to the road opened, causing a gust of cool air to rush in, and we turned our heads to it. Two men, father and son perhaps, stepped inside. I did not know them, and looked back to my cup.

The men did not sit, for from the tail of my eye I saw them pause and then look round the brew-house. Then they walked rapidly past the crowded tables, quickly enough to make me look at them. Tindr had just come in through the split curtains at the other end, and both men were now before him. They stopped abruptly in front of him, barring his way, and the younger man now clamped his hand upon Tindr's shoulder. The man's anger was clear upon his face; the elder too was grim.

Tindr's face was towards me and I saw his eyes widen. Sidroc had seen the men approach him, and now dropped the dice from his fist and came forward. Rannveig too saw this, and put down the pitcher she held, and came to her son, wiping her hands on her apron. I rose and came over to them, standing by Rannveig.

Sidroc had stopped level with the younger man, who still held Tindr by his shoulder. Sidroc reached his hand out, closed it over the man's wrist, drew it away from Tindr, released it.

Sidroc spoke, his voice low, and his eye trained on the man's face. "He is my man," he told him. "If you have trouble with him, speak to me."

The younger man stared at Sidroc, gauged his size, and let his hand drop. Sidroc looked from younger man to elder.

"If you have trouble, tell me of it," he repeated.

It was the younger who answered. "It is Sigvor. My sister."

Sidroc glanced around the crowded brew-house. Those nearest had all stopped in their drinking and gaming, and were looking at us.

"Where is Sigvor now," Sidroc asked. She had gone home in the afternoon for a visit, and had not eaten with us.

"We left her at your hall," said her father.

"Then we will go to Tyrsborg and talk about this," said Sidroc.

Tindr was ashen-faced. I could not tell if he knew who these men were, but thought certainly he must. What was clear is that he did not understand their anger.

Rannveig pulled her apron off, and Sidroc and Tindr and I swung our mantles over our shoulders. We all set off in the dark up the road to Tyrsborg, a single rush torch Rannveig held lighting our way. The voices of those drinking inside the brew-house resumed, and then faded as we climbed the hill. Sigvor did not have a key to the box-lock, and was sitting in the dark on the bench outside the door. She was swaddled in her mantle and looked both cold and frightened as we approached.

We stepped inside, and Sidroc thrust a few pieces of fire wood into the banked fire pit. I lit cressets to give us more light. I knew no one would sit and did not offer; this was talk that need be said standing.

"Now. Tell me of your trouble," Sidroc began. His voice was still low, and he looked from father to son, and then to Sigvor.

It was the father who spoke. "Sigvor will have a babe in Spring," the man said. "She tells us it is Tindr's."

Sidroc's eyes flicked up to the darkness of the rafters. He had noticed the change in Sigvor towards Tindr, but it was clear had never expected this. Nor did I. Sigvor had shown no sign she was with child, displayed no queasiness; or if she had she had hid it well. But then some women only felt so for the first few weeks.

I know my mouth opened in a gasp, and Rannveig stepped forward, her eyes flashing. Her son stood before us, seeing us speak and not knowing. Rannveig's hands moved quickly through the air. She pointed at Tindr and touched her ear, pointed to Sigvor, then held her elbows as if she cradled and rocked a babe. Then she pointed back to Tindr.

A sound came from Tindr, a sort of squeal, and he lifted his own hands. He looked to Sigvor, standing across from him with downcast eyes. Then he took his clenched hands and crossed them at the wrist – Do not do.

"He is not the father," said Rannveig, turning on her heel to Sigvor's father and brother. I had not seen her angry before, and saw she would defend her son to the end.

Sidroc looked to Sigvor, about to speak to her. The girl was quaking and tears began to run down her cheeks. Both she and Tindr were in my keeping, and tho' I fully believed she lied, I did not want the girl shamed. I raised my hand to stop Sidroc, and spoke myself. I stepped forward to her.

"Sigvor. You are with child, já?" I began, trying to get her to raise her eyes and look at me.

She nodded her answer.

"But the father is not Tindr, is it? It is your sweetheart, is it not?"

She shook her head so vigorously that her tears flew from her round cheek. "It is Tindr," she choked out.

130

I glanced at Tindr, still white-faced, his hands clenched at his sides. I did not believe her.

"How many months, Sigvor. How many?" I asked, drawing nearer her.

The man she was to have wed had been gone since mid-Summer. She was plump and her gown loose. I did not want to take my hands and pull her gown tight about her waist to show she was four months gone. I did not want to, but as I moved towards her she saw in my face I would do so if she did not tell us the truth.

"Three. Four," she spluttered out, her tears falling freely.

"And you have been at Tyrsborg only a month," I reminded her. "The babe is not Tindr's," I ended, turning to her brother and father.

They shook their heads and glared at Sigvor. I did not understand it, and need say so.

I turned back to the weeping girl. "Sigvor," I said more gently, "there is no shame in this. You and he were to be wed. Surely his people will welcome you and your babe into their family."

Fresh tears came to her eyes, and she shook her head. I turned back to her father, who also shook his head.

"They are of the fishing family that own most of the stockfish on the drying racks," he told us. "It was not a match they approved."

I could do no more than sigh and drop my hands. Even in Christian Angle-land there was no shame for a girl already with child to join hands with the father before a priest. Cottar girls would often purposely do so, to prove they were fertile. For the poor folk their only wealth was in their children. It was only in the high-born that a woman was expected to be yet a maid upon the wedding night. Here in heathen Gotland there was no fear of sin or loss of face if a man and woman knew each other before the hand-fast. But common to both places was the sorrow caused when one family refused to accept the match.

Rannveig had been gesturing to her son what had been said. He now stood with eyes downcast as well. He had had the fright of having hands set upon him, of being unjustly accused, and now learning that the girl he cared for had tried to trap him. The pain he felt shown in his furrowed brow and slumped shoulders.

Sidroc took a breath and ran his hand through his hair. He looked to Rannveig. "How do I ask him if he wants her," he asked. She did it for him, pointing to Sigvor, pointing to her son, then clasping her hands together. Sigvor raised her eyes to them, watching.

"Nai," said her brother, and took a step forward. "He could not give her a sound child."

We all turned to him, but it was Rannveig who answered. She made no effort to hide her anger. "That he could! Tindr was born sound as you or me. It was fever that took his hearing, when he was two."

Sigvor's father reached forward to rein in his son. "It is not your decision, but Sigvor's, to make," he said, and I was grateful for the reason in his words.

"Ask him," Sidroc said again. "Does he want her?"

Rannveig repeated the gestures. It was terrible to make him declare himself thus, after the shock and hurt he had suffered, but I knew this must be settled as quick as it might.

Tindr stared at his mother, then looked past her to Sigvor. She had wiped her face with her hands, and tho' her eyes were red they met Tindr's.

Tindr lifted his hand to her, pointed at her, then clasped his hands together. I thought his own eyes were full as he did so.

Sigvor looked back at him, her chin quivering. It took a long moment for her lips to gather and her answer to come. She fairly spat out her reply.

"Nai," she said.

Sidroc and I stood alone in the empty hall. Sigvor had left for good with her father and brother, her belongings in their arms. Tindr had left first, gone down the hill to the brew-house with his mother for the night. Alone as we were, the wind soughing through the spruce boughs outside made the quiet within the greater.

My heart ached for Tindr, yet I could not help but feel that Sigvor was not suited to his happiness. Sigvor had been unkind to lead him on, foolish to accuse him, and cruel in her rejection of him. But it was not possible for me to judge her harshly. She was young, had lost the man she hoped to wed, then found herself with his child. His kin did not accept her. She had been frightened and had acted from that fear. Tindr had acted from his courage, for truly it had taken much to declare himself to her as he did in front of all.

I went to the rank of shelves by the kitchen passage and dipped out cups of mead from the crockery jar there. Mead was drunk at the gladdest of times, but tonight I felt need of its heady strength. I joined Sidroc as he stood by the fire pit, and pressed a cup into his hands. He and Tindr had dragged several large stones to the edge of it and built up a kind of bench on which it was pleasant to sit and warm oneself when the fire was not high. I dropped down upon it now, glad for the warmth of the embers at my back, and the warmth growing in my belly from the sweet and strong mead.

"Perhaps when the dead man's family learns Sigvor bears his child, they will welcome her," I hoped aloud.

Sidroc shrugged, his eyes lost in the fire. "Even if not, she will find a man before the babe is born," he said. "She is comely, a skilled weaver, and her family is known." He looked to me and went on, "But you have lost your serving woman, just when you were making all ordered here."

I nodded, and had to sigh. Part of the running of a hall, however small, was the dealing with the folk who lived there and served as part of the household. If they be young and away from their homes for their first time, as Tindr and Sigvor had been, so much greater was the chance that they might come to love, or to grief.

"I do not want Tindr to have to go through this again," I said. It was his own mother who had chosen Sigvor for us, but I felt guilt too, and true sadness at his own sorrow.

Sidroc was looking back into the fire. "Tindr will not find a woman in a hall," he said. His words were low, as if he made a foretelling of Tindr's Fate.

I had heard tales of the skogsrå in the brew-house. This was the Lady of the Forest, a wood-spirit who came in womanly form, who guided and helped those hunters upon whom she looked with approval. Sometimes she would invite one to her woodland bed chamber, and give her love to the man under the leafy boughs. Such a gift was the sign of highest favour, but also a doom, for after this he could never lie with a mortal woman. Some said the man would even die shortly after.

The old women who told such tales did so with fervor, and I had watched men nod in agreement as they listened with me. I did not know if the skogsrå was a form Freyja would take, and that to a young hunter devoted to her.

Sidroc had heard these stories too. I could say nothing. I clutched my cup and lifted my eyes to him.

But he smiled and reached his hand to me. "Come to bed," he invited.

A full pail of milk sat by the door to the kitchen yard when we rose: Tindr was already back. He did not join us at table that morning, but went about his chores with the animals as he always did. Later in the day while I was at my loom he came into the hall with more logs for the fire pit. After he finished stacking them he turned. Sigvor's alcove, empty and bare, stood across from him, its curtains drawn open. He looked at it, and then made a quick movement towards it. Something had been left behind on the platform. I saw it in his hand before he crushed it in his palm and flung it on the smouldering logs. The lump which been the little beeswax flower took fire and flared up like a torch, then died out just as swiftly.

Chapter the Ninth: Grindstones and Crystal

"THERE is good stone in the South of the island," Sidroc told me. He spoke to me in Gotlandic Norse, as I had asked him to, the tongue of our new home. The more I had heard and used it, the easier it fell into my ear; and in all things, save my dress, I wanted to be of our new land.

I had been standing in the afternoon Sun, holding my mantle close about me, thinking of the fruit trees and herbs I hoped to plant at Tyrsborg in the Spring for a garden. He had just come up from Rannveig's, and I walked a little way down to meet him.

We stood facing the stone front of Tyrsborg. There was a great deal of stone everywhere around us, from what I had seen; from the twisting towers of the raukar at the water's edge that we spotted from our boat, which told Sidroc we were at Gotland, to the grey-white limestone from which parts of our hall was built, to the many rocks and stones thrusting up from the soil in the forest depths or edging the grasslands.

My face must have asked my question, for he went on, "Sandstone. Querns and grinding stones are quarried and shaped in the South."

We did not have a quern, tho' we had seen several for sale along the trading road. We waited to buy one until we had a cook, but by waiting we must buy sacks of barley and wheat and rye flours, and ground pease, too. We need not travel to buy a quern, so I asked, "Querns and millstones for trade, for next Summer?"

He nodded. "Millstones will bring us real silver. I want to go, before it gets colder, to the quarries. I can buy a quern for us, and order up millstones to send out to trade."

We were now inside the hall, and he went on, "Rannveig and Tindr have kin that way; I will take Tindr with me. We will be gone five or six days. You can stay with Rannveig, or come with us."

"Of course I want to come," I said at once, glad to think of the trip. It had been two days since Sigvor had left us, and I knew such an outing would be good for Tindr as well. Then I thought of sleeping outside. "But…will we be making camp at night?" It was growing sharply cold as soon as the Sun went down, and that happened earlier each day.

"Rannveig says any farm will take us in for the night; it is the custom of the folk. Farms are not many, but Tindr will know where they are. We need only bring food, to share with our hosts."

"Já, já, I want to come," I said, and he took and squeezed my hand in reply.

"Good. Tindr will go to his cousin and borrow horses, one for him and one for pack. Rannveig will take the cow for the week, and Alrik's wife will care for our fowl."

So we made plans to leave the day after next. It felt strange to set out on horseback, full saddlebags slung behind us, and walk away from Tyrsborg. I kept turning in my saddle to catch a glimpse of it, but the trees closed up so quickly that soon only the tip of the gable-peak met my eye. The hall meant so much to me that to leave it even for a few days was far harder than I had thought, eager as I was for the trip; and only my reminding myself that we would soon be back eased my way. Sidroc was mounted on his black stallion, I on my dun mare, and Tindr had charge of two horses, both chestnut geldings, one he rode and one he had loaded with our provender. He brought deer hide ground-cloths with him, so even if we must spend a night afield we should have some shelter from the damp.

He did not lead us on the same path we had taken to Ragnfast's farm. Instead we took the first forest turning, and began heading South at once. We quickly came to Ketil's farm and its fields of shorn barley, but skirted his fields and once again entered the forest. There was no path or track-way here; Tindr took us though the broadest ways he knew, sometimes walking in or by a rivulet, other times through the slender openings in the dense stands of fir trees. These rose above us, straight and tall, in such numbers that the air itself seemed dark green from the shadow of their reaching needles. Our horses' hooves ploughed up tiny hillocks of dried needles as we drove onward.

It was just after dawn when we had left, and when we came to a clearing the Sun was lowering in the sky. It was not a clearing made by man; there was no farmstead near, but rather a boggy place of sedge and other plants that love the wet. As soon as we came out Tindr stopped, and raised his arm in front of him. Against the dark background of the far trees I saw an old hart, broad-chested, thick necked, his dusky muzzle raised to the air and sniffing. The rack of antlers was huge; as great as that which topped Tindr's memory-stone. Tindr raised his hand to it in a sort of salute. He was not hunting, the animal need have no fear; and I thought it might give Tindr pleasure to gaze upon such creatures as had lived to a great age and size; they too must be beloved of the Goddess. We came forward and the beast bounded away, lost in the dim recess of the trees.

We skirted the bog, which took some time, as the ground was soft, heaved up in low but spikey-growthed mounds, and our horses liable to stumble if we rushed them. But they were sure-footed, and picked their way around to the place Tindr chose. I wondered if it was almost where the hart had stood; no track could be seen, and the firs here rose just as thick as they had been on the other side. But he chose an opening and urged his horse in.

When the way was broad enough for me to turn in my saddle, and for him to come up a little closer to me, I turned to look at Sidroc. By the way his own eyes scanned the dense tree tops I knew his thoughts ran close to mine. In this deep forest the Sun could no longer be seen, but Tindr went ahead without it.

"He is a way-finder," said Sidroc.

I had not heard this name before, but nodded just the same. When I had travelled with Gyric, heading South and West through the woods of Lindisse, Mercia, and finally Wessex, I had had to use the Sun to guide us, and depend on Gyric's knowledge of the rivers we might meet. It was difficult and slow, and we could not travel if the day was wet or cloudy. Tindr followed no track, and had now not even the Sun to direct him, yet we moved on with almost as much sureness as if he walked the wooded path to his memory-stone. Once in a while he would pause, and lift his arm to signal he was stopping. Then he would look about him, tilting his head as if he listened, which I knew could not be; and then his knees would squeeze his horse's barrel and we would move on.

The dark firs gave way to groves of oak and elm, the oaks still grasping their leaves of withered brown, the elms nearly bare. Open sky, paling quickly to a light blue, was above us, and we crossed a path, well-worn and rutted, that told us waggons passed there. We went on a little way, towards, I could see, a clearing, for the light was stronger there. A few waggon-ruts showed that carts too came here, off the well-worn path, and I wondered why. The light grew stronger as the sky appeared above us. Tindr stopped his horse and let us rein up alongside of him.

Before us in the centre of the clearing was an immense ash tree, its huge and reaching grey boughs almost bare of any leaves. The girth of the mighty trunk was such that I thought two men could not reach hands about it, and it was so tall that when it bore all its leaves it must cast the clearing into deep shade. Even now the boughs were not wholly bare, tho', for hanging from the lowest of them were the ragged remains of animals which had been Offered here.

"It is like Yggdrasil," I murmured, the great ash whose roots formed the basis of the realms of Asgard, Midgard, and Niflheim, those worlds of the Gods, the Middle-Earth of Men, and that mist-home of Death. My kinsman had told me of Yggdrasil, it was sung of in the sagas I had heard, and Sidroc too had spoken of the fabled World Tree.

Sidroc had turned in his saddle to look at Tindr. Tindr made a sharp poking movement towards his own eye, and Sidroc watched and nodded. He swung down from his horse and stood upon the ground, making a gesture with his hand that I stay. He handed his reins to Tindr, and reached to his belt and the silver-pouch tucked there.

"I will make Offering to Odin," he told me.

He walked slowly towards the tree, his arms slightly open, palms forward. We watched as he neared the foremost bough, and placed his silver on one slender reaching tip. I could not tell what it was, a piece of broken jewellery or a ring, but saw it glint as he threaded it as gift to the God.

Odin, All-father, had given up an eye in return for one drink at the spring of wisdom which watered Yggdrasil's roots. And that same ash was the place on which the God had hung himself, upside down, for nine days and nights while he received the knowledge of runes and the gift of writing.

I looked steadily at Sidroc as he did this. The bough he gave his silver to, and those spreading out around it, had

140

not only the remains of sacrificed beasts upon them, but bore signs of supplication too. Some of what was hanging were garments – tunics, leggings, gowns, even shoes, left by those who asked the Father of All Knowledge for healing.

Sidroc returned to us. From the way Tindr nodded at him I knew Sidroc had made good on the charge. The tree must be the site of important Offerings, but beyond that perhaps all who passed into this part of the island stopped here as we did, a bounden duty to Odin.

Sidroc pulled himself back upon his horse, and looked to me. I knew he thought Odin treacherous, and indeed the one-eyed one was the master of every form of dark magic. Sidroc had ever been pledged to Tyr, the law-giving God of battle, and to Freyja, Goddess of battle and lust. Yet Odin was All-Father, and demanded his due. Sidroc's next words to me signalled this.

"All warriors recall Odin when the battle-horn calls," he said. "I do not forget him, tho' it will be to Freyja's hall I will go to in Asgard, not his."

He turned his eyes back to the ash tree. "But I am glad to have seen this great tree, and glad Tindr thought to bring us here to ensure the success of this journey. All things have their price, and Odin is ever welcome to my silver."

Tindr led us out, away from the rutted track, and once more overland, the fastest way to reach our goal in the short daylight.

We came to a broad stream, and travelled some little way along it, until at a bend in the stream-bed five white, tall, and slender stones were set upright. Just across from this bend on the other side were their fellows, another five tall white stones. On that side also stood a single stone, tall as well, but flared from top to bottom, as an axe blade is flared. In the little light I could not see if it bore pictures. Tindr urged his horse and the following pack animal into the water just at the point where the white stones rose.

"It is a marker, to show where the stream is safest to ford," explained Sidroc. At this time of year the water only came a little above our horses' fetlocks, but in the Spring melt it must be deep as their knees.

The flared-shaped stone indeed bore pictures, for in the centre was a big circle with a swirling spiral design in black and white, the same as was painted on Sidroc's shield-face; and above and below this were paired horses, facing each other and rearing as if about to fight. A gift to Freyr, I wondered to myself, and wondered too if he who had raised the stone perhaps had placed the guide-stones in the water.

We smelled the fire of the farmhouse before we saw it. The air was thin and cool and the dark gathering fast, and the tang of wood smoke and the promise of warmth and shelter led us on. I could see the dim rails of fencing in a clearing, with a flock of sheep nestled within, and the shadowy shapes of the farm buildings behind this. A dog began to bark, and a patch of sudden light shown in the dark as a door was opened. The dog came barking, running to us, but when it saw we were folk on horses and not the fox or other threat it feared the tail began to wag as it yipped its welcome. In the glow of the open door we saw a man come forward.

Tindr jumped off his horse and went to him. In the low light I do not think the farmer could make him out, for he began to speak, and speak so rapidly that I could scarce hear one word of what he said. He moved his head about as if trying to see Tindr's face better, and then clapped him on the shoulder in greeting. Sidroc and I got down and walked to join them. Tindr cupped his hands together in request, pointed to the farmer, and gestured to us with them.

We both bid the man good evening, and Sidroc spoke. "We are Rannveig's and Tindr's friends, traveling South to buy quern-stones. Could we pass one night with you?"

Another form had appeared in the open door, that of a woman, and she too came out. Almost in one voice they answered, "Já, já."

We told them our names, then Tindr and the man led the horses to their barn. The woman stood in her threshold, smiling and nodding at us, holding open the door in welcome. Four children were within, three boys and a girl, the eldest about twelve years, the youngest perhaps five. An older woman came forth too, from where she stood at the great cauldron hanging over the fire pit in the middle of the house, for now it was growing colder most cooking would be done inside. The smell that rose from her pot was of great savour, a rich meat like pig or goat, with onions, turnips and round oats, all billowing to us in the steam.

Their house was too small to hold a table, and the younger woman gestured to us to sit on the platforms of the sleeping alcoves that lined both long walls. These were covered with sheepskins, and the plank floor too was laid with their fleecy pelts. She moved to dip out ale for us from a red crock, and poured out water into a basin so we might wash our hands. The door opened again, and Tindr came in with the farmer. Tindr's hands were full with the smoked deer haunch he had taken from the pack horse, but on top of this he balanced a small jar of something, which he nodded with a smile to me to take. As I did so I saw it was one of the small pots that Rannveig put her mead up in; I had not known that Tindr had brought any. I passed it to the farm wife with a smile. She sliced the wax sealing the wood stopper and brought the jar to her nose. She grinned to us, and said, Þakk, and so thanking us passed the jar to her husband so he might see.

We made a merry feast of it in the small farm house. Anund and Tofa were our hosts, and Tofa shared out the mead amongst us in her thick-walled pottery cups. Even the youngest had some, well-watered, and the enjoyment they all had from this treat was plain. Anund the farmer carved off slices of the deer haunch, one for each, understanding that this gift was to last us our entire trip, and only shaving off a bit more for himself when Tindr pressed him to do so. Their browis was served up in oaken bowls which we ate with wooden spoons smoothed and thinned from long use. The old woman, Anund's mother, was a good cook, and I tried to tell her so.

They did not question who we were, tho' it was plain we were from afar. I thought they knew, as all Gotland folk seemed to, that Sidroc was a Dane, but the way that Tofa looked at my gown and listened to my speech I knew she puzzled over from whence I had come. I was grateful for their open-heartedness, and grateful too that they questioned us not. After we had supped, Tindr with his knife carved tiny faces in the ends of kindling sticks, and set them upright, like marching men, in the cool ashes at the edge of the fire pit, which pleased the little ones. Sidroc and Anund spoke of the stones he hoped to buy, and Anund listened with approval to the stone-shaper's name we would visit. Sidroc asked if there be any other man known for his skill in hewing sandstone, and nodded his thanks when the man offered a second name. I saw this pleased Anund, as most folk take pride in being asked advice of, and Anund was one. I thought this farm family did not often travel to the trading town, and that visitors might be rare, and thus valued, and for our part we tried to answer the questions they had about certain of the tradesmen and merchants there.

They had but one spare alcove, but one of the boys gave his to Tindr and crawled into the one in which his little brother slept. The early setting-out, long hours on horseback, and hearty fare made sleep come early for me. Tofa saw me

stifle a yawn, and with a smile made ready our alcove. She
had no sheets of linen, for we slept on rush matting, but her
wool blankets were thick and warm, and the sheepskin fleece
that touched my skin soft. I crawled in and drew the curtain,
content to listen to the fire-side talk as I fell into sleep.

We were up and away early, with thanks to our hosts.
Tofa gave us bread and cheese that we might eat upon the
road as a parting gift. We were, they told us, nearly a full
day's ride from the next farm, which was that of Tindr's
father's kin, and I was glad that the day promised to be a fair
one. We rode past their pasture lands, and I saw in the light
the great number of long-haired sheep they kept, both rams
and ewes horned, as I never saw in Angle-land. Then we
crossed into higher ground dotted with thickets of hazel, and
open stands of aspens. Clumps of white birch stood out, vivid
against the shadowy backdrop of spruce and pine.

At times in the clearings great birds circled above.
Tindr pointed to them and then to his wrist, telling us he
knew of these birds being trained to hunt for men, tho' those
above us be wild. I had seen no hawks or falcons for sale on
the trading road, but precious as they were few might pass
through. I knew they were one of the things Sidroc thought of
trading, but it took time and skill to catch and train them. He
had kept falcons at Four Stones, and his eye now followed the
bird as it swooped in long circles over the tree tops.
"Goshawk," he said with a nod, and turned in his saddle to
watch the great passes the bird made.

We rode all day, almost always in forest lands. But
there was water everywhere, in rivulets and streams and dark-
watered, deep-looking ponds, so we and our horses need
never grow thirsty. The sky was bright and blue above us, and
we made good time, so that the raking Sun still shone on us
as we came to the farm we sought. I hoped to see the standing
stone that Rannveig told me she had put up for Tindr's
father, sorry only that I must view it without her. The stone

stood well before the farm, and what captured my eye was
this: behind the stone was set two long rows of square white
rocks, joined at either end and bowing out in the middle, the
outline of a ship's hull, and just as big as a ship too. He had
not been lost with his ship, both it and his body had come
back to her, and she had remembered both by having this
outline of a hull set in his memory.

Tindr swung down from his horse and walked up to
the tall painted stone. He set his hand upon it, and bowed his
head. We came up to him, and he turned and looked at us. I
did not know the gesture for 'father', but I put my fingers to
my waist, as if fingering keys there, his sign for Rannveig, and
then clasped my hands together. He nodded. Then he
pointed to the ship outline, and drew his hand down in front
of his face, closing his eyes as he did so.

"Is he then buried here, beneath the ship, or this
stone," I wondered aloud.

"He is a dead man who has all," considered Sidroc,
looking over the length of the ship-stones. "A ship to sail,
and the comforts of his boy-hood farm."

We stood looking at the pictures on the stone. The
top most of them was of a great ship, its billowing sail full of
wind. Fish flew out of the sea around it as if landing on its
deck. It was a fitting image for a man who had fished and
done well at it. Beneath this was a man standing amongst
waving lines, reaching his hand to a woman who stood on a
hill. Was it a man drowning, I wondered to myself. But no:
Looking at it, Sidroc began to laugh.

"It is Njord, the Sea-God, reaching to his bride, Skaði.
She was of the mountains, and they could not be happy, for
when he went to her lands of snow and forests he longed for
the sea, and when she tried to live in the sea with him she
hated the wet. In the end they went their own ways." He
looked to me. "I think Rannveig and her husband were

happier than this, but it is a reminder that he loved the sea, and she, her life on the trading road, brewing."

Tindr was watching Sidroc good-naturedly, and I wished he could know what he said. He seemed to guess some of it, for he pointed to the figure of Skaði, and then drew back a bowstring from the air. Sidroc nodded. "Skaði is a great hunter, like Tindr," he told me.

The lowest rank of pictures was of a line of people, a few sheep and cows at their heels, walking towards a great tree. "The Blót," Sidroc said simply. This word, blood, meant the sacrifice the folk would make to ensure a bountiful return of beasts, grain, fish, and game, and to hope for hale and hearty children to be born.

Now my eye fell on the braided border which travelled the length and height of the stone, outlining the drawings. Within the border were carved runes, scores of them, running the whole way, from where the base of the stone sat in the grass, up, and around to end in the grass again.

It had been a long time since I had read rune-writing, and I had already seen that the runes of Gotland, like those of the Danes too, could differ from those used by my kin in Mercia. Some runes I knew, but here were drawn backwards, or on their sides, and this made my understanding of them the harder. Sidroc knew the runes; the meaning of each, their names, and how to draw them, but he did not know how to read or write with them to make words. And each rune carried its own message, so that a single rune could mean more than its name, just as Feoh, one of the runes Tindr marked his hands with when he hunted, meant cattle, and also therefore wealth. But used alone it could mean the Goddess, Freyja; just as Sigel, which Sidroc used to sign his name, meant Sun.

I bent down to get a better look. The first rune was Rad, ᚱ, which meant riding, or road. The second was Os, ᚠ, then two together of ᛏ Nid. Several others followed them.

"Rannveig," I said aloud. Now that I saw her name it gave me sureness that I could read the rest. The runes were all run into each other, with no spaces, but by sounding things out and Sidroc helping, I was able to read out what I thought it said.

"Rannveig set this stone for Dagr her husband the best fisherman in Njord's great sea. Ingmund carved the runes."

I thought these picture stones the grandest way to recall and remember a person or a story I had ever seen; as wonderful in its way as the parchment books with tiny paintings Modwynn owned at Kilton. This that Rannveig had made had majesty in its size and force, and yet here too upon its face was the story of a man and woman who loved each other.

We walked our horses the rest of the way to the farmhouse, and as it was still light, some folk who were about saw us and came out to meet us. Tindr was greeted as warmly as he had been at his cousin Ragnfast's farm, for a number of children came forth and swarmed him, and the man and woman who welcomed us both embraced him. This was the farm of Dagr's elder brother, who tho' aged, still lived here with his son and his family. They had several serving folk as well, and between the flocks of sheep and penned red haired cattle I saw they were blessed with plenty. Their kitchen yard was full of squawking yellow-footed geese, and beneath the long eaves of the barn they had a fowl house from which strutted numberless spotted hens. Dagr had been born here, but as he was a younger son it had fallen to his brother, and he and his other brothers had built farms of their own, or gone to be faremen by taking up a trade. Dagr chose the sea.

We supped well, and afterwards Tindr's old uncle sang to us in a deep and unwavering voice. He sang songs of the island's rich forests, of the spirits that roamed there amongst the beasts, and sang of the sea and the treasures of fish and walrus and seal it brought forth. I had seen fish aplenty since coming here, fresh and glistening or flayed and drying, and knew both wealth and sustenance came from them. At the pier on the trading road I had seen the massive body of a walrus, bigger than a horse, lashed to a ship deck which had come from far up the Baltic, but I had no idea of the second creature he named.

We need not hurry away in the morning, for we could reach the stone-shaper's quarries by noon. As we left Dagr's farm the land we rode through changed, for there were no woods to re-enter. Instead we picked our way through vast grasslands, not made so by men or cropped by animals, but almost free of trees just the same. Rocky outcroppings, showing the same grey-white stone as the walls Tyrsborg were made of, thrust up from the brown soil. In places no grasses grew, just the scraped whitish surface of the stone, dotted here and there with ringed lichen. In the weak morning Sun it had an odd and eerie beauty, and we threw huge pale shadows against the rock as our horses crossed it. The sky loomed above us after being so much under the shelter of boundless trees, and under its expanse I felt small despite the long shadow I cast.

We came to the quarry as the Sun was at its highest point. I had seen deep quarries in Mercia, but this of the Gotland sandstone was new to me. There was such abundance of the stone that the shaper and his men had hardly to scrape away soil to find a vein which then yielded to their sharp chisels and iron hammers. Several sheds with roofs but open walls gave two or three workman shelter as they fashioned pieces of the stone that had been dragged to them on rollers of smoothed fir trunks. The stone-shaper, Thorfast, rose from his work in one of them and came over to

149

us. He was as big as an iron-smith, with shoulders and arms that proclaimed the heavy stuff he worked with, but his eyes were friendly. Now he slapped the stone-dust from his hands and greeted us. Not far away was a small farm house where he and his family must live.

From his hard stone he fashioned querns, which he brought to the trading posts on Gotland each Spring to be sold. These would be bought both by Gotland folk and by merchants who shipped them to the large trading towns and posts along the Baltic. They were of two pieces, a flat round stone bottom, and another round, domed stone which fit over it. Thorfast was drilling the hole in which the wooden turning handle would be set, which would move the heavier top stone around and around the grain that lay between it and the bottom stone. He made as well larger millstones, all for merchants to carry away, for the folk of Gotland used no mills, each family grinding their own grain each day. We selected a quern, which were all alike, and as much like Rannveig's that only the greater smoothness of hers would proclaim its age, and he packed it in straw to give the horse that must carry it greater comfort. Sidroc paid him his silver, and then began to look at a thick and flat millstone another man was fashioning.

"How much for a pair?" asked Sidroc, for like a quern the stones must be used one upon another to grind the grain.

Thorfast saw he was now speaking to a merchant, and not just a man setting up a new household.

A pair of such stones was five times as much silver as we had paid out for the quern, and next to the big iron cauldron we had bought, the quern was the most costly single household purchase we had made.

"Will you make me two pairs, that I may have in Spring," Sidroc asked, and then took the same tack he had with the amber-worker. "I will pay you now in full for one,

150

and next Fall I will pay you one-quarter more again for the second pair."

"I do not know that I can make four such stones by Spring," Thorfast said. "This is one of a pair I have just begun, and it is spoken for."

"There is light yet," Sidroc answered, raising his hand to the mildness of the noon, as if it would last forever. "You have men. I will not need them for months. Or you can let me go to Abi, who I hear works stone well."

Thorfast straightened to his full height. "Abi's stone is not as hard as mine, and he splits more than he spares. The pile of waste-rock in his work-yard would shame his dead father, who was a man who knew stone."

In this way Sidroc obtained the promise of two pairs of fine large millstones for the coming trading season.

We now turned back, but Tindr did not lead us the way we had come. He knew that Sidroc was pleased with the deal he had made, and I think he wished to show us that which we had not seen, for we turned East, following at first a well-rutted ox cart track. Soon we left this, and the barren stone face of the land about us began to show grasses and shrubby growth. I thought too, I smelled the tang of the sea, and then we saw glimpses of its shining waters through the clumps of bushes. The coast here was marked by the same shingle as formed the edge of the trading town, but here there were as well beaches of hard grey sand, rippled and blowing in the steady breeze. As the blue sky was paling to white we came to a farm set up on a rise above the water. Plots of stubble remained where oats and wheat had been cut, but the rows of vegetables showed the tops of beets and carrots and turnips still waiting to be pulled. A great speckled pig lay

snuffling in a pen by a small shed. A stout boat shelved on
the sandy beach told us this was the home of fishing folk, as
did the drying rack on which white fleshed fish lay, pointed to
the Sun.

Tindr did not know them, but they opened their door
to us just the same, and were glad of the smoked deer haunch
and jar of mead. They were older folk, alone it seemed with
no grown children about, but they looked content and well
fed in their home perched above the sea. The woman dished
out a fish stew, and then ladled over it a sauce of parsley,
mint, costmary, and other pot herbs, giving brightness and
savour to the whole. She had also large sharp crystals of salt,
clean and white, which she sprinkled over all. I asked her
where she had gotten such salt, and she laughed and took me
to the door of the house and pointed down to the flat sea
rocks below. They had slight hollows in them where it might
be easy to dry the sea-water, and even now I saw white flecks
as they gleamed in the setting Sun.

When we set out in the morning we kept to the coast.
I was glad to see the sea again, and to travel by its pebbled
edge. There was a good wind ruffling its surface, pulling
endless rows of white tips into peaks only to rise and sink
back, lost into the tossing seas. The air was fresh with the
smack of its salty brine, and I was thankful for my warm
mantle, and for the brilliant Sun which beat upon my
shoulders. In the forenoon Tindr stopped, and pointed down
to where the waters foamed around wet rocks. I did not know
what he wanted us to look at, and then I saw something in
the water. It looked like a man's head, bobbing of a sudden
above the surface, and then vanishing below, and I stifled a
cry of fear for him in the rough waters. Then the head
appeared again, much closer to the shore, and a sleek creature
hauled itself glistening onto the rocks. Another creature like
it, which I had not seen, now moved to make way for it.

"Seals," said Sidroc, and he was smiling, as was Tindr. "They are not good eating, but their hide is tough and warm. Also they have much fat to boil down for oil."

"Have you them in Dane-mark?" I asked.

"They swim by. They are hard to hunt, fast and wily. They live further North, where the men there hunt them with barbed spears, make their tunics from them, and eat them too."

He turned to Tindr to question him. He pointed to Tindr, made as if he drew back a bow string, and pointed to the glossy seals below.

Tindr shook his head and crossed his clenched wrists. Then he pointed far into the sea.

"They are sea-creatures; they must be sacred to Njord," I suggested. I thought of Dagr, Tindr's father, and half-smiled to myself, wondering if he had sent these wet and shining creatures as a greeting to his son.

We came back to the trading town two days later, riding through the place of burial and along the fish drying racks, past the mighty carving of upright Freyr, and then onto the main road fronting the sea. I was eager to see Tyrsborg again, to heat water and to stand in our large copper basin and bathe, and to again sleep in our soft bed with the great knot design carved in it. But as we made our way down the road a ship sailed into view from the low bluffs past Rannveig's brew-house. Sidroc, who was in front, reined in at once, and we stopped and gazed on it.

It was a long ship, much like that of any Danes on a raid, for it was slender and built for speed, not broad-beamed like that of many of the knorrs, or merchant ships. As it grew closer I saw it was longer than any other I had seen, longer than that of the red-bearded Dane who we had sailed with, and longer even than that of Ulf, the yellow-haired Dane who had taken us from the Idrisid ship.

The sail was furled and the mast down, and lines of oars rose up, curved, and fell into the still water. A row of vivid painted round shields lined the ship-rail above those oars.

"A drekar," breathed Sidroc. A dragon-boat, the largest of any of the long ships, built to carry the greatest number of men, and not cargo.

"Danes?" I asked, turning to Sidroc. I tried to keep my voice steady. "But are they trading, or raiding?"

His eyes were still trained on the ship. "Nai," he said at last. "Not Danes. I think they are Svear."

The Svear were the people who lived above and just to the East of Dane-mark, and across the Baltic to the West from Gotland. All I knew of them is what Sidroc had told me on board Ulf's ship after we had escaped the Idrisids: That the Svear were warriors, of the best.

Now he looked to me. My fear must have been in my face, for he quickly said, "They are not raiding. One ship against a trading town is a dead man's wager."

There were not many people about on the road, but those who were stopped and stood and looked at the ship as it beat closer. The oars on one side lifted high as the man at the steering-oar turned her prow in line with the pier. In busier times men would be about the pier or close by, ready to grab a line thrown from the approaching ship and haul her close. Today no man did.

The ship looked new and tight, its sides unscraped. The prow indeed bore a carving of a ravening dragon or sea-bird, talons spread by the gaping beak; a dread-full thing to have bear down on another ship.

We could see the men aboard now, as they began to rise from the oar-wells. They were all tall, with yellow or light reddish hair. They wore tunics and leggings such as Sidroc or the men of Gotland wore, with leathern leg-wrappings, and now some threw mantles over their shoulders. They bore no weaponry save their long knives hanging at the waist, tho' up high as we were on horseback we could see their ring-shirts and swords, lying in neat order, in the centre of the narrow deck, ready if needed. Spears lay lashed together in two straight piles on either side of the mast. None of the men reached for their weapons, which gave me more ease.

Their clothing was as brightly coloured as the shields which hung from the rail: blue, green, red, yellow, and a deep russet blended from the last two. They were all young, and the yellow-haired man at the steering oar had the hawk-like glance of their leader. Those eyes were of a clear blue, deeply set over a nose which had never been broken. His long hair fell in two braids on his shoulders, his brow was broad, his face unmarked by any scar.

Sidroc turned to us. "I am going to speak to them. Tindr will come with me." He touched his ear, then made a slight gesture with his hand, telling Tindr to follow him. "You stay here," he told me. "And –"

"I know," I said. "Do not look at them."

He nodded, and grinned just a moment. "Já. Do not look at them."

He nudged his horse forward and onto the pier, Tindr behind him. The men had not yet slid a gangplank from their ship. Sidroc reined up and stood his horse even with the man

155

at the stern, who paused in the tying up of his steering oar to look at him. The captain saw a tall warrior perhaps ten years older than he, a man with flint blue eyes which narrowed over the long scar on his left cheek; a man who in his dark brown hair had one strand of grey at his left temple above that scar.

"Welcome," Sidroc said, looking down on him. He lifted his hand as he did so, moving his mantle so that the glittering hilt of the long seax strapped across his belly was in plain view. "Here in Gotland you will not need your swords."

"I thank you for your welcome," said the leader. He spoke slowly enough so I could understand, and with a different accent from the folk of Gotland. His eyes went swiftly from Sidroc and his fine horse to Tindr, and then beyond to where I sat on my dun mare, with the pack horse behind me. I lowered my own just in time. The stranger took in the wealth in horses this man before him travelled with. When I glanced up again, head lowered, I saw he looked again at Sidroc.

"I am Eskil. I have iron to trade for salt."

"I am Sidroc. There are two iron-workers who will welcome your bars up there," and here he turned in his saddle to point to one of the side roads reaching back from the main trading road, where the smoke from the hot smithing fires could be seen.

"As for your salt, if you seek the grey kind to cure meat, you will find several folk on the main road to supply you. But if white salt in flakes for the table is wanted, go only to Asfrid, the salt-seller in the stall with the green awning; hers is the finest we offer."

Eskil listened to this counsel and nodded, a grin on his face.

"And you Sidroc, what do you trade?"

"At this time of year, nothing. But I do play dice. There is a brew-house there," he said, pointing the short distance to Rannveig's. "The ale is good. And I will be there tonight if you care to lose some silver to me."

"I look forward to taking your silver," answered Eskil. "For now I take your advice about who to see about my iron."

We rode up the hill towards Tyrsborg. Sidroc began whistling. "They are Svear," he told me, interrupting his song. "I am glad they are here in one ship and not many. And I am glad," he went on, turning his head to look back to Rannveig's, "that tonight I will be the richer for their coming."

It was late when Sidroc started down the hill. "Will not Eskil grow restless, waiting for you?" I asked him.

"Já," he said. "And as he is a good player, he is winning now. So I will have the more to take from him when I finally do show."

I had to shake my head as I smiled at his sureness. In truth in I did not much want him to go, even tho' he felt the Svear safe. Tindr would stay at Tyrsborg with me, as Sidroc did not wish me to go to the brew-house. As he set off I kissed him and he pulled me close. "I will wake you up with silver," he promised.

I locked the door of the treasure room behind him, as we always did, for it was the strong-room of the hall. But sleep did not come easily, tired as I was from the long trip to buy the quern and millstones. I began to wish that Sidroc had taken Tindr with him, then had to smile at this thought as I lay in the dark in our big bed. Tindr was so gentle that I could not imagine him in a fight. Like all folk of Gotland, he wore a knife each day, which he used for eating and every other ordinary task, but other than his bow used no weapons. Sidroc had made a target on the side wall of the stable, hammering up boards and marking them with squares. He used this to practice his spear-throwing, both with his heavy Danish spear and the lighter, shorter one he had taken from the Idrisids. He had tried to interest Tindr in this, but after a few tries Tindr made it clear he would not hunt that way. I was struck by this; he could not think about hurling such a weapon against a man, as Sidroc did.

Sleep came at last, fitful as it was, for I awoke hearing the low whistle Sidroc used to tell me he was near, and heard his key turn in the treasure room door. I threw off the coverlet and ran to him, naked and shivering in the sudden cold. He held a few straws with flaming tips to light his way, but caught me up in his other arm and drew his mantle around me.

"I am glad you are back," I told him. He shooed me into bed and I pulled the feather coverlet up over me. He sat down at my side and lit the oil cresset by our bed. I waited for him to tell me what he had won.

"I did not bring you any silver," he said. His face was grave enough to make me believe him.

I blinked in my surprise. Sidroc was a very good dice player, and even better at making men wager more than they should.

"Then you lost?"

"I won," he said, and then he smiled. "But it is not silver I bring you." He moved the oil cresset a little closer to the bed. He reached into the lining of his belt and withdrew something, which he held up between his thumb and forefinger for me to see.

It was a small flattened round of clear stuff, rounder in the middle and tapering at the edges; like the clearest glass I had ever seen, clearer even. He turned it slightly in his fingers and it caught the light of the cresset flame in its eye, making it blaze up within its clear heart.

I gasped.

"A crystal," he told me.

I had only seen one this size before, and that upon the greatest treasure of all the books at Kilton. Modwynn and Godwulf had been given the four Holy Gospels, copied out on parchment, and encased in a silver binding studded with gemstones. The largest of these was a great crystal in a silver mount in the centre of the cover. The book and its gemmed cover had been a gift from Ælfred, King.

He passed the disc to me. I too held it up to the light, delighting in how it made the small flame look huge. Then holding it near the lamp's glow, I passed it before the fingers of my other hand. My fingernail looked twice its size.

"Everything is bigger and clearer, seen through this," I said. The crystal on the Gospels had been fixed in its mount, so I had never seen this part of a crystal's nature.

"We will take it to the silver-smith, and he can put it on your neckchain for you," Sidroc said.

I wrapped my arms around his neck and hugged him. It was not any piece of jewellery; the crystal in its clearness and ability to capture and throw light felt as if it had a power of its own. All gems had their own magic, and this one, of such great size and clarity, must possess great magic.

I held it now, smooth and hard, firm in my closed hand. "It will help me to know what to do," I told him, not really understanding what I said.

But he just nodded. "It will be a talisman to you," he agreed.

"That is not all I won," he went on, rising and beginning to undress. "Eskil told me much. Knowledge can be as valuable as silver."

"Still, he could not have been happy to lose such a prize as this," I answered.

"He knows I give it to you," he said, and grinned. He unbuckled his seax belt and hung it on a peg. "We spoke of you."

"Did he ask to buy me?" I could not help but smile.

He shook his head and gave a short laugh. "Eskil has better manners than that. But he worked his way around to you. He told me he admired the dun mare he saw with me today. Then he asked about she who rode her."

"And – ?"

"I told him the truth. That you are my wife. All he could do was shrug and let me call for more ale."

"You must have drunk a lot," I said.

"Not as much as Eskil, for he had been drinking all evening, playing dice and taking silver from Ketil and a few others. When I began winning Rannveig brought us mead, which helped me play better."

"And Eskil, worse."

"Ah – já," he said, smiling. "Rannveig does not earn her silver without cause. But drink makes a man more willing to talk as well as more willing to wager, so I welcomed it."

"So what is the knowledge you gained?"

His face darkened a little, and he no longer joked. "The first I knew already: That we had the favour of the Gods to make it here. Eskil sailed here from Birka, a big trading centre in the land of the Svear. He was chased by two ships on his way to Gotland, one of them Danes, one he could not tell. His ship is fast and he has many men rowing, so he outran them both."

For several years much of the raiding had taken place solely at sea, for lands like Frankland and Angle-land were now mostly at peace. Those who were native to those lands had shared out parts of it to the Danes who had landed and settled there. Young warriors seeking treasure had to take their chances chasing down merchant ships or even the long ships of other warriors.

"We ourselves were chased and caught by two warships in the Baltic." I reminded. He nodded, and I thought again how Fate had guided us, bringing us safe through it all. But these were the same waters he hoped to send out our amber and millstones into come Summer. Our eyes met.

"The ship I hire must be fast, the captain able, and the men aboard it, trained," was what he said.

I had not seen one man of Gotland wear a sword, but then in a place of peace there was no reason to. Swords were dear, and only those who had cause to use one would invest so much silver in such a weapon. I had seen spears inside the workshops and stalls of tradesmen, and knew one of the iron-workers was a swords-smith, but how Sidroc would find men trained in arms I did not know.

His thoughts had moved on. "The other thing I learned was that my homeland needs salt."

"Salt?"

"Já. Eskil will take the salt he buys here and carry it to Dane-land. Our salt-making has not been good due to much rain these last months, and there will be a need for salt next trading season."

"But the ship you will hire – you will ask it to sail both to Frankland and to Dane-land?"

"That I do not yet know," he said, sliding in next to me. He reached out and snuffed the cresset wick between his fingers. A pale patch of moonlight fell upon the bed from the high window. He turned to me and drew me close. "You will ask your crystal that for me."

Chapter the Tenth: Sparrow

I had gone down to the trading road to pay the grain seller, and ask him for another few bags of wheat, rye, and barley to be brought up to Tyrsborg. As I came out Tindr joined me, and we began the walk back together. I glanced down to my shoes and saw the white flour clinging to the hem of my gown; the grain seller's store house could not help but be dusty with it. As I shook out my hem to free the flour I saw something move on the water from the tail of my eye. A long ship.

It was mid-morning, and those stalls still open had folk in and about them. The pier was empty of any ship, and as this one oared closer I saw it to be that of Eskil, the Svear. He had left several days ago, and I did not expect to see him back here in Gotland. But here he was. Perhaps he had gone to another Baltic post and found something else to trade here for; or he might need water or ale or more food for the voyage home. Tindr and I paused a moment to look as his ship came in, oars lifted. I knew such ships had their own beauty, and this one, with the round faces of the bright shields rimming it, even more so; yet it was not a thing I could easily look on without a knot forming in my throat. Tindr looked at it long, and in his light eyes I thought I saw him admire it, but admire it perhaps as something far from his own realm, as if it were Freyr's magic ship.

The folk about us went on their way after stopping to look, and we too resumed our walking until we reached the pier. All oars had been shipped, and the men worked to make all fast. Eskil was knotting up the steering oar tie. His back was to us, and as I watched him do this a small figure, not of the Svear, rose up from the deck near where he stood in the stern. I could not tell at first if it was man or woman, but the mantle it had held over its shoulders slipped and I saw it was a young woman. Her gown was little more than a rag, torn and filthy, and I saw her mantle was but a strip of blanket. She stood and looked out at the place they had landed, and as she did so looked straight at us. She wore no head wrap, and her brown hair lay free upon her shoulders. Her face was pinched, her lips pressed tight, but her dark eyes moved wildly about. I saw she was very young, no more than fourteen or fifteen years.

I stopped in my tracks; I had to. Eskil finished his work and turned and saw Tindr and me standing at the foot of the pier. He glanced back over his shoulder to the girl, and saw she was what we looked at. His men were already coming across the gangplank onto the pier.

I resolved I would buy the girl from him, regardless of cost. I had not much silver with me, but plenty back at the hall. Even as I thought this I knew I should wait, tell Sidroc of the girl, have him go to Eskil and buy her. But I could not.

I took a breath, gathered my skirts up in my hands, and stepped onto the pier. Eskil stood still awaiting us, his hand resting on the leather-wrapped handle of his steering oar. I thought he would remember me and he did.

"The wife of Sidroc," he said, and tipped his head a little to one side. He did not know my name, and I did not intend to tell him. Now he gave a little smile and made bold to let his eyes sweep across my face and body.

"I will buy your slave," I said, without any word of greeting.

His face fell, and he looked almost startled. "O," he said. "I bring a couple lengths of silk with me, and thought you, of all the women of rich Gotland, should have first pick of them."

I said nothing. The girl was looking at me, and did not, I think, understand our speech. Now that I was nearer I saw how fine-boned she was. A shivering thrill ran up the back of my neck: I wondered if she might be of the Welsh.

Eskil shifted where he stood. He looked me full in the face.

"But you are not truly of Gotland," he went on.

Even my gown would have told him that, for I did not wear the over-gown of the Gotlandic women, with the paired bronze brooches at the shoulders; but the long-sleeved gown of the women of Angle-land.

"You are from Frankland," he guessed.

So their women too wore such gowns as mine. I would tell him nothing, and only wanted to rescue the girl. Some of Eskil's men had passed onto the trading road, while a few others stood around us on the pier, watching. Eskil waved them away, and they began to move off as well.

"If you want to buy her you may have her," Eskil said with a shrug. Then he gestured to the gangplank. "But come aboard and I will show the silk I have." His smile told me he knew just how handsome he was.

I had no fear he would try anything with me, but his confidence I would be lured aboard by him on the hope of securing a bolt of cloth, even if it be silk, angered me.

"I will not come aboard. Send her to me," I said. I knew my tone was cold and I did not care.

He took the girl, who was still looking at me, by the elbow, but she tried to jerk herself away from him. He only tightened his grasp; I could see he was hurting her. I stepped forward, and he let go of her and looked up at me. Now that I was nearer I saw his face was scratched. Human fingernails had raked across his right forehead and left cheek.

I forced myself to keep my voice steady, but could not stop my words.

"Do you keep a cat on board, Eskil?" I taunted. "Because your face is badly scratched."

He flinched, and began lifting his hand to his face before he stopped himself.

"I keep no cat. Or rather, she is yours now," he told me. He kept looking at me, and a grin spread across his face. His next words were meant not to praise, but to shame me. "Sidroc is a lucky man," he said.

I would not answer this and just stood there, staring at him. Finally he gave the girl a poke in the back, trying to propel her to the gangplank. She dropped the blanket she clutched.

"Come," I said, and extended my hand. The dark eyes shifted between the deck of the ship, up to me, and then beyond to the trading town. She would not even raise her eyes to Eskil; she knew what she was leaving, but not what she was going to. She put her foot on the narrow gangplank. The tide was at the full and the gangplank steeply pitched to the pier. We saw she was barefoot, her browned legs as thin as sticks.

I took a step closer to her, and again said, "Come," as gently as I could.

She trembled as she took her first steps, and Tindr, watching at my side all this time, jumped lightly forward to take her hand. She pulled back from him; her fear was terrible to see. Eskil looked on, still grinning. Tindr moved closer to the girl and slowly extended his hand to her. She took it only for a moment to steady herself, then hopped down upon the wooden planks of the pier.

Her rag of a gown told me little; I think it had been merely her shift, for it was of undyed wool, coarsely woven. She wore no over-gown. The sleeves were long and one of them almost torn off. I reached to her and pulled her in under my mantle with me, wanting to give her what little shelter I could. I had my arm about her waist and felt her pitiable thinness, her hip bone sharp against my palm.

I was not thinking of buying a slave, only of saving a young girl. I had not seen any men or women I could identify as slaves on Gotland, and did not know if they were kept. Slaves were for sale at Baltic trading posts, I had seen them myself; and some must, I thought, come through here in high Summer, even if the Gotlandic folk themselves did not buy them.

In Mercia and Wessex the keeping of a slave was a grave burden. The owner stood liable for any hurt or damage a slave committed. Ælfred had laws about the treatment of slaves, and that they be allowed to earn their own money when their day's duties were done so that they might hope to redeem themselves. At Kilton most of the slaves were cottars who had fallen on hard times and feared being able to feed themselves; they were sometimes at the point of starvation. They had come to Godwulf or Modwynn and now Godwin and asked to be taken into their care. Godwulf had freed many on his death, and Modwynn too freed slaves each year, at Eastertide. Even freeing a slave was costly. In freeing them the owner had by law to equip them to feed themselves, and give them once again a seax, the sure sign of a free man. Folk were also made slaves as punishment for wrongs done by them; then there was always the fear they would repeat their crimes while in your keeping. I knew all these things yet at that moment was thinking none of them, nor did I know what my obligation by Gotland law would be to her.

Eskil now put his foot up on the gangplank. He leaned forward and again smiled at me. "Do not just buy something ugly from me, wife of Sidroc," he began. "I want to show you the red silk I –"

He stopped, and looked up and over our heads. I turned too. There at the foot of the pier was Sidroc on his black stallion. That morning he had ridden down to where the ships were beached past the great carving of Freyr to meet with a man he thought to hire to sail for him. Now he was come back. He stood his horse, looking at us, then quietly nudged the beast along the wooden planking to the ship. He came up near me. The girl was peering out from underneath my arm, and as he neared us she stiffened up against me.

I wanted to be the first to speak and did so.

"I have bought this girl from Eskil," I told him.

He glanced at her and then back to me.

"How much did you offer to pay for her?" he asked me. His voice was calm and his way, easy. I knew he could not be pleased to see me before a man such as Eskil, but I knew too he would not show his displeasure in front of him unless he must.

"We have not yet spoken of the price," I admitted, stricken that I had leapt to buy her without knowing.

Sidroc took a breath, looked up at the sky, then leaned forward over his saddle to look at Eskil. "How much?" he asked.

Eskil paused just a moment. "Two marks of silver."

"Two marks. For a ragged girl you won at a dice game."

The look on Eskil's face showed that this was not far from the truth.

"Or you can play me for her," Eskil offered.

Sidroc did not spend long considering this. "I will not play for her. My wife said she would buy her, and your price is two marks. Therefore I give you two marks." He was already reaching for his belt.

"One mark," countered Eskil, which made me turn to him. I looked at his face, intent on Sidroc's. I knew Sidroc did not want to be in any man's debt, and had, for all his years of raiding, a sense of fitness about how he dealt while trading. I thought Eskil must feel the same. If he took more silver than he thought the girl was worth he would debase himself in Sidroc's eyes.

At this Sidroc had to smile. "One mark," he agreed, and tossed a doubled coil of silver to Eskil.

Sidroc looked down at us and inclined his head toward the road. Without a word to Eskil I turned and began to move the girl along with me. Tindr was still at my side and I was glad for it.

A knot of Eskil's men had gathered, waiting and watching, at the end of the pier. They moved back as we walked through them, some of them snickering at us. I pulled my mantle up around the girl's face as we went, but I looked at them with the angry boldness I felt. I could not help but wonder if she had been passed around amongst them.

When we gained the road one called out. I could not catch his words but Sidroc turned quickly in his saddle, the scowl he bore telling me much. He yelled something back, but all I could hear were the words "mare" and "bargain".

We went on a little way. Rannveig came out of her brew-house; she must have seen us from her brewing yard. I stopped in front of her and opened my mantle.

Rannveig bent down, placed her hands on her knees, and studied the girl.

"She is just a child," she said.

I looked down at her once more and felt she was right; she might have no more than twelve or thirteen Summers. The girl was again trembling; I wondered if she thought she would be sold yet again. Rannveig straightened up, then took one of the bright strands of coloured glass beads from around her plump neck. She held it out to the girl, and smiled at her. She gestured it was a gift, and said as much too.

"I do not think she knows our speech," I told Rannveig. But the girl bowed her head and let Rannveig drop the necklace around her neck, a pitiful contrast lying on her ripped and dirty gown.

"Let me know if you need help," Rannveig told us, as we turned to begin the climb to Tyrsborg. She could not help but shake her head as we moved away.

Once off the well-travelled trading road the way up was full of sharp stones, and from the cautious way the girl stepped it was clear they hurt her naked feet. I could not see how she could walk even so far as Tyrsborg. Sidroc's horse skittered along next to us, side-stepping and tossing his glossy neck, impatient at our slow pace. Sidroc looked down and said, "Pass her up to me; I will carry her before me."

He extended his arms, and Tindr came closer to boost her up, but she recoiled into me. The fear of being passed to such a man as Sidroc was clear; it might have been the way she was first carried off from her home.

I could only look up at him. I need not say the next, but did anyway.

"She fears you. She fears all men; she has only been hurt by them."

Sidroc swung down from his horse. He patted the saddle, and pointed to the girl. She still clung to me. I tried to lead her to it, talking to her the whole time. Tindr came forward and made a little bow to her, cupping his hands together to ask Please. Then he opened his hands and showed she should step in them and so be able to reach the saddle's height. At last she did so. Her thin legs swung over the broad back. Sidroc stepped away from the stallion's head and gestured that Tindr should lead her so she had less fear.

In this way we made our way to Tyrsborg. Sidroc came up even with me as we neared our door.

"Tell me what happened," he invited, as he turned the key.

I had to sigh.

"Tindr and I were heading back to Tyrsborg from the grain seller. We saw Eskil's ship sail in. When we got even with the pier, the girl stood up and I saw her. She was so wretched…"

I did not have to go on; he looked at me and nodded. If Fate had dealt differently I could have been her, and he knew I felt this keenly.

"That man – the one who called after us. What did he say?" I asked.

He shook his head. "That the babe would look like him."

I had to bite my lip to keep my anger from rising. "And what did you yell back?"

171

He waited a moment. "The only thing I could. That a bred mare was a better bargain."

I felt almost sick with anger at the men.

"Eskil has silk," I told him now. "Please do not buy it for me; I do not want it." He had turned his head slightly towards the town at this, as if to Eskil's ship.

"Or rather," I went on, realising what I asked, "if you want it, buy it only for Frankland. Not for me."

He nodded. We turned to where Tindr waited at the head of the horse. The girl was clutching handfuls of the thick mane, and looking up fearfully at Tyrsborg's high-peaked roof.

Sidroc gestured that she come down. Tindr reached up and plucked the girl from the saddle, as gently as he could, and placed her upon the ground. He took the horse to the stable, and I took the girl's hand in mine and led her in.

Once inside with her I hardly knew where to begin. I led her to Sigvor's old alcove, and made her sit down there, and went first for food. I brought her a slice of bread, thick with sweet butter. She wolfed it down, swallowing so quickly I thought she might choke. I brought her another, this time spread also with Tindr's golden honey. She licked at it and I thought I saw the faintest smile form as she tasted it. This too she devoured, as she did a bowl of warm browis. Tindr had brought us two large hares yesterday from the snares he set in the forest, and I had boiled them up with barley and skirrets. She held the bowl to her mouth and spooned it in, her eyes never leaving me.

I had been speaking to her this whole time, first in Norse, then in the tongue of Angle-land, and although she made answer I could not understand what she said. Sidroc had left us alone, and I thought again of how I had felt when I first looked at her face – that she might be of the Welsh.

I knew very few words of my mother's tongue, for my father and kinsman had been of Angle-land. I squatted down next to her and asked, "Cymru?" – Wales? almost fearing the answer if it be Yes. If she be Welsh that meant war might be there once again.

But she just shrugged and looked blankly back at me. Eskil thought I might be of Frankland. She did not wear a gown like the women of the Danes or those here in Gotland. I knew that could mean nothing; she may have lost all her clothes long ago. But I began to wonder if she herself might be of Frankland.

I knew no one who spoke their speech; only knew it was different from my own. All this would have to wait until she could tell us herself where she was from and what her name was. To do that we needed a common tongue. Gotland was her new home, so I spoke Norse to her.

"Mitt nafr ir Ceridwen," I told her, pointing to myself. "Ceridwen."

"Ceridwen," she answered. Her eyes were beset with uncertainty.

The door to the kitchen yard opened, and Tindr came in. He had in his hands a tanned boar skin. I saw at once what he meant to do, and blessed his goodness in my heart. He came slowly up to us, then bowed to where the girl sat perched on the alcove platform. He knelt down before her, set the boar hide on the floor, and smiled at her. He pointed at my shoes, then pointed at the girl's bare feet. He would make her shoes.

He turned to the fire pit and picked out a piece of cold charcoal. Her eyes opened wide as he reached his hand forward for her ankle; he meant to place it on the hide and trace around her foot. She shrieked, pulling back as he touched her. He withdrew his hand.

"He will not hurt you, little one," I soothed. "He will cut shoes for you. Please let him help you." I extended my hand to draw her near again, and after a moment she took it, and sat back up.

Tindr looked up at me, and I nodded he try again. He cupped his hands together, Please.

I touched my ear, and said to her, "Tindr is deaf. This is the way he speaks. Now he asks your permission to touch your feet." Her eyes were fastened on my face and she gave out a breath. She moved one foot onto the boar hide. Tindr went to work, and in three quick strokes outlined first one foot, and then the other. He touched his heart and opened his hand to her.

"Now he says, "I thank you," I said.

Tindr rose, and smiled at her. He lifted his hand and made sure she watched. First he touched his own ear.

"Tindr," I told her, and pointed to him.

Then he touched the tips of his hair and opened his fingers fast. "Me," I told her. "Ceridwen."

Now he placed his fist into his cupped left hand, and extended the thumb and index finger of the fist. He moved the two fingers open and closed, like the beak of a bird on a nest. Then he pointed at her.

"That is his sign for you," I told her. "A bird – a little bird." I smiled at Tindr. "Já," I said. "She is like a little brown sparrow."

It was not a real name, but until she could tell us herself, it would suit her well: Sparrow.

Tindr went back out, and I considered what to do next. I wanted to bathe her, and to burn her rag of a gown. I went to the treasure room and brought forth one of the new gowns I was making myself. This one was of dark blue wool, and as I had yet to hem it chose it for her. I held it up to her and gestured it would be hers. Her eyes opened wide once more. I began to wonder if she had always been a slave. If not, I thought she was from poor folk indeed. The way she crammed her food into her mouth could not have been just hunger. Her fingernails were filthy and she made no effort to braid up her hair. Tomorrow I would give her a spindle and see if she could spin; that would tell me something. Just now I wanted her clean.

I took up my golden bird-shaped shears and then held them up so she might see them. Her eyes opened wide in wonder. Then I edged the shears into the gown, cutting off a hand's length or more from the bottom. From the piece I could make her a sash as well. She was content to sit there in the alcove as I did my hemming, and I spoke to her as I did so. As I neared the end of my work I went out to the stable and found Tindr bent over the boar hide, cutting out pieces with his knife. I asked him to bring two buckets full of water to the closed kitchen shed. I set out a large basin there, and put a pot of water on to boil.

I held up the finished gown, again telling her it was for her. I laid it over my arm and led her to the kitchen yard door. Every new thing seemed to awaken a fear in her. She looked out over the kitchen yard with the same wild eyes she had used when she stood on the ship. I took her hand and tried to lead her to the kitchen shed in which I had the basin ready. But she pulled back; I think she feared the closed space. I opened the door to the shed and showed her no man was within, just kitchen stores and the big basin awaiting the water now on the boil. Tindr had poured in the well water, and now I took the pot from the cooking-ring and poured it, steaming, into the cold water. I shut the door behind us. I would not move to strip off her dress, and only gestured to her to do so herself. But she would not, and I would not force her to do so before me.

I had brought linen that she might dry herself, and laid it and her new gown down on a barrel. I again entreated her to bathe, and stepped outside, staying just by the closed door. After a few moments I heard her move, and then the welcome sound of her splashing about. It was not long before the door opened and she peered out. Her hair was wet and her fingernails still dirty, but the rest of her, I trusted, was cleaner. The new gown, tho' big for her, suited her well; her eyes were dark brown like her hair, and the rich shade brought out green flecks in her iris. She wore Rannveig's many-coloured beads around her neck, and no longer looked a slave.

The four of us ate together that night at table. I had her follow me about and bring spoons and the cups. When I gestured she should sit with us she froze. Now I thought again she might have always been a slave, or at least the time when she was not must be beyond her memory.

"I am going to the brew-house," Sidroc told me after we had supped. Left unsaid was that I was not to go with him.

Nor did I need him to tell me that Eskil would be there. I did not want him to go, and was at the point of saying so when he spoke again.

"I want to get my silver back."

"Go then," I answered, more sharply than I meant.

He looked up into the gloom about the timbers which held the peaked roof, then ran his hand through his hair. He said no more, just nodded, and left.

I was angry at Eskil and his men, angry that we had been forced to part with good silver to rescue the girl, angry with Sidroc for wanting it back and so having to deal further with Eskil. And I was angry at myself for how I had parted with Sidroc. I almost thought of going down to Rannveig's myself, but knew that seeing me walk in would be the last thing he would want.

Tindr went to the stable to check on our beasts. I tried to put myself to rights as I moved about the kitchen yard and hall, washing up and ordering things. I took care to show Sparrow where to put the cups and how to stack the salvers. I spoke to her but she kept her chin down, not seeming to attend.

I showed her once more to Signor's old alcove, and told her it was hers. She touched the feather bed and lifted the woollen blankets. "You are safe now," I told her. "Tomorrow you will start your new life here." I pulled the curtains closed and bid her Good night.

Tindr came and sat with me by the hall fire pit. Each night he banked the fire to keep it burning low through the dark, but tonight, seeing me settle on the rock bench he and Sidroc had built, he kept the fire going. He sat down cross-legged on the floor upon one of the many sheepskins he had brought us from his cousin Ragnfast's farm. Tindr wore each day the long straight-bladed knife which all men of Gotland wore, one like that which Sidroc had carried before he cut the sheath of his fine seax from the body of a Saxon thegn.

Tonight Tindr sat carving a small wooden figure with his knife, a figure of a deer. He sat close to me, and close to the fire for the light it gave him. I watched him bend his head over his work, and watched too the dull gleam of his steel

177

blade as it turned in his hand. Finished, it would be a little bigger than his hand. He had made such carved deer before, like unto a toy for a child, but I knew they were not. He did not keep the figures, nor give them to children. I wondered if he took them to the forest glades and left them there in homage to Freyja. I had not seen him carve a sow or boar.

There was ease in sitting with Tindr. In his very silence was a sort of company, tho' I knew, and had myself seen, that some did not feel it; that some in fact ignored or avoided him. I rose and lit an oil cresset and brought it near to give him more light. He lifted his head, gave me his smile, and touched his heart with the fist that held his knife. I did not wish to wait for Sidroc in the treasure room, and knew I should take up my spindle and work as well. But I could not.

The fire hissed and crackled. I heard the wind outside in the spruce trees when a strong gust blew through the heavy boughs. I thought of Sidroc gaming with Eskil, and the girl Sparrow, who I hoped was asleep in her alcove across from where I sat. Less than three months ago I had been captured and marked as a slave. The Idrisid woman who had claimed me as such placed about my neck a strand of glass beads. Now I sat in my fine hall while my husband threw dice with a slaver. Loki the Trickster God must be smiling at me now.

Whenever the fire burnt low Tindr would rise and shove a few more logs into it. I felt myself drowse where I sat, but did not wish to be alone and wakeful in the treasure room. Tindr finished his deer carving, and placed the little figure on one of the low stones bordering the fire. The flames cast their dancing yellow glow upon the bright white wood.

At last I heard Sidroc's key turn in the box lock. He stepped in, and looked his surprise to see us still up and waiting for him. He turned and slid the iron bar across the oak door. Tindr rose and lifted his hand in greeting, then picked up his deer, nodded, and made his way to his alcove.

I could tell Sidroc held something under his mantle. I filled one of the brass braziers with glowing charcoal and carried it to the treasure room, where I laid it near our bed. Sidroc followed me in and cast his free arm about me, pulling me to his chest. I did not know what to say and was only glad that he wished to kiss me as he did.

Then he pulled forth the folded red silk; even in the low light I could see it was that. He had wanted his one mark of silver back, and returned with something worth ten or more marks.

"Do you never lose?" I asked.

He grinned so that I too had to smile.

"Not to such as Eskil," he said. "He is young; he does not know when to stop."

He gave a shrug. "Ketil has taken silver off me. Alrik too."

I knew the sums he had lost on occasion to them were slight compared to his own winnings from the same men; and nothing he had won from any man of Gotland could match the richness of either the rounded crystal nor the length of red silk Eskil had forfeited.

"It is for Frankland," he assured me.

I nodded and began to undress. But tired as I was, I would not sleep well, wondering and worrying about Sparrow. I hoped she had been sleeping while Tindr and I sat by the fire pit, or if she had not, that she had felt safer knowing I was there. I feared she would be frightened during the long night by herself, yet did not wish to startle her by checking on her. Tindr's alcove was nearest to the kitchen yard, and I hoped she would not fear his presence. At last I fell asleep, but the night-mare came for me, and carried me fitfully back to the ships I dreaded. The girl and I were there together, and alone. Sidroc woke me; one hand placed on my heart, and the other wrapping my shoulders to turn me and draw me close.

"You are safe, shield-maiden," he whispered into my hair. "No one can harm you. I am here."

I clung to him and steadied my breathing. He laid back and pulled me against his chest, heart to heart, and I tried to match his slow and steady breath. When I felt I could speak I raised my head. The Moon was full. A sharp square of light fell on the deerskins on the floor, and onto my plush weaving, its colours dark in the imperfect light. I saw the length of folded silk lying upon a chest, and looked away from it.

"Was it of the ships?" he asked.

I nodded my head, and laid my face to his chest. "But you were not there with me. It was the girl – Sparrow – and me."

"You will never take ship again," he promised, as he had before. "I will always be with you if there is danger."

I was silent a little time, thinking of Sparrow, and of the ship I had found her on. "I am sorry," I told him.

He moved his head in a way to question my words, and I went on.

"Sorry about Sparrow. About the silver you paid for her, even if you won it and more back. And – you have said nothing about my speaking to Eskil; thank you."

He gave a short laugh. "Já. I would rather that you had not gone to him. I saw you from afar as you walked to his ship."

"I had Tindr with me," I murmured, in feeble defence.

He paused. "I do not want you to depend on others to protect you, but on you yourself. Gotland is safe. A young buck like Eskil is not. The Gods have smiled on him so far. He has a fine ship, many men behind him, and is smart enough to trade as well as raid. He has the sort of boldness that forces him to try anything. He is good-looking too; I know that."

I began to speak, but he went on in his steady way. "But I have learnt that if there is something you wish to do, you will do it. You saw the girl and wanted to free her; you could not do so without talking to him. But," he ended, kissing my forehead, "next time ask the price, before you say you will buy."

I woke early in the dark; the Moon had set. Sidroc still drowsed, and I drew on my shift and a gown and went out into the hall, a burning cresset in my hand. Tindr was already up and in the stable, his bow hung by his open curtains so I knew he was not out hunting. The curtains were still drawn in the alcove where the girl slept. I walked over and when not too near called to her.

"Sparrow?" I asked. I called again, growing closer, and set the cresset on the fire pit stones. I stood outside the closed curtains of her alcove. I heard nothing, no sound of breathing. "Sparrow?" I called again, and slowly parted the curtains with my hands.

She was gone. So was the blue gown, and the blanket from her bed. I sunk down a moment on her bed; it was cold. She had run off. She was a child in a strange land, could not speak to folk, and had no shoes.

I rose and went hurriedly to the stable. Tindr squatted there in the gloom, milking the cow. On the work bench sat the cut out soles for Sparrow's shoes, and the pieces he would sew to form the top and straps. He looked up and saw my face. I put my fist in my left hand, extended the thumb and index fingers to signal Sparrow. I asked Where? – a hand shading the eye, as if looking for something against the Sun. Tindr made a little grunt and jumped up, scattering the two skogkatt kittens who had been waiting for milk at his side. I followed him as he ran to the hall and stood looking, open-mouthed, at her empty alcove. I asked him if the kitchen door was locked when he awoke. He told me that it was.

She must have waited until he went to the stable and then snuck out. He shook his head, then signed he was going to Rannveig's to alert her. She could tell the town folk to keep an eye out.

I looked quickly about the hall, then opened my work box with a catch in my throat. My bird shaped shears were there, as was the tiny ivory comb, and all else. I went back into the treasure room. Sidroc was just stirring, and I sat down on the bed.

"Sparrow is gone," I told him.

He blinked himself awake. "Gone?" He pushed himself up. "Did she take anything?"

"Her gown, and the blanket from her bed."

He leaned against the headboard, and reached his arms to stretch them. He blew out a long breath and shook his head. "That will not keep her alive through Gotland's Winter."

"Can we look for her?"

He gave a little laugh. "She is not lost, shield-maiden; she ran away. She does not want to be found."

This was all too true, but I felt we must do something. I had not rescued her from the ship of the Svear only to have her perish from cold or starvation here.

"Tindr has already gone to Rannveig," is what I said.

"That is all we can do. All on the trading road will know by noon; if she is seen we will learn of it."

"Perhaps she will return when she grows hungry," I hoped aloud.

He only looked at me. "If she realizes she has stolen from us, she will be too fearful to return."

I put my hand to my face. When I had looked to see if she had taken my shears, I did so only fearing the loss of them, and not thinking beyond. Theft was ever a serious crime, but a slave who stole could be killed with impunity. The gown I had given her, but she had taken the new wool blanket. She did not know we would not harm her. My thoughts leapt on.

"If she grows hungry and steals from a stall on the trading road, or a farm…"

I could not believe that any of the Gotland folk would be cruel to her, yet no more could I be certain they would not.

But perhaps this was not even the greatest danger she faced. "If she ran into the forest…"

"There are no wolves or bears here. She will be hungry, will have to forage as she can, and with no shoes she will be cold. But she will not be eaten alive." He shrugged. "I think it is more likely she will hover around the trading road, keeping hidden but nearer to food."

He reached out and took my hand, tried to make me smile. "You and I have not had good luck with slaves," he said.

He spoke of the Saxon whom he had claimed as part of his plunder from the fight on the Idrisid ship. But the Saxon had cost him no silver, and Sidroc had at last driven him off.

In my helplessness I scarce knew what more to say. We had freed the girl from the wretchedness of being a flesh-slave only to have her run from us, who sought to help her.

So we began our day. Sidroc was once again riding out, going to speak to ship owners who he might hire to take our goods next year. All he met he would tell about Sparrow. Tindr took my mare and was gone much of the morning, and when he returned told me he had been to the neighbouring farms, as far even as his cousin Ragnfast's, to tell them of the missing girl. I went about my morning as best I could. Past noon I came out to the stable to see if the hens had left me any eggs; sometimes they did not lay until late. Tindr stood, back to me, at his work bench, lacing up the top part of one of Sparrow's shoes to the sole he had cut. I felt a twinge in my heart watching him, not only for the loss of the girl and the danger she might face, but for his goodness. He trusted she would return; I must do the same.

When morning came again I saw the completed shoes resting on Tindr's work bench. He had worked the warm brown of the boar skin into a handsome pair. There was a boot maker on the trading road who had made Sidroc and I each a new pair; mine short, just above the ankle, and his a little taller. This pair that Tindr had fashioned was nearly as well made. I took one in my hands and saw he had used a boar's tooth for the fastening toggle at the ankle-strap, just as he did with his own shoes. Later that day the shoes were

184

gone. I looked to see if he had placed them in Sparrow's alcove, but he had not.

The following day Tindr was gone all morning, not hunting, for he left his bow behind, but it was nearly noon before I saw him emerge from the forest path and into the kitchen yard. He had not broken his fast with us and I gestured he should get himself something; he knew he should help himself to our food stores, but he only shook his head. Yet there was one less loaf in the food chest when I opened it later; he must had grown hungry and eaten it after all.

The new day brought an answer. I saw him slip into the trees, clutching a loaf and a pottery flask. I had never seen him take food into the forest before. The shoes he had made for Sparrow were gone. Had he then found her in the forest, tracked her somehow, and was feeding her there?

I asked him when he returned. It was nearly dusk, and I stood by the cooking ring, tending the big pot of boiling fish. Rannveig had showed me how to mix a savoury paste of parsley and mint, pounded with verjuice I had made from grapes, and I was stirring that in. It had been several days since Tindr had been hunting, and he came to me and signalled that in the morning he would go out. I looked at him for a long moment, until he dropped his blue-white eyes.

"I think you have already hunted," I said aloud. I made his sign for Sparrow, then pointed to the forest behind us. I put my hand above my eye, for Look, and then closed my open and extended fingers: Find.

He lowered his chin and nodded. But he lifted his hand to his eye, and shook his head. He had found her, but had not seen her. I pointed to my shoes. He nodded yes, and gestured he had carried them into the woods, and that they had vanished. He had gone there again, to the same place, and left food. It was taken. But he had not seen Sparrow.

185

Chapter the Eleventh: The Sacrifice

A small bird is hard to capture. Each morning Tindr took food and drink into the forest and left it for Sparrow. But wait as he would he had not seen her. He might stay for hours near where he left it, and would for pity's sake finally leave so she could slake her hunger, for she would not draw close if she saw him.

One morning I opened Tyrsborg's broad front door to see the withered grasses sparkling with hoar frost. A thin rime of ice had formed too on the surface of the well water, so that it make a tinkling noise against the stone well-walls as I dropped the wooden bucket down and shattered it. The sky was a watery blue, with no strong Sun, and I felt that day that true Winter must be nigh.

We now had a good cook and a steady serving woman, so I need have no concern when I asked Ragnfast and Estrid to come to Tyrsborg for their promised visit. Gunnvor was our cook, a woman of perhaps five and forty years, cheerful, hard-working, and a good manager of stores. She was the younger sister of Gudfrid, Rannveig's cook, which is how she came to us.

Gunnvor's husband had died two Winters past, and she had been living, not too happily, with her eldest son and his family on their farm in the northern part of the island.

"Gudfrid will vouch for my cooking," Gunnvor told me when she came up the hill the first time. "Rannveig too knows of it, will speak for my cheeses and bread. And there will be no waste in the kitchen yard. My husband was spare with his silver, and we always ate no less for it."

Helga had also been part of the household, and wed to
a shepherd there. She was as tall and thin as Gunnvor was
stout and short, with a kindly, faded face, and great strength
in her large hands. She was a skilled spinner, quick to see
what needed to be done about the hall, and got on well with
Gunnvor, who she regarded with marked respect, as befit her
former role. She too had been recently widowed. Her
husband gave himself a cut shearing sheep, and it had turned
hot and green, and he had died of it. Helga had no children,
and tho' she was no more than thirty years, did not look to
wed again. Gunnvor and Helga were glad to be in town,
thankful for a home, and willing to prove their worth to us.
And they knew Tindr, especially Gunnvor, who had seen him
yearly on visits to her sister at Rannveig's, and were quick to
show their like of him.

We were all busy. With Gunnvor's help I tried to
assure our supplies of grain would last through Winter, and
she went with me to the grain seller's to make our final
purchases before he closed his storehouse and left for his
upland farm. We could now buy whole grain rather than
costly flour, and Gunnvor grind it in our quern. She was as
skilled, I think, as her sister Gudfrid, and laid up great crocks
of deer and boar meat in brine, bargained for and bought
boxes of dried flayed herring, and dug a shallow trench
outside the larger cooking shed in which she laid straw-
wrapped cabbages, then buried them in soil to keep them
fresh. She slaughtered one of our fattened geese, rubbed sage
and butter between the skin and flesh and roasted it to great
savour, catching every drop of the precious fat as it fell from
her turning spit and using that next day to fry eggs in. She
used Rannveig's good ale to flavour her browis, and could
turn our cow's milk into the thick and tangy skyr, which
Sidroc and I had first tasted at Rannveig's. And she promised
come Spring and richer milk she would make fine cheeses.

Helga took over much of the tidying and ordering of
the hall, served us at table, helped Gunnvor when needed,

and in every spare moment took up her spindle to keep me in yarn. I worked steadily at my looms, one warped with linen, the other with wool, and spent time too sewing new clothing for Sidroc and myself. Gudfrid grew dye plants down at Rannveig's, and had skill at the dyer's craft. She had taken my first lengths of linen and wool and given them rich hues of blue from dried mulberries, deep green from copper and lye, and light brown from chestnut bark. I made three linen tunics, one of each shade, for Sidroc, and two pairs of leggings in blue and brown, and for myself a new blue woollen gown to replace that which I had given to Sparrow, as well as two new shifts of undyed linen.

Tindr took on a new task. Out past the end of the kitchen yard he set a big rick of firewood to smoke into charcoal. He laid the makings of a fire, then set lengths of wood upright on end all round it, building it into a conical mound, layer after layer, until it rose ever higher. When it was nearly as tall as him he covered it all over with turves cut from grassy ground. Then he lit the fire he had set deep within by taking a flaming brand and sliding it through one of the air holes left at the bottom. He tended this for several days, sprinkling water on the turves to keep them moist. It gave off no smoke; it was all confined within, and when he pulled back a block of turf to check below we saw the wood beneath had hardened, turned black, and into the long-burning charcoal we would use in our braziers to warm the treasure room and the floor at the feet of the table in the hall.

The full Moon waned, and vanished, and so began the month of Blót, blood-month; that time when animals not kept over 'til Spring were slaughtered, meats set up in brine to cure, the haunches of pig smoked to keep over Winter. Here at Tyrsborg tasks such as these were underway, as it was with all our neighbours. It was a great feast time, and friends and neighbours called to join in the bounty. And here in Gotland it was the month of sacrifice.

The Hall of Tyr

I still had memory of my kinsman Cedd, of him carrying me to the grove of oaks that served as place of Offering at our hall, and how there I would pour out gifts of honey and milk for the Goddess of the Welsh I had been named for, Ceridwen. In that same place I had watched him kill pigs and rams as sacrifice to Thunor and Woden; and had stood with Sidroc and Yrling ten years ago at Four Stones when Ælfwyn and I went to watch them offer to the same Gods, Thor and Odin.

I had made Offering once with Sidroc, when we had killed the cock he had bought in thanksgiving for our safe arriving at the Baltic trading post we had landed at. Now he planned one far larger. He and Tindr took our horses and rode away in the morning. They came back when the Sun was lowering leading an oxcart driven by a farmer; I heard the bells on the oxens' horns and came out of the hall to meet them. Seven sows swayed between the rails of the waggon bed.

Sidroc looked down at me and smiled. "What I owe to Freyja," he said.

When, in our little boat, we had sighted the safe haven of Gotland and I had told him I had gold he had raised his arms and made a sacred boast: That he would sacrifice seven sows to Freyja. Here they were.

Tindr brought planks from the stable and the farmer drove the sows down. They were young, fat and sound, perhaps just after their first farrowing, and now they would be Freyja's. Each had an iron ring through the nose, and Tindr looped rope through them and led them to the stable.

Sidroc would make Offering the next day. He and Tindr had chosen a glade in the forest, not far from the dell in which Tindr kept his bee skeps. The sows were too big to hoist high onto the tines of rakes, but they had crafted simple open-sided boxes on stands, one for each, to lift the beasts

189

from the ground and thus offer them to the Goddess. Ravens and crows and other large birds would feast there, partaking in the Goddess' bounty, as would foxes and even the wild skogkatt, the thick-furred forest cats, cousins to those in our stable.

Tindr had the sows in his keeping for only one day, but he watered and fed them as if he meant to keep them over Winter. I heard him singing to them as he tossed the leathery outer leaves of cabbages to their snorting snouts, and could not help but wonder what he sang of.

That night by the fire pit Sidroc sharpened his seax, drawing it over and again across a whet-stone, polishing the blade to a razor's edge to ensure the quickest end. The rhythmic scraping seemed to me the bright blade's own voice, carried to a higher pitch by Sidroc's strong wrist. He himself was silent as he honed; the carrying out of Blót was a solemn obligation, both a needful ritual and a gift to the intended God, and I thought he readied himself inwardly with each stroke.

When the Sun neared its highest point in the sky next day, Tindr led the sows by twos to the chosen place, staking them there. He returned from taking the seventh one and filled a bucket with plump grains of oats. I watched him take a jar of his mother's strong mead, warm it by the cooking-ring, and stir it into the bucket. This too he took to the place of Offering.

Sidroc had asked Rannveig to witness, and she walked up the hill to us, as much a part of our household as her son. Helga and Gunnvor took off their aprons and we all followed Sidroc up the forest path. We passed the dark spruces at Tyrsborg's edge and stepped into a bright forest. The reaching arms of trees stood bare over our heads, and the sky was clear and light blue. The forest floor lay open all about us, littered with leaves of bleached green and pale gold. Moss-topped stones and lichen-spotted round boulders thrust up amongst faded and torn leaves. My feet sank into a newly fallen layer of brown fir needles. I could not help but think of Sparrow, and wonder if she somehow watched us from afar.

We heard the sows snuffling and snorting, and came into the place of Offering. Tindr went to the sows, bucket in hand, and scooped out ladles-full of the mead-soaked grain. The sows butted and challenged each other, but Tindr shared it out amongst them. They ate greedily, ploughing up the soil where the grain had laid when they were done. It did not take long for the mead to slow their movements.

Sidroc came forward, but before he pulled his seax Tindr raised his hand. He took a piece of charcoal from the pouch at his belt, and drew a rune on the back of each of his own hands. He passed the charcoal to Sidroc, who did the same. He drew Tyr on his right, weapon, hand, the hand that would slay the beasts, and the rune Feoh for Freyja on his left, to receive the Offering.

Sidroc stood, back to us, looking up at the sky above where the sows were staked.

"Freyja!" he cried. "You of the White Arms, of the running forest beasts, of every tree and sacred place where animals shelter, hear me! Freyja of lust and of war, who haunts men's dreams with desire, who gives hope to women, who comes as a hind, who comes as a sow, who sends new life to fields and beasts and folk. Who sends her Shield-maidens to hover on the plain of battle and carry the fallen to new life in her shining hall.

"I, Sidroc made a boast which I fulfil: These seven sows are yours! Look kindly upon your shield-maiden daughter, and upon Sidroc, son of Tyr who has honoured you these many years. For guiding us here, I give thanks. For food and friends, I give thanks. For the Circle of Life, I give

191

thanks. Take these sows into your keeping – I send them to you."

He paused a moment, hands upheld.

I closed my eyes. Time folded in. Those at Kilton who I had cared for were all Christians; they believed that the Gods had founded us as folk, but were now long dead. The Prior who had raised me had taught me that the Gods were false, and had never even lived. My father Cerd and my kinsman Cedd had been heathen, as was my Welsh mother. I had tried, and found that I could not be Christian, but having been made to forsake the Gods as a child I feared I could never know the ardency I saw in the man who stood before me.

Yet I felt this thing was deeply mine, and could not be taken from me, this draw to those earliest I had named as Gods, had prayed to, made Offering for. They stirred still in my blood, after all I had been made to renounce. The bright gladness I had felt in my heart as I poured out milk or honey as a girl flared up like an ember in my breast. I remembered much of what my kinsman had told me, and all of Sidroc's precious words to me about my luck-spirit hamingja and guardian-follower fylgja. I wanted these spirits strong and vital in my life, guiding and guarding me.

What good folk believed could not be unholy if their lives be just.

I said it to myself again: What good folk believed could not be unholy if their lives be just. Yes, there was the blood of sacrifice, but to me it was akin to the king or warrior-chief who dies for his folk: a needful death, a worthy and good one. As I had always given thanks for those beasts who died so that I might eat, I gave thanks to those beasts who died to honour the Gods who sent them to us.

There was blood as part of these rites, but subtlety
and mystery was here too, and the direct connexion with the
Gods that needed no trained priest or go-between. Tindr,
Rannveig, all the folk of Gotland were alive to each water and
wood-spirit and God which surrounded them, walked
amongst them, interceded for them. I wanted this for my life.

I opened my eyes to Sidroc as he stood, arms lifted.

The echo of his words hung in the still air, and rang
deep within me. He had spoken with power, spoken freely,
with an open heart and with the potent certainty that his
honouring of the Gods gave him. Gazing on his back, I
blinked away the water in my eyes. My love for him was never
stronger than at that moment. I felt we stood knee-deep in a
fast flowing river, the current streaming past us and yet
connecting us, and that he pulled me along with him. I
wanted his strong and pure belief, I wanted his sureness, I
wanted everything that was of Sidroc. I wanted to open
everything to him, and to the Gods. Everything that he had
given me, and brought me to, I embraced.

Freyja, I begged wordlessly. I give myself to you. Make
me yours.

My own hands had raised, palms upward, as he spoke.
I felt the tears run down my cheeks but did not brush them
away. I kept my arms lifted and let my tears water the waiting
Earth, just as the blood of the sows would do.

A cloud had passed before the Sun and now shifted,
so that sudden warmth struck my face. I felt something shift
within me, something which had been covered and was now
set free.

My hands were still uplifted, and those too I saw of
Rannveig and Gunnvor and Helga. Tindr had stood rapt,
watching Sidroc, hearing with an inner ear the words he
spoke. Somewhere above us a bird called out, sharp and clear,

lifting my eyes higher where the pale sky was hatched with the dark and reaching tips of bare tree branches.

Now Sidroc lowered his arms, drew his seax, and stepped forward. The mead-soaked grain had acted. The sows staggered, heads lowered, in a stupor; two of them were already lying down. Tindr squatted by the first and placed his rune-drawn hands upon the beast, first its shoulders, then the head. His eyes lowered for a moment and I know he laid his own blessing on these now-sacred beasts. Sidroc nodded to him, and in a quick action Tindr pulled back the sow's head, exposing the cords of the throat to Sidroc. His blade flashed in the air before it was lost in the thick neck. The sow had no time to squeal. The back legs kicked out, and an issue of blood poured forth upon the waiting forest floor.

We women stood with our hands upheld as six more sows were sent this way to Freyja. When they were done Sidroc wiped his seax on the curled fern bracts dotting the glade. He and Tindr took each sow by the front and back legs and swung them into the open framed boxes they had made. There they were held to the sky, where any bird or other forest creature could partake of the Offering. Dark stains lay in the dried grasses and ferns where the sows had bled. The Earth had received its share of the gift.

We were silent walking back to Tyrsborg. We had mead ready waiting for us, and Gunnvor had baked honey-cakes. We all took up our cups, and Rannveig's face, looking at Sidroc, told of her admiration. It had been a rich and costly Offering, but I knew it was more than the price of it that struck her. Sidroc had shown his dedication to the Gods, not before many, so that the richness of his sacrifice might be spoken of, but only before those of his own household, who he hoped would share in his blessings.

"Sidroc the Dane," she said, when we had lowered our cups. Rannveig did not often smile, but she smiled now at

Sidroc, and he grinned back. "You are a canny bargainer, and shrewd at dice. You keep your word, and are generous." She tilted her chin at me. "You have got this fine woman to be your wife, which says much. I can guess, too, that you are a warrior of some fame, and I think you have led many men. Whatever has brought you here I cannot know, but I am glad to have you amongst us."

That night we gave our bodies to each other with special ardour. We had not coupled the night before, and when I laid my head down upon Sidroc's bare chest the sound of his heart filled my own chest. I felt I heard the beating wings of a raven as it hung over the Offering, the rhythm of its reaching and folding wings replacing that of the stilled hearts of the sows.

Tindr went out with his bow next morning, but he did not bring us a deer. I was in the hall with Gunnvor when Helga came in through the kitchen yard door.

"Mistress," she called. Helga and Gunnvor did not call me Lady, for in Norse that was the name of Freyja, just as the word for Lord was that of her brother Freyr.

"Mistress," she called, and her voice, always low and calm, carried a note of urgency. She gestured me to come, and I did, Gunnvor at my heels.

We stepped into the kitchen yard. There at the mouth of the forest path stood Tindr, his bow on his back. Sparrow was at his side.

She lowered her head when she saw us. Tindr was not holding her hand and I feared she might run back into the trees. I took a breath and walked slowly towards them. The relief I felt at seeing her alive mingled for a moment with anger for the worry she had caused us, but having her whole before me once again I could be nothing but gentle with her.

"Sparrow," I said, and bent down to her, arms extended, as one does to beckon a young child or pet dog or cat. Her hair was matted and tangled with bits of leaves and twigs, and her new blue gown was rent with tears at the hem and sleeves. The blanket from her bed lay upon her shoulders, stuck over with burrs. She had lost her sash, but somehow the string of glass beads Rannveig had given her still hung about her neck. The boar hide shoes Tindr had made for her were safe on her small feet.

She raised her filthy face to me. Tindr placed his rune-drawn hand gently on her shoulder, bidding her go to me. She did so, stopping just before me. I straightened up and placed my hands on her thin shoulders, then touched her cheek.

"Do not run from us again, Sparrow," I told her. "Without Tindr you may have died."

I knew she could not understand my words, but did, I think, my tone, and all of our acts.

I turned to Gunnvor and Helga. All knew of our runaway slave, and tho' Gunnvor and Helga had never met her, had shared in our concern for the girl.

"Gunnvor, will you feed her. Then Helga, do you bathe her; I will do what I can with her gown."

Gunnvor was already coming forward to take her, making a clucking sound like a mother hen. I spoke to Sparrow once more before she did.

"We are glad to have you back, little bird," I told her, and just touched the tip of her nose with my finger. "You are slave no longer."

I turned to Tindr, placing my hand on my heart and then extending it to him in thanks.

He nodded to me, a slight smile on his lips. He had watched all this with a furrowed brow, not certain how the girl would be received, or how she herself would act. I knew that over the days she had been gone he had spent hours in the forest, waiting for her, showing her the same patience he had with animals. The dark had come earlier every night, and with it the cold; I could not imagine where she had been sheltering, and even with the food he left for her she had to have known hunger, and, I was certain, fear. Yet here she was. Tho' he be a man, somehow she found the courage to trust him, and to come with him back to us.

Sparrow had paused, Gunnvor's arm around her shoulders. She had been watching us, and now looked at Tindr. She touched her fingertips to her chest, then held them towards him. "Tindr," she said, in a soft voice.

Chapter the Twelfth: Snow

RAGNFAST and Estrid arrived in a horse drawn waggon for their promised visit. They would only spend two nights, as the days were short and they could not for long leave their farm. To have Tyrsborg come alive with the ringing calls and scampering feet of little ones deepened the pleasure I felt in welcoming them all.

Sparrow had been scrubbed, her hair combed smooth, and was learning to help in both kitchen yard and hall. Helga and I had been at work readying sleeping alcoves, while Gunnvor laboured over a feast for us. Gunnvor's work over her cook-fires did not disappoint. She had again baked honey cakes, dripping with Tindr's amber honey, of which Sparrow, and Estrid's older girl and boy would have been glad to have eaten nothing but. She baked many loaves of tender bread, and made pies, too, filled with minced deer-meat, spiced with juniper berries, like unto a pasty. She filled the big iron cauldron with a steaming fish stew, tangy with verjuice, and roasted parsnips and beets in a shallow pan in the cook-fire ashes until they grew nearly as sweet as her honey cakes. Rannveig came up the hill with Tindr, who wheeled a barrow holding a crock of her mead and a crock of her ale. When they crossed the threshold she paused a moment to take in her old hall, and nodded in approval at how we had filled it. The mellow golden brightness of our new tables and benches lent a pleasing contrast to the dark floor boards. She had brought us beeswax candles to grace the big table, soon to be laden with Gunnvor's good food. We all settled down to this bounty with high and happy hearts.

We had new cups to drink from, for an upland farmer had brought to the trading road an array of drinking horns, cut from the large horns of cattle, to which the silversmith had added narrow silver rims. These we would use for such festive meals as this, when guests would linger and drink deep. Indeed, there was little choice in that, as the tapering horn could not be placed down again until it was empty, and I had chosen horns of greater and lesser size for that. The one I liked was small and dark, the veining a butter yellow against a rich brown field.

Estrid and I sat together after we had feasted, her babe Alvild in her arms. She was a cheery child, waving her fat little hands as she sat propped up on her mother's lap. I had not held her that day at their farm, and now seeing her again, and here at Tyrsborg, I found my arms almost lifting to her. A lump rose in my throat. Estrid saw this, and on a gentle pretence passed her to me. "Could you?" she asked, rising from where she sat to check on her son who had vanished inside one of the alcoves. Her own eyes grew soft as she looked at me. She did not ask, but I think she knew I had once held babes of my own.

Alvild watched her mother move away, but then brought her round blue eyes to my face. I shifted her slightly in my arms, and her head turned, mouth opening, as her hand patted my breast. I felt a pang centred in my body. It was not a twinge of contraction, pulling me in, but one of reaching out, of opening towards that which I yearned for. In truth I did not know why I was not yet with child; Sidroc and I had been so much together. Yet my Moon flow had come twice, and would I thought, come again soon.

Alvild's pink mouth still sought my nipple, and I brought my finger to her face. She grasped it tightly with her tiny fist. Holding a babe was good luck for any woman who wished one of her own. I lifted her higher in my arms and kissed the crown of her downy head as her mother came back to us.

The next morning Tindr and I rode down to the trading road with Ragnfast and Estrid. They needed a larger soapstone cooking pot, and Ragnfast wanted to buy iron bars from the smith, from which he would fashion new farming tools over the Winter. A light snow had fallen over night, just frosting the dark roofs of the neighbouring crofts. Here and there we saw the corpses of sacrificed beasts, lying in open wooden platforms hammered to the steep eaves of our neighbour's houses. All were making Offering for Blót.

A few folk moved along the trading road, well-wrapped in their mantles against the cold. A layer of sparkling frost whitened the dark grey planks of the empty pier. Soft ridges of slushy sea ice formed growing pools, rimming the pebbly beach. Even the mewling sea birds circling our heads sounded cold, their cries seeming distant in the thin crisp air.

We got off our horses and went from stall to shop, partly for the pleasure it gave Estrid to see what lay for sale there, and partly too to satisfy their need for things such as steel needles and a sheep shear.

I wandered near the door of the shop as they bargained for and bought a large pair of shears. A lone woman stood before the closed awnings of the stall next door. Her back was to me and she looked out over the blank and empty sea beyond the pebbled beach. Of a sudden she turned and looked straight at me. It was Sigvor. She was six months swollen with her child, her mantle clutched tightly around her. Tindr was by my side and he too stopped. She looked from me to him. I thought she might open her mouth to speak, but she did not. I looked to Tindr. I did not know if he still felt hurt at how she had dealt with him. If she would not greet us I wondered if he would make greeting. He nodded at her and lowered his eyes. He was raising them again to her when a man came out from the next shop. He took us in at a glance and glared.

"Sigvor," he called. She looked then that she would speak to me, but instead turned her head over her shoulder to him, and the moment slipped by. She went to his side, and they moved on. I watched them, as did Tindr, as they went. If I had not already met her father, I would have assumed this was he; he was twice her age. I wished I could speak some word of comfort to Tindr; his face was downcast and all the high spirits he had shown with Ragnfast and Estrid were lost.

On our way back we stopped at Rannveig's. Tindr wanted to give his cousin jars of his honey to take back to the farm with them. While they were out in the kitchen yard getting this I sat with Rannveig in her house. She asked about Sparrow, as she always did, and the girl herself had not forgotten Rannveig's kindness to her, for each time she saw her she gave a quick smile and fingered the first thing she had been given, the glass bead necklace. This reminded me of something I wished to know.

"What must I do to free her?" I asked. Her livelihood was assured, as long as she was willing to stay at Tyrsborg, but I wondered if by Gotland law there was some other act I must perform. When I was a girl at the priory the Prior spent much silver redeeming worthy slaves from unkind owners. They came and lived with us, working about the priory or in the fields. Each Eastertide he would bring any he had bought the year before to the crossroads that stood not far from the priory gate. There he would proclaim them free, making the Sign of the Cross over them, and, as standing at the crossroads signified, letting them go their own way if they wished. Almost all chose to come back with him to the priory, where they returned to their labours, but as freemen.

"Only to declare her free in front of a witness," she answered.

"Tindr and Gunnvor and Helga were there when I told her she was free," I said.

"Then she is free," she assured me. "Even if she does not understand that now." She paused a moment, and I thought she remembered the first day Sparrow had passed before the brew-house, bedraggled and terrified. "Fate is kind, to have finally brought her into your keeping."

"But it was Tindr who saved her too; without him she might have perished in the forest."

She nodded. "Tindr has always tamed wild things," she said.

Now I told her who we had just seen.

"Já," she sighed. "I heard last month that Sigvor had made hand-fast with a cousin of her sweetheart's. His farm is just north. His wife died last Spring; he has four children, the eldest as old as Sigvor herself."

"It is perhaps not the happiest end for her," I found myself saying. "But I do not forget how unkind she was to Tindr, whom she could have wed."

It began to snow. The flakes were as fluffy as the down I had stuffed our featherbeds with, but could fall thick and fast. In Angle-land I had seen snows sometimes reaching to my knees, but often it would rain just after and soften it to frosty slush. Here the cold was dry and sharp and the snow lay dazzling and unmelting under the blue sky. I understood why Sidroc had been eager to buy horses, for their long legs moved easily through it. But I was cold. Sidroc bought another brass brazier from the trading road, so that we might have two by the table in the hall as well as the one we kept fired in the treasure room at night. Tindr had given me the skins of the hares he had caught to line my boots with, and tho' they were warm their skin was fragile and did not last long.

The Hall of Tyr

Gunnvor had moved her cooking gear inside to
Tyrsborg's fire pit, and as the fire was kept high in the late
afternoons and evenings it made the hall snug, and filled the
place too with the savour of her good cooking. But while
riding or walking out I was cold.

Sidroc rode out one morning on his stallion, saying he
would return before nightfall, but not telling me where he
went. Snow was swirling through the air as he left, and I bit
my lip rather than tell him not to go. Helga and Gunnvor
were out by the cooking sheds when he returned, pushing
open our front door while stamping the snow from his feet.
He swung off his mantle and clumps of snow dropped to the
floor boards. Now he heaved in two of the largest leathern
packs I had ever seen. Whatever was in them was mounded
up to the drawstrings that laced the openings. I knew they
were not heavy by the ease with which he pulled them, but
could not guess what might be within. His grin told me they
were for me, tho'; and he looked around the hall quickly as if
deciding something.

"Go into the treasure room," he said.

We did not keep a brazier burning there by day, and I
said, "But it is so cold in there."

He kept grinning and answered, "You will not be
cold."

I left my loom and unlocked the door, and he followed
me in. A wall of cold air greeted me. The day was a grey one
and the afternoon far gone, and it was dusk within.

"Ah – lie down on the bed," he told me. "And shut
your eyes."

I was shivering but did as he asked. I heard him pull
the drawstring from the mouth of one pack, then the other. I
felt a whoosh of cool air and then something like the softest,

lightest cat's fur on my face. This was followed by another, and a third, across my body; and then he was laughing and I opened my eyes to see his arms full of furred pelts, which he cast over me, layer upon layer. I sat up, laughing now too, as he showered me with skin after skin, large and small, black and white, tan and brown, red and grey.

"I told you I would keep you warm," he said.

I did not believe the wealth of furs covering the bed and sliding down upon the floor. Some were easy to name, pelts of red foxes with long full tails and white-tipped legs, and the big pelts of grey wolves, their fur so dense and thick that it stood up like bristles. Two soft glossy pelts of darkest brown, nearly round in shape, were beaver, Sidroc told me. There was a mound of long slender dark brown pelts, and when I touched them I cried out, "Otter," for their sleek fineness was the same that once had trimmed my green mantle. There were small pelts of squirrels, both grey and red, with fluffy tails of surpassing softness; and two pelts, mid-sized, startling in their whiteness, and with thick tails like that of the red foxes. I picked these up and stared at them in wonder. Sidroc answered my unasked question.

"They are fox, the kind that live here in the North, in their Winter fur," he said. His eyes scanned the mass of pelts. "You will have enough to line your mantle, to trim your hood, to cut gloves from, to place in your boots to warm your feet, to –" but I stopped him now by reaching for him. He bent down and I wrapped my arms about his neck and kissed him.

"I thank you," I told him, as he smiled back at me. The day when he had made that promise to me felt very near, when he had asked would I be his wife if he kept me warm in the long Baltic Winters.

"But how –" I began to ask.

"They are from a friend of Ragnfast's, a trader named Gautvid. He sails North each year to buy and to sell, so I went to see him."

He reached down with his hand to the second pack. Something remained within, and he drew it out. It was a bearskin, dark brown, immense, the fur so thick upon it that it curled in places. It was indeed handsome, and had especial meaning, for the power of the bear was revered amongst warriors.

"This one is for me," he said, and drew it on over his shoulders. The fur of the front legs dropped down across his chest, and the back of it reached past his knees. He looked like a great lord of some wild kingdom.

"I will line your mantle with it," I said. "I do not think you will need more warmth than that."

"Nai," he laughed. "It during the day and you at night will do nicely."

There was other preparation made at Tyrsborg for the deep Winter snow. I saw Tindr in the kitchen yard one day, his right foot strapped to a long thin plank of wood. On his left he had a much shorter piece strapped to his boot, only slightly longer than his foot, and he was pushing himself around on the packed snow. He held a peeled wood pole in his hand for balance. Helga was with me and I turned to her in wonder.

"They are skis," she told me, trying not to laugh at my surprise. "In Winter we use them to glide over snow, when it is hard walking."

Sidroc had seen men use them as a boy, but had not done so himself. Tindr made us both a set, making the long ski as tall as we each were, and the short one just a bit longer than our boots. Small wooden blocks held our toe and heel, through which he augered holes and then passed leathern cords to bind the feet fast to the blocks. Tindr went so fast and well on them that I was eager to glide about as he did. But when he laced them on my feet and I tried to push myself forward, I fell over into a drift near the stable. The snow flew up in clouds about me, and both Sidroc and Tindr laughed as they reached to pull me up. I did not find it easy to stand up with such things on my feet, one long and one short. I brushed the snow from my mantle with my left hand, jarring myself and almost falling again. Snowflakes frosted my eyelashes, and the red fox tails I had rimming my new hood were tipped white with it.

"It will take practice," Sidroc said, and then set off, the pole in his right hand. He lifted his left foot and pushed with that, leaning forward a little on his right where the long ski was. He went several long strides. "It is easy if you –", but here he tried to make a turn to come back to us, and fell himself. Tindr's honking laugh rang out for a moment before he reached where Sidroc knelt in the snow, trying to get the skis beneath him.

Before we stopped that day I was able to go slowly across the kitchen yard, and then back, but I could not make the skis turn as Tindr could. I had to stand and stomp my way around my long right ski to head back. Tindr was merry as he showed us how to stroke and use the pole to advantage, and soon Sidroc was making long smooth glides, and could turn too. Tindr showed me how to lace and unlace the cords holding my boots, and then, smiling, began to gesture to the sole of my foot, making the sign for Ice, which was the heel of his palm moving swiftly away, as if it slipped on ice. I could not understand what he told me, but Sidroc did.

"Ah – he thinks you would do well on skates."

Sidroc and Rannveig both had told me of skates, that some took the leg bones of deer or oxen and fixed them to the soles of their shoes to travel over frozen lakes and up rivers.

I nodded my head vigorously to Tindr. "When may we try that?" I asked aloud. They both looked at me, and I began to laugh at myself. The wool of my mantle was wet from the snow that I had picked up falling, and yet I wanted to do something even more difficult.

The year drew closer to Yule. Sparrow settled in, spending her days with Gunnvor and Helga, both of who were teaching her much. Her Moon-flow had come, greatly relieving my mind when Helga told me of it, for to have the cruelty done to her multiplied by having to bear the child of her captors' was nothing we women looked forward to. Gunnvor spoke to her all day long when the girl was at her elbow, helping with cooking or scrubbing up, and in this way Sparrow soon came to speak Norse. She could not tell us which land she had come from; she had no name for it. She told us her own name – it had been Bova or Bona; with her accent it was hard to be certain; but she did not ask us to call her this. Instead she remembered Tindr's sign for her when he first saw her – that of a little bird. When I stood with her in the kitchen yard one day and pointed to the sparrows that darted in and out of the thick branches of the spruce trees, and said "sparrow" she smiled back at me and touched her chest. "Sparrow" she answered. So in this way was she named, by Tindr and me and by she herself. She was fond of birds, and took to feeding her namesakes, crumbling bits of bread upon the snow so that they rushed down cheeping, wings outstretched, when they saw her. She took over care of the hens as well, feeding and watering them, and carrying in the still-warm eggs. Helga taught her to spin, and her thin and nimble fingers took readily to it.

I made her a mantle of red from the sturdy wadmal woollen goods I had bought. For Winter warmth most Gotland folk wore the skins of their abundant horned sheep, both cut and pieced into tunics and mantles with the fleece inside, or simply as full hides fastened around their shoulders, fleece side out. Tindr had both, and one day brought in two lambskins, that I might make a warm garment for Sparrow. They were soft and fluffy, and I turned them into a long vest for her, which she wore over her gown going from hall to kitchen yard or stable. Gunnvor was ever urging her to eat, and she gained some needed flesh on her narrow bones. She was not a pretty girl, but her face began to look less pinched, and she lost the furtive, hunted look which had so marked her.

She even grew more at ease with Sidroc, who she had feared most. I could not blame her for this; to her he must have seemed so like the men on Eskil's ship. Sidroc acted to her just as he did to Helga and Gunnvor, accepting food and drink they brought him with a nod or word, helping when anything wanting great strength was needed, as when we brought in the cooking gear and great cauldron and frame to the hall, but otherwise leaving them to my care and management. After what she had been through I did not know if she could become a girl again, but at least she knew she need no longer fear abuse as a flesh-slave.

Sparrow was not the only one to learn things. Helga and Gunnvor taught me the art of making warm stockings, far warmer than those we had cut and sewn of fine wool in Angle-land. They made small loops of soft wool yarn around their left thumbs, and holding a blunt bone needle in the right hand, built loop upon loop of soft and sturdy links. They called this nålbinding, and showed me how to easily join ends and shape stockings to fit the leg, with no cutting or sewing. It was so clever, and the result so soft and warm, that it made me wonder why we did not have this art, which here every child, boy and girl, could do. But as I had seen with the skis, these Gotlandic folk had many ways which were unknown to me to help them bear, and even enjoy, the long and cold Winters.

I had my new furs against the cold, and lined the body of my thick green mantle with a patchwork of smaller pelts, using strips of the otter skins to once again edge it all the way up the front, for show as well as the comfort they gave. Besides my hood of russet wool trimmed with red fox tails, I sewed a second of green wool, trimmed with white fox tails. The strong silk thread from my Idrisid workbox served me well in this, as did the thin and long steel needles. The huge brown bearskin I cut and pieced to line Sidroc's dark mantle, filling it completely, so that he should be as warm as me. Tindr, handy with any leathern goods, made us both deer hide gloves lined with hare fur, so that even our hands were ready for true Winter.

One night when Sidroc and I sat long before the fire Tindr came to us. He had been out in the kitchen yard for something, and now we heard the door swing shut again. It was sharply cold and he was heavily muffled against it, but he flung open the long ties of his hood which covered his face. He gestured Come to us, a smile below his shining blue-white eyes. I did not look forward to leaving the warmth of the fire, or the woollen lap robe covering my legs, but rise we did. We took our mantles and hoods and followed him out the kitchen yard door.

As soon as he opened it I made a cry of surprise, and when he closed it behind us and I saw fully what he had called us to I stood gaping. The night sky over the spruce trees, always black and dotted with tiny stars, was a shimmering curtain of bright green light. The light danced and pulsed, long rays shooting up straight above the trees, then gently curling in. Now a glimmer of pink light joined it, the warmth and brilliance of which made me cry aloud. I turned to them both, seeing a shadow of both pink and green upon their upturned faces.

"Northern lights," Sidroc told me. "I have missed them."

I still could not speak, for the wonder and beauty of it.

Sidroc did, for me. "When we see them, we say all the hall doors are open in Asgard, so that we see the glory of the jewels kept there."

As all the Gods kept their own halls in Asgard, that treasure must be great indeed.

We stood there long, until our toes were numbed and noses frosted, gazing upon this glory. I felt again the deep magic of this land, that the skies themselves should bear such messages from the generous Gods.

We held more feasts at Tyrsborg, welcoming in our new friends, and meeting their kin. I wore my red gown on these days, and was proud to wear my new crystal too. The silver-smith had built a scalloped mount which held the rim of it, with a silver loop to hang from my thick necklace of twisted silver braid. The smoothness of the crystal made it a pleasure to touch and hold, and often my fingers would go up to it. And it made everything large when you looked through it; I used it to find and pluck out a thin splinter from Tindr's hand, so it was as useful as it was beautiful.

All wore their best on these feast nights of Blót; for Sidroc, his new tunics of dark blue and of green. He had no ornamental pin, no cuffs of silver or gold, and would not buy such until the goods he planned to trade brought silver back to him; but his seax and its sheath was of the finest, and gave their own show against the dark wool of his tunics.

Ketil the rope-maker came to Tyrsborg with his wife Tola, and brought their four young sons, and brought too Ketil's elder brother Botair. Botair was a fisherman, but when he was younger he was a merchant-man also. At his side were his two sons, Runulv and Ring. Sidroc had already met both of them, for Runulv had a ship of his own, and I knew he had spoken to them. They were fine-looking young men, not much above medium height, broad-shouldered and well-formed, with light reddish brown hair worn to the shoulders, Ring's a little darker. They had blue-green eyes under smooth and untroubled brows, and the forthrightness of expression that marked so many of the Gotland people. Each wore silver pins to fasten their wool mantles, and Runulv bore a bracelet of twisted silver cuffing his right wrist as testament to his success in trading.

Runulv was wed, and came with his wife Gyda, a sweet-faced young woman with eyes of cornflower blue and long yellow curls. She wore a triple strand of polished amber beads about her neck, and her over-gown was pinned not with brooches of bronze, but of silver. Ring was the younger brother, as yet unwed, but as we settled down to watch the men at dice Rannveig told me Ring hoped to change that. I had taken up a ewer of her fine mead and had finished refilling all the drinking horns.

"He has a sweetheart, she is Gyda's cousin, and is only wanting enough silver to make his hand-fast," she said, as we sat down together on a bench.

"His brother Runulv has silver in plenty, to look at pretty Gyda," I answered.

Rannveig nodded. "He is the elder, and Botair gave a ship to him; Ring must make his own way."

I watched Sidroc as he leaned forward, cup in hand, urging Runulv on as he readied himself to throw the dice. I had once asked him how he would find ship captains to take the amber necklaces and millstones we would send out to trade. He would not be sailing with them, and could not know if the silver they returned with was full value for what was sold. What if they failed to return at all, and ran off with the costly amber and millstones?

"How will you trust them?" I had asked. I remembered his answer as I watched him now.

"I will drink with them, and I will game with them," he had told me. "You can learn most things about a man from these two things."

As I watched them now I thought Runulv a good bet, wed as he was to a young wife; he had much to return for.

It had begun to snow during our feast. The wind shifted and a little blew in through the open gable end, so we knew it was falling. When we let our guests out into the night the rush torches we handed them sparked and frizzled at the clumped snowflakes swirling about the reaching flame.

I was thankful to stay inside with the great fire that blazed up in the hall fire pit, and filled both braziers with burning coals and carried them to the treasure room to warm it. Soon the remnants of our feasting had been cleared away, the fire banked, and the hall fell quiet. It had been a day filled with the pleasures of good food and drink, of new friends and those who might become friends, of feeling Tyrsborg cared for by Tindr and Gunnvor and Helga and even little Sparrow, folk who all wished to be here with us. And I felt deeply cared for. I drew my silver neck chain over my head, and held the crystal a moment in my hand.

Sidroc came in, closing the door behind him. He stood and looked at me by the light of the oil cressets.

"You wear your red gown," he said.

A slow smile was spreading on his face; the gown would ever be for him what it was for me, symbol of our first nights together. I wore it rarely to keep it, and the memory of those first nights, fresh. He came closer to me and placed his hands on my shoulders, then drew me near. The gown had always been snug over my breasts, and as he pressed me to him I knew my nipples hardened. He lowered his head to my ear. "The only thing better than seeing you wear it is knowing that now I will take it off you."

He lifted my chin in his hand and lowered his face to mine. Our mouths met, and clung. When the kiss ended he spoke again, his hands at the small of my back.

"I knew you would be like this," he told me.

"How did you know?" I breathed back.

"I always knew. Your fierceness when you were a girl. The way you stood up to me, to Toki, and even Yrling. And – ", he paused, "your body told me, even then."

I had but fifteen years when we had met, but my body was womanly from a young age.

"I could sometimes see your hips and breasts move, under your gown…I thought you favoured by Freyja from the start. That you would know how to give to a man. That you would want to give."

"I want to give to you," I murmured.

He closed his eyes and tipped back his head a moment. "That is all to me; that is everything, to hear you say that, and know you mean it."

He shook his head, remembering something.

213

"After I saw I could not have you, I worked hard to gain everything else I ever wanted – land, men, silver, horses, even gold. And I worked hard to keep myself alive, so that if I one day had the chance of having you, I could take that chance. Now I have both you, and the hope of building new treasure. The Gods must envy me."

I smiled, but shook my head. "You have only what you have believed in for so long – yourself, and now, me. They will honour you, not envy you, for that."

Fate had not made it easy for us to be together, but we had each played our part as best we could, he in the settling of Lindisse, and me at Kilton. At that moment, standing in his arms at Tyrsborg, with the snow falling in silence outside, even the names of those places felt distant, and lost in the past.

"We were brought here to begin anew, and for each other," is what I said, and what I now truly believed.

He lifted my hand to his mouth and kissed the palm, and as he did so my spiral disk bracelet caught a gleam of light from the cresset, a gleam that looked like a tiny, guiding, star.

When I awoke I thought that it had snowed heavily; it was so quiet that I could hear neither the wind blowing in the spruces, nor the birds that chirped from the shelter of their thick branches. But the cool dim light of the late dawn shone from the high window above us, so I pulled on my shift. The braziers had long ago burnt the last of their charcoal, and the room was so cold that as I shrugged my furred mantle on I saw my own breath smoke in the air. Sidroc was sleeping soundly. I thought to take one of our braziers to the fire pit and gather a few coals to warm the room.

I left the door to the treasure room open and stepped into the hall. Tindr had been up early, as there was a good fire starting to catch in the fire pit; and the curtains to his alcove, closest to the yard door, were drawn open, telling me he was already in the yard or stable. But all was still dim; the room was lit only by the fire and the little light coming from the two windows. The curtains to the alcoves where Gunnvor and Helga and Sparrow slept were drawn, and I moved carefully in the early dusk so as not to wake them. I set the brazier down on the flat rocks rimming the fire pit, and was again aware of the intense quiet. I felt drawn to go to the front door of the hall and look out to see how much snow had fallen.

It took both hands to slide the iron bar which was shot across the back, but tho' it was heavy it worked smoothly, and I pulled open the oaken door so I could greet the day. I pulled it open, yes, but instead of seeing the mounded forms of the wooden bench and the well-head covered in snow, with the awakening town before us and the sea beyond, I saw nothing. I had opened our door to a wall, a wall of snow, as greyish-white in the little light as was the stone wall in which the door sat, and looking just as solid. It sealed the door completely, far over my head; I could see no sky.

I could not believe it, and pressed the palm of my hand to it to prove myself wrong. It was real. We were buried in snow, and my mouth opened in a scream.

I heard a yell from the treasure room, but I was rooted to the spot, staring at the snow trapping us. Gunnvor and Helga thrust their heads out of their curtains, and Sparrow popped out of her alcove with a cry. Sidroc came running from behind me, and I turned to see him, barefoot, wearing only his leggings and with his spear hoisted in his throwing hand.

"What?" he cried, yanking me away from the door. I did not have time to speak. He looked at the wall of snow, and looked to me. He lowered his spear, then shook his head. He began to laugh. He set the butt end of his spear on the floor, and ran his other hand through his hair to get it out of his eyes.

"It is only a drift," he said, and laughed again. Helga and Gunnvor and Sparrow stood huddled together, facing us, and seeing what he pointed to, their worried faces relaxed.

I was glad to see him laugh, but was speechless at the wall which sealed us up.

"You have seen such snow before?" I finally asked. "You told me there would be much snow here, but this much…?"

"Ah – nai. It does not snow this much in Dane-mark; my home was on the coast there as well. But we know of it."

To be buried still frightened me, and I stood there clutching my shoulders as I looked at the snowy wall. I was about to ask how we were going to dig ourselves out, when sudden light flooded the hall. The yard door had opened, and we turned to see Tindr come in, stamping his feet to free the snow from his boots and leggings.

He came forward as he did every morning, his shy but ready smile on his face, rubbing his hands to warm them from his morning chores. There was no worry on his brow. He stopped when we saw us all clustered at the front of the hall. Sidroc waved him over, and when he grew closer and saw the opened door, he too began to laugh, that sound like a honking of a goose. Then he saw my face, and stopped. He shook his head at me and pushed his fingers at the corners of his mouth, telling me to smile. He gestured we follow him, and we closed the door on the snow and went to the yard door. Tindr pulled it open, and I saw why he smiled at my fear. The new snow which had fallen raised the level of the snow in the yard to just below my waist; far more than I had ever seen, but Tindr had been at work with shovels, and then with the stallion and the wooden snow board, smoothing and flattening a clear path through the yard to the stable and other out buildings.

"The front of Tyrsborg faces the sea; the wind blows from there, and that is why it drifted against the door," said Sidroc.

"I am grateful for two doors," is how I answered, and had to smile too.

The light of the days dwindled as the cold and snows increased; Yule had come. To herald the shortest day and longest night we held a feast, and Rannveig and Gudfrid, her cook, walked up the hill and stayed the night with us. Gunnvor made us special treats, not only her loved honey cakes, but a pudding as well, made by stirring eggs and milk together over a low fire. When it thickened she added honey and the crumbled flecks of lavender blossoms from Rannveig's garden, and I thought I had never eaten anything so good as that. Eggs were precious, as our hens gave us few in these dim days, but she had saved what Sparrow had gathered and used them to full account in this pudding. Gunnvor and Gudfrid laughed and chaffed at each other, the two sisters teasing about who was the better cook; Gudfrid claiming it was only Tindr's honey and Rannveig's lavender that had made the pudding so good; Gunnvor saucing back that it took a deft hand to preserve eggs until Yule, and an even better one to stir up such a smooth pudding from them.

Sparrow followed them about the hall and tramped with them to the kitchen outbuildings, watching everything they did as she helped, and I thought she might herself have the makings of a cook. Sitting together around our big table laden with smoked deer meat, roasted goose, a barley browis of turnips and carrots, wheaten loaves and butter, honey cakes and the grand milk-pudding we were all gladsome. I felt a deep liking for the ways of my new land, for here in Gotland we ate all at one table, Sidroc and serving woman alike. This made us like unto a family in my eyes, and in my heart as well, and within that heart I gave thanks to Freyja and all the Gods to know such bounty as this.

The Sun died, the Sun was reborn. From here the days would grow steadily longer, tho' it was hard to see the stretching of them. A few days after Yule I awoke snug and warm in our bed. Drawing breath I could tell how cold the room was, and snuggled in again a while longer. I reached out to touch Sidroc's shoulder, and then raised myself as I turned towards him. Of a sudden my stomach lurched and my head began to spin. I shut my eyes tight and rolled into a ball at his back. My Moon-flow had been late and now I knew why.

"What...?" he asked, waking up. He put his hand on my shoulder as if to turn me to him. "Are you laughing, or crying?" he asked, for with my face muffled he could not tell.

I raised my face to him. "Both. And for joy," I told him. "I have got your babe."

"Ah," he cried out, and pulled me close. "The Gods will withhold nothing from us."

"Já," I said, and kept my eyes closed a moment, savouring this discovery, the beauty of his answering words, his warmth about me. "I think – I think it was the night you made Offering...I made Offering too. Of myself, to Freyja."

My thoughts floated back to that night, hearing the beat of Sidroc's heart echo in my own chest. "I am sure it was that night."

He smiled, and then bent over me and kissed my belly. He kept his hand upon it and he kissed my lips. "It is one of the girls the old spice merchant promised you."

I put my arms around his neck. "We will have time enough for the second girl, and for sons too," I promised.

Chapter the Thirteenth: The Letter, and the Lord

Four Stones in South Lindisse, Angle-land

The Year 882 Spring

I had wished to spend Eastertide at the foundation at Oundle amongst the holy sisters and brothers, with my own dear mother, and with Sigewif, Mother of them all. Eight months had passed since that fateful St Mary's Day when Sidroc and Ceridwen had been taken. Spring was here, and Christ's promise of Resurrection, of great joy after great sorrow, drew me to Oundle.

I brought Ashild and Ealhswith with me, and Burginde of course, but Hrald I left at Four Stones in Asberg and Æthelthryth's keeping. Hrald was a Winter's child, now of eight years; still so young. Yet he was heir to Four Stones, and I would not have both he and I away at the same time. Asberg had become as a second father to him, and three-fingered Jari a huge and looming body-guard. There was, perhaps, scant cause for worry about any of Sidroc's men attempting to usurp Hrald's claim as rightful heir; those who had been prone to trouble had been sent off years ago, and all who remained had shared fully in his distribution of land and goods. As long as we enjoyed peace in Lindisse few, I hoped, would grumble about a child holding the place of their missing jarl. If Lindisse was threatened – a thought I could not allow myself to dwell upon – then Asberg and Jari and the others who had sat at high table with Sidroc would have to defend it.

Eanflad was also with me at Oundle. Since she had regained her speech she had come several times with me to see our mother, who rejoiced in her return to us. Sigewif had prayed over her in celebration, a fervent prayer of thanksgiving replacing that of beseeching supplication. Eanflad was calm, steady, thoughtful; but now she spoke once more, responded to all about her, and most precious to me, smiled. Yet a gentle reserve hung about her, and all she did. It made me wonder if she would not wish to go to Oundle and profess there. That place of quiet and peace might suit her far better than the bustle and noise of a fortress like Four Stones. She listened carefully when I told her I would gladly make a dowry over to the foundation so that she might live there.

"I have come from a place of great stillness," was Eanflad's answer. A small smile rose upon her lips. "Mother is there at Oundle, yes, but she is a nun, pledged to silence most of the day. Here I have not only you and Æthelthryth, but your little ones. They are dear to me. I would miss my loom," she went on, for we stood in the weaving room, where she had always woven such good cloth. "And Burginde –" she ended. "I could not leave Burginde."

As she said this I felt she was nearly fearful of being sent to Oundle against her wishes, as sometimes happened to youngest daughters, and I promised her that she should live with us at Four Stones as long as she wished, with no expectation that she either wed or profess as a holy woman.

"I have silver enough to spare us all from unwanted ends," I vowed.

Over Easter week at Oundle we celebrated the Tenebrae meal honouring the Last Supper of Christ, spent Good Friday in silent prayer in the stone chapel, and Saturday in private reflection, walking in Oundle's garden or its greening fields. Easter morning Mass saw the stone church bedecked with blossoming boughs and Spring flowers. As I stood listening to the priest my eyes skipped from the altar, where silver candle holders rested atop blanched linens, to the carved and painted cross, brought with great effort from Rome, which hung above it. The crucified Christ looked down with serene eyes upon us, arms outstretched in welcome. My eye travelled then to the statue of St Mary, His Holy Mother. It was her son's suffering and death we had remembered in our prayers, and his jubilant rebirth we celebrated this morning. Her unchanging face was ever placid and strong. The nuns had dressed her in a new mantle as was their custom; it was always blue, but renewed each year at Eastertide, and she wore it every day save for that late Summer holy day commemorating her assumption into Heaven, St Mary's Day, when the cloak was for one day replaced with one of white.

Around the statue's neck lay the gold necklace of linked, gemmed disks which I had given to Oundle; the same which a lifetime ago my first husband Yrling had placed around my throat after our heathen hand-fast. I had been heart-sick with grieving going to wed him, frightened by the fact that I must lie with him, alarmed that I must try to weave peace between enemies; yet by the time of his death I had begun to care for him. When Oundle had re-opened with the coming of peace it had been the first large gift I had presented to Sigewif; in truth I was eager to free myself from it and the memories it carried. Yet now I could at last look upon it without wincing. Time had been the salve, as had new cares and demands and even joys. I had grown up, and grown, I hoped in faith as well.

Our Easter feast was enriched by many ewe's milk cheeses I had brought from Four Stones, and the brother who was the baker at Oundle had made small spiced cakes to serve them with. Sigewif, dressed herself in pure white for the holy day, made blessing over the tables we sat at, and after the sombre recounting of the days leading up to this Resurrection day all gathered before her, priests and brothers, sisters and lay-women, serving folk of all ages, and we as guests, all had cause to be light-hearted. At Four Stones there would be a special meal as well, and Wilgot the priest would have held his Masses, both at the preaching cross in the village and at the little wooden chapel within the palisade walls. In the morning I would return there, to Hrald and my sister and brother in law and all else; all else save one.

The morning meal was always taken in silence, but Sigewif had asked me to meet her in the herb gardens before I took my leave. Burginde was with Ashild and Ealhswith in the kitchen yard, for the girls were too young to keep silence through a morning meal. I ate in silent company with Eanflad and the rest of the foundation, and rose when Sigewif did, signalling the end of the meal. Eanflad went off to Burginde and the girls, and I followed Sigewif out the side door and along the gravel pathway to the largest of the herb plots. I came up beside her and we began to walk.

"I found a casket of jewels in the church this morning," she began. Her hands were clasped together at her waist, and she walked forward without looking at me, yet I know her lips bore a faint smile.

"I beg of you to accept them," I answered.

In a small bronze box I had carried the last of the gems that Yrling had given me, or had been left to me from his store at his death, and late last night had laid them on the floor before the statue of St Mary.

She paused but a moment. "In the name of St Mary and her blessed Son I do accept them." We turned on the gravel pathway, following the outline of a twisted knot formed of low rosemary plants. Their spiny green-grey leaves gave forth their odour of resin as we brushed against them.

"But," she wanted to know, "Ashild and Ealhswith, and now Eanflad too – are these not jewels that would serve them in marriage?"

Sigewif had shown her fondness for my children and sisters time and time again, and now did so once more.

"I have a great amount of silver, and gold, too, to serve as dowries for all," I said. "These – these are from my first marriage, and I have a boon I would ask…"

Now she looked at me. It was not the custom to make requests concerning any gifts presented to a nunnery.

"I would ask that you use the jewels in the redemption of slaves," I went on, "here, or anywhere – in Rome – or any land in which such sums could be so used." I said no more.

She resumed her walking. She knew my husband and my dearest friend had been taken by slavers, and knew as well that Yrling had enslaved those at Four Stones when he had conquered it.

"I shall do as you ask with your treasure," she told me.

"Thank you, dear Mother," I said. I was aware that my voice quavered, and suddenly felt near to tears. She took this in, silently, and then spoke.

"Can you not stop with us a while longer?" she offered. We had paused again by some rose bushes, their tight buds showing promise.

"I wish it could be so, but as much as these past days have meant to me, my place is at Four Stones. Hrald is waiting for me, and the lambing is still going on…"

She turned to look at me. "Mayhap one day you will come to stay."

"That is a beautiful dream."

She smiled and lifted her hands to all about us. "And dreams can come true."

Oundle had been ruined during the wars; Sigewif's will and my silver had rebuilt it.

Sigewif considered a moment longer. "When you are by law free, and if you are called by God, I will welcome you."

By law free. That could only happen if Sidroc did not return for five years. I reached out to a budded rose and pressed my finger against the barb of a thorn, not to break the skin, but just to recall myself to the present moment.

She glanced towards the end of the woman's hall where she kept two private rooms for esteemed guests. A smile was in her voice. "But you shall not stay where you do now; you will have a cell just as the other sisters."

I had seen the simple cell in which my mother lived, and that of a few other of the sisters, and Sigewif had invited me into her own, no larger than theirs, and with scant greater comforts.

"I would welcome that, to be as other women. My father marked me to be a Peace-weaver, against my wishes. I wed the man he chose for me, and when he was killed had little choice but to wed again, for Oundle was destroyed and I had no place of refuge. To come here as my mother has, renouncing all but prayer and contemplation –"

"And work –" Sigewif smiled.

I smiled back. "Yes, and work – that would seem the greatest freedom of my life."

She was smiling still, and then I thought of who I told this to. Sigewif had been the sister of a powerful king,

Edmund of East Anglia, who in the defence of his people had been shot full of arrows by Danes. I could tell her nothing about the bounden duty of a high-born woman.

"But I do not know if such a life would truly suit me. I am not made of such strong stuff as my mother, or of the sisters and brothers already here with you…"

I shook my head, thinking of my own short-comings. And I had children I loved dearly and who needed me; Ealhswith was not yet three.

Sigewif was about to speak again when a serving woman appeared at the edge of the garden, raising her hands in request that she be allowed to approach. Sigewif signalled her to come.

"A messenger for the Lady Ælfwyn, dear Abbess," she said as she curtsied. "A letter that he must place in her hands only."

Sigewif's hand closed over mine in a firm grasp.

"Show him to the hall. She is coming now."

A letter. One hand I had lifted and pressed over my heart; the other still was held in Sigewif's own.

The woman hurried away. Sigewif looked at me.

"Will you take your letter alone, or would you have me with you?"

I feared its contents and clutched at her hand. "Please to stay with me. And – may I have my mother too?" Again I asked something beyond the rules of the order; my mother had left the world and now should be but another woman dedicating herself to a holy life.

Sigewif's grey eyes looked at me from under a slightly furrowed brow.

"Her task this morning was to clean the church with another sister," she reminded me. Her tone softened. "But I think she will be done by now."

I tried to smile, and nodded. She left to fetch my mother, and I took a moment to go to the kitchen yard to get Burginde. When the four of us entered the hall we saw the man, standing near the high table, and facing us. A few serving folk were about the room, as were two sisters, replacing the tapers in the iron candle holders which sat on the floor. The man put down the cup of ale he had been brought and came towards us, glancing quickly from one to the next.

"My Lady Ælfwyn?" he asked me. "A letter from Lord Godwin of Kilton."

He was, I thought, a thegn of Kilton, young and fully armed with seax and sword. We had seen his shield and kit near the door when we came in.

I nodded, and he took a leather pouch from his shoulder. Inside this was a linen sleeve, which he handed me. I could feel the rolled parchment within just flexing in my fingers.

Sigewif looked around us. "Please to finish your ale," she told the thegn. "We will take this in the writing room," she said to me.

I could barely feel the parchment in my hand, and was glad to move away where I could open it with no one but we four women to hear its contents.

Inside the writing room I stood at one end of the long table at which I had watched Ashild and Hrald and later

Ceric copy out the alphabet, the table at which Sigewif herself wrote missives to other abbesses and abbots. I did not think I could sit, and turned and just looked at Sigewif, my mother, and Burginde. Sigewif raised her hand to gesture they be seated, then sat down in her carved chair, her blue-veined hands firm on the armrests. Burginde slumped down on the table's bench, but my mother stood near me, her pale face made the paler against her dark gown and veil.

I looked at all three faces in turn, Sigewif with her calm resolve, Burginde, whose brow was knitted, but eyes trained on me, and my mother with her tender gaze. Even in my fear I knew I was blessed to be surrounded by such women as these, all of who were strong, and all of who loved me.

I pulled open the linen sleeve and drew the roll out. The large wax seal had been cracked with handling, but was intact. I snapped it with my fingernails. I resolved I would read it silently to myself first, and then read it aloud.

TO MY LADY ÆLFWYN, and asking the discretion of the priest that reads this to her, that she may hear it in private.

– I paused here, swallowing back the impatience I felt at this; had he forgotten I read and could now even write? Ceridwen and I had exchanged several letters –

Lady, know that my Lady Ceridwen and Sidroc live.

– I made a sound at this, one of gladness, and glanced up a moment and nodded to those who watched me –

Word has just come to me of this, brought from one who, if dishonourable, I could not yet discredit. The message came from a Saxon, a man of Wessex, and a thegn of Odda's; likely an outlaw to his own people, but one who offered such proof in his words that I must believe him. This man was aboard a red-sailed ship, a slave at the oars, on St Mary's Day last when Ceridwen and your husband were last seen. He watched them come aboard, bound, as prisoners, and from his description of them there could be no doubt of the truth of it. The ship was one of a southern tribe unknown to me, the Idrisids, known for their slaving. They sailed due East, past Dane-mark, and into the Baltic.

– I had never heard of Baltic and knew not which land that was –

Once there the Idrisid ship was chased and overcome by a ship of Danish raiders. In the battle that ensued Sidroc and Ceridwen were freed, and your husband claimed this thegn as his own slave. The three put ashore at a trading post on the Baltic coast, and travelled steadily East-wards from there.

I fear I do not need to tell you that the Lady Ceridwen has been driven far away from her rightful home by your husband. He has made of her an abject captive, with all that entails.

She implored the thegn to help her return to Wessex, and he agreed to do so, but before they could make their escape Sidroc learned of their plan. The thegn barely escaped with his life, but could not free her. Her parting words to him were to beg him to come to me so she might be released.

All that is known is that they are on the southern coast of the Baltic, an unsettled and wild place, save for the Summer trading posts. Knowing Sidroc

– here I had to bite my lip; Godwin knew almost nothing of Sidroc –

Knowing Sidroc I think he will seek out a place without laws, gather men about him, and begin to raid, and thus build up treasure. If he has taken her deep into the lands

229

of the Rus, a place known for sheltering renegade Danes and Svear, it will be nigh impossible to find them. But if they remain on the southern Baltic coast there is some hope, however slight, that we might learn where they are.

As soon as ships can sail this Spring I will send a picked group of men to the Baltic, asking after them. The waters are filled with peril and the coastal settlements suffer from many dangerous and lawless tribes.

I entreat you to send your own men as you can to ask after them. None should approach him as the safety of my sister in law must be assured. If they are found I shall go myself to fetch her home.

If I learn more I shall send to you, and you, I know, shall do the same to me. I further ask that due to the nature of its contents you return this letter to me, with your response on the reverse. I bid you health, Lady.

I am GODWIN.

I knew I must speak, and knew as well that I could not read this letter aloud as I had thought I would.

"Godwin says they are alive," I began. My mother gasped and crossed herself, Sigewif gave a firm rap on the table top with her knuckle, and Burginde clapped her hands together.

"A thegn of Odda's of Wessex came to Godwin. This thegn had been enslaved at the oar of the red-sailed ship." I scanned the letter again. "The sailors were a slaving tribe called Idrisids. The thegn saw Sidroc and Ceridwen brought aboard as prisoners on St Mary's Day, and described them so well to Godwin that he knew it was they.

"They were taken due East, to a place called Baltic" – I looked to Sigewif, who had wide knowledge of the world.

"It is a great and cold sea, far to the East," she said.

"There the Idrisids were set upon by a Danish ship, and the Danes took the victory."

"A sea battle?" asked Sigewif, her eyebrows raising in horror. I nodded to her, unwilling to think just then what it had all meant.

I went on. "Sidroc and Ceridwen were freed, they landed on the Baltic coast, and Sidroc took the thegn with them.

"The thegn left them and made his way back to Wessex, and to Kilton."

"Aye, seeking silver for his news," chimed in Burginde.

I nodded at her, and Sigewif said quietly, "No doubt."

I hardly knew what more to say, but did the best I could.

"Godwin will send men of his own to the Baltic to try and learn where they are."

I lowered the parchment. "Please, Abbess Sigewif, may I have a piece of parchment to make my answer – a small piece will do."

My mother was embracing me, yet I hardly felt it. "Praise God they be alive," she said.

"Yes," I told her. "Alive, and free; that is what matters most."

I would not comply with Godwin's request that I return his letter. I took the sheet of parchment and wrote out my answer.

The Hall of Tyr

MY LORD GODWIN OF KILTON

Know how grateful I am to learn that my Lord Sidroc and my dear Lady Ceridwen live, and are free. If I hear more of them I shall send to you, and you to me. Until then I bid you health.

LADY ÆLFWYN OF SOUTH LINDISSE

I added a post-script to this:

Know, sir, how sorry I am not to return your letter; I could not part with so dear a parchment assuring me that they live and are well.

I read my answer aloud so that Sigewif, my mother, and Burginde knew what I wrote, for it was truly what was in my heart. I slipped the parchment into the linen sleeve and looked up at them. My letter was indeed short, but said what it needed: that I rejoiced to hear they lived, and were free. I did not urge Godwin to look for them; did not say I would send men for them. It said only what I felt, my joy in their being alive and free; the answering of my prayer.

"Forgive me, dear Abbess, for what I shall ask now. I beg of you all not to speak a word of this; I have need to ask Asberg and Jari their counsel." I had to pause as I thought how to say the next. "I must think of Hrald, and his future. If the men of Four Stones know Sidroc lives, and does not come back, that perhaps is different in their eyes than thinking he is a captive somewhere, trying to come back..."

Sigewif gave her sturdy writing table another rap. "This table shall not speak, and no more shall we," she promised. I embraced her, and gave her my thanks, and kissed my mother.

I gave the answering parchment to the waiting thegn and thanked him, and we took our leave of Oundle.

We had come and would return by horse-drawn waggon, and our slow progress gave me time to compose myself. We reached Four Stones in late afternoon, and after I had kissed Hrald I told Asberg I wished to see him alone. But first I went into the treasure room with Burginde.

"I must read this to you," I said, and unrolled Godwin's letter and read it all aloud. She listened without speaking until I reached the line which said "He has made of her an abject captive…" at which she broke in.

"'Tis a lie," she said flatly. "A lie. The Lord would never harm her, I lay my life on that."

"I know you are right, Burginde; it is why I could read this only to you and not even to mother. No one except me knows Sidroc as well as you do; you have known him as long as I have. You know he would not hurt that which he loved." I took some little solace in having said this aloud. "That which he loves…Ceridwen. He will not hurt her."

"Let us look to the source," she returned, warming with her words. "The Lord Godwin himself calls this Saxon thegn dishonourable. Yet he seems ready enough to believe all the blaggard told him!"

I went on with the rest of his letter. She listened quietly to it, making no more comment until I reached the end.

"That thegn sized up Godwin and told him what he wanted to hear, made sure he got his silver's worth for the tale," she decided. She shook her head, then looked back to me. "And will you send men to look for him?" she asked. "You did not tell him that you would."

"Nor will I," I said. "Or if I did, it would be to warn them that Godwin looks for them."

She thought a moment. "Aye,'twould be far better; think what could befall if he finds them," she said.

Suddenly the defiance that flared in my breast against Godwin was gone. The strength it had given me was replaced by the fear I felt at Burginde's words. I had written to Godwin the truth of my heart: That I rejoiced to learn that Sidroc and Ceridwen were alive and well – words that would surely anger Godwin. I wanted them to have that much after the ordeal of their capture and the sea-battle. Now he threatened to find them so he could seize Ceridwen and punish Sidroc. I must hope that this was but a bootless threat. The land sounded so vast, the way so full of danger. I wanted to believe Godwin's spies would never find them, but I had myself seen the resolve he possessed.

But what did Ceridwen want in all this? I had felt her reluctance to return to Kilton, only to be sent away to Sceaftesburh to wed. "He must use me as he can" – her words sounded once more in my ears. I felt my defiance to Godwin's will rise again, and deepen.

I had always known of Sidroc's desire for her. What I could not judge is if she could return that desire, and bear the sacrifice of losing Ceric as part of its fulfilment. With the hazards of the journey, could they return if she insisted? If they were spared, and made it back, what would happen then? She would be sent to Sceaftesburh, if the man there would still have her. But Sidroc – Godwin would seek revenge; surely he would. I felt the fine hairs on my arms stand as I considered this. Blood would flow if they returned.

"They must never come back," I said, knowing my words were scant above a whisper. I was staring at the shelf that held Sidroc's wooden comb, and looking at that commonplace object he handled every day grounded my thoughts and gave me the end I sought. Fate had offered him a path, and he had taken it. I would not have him hunted down like a felon. I turned to her and spoke again.

"They must never come back, Burginde."

She heaved a sigh and nodded her head in assent. "'Tis death to return," she murmured.

I unlocked one of my clothes chests and dropped the scroll inside, locking it after. A few hours ago I had no assurance other than my own heart that Sidroc and Ceridwen still lived; now I knew they did. Beyond that I knew they were free, and Sidroc was forging a new life for them far from Angle-land. The anger and threat of revenge in Godwin's letter awoke me to this new danger he posed to them, and I had rebelled against him.

Now I had immediate need here at Four Stones. I must speak with Asberg. Burginde went up to the weaving room to unpack our things, and I walked to the stable yard where Asberg had told me he would be.

I found him at the paddock fence where Sidroc's bay stallion was kept. The horse had not been ridden since Sidroc himself had left him at the foot of the bluff at Saltfleet. Asberg had not found it fitting that any other man be seen on his back, and the horse had become almost half-wild at not being ridden for so many months. The animal was old and wilful, but vital and eager for life. He was still the handsomest stallion at Four Stones, despite the few white hairs frosting his lips and eyes.

Asberg greeted me with a raised hand and a smile, all unknowing what news I bore. He cocked his head to the bay, who had thrown himself down in the mud and was thrashing his dark legs in pleasure to the sky above.

"I think we should let him in amongst the mares at the valley of horses," Asberg said, eyes upon the stallion.

Sidroc had always bred him up only to the best of the mares, taking care that neither stallion nor mare was hurt in the process.

"Will be the best thing for him, to have his hands full of a lot of females," Asberg went on, only partly in jest. "He has much life in him still, and to be neither ridden nor bred serves him not."

"Then do that, please," I told him. "Sidroc would not want him confined like this."

He nodded in agreement. There was no one near us and so I began, still looking across the paddock where the bay was now standing and swishing his long tail against his muddied flanks.

"Sidroc and Ceridwen are alive," I told him.

He turned to me, blues eyes wide.

"This morning a letter came to me at Oundle, from Lord Godwin. A thegn of Wessex travelled to him, a thegn who was himself a slave at the oars upon the red-sailed ship. This man saw Sidroc and Ceridwen brought on board. The ship is one of a tribe called Idrisid."

Asberg's face told me he did not know of the name, but he nodded just the same.

"They sailed East, past Dane-mark, and were in the Baltic Sea when a ship of Danes attacked."

"Ha!" cried Asberg, his eyes shining.

I went on and told him the rest, much as I had at Oundle.

"The Lord will send men to look for him?" he asked, thinking on what Godwin had said.

I nodded. "But I will not," I told him.

"It is too early for any ship to sail from the Baltic to Lindisse, for him to reach us," he thought aloud.

I said what I must. "Yes, if Sidroc thought of coming back."

His eyes were now fixed on mine.

"I do not believe Sidroc will come back," I said.

He turned his chin slightly away, and his eyelids lowered. I could not help but read the thoughts running through his mind; they were there upon his honest face. Sidroc had been forced away from Four Stones, but now would take what Fate had offered him and stay away. He would leave not only me and our children, but his men with whose help he had won all that he now forfeited.

Asberg reached out his hand and placed it on the top rail of the paddock fence. He stood there, lifting his gaze so he seemed to look at the back of his hand, but in truth, I thought, seeing far beyond that.

"When you and the lady first came here," he began, "I remember how it was. Yrling had won you and your treasure, was eager for both. When you came he saw you were beautiful; this he did not expect." He looked over to me, a smile crossing his face, and then went on. "His bargain was better than he thought.

"Then he saw you had brought the lady with you. She too was beautiful, and not kin nor a serving woman to you. We needed women, had none here. We all wanted her; she was part of your treasure and would raise whichever man she went to in Yrling's eyes. We knew Yrling would decide whose woman she would be."

Those early days when Ceridwen was so watched by Yrling's men, when Sidroc and Toki vied for her time and company, felt as near to me at that moment as solid Asberg did.

"I saw Sidroc almost kill Toki over her," he went on. "And he told me that he would take the lady with him when he left Yrling. I had already thrown in with Sidroc, knew I would follow him. He told me this so I would be ready to ride with them when he went."

He turned to me again. That day had not come as he or Sidroc had expected, but it was here now.

What I said next could decide the future of us all. Asberg's past was bound up in his loyalty to Sidroc. I must find out if this loyalty would extend to Sidroc's son. I almost reached to take his hand, but stopped myself. He must hear what I would say without my seeming to plead, or borrowing on the affection I knew he bore for me.

"I tell you this next because I need your trust, and all may depend on you. Sidroc will not come back. For him to return would mean war with Kilton."

His head tipped back and his mouth opened slightly. I saw he understood, and I went on.

"You and Jari could take Four Stones for yourselves; your king Guthrum would back you in this, I think. Or if you believe Hrald will grow to be a fit leader under your care, you can go on as you have, ruling in Sidroc's stead until Hrald is of age."

He turned from me to look at Sidroc's bay, now tossing his head at the far end of the paddock. When he turned back he had made his decision.

"I will not break faith with my war-chief," he proclaimed, and shook his head.

"Sidroc saved my life twice in battle. He earned my service to him. He made me rich in horses and weapons. He gave me your sister as my wife. When Hrald was born I made a blood-oath to protect him," he went on, pointing to his left wrist, "swore willingly with my blood, tho' such oaths were forbidden to me, as I was then a Christian."

I had not known this, that he had offered such a pledge to my son, but I rejoiced to hear it now.

He shook his head again as he ended. "Sidroc named me to watch Four Stones. I will not break faith with him."

Chapter the Fourteenth: Honey

Island of Gotland

I had never seen so many Spring wild flowers. They came as quickly as the snows left, and in great drifts blanketing the grasses all around Tyrsborg. The nodding heads of white snow drops were first, and then the lapis blue of the little star-like blästjärna. The yellow disks of vintargekko and white blooms of hvit fagningsblóma pushed through under trees. I walked about delighting in them all. The soil they spouted from was cool, but the breezes that bent their heads were beginning to warm, and the Sun that grew higher and stayed longer above us was hot upon my back.

I was four months along with our child, well, and happy. It would be a late Summer's babe, as I had been, born at the peak of Summer's abundance. Now with the growing light our hens had begun to lay again, and our cow, wandering about the flowers and vibrant green grasses, to give us her richest milk. Gunnvor made skyr and butter and puddings and the soft and creamy cheeses she had promised, and fed me up until I laughed that she mistook me for a goose. Sparrow and Tindr had cared well for all our fowl, and we had chicks and downy goslings fluttering near their feathered mothers, or sleeping nestled upon their backs. Our two skogkatt kittens were now near as big as foxes, and just as fluffy. They not only kept the stable free from mice but even brought Tindr young hares and squirrels, which he skinned and fed to them along with the cow's milk they still begged him for.

During the Winter Ketil's nephews Runulv and Ring had come several times more to Tyrsborg. Rannveig's brew-house had closed during the depths of the snows and cold, so folk went to each other's houses or farms to visit. Ketil and his brother Botair were both good men of business, Ketil with his rope-works, and Botair with his fishing, and the younger men were eager to make their mark. For three Summers now Runulv had taken Gotland salt on his ship to the Baltic shore, to the trading posts of the Pomerani and the Polanie. That he had done well in these ventures was shown by the silver and amber his pretty wife Gyda sported on her gown and neck.

One night Sidroc, Runulv, and his younger brother Ring sat throwing dice at Tyrsborg. Gyda and Rannveig and I watched them, as did Tindr, who never played but would sometimes sit and carve and watch as the spotted ivory dice tumbled out of hopeful hands. We had had a fine meal; Helga and Gunnvor and Sparrow were clearing away what was left of it, Gunnvor smiling as she glanced over to where the men called out their wagers and urged each other on.

Gyda, at my side, smiled to me. I liked her; she was not only pretty but thoughtful, and her love for her husband was clear. And she was kind to Tindr, knew how to speak with him, and did so often. Her girlhood farm had not been far from that of Ragnfast's, and I thought perhaps she and Tindr and he had played together as children.

This made me think of her own little boy, coming two years, blessed with the same yellow curls as his mother. I had seen him clutching her skirts on the trading road earlier in the day, and asked her where he was now.

"My sister lives with us, and she is home with him," she told me.

"How old is your sister?" I wanted to know.

Gyda spent a moment considering. "She has seventeen Summers," she decided.

Seventeen Summers, I thought, and so of an age to wed. "Does she – know Tindr?" I asked next.

Gyda smiled. "Já, of course. We all know Tindr; we grew up together," she said quietly. She kept looking at me, and then glanced over to where Tindr sat, watching the men game. Her smile broadened as she looked back to me.

I had to laugh at myself. "I am sorry," I said, and think my cheek grew red. "It is just that I am so fond of Tindr, and wish he had a sweetheart."

She smiled back at me. "Do not be sorry. You and I are happily wed, and it is natural we wish that for all we care for."

I had to take her hand at this in gratitude. My eyes went back to Tindr, his profile sharp in the firelight.

"He is handsome," I said. "He is kind. Children love him. Rannveig told me he is the best hunter on Gotland, and I believe her. I think most girls would be proud to be at his side, proud to wed him."

Gyda looked down a moment. "Já," she agreed. "But…"

"He is deaf," I answered. "He makes odd sounds when he laughs, or tries to talk. But he was not born so; his children will be whole."

She only nodded. "Tindr is…"

I did not know why she hesitated, or what she could not bring herself to say. I did not understand it, and did not know what more I could myself say. I looked again to where Tindr sat, working on making a new handle for a cookery knife, his eyes lifting from his work now and then to see how the dice fell. I could not accept that through his deafness he would be forced to live his life alone, or that maid could not be found to love him.

Gyric had been cruelly maimed, his life made trying from the loss of his eyes, yet I could not help my loving him. I took him from Four Stones without his knowledge or consent, and from thence we travelled weeks together. Day by day he let me know him; indeed, thrown together as we were, and often in danger, it was not possible that he should not. Our nearness led to knowing, and knowing, to caring. I had no choice, and soon no goal, but to love him. Folk at Kilton, and Ælfwyn too, had often praised me for what I could not keep from doing. Yet I did not feel that Gyda or her sister or any of the maids of Gotland were so different from me.

Then I thought of something else. Gyric had told me there were some men who did not want women, men other than Christian priests who had foresworn them. This was said to be a great sin to the Christians, and to the Danes forbidden as well. But Tindr, I felt, was not such a man. His attraction to Sigvor and willingness to wed her seemed proof to me of this.

"He is different," Gyda finally said. "To think of living with him…" Her voice trailed off. "Not to be able to speak with him…" She shook her head. "He will need a special woman. And I hope he finds her."

I could only agree with this, and nodded. Sidroc had claimed that Tindr would not find a woman in a hall, and he must be right. We turned our eyes back to the gaming men.

Both Runulv and Ring were able players, Runulv in particular, and Sidroc had a worthy opponent in him. Runulv had skill, and Sidroc could not tempt him to wager more than he thought he should, so they were well matched. They played, as they usually did, with hack-silver, broken bits of jewellery, bent coins from afar, or chopped lengths of plain silver coils. Runulv, being a merchant, had always his small folding scales with him, and he would weigh the metal to make sure all men had put in equal shares.

Each man had a pile of hack silver before him, which grew larger or smaller with each completed wager. At times Sidroc's was the greater, and at others, Runulv's. Ring's pile had grown so small that he laughed and pulled it aside, letting his brother take on Sidroc alone. I watched Sidroc make a large bet on his next throw, for he pushed more than half of his pile forward. Runulv took up the dice, called out his wager, and cast the dice down. He had won.

He threw back his head with a laugh. Sidroc laughed too and pushed his silver pile to him.

The three men were talking and laughing. Runulv had both hands clasped around the pile of silver Sidroc had lost to him. Then he looked down and paused. He plucked out half of a man's arm cuff.

"This was not in your wager; it was in your reserve," he told Sidroc, dropping the piece back into Sidroc's pile.

I was surprised. Sidroc always took careful note of what he wagered and what he held back, and they had been drinking only ale, so it was not that that had made him careless. Sidroc nodded his thanks, and said no more of it.

The game went on a while longer, with Runulv in the end coming out with slightly more silver than his host. Sidroc did not seem eager to even the score, but looked content with a good evening's sport. The men were beginning to stretch and roll their shoulders, and then to sweep their winnings into their hands. Sidroc looked at Runulv as he did so, and spoke.

"You know I have been looking for a man who likes silver to sail to Frankland for me."

All the ship-owning men of the trading road knew this, and several had put themselves forward for this adventure. Both Runulv and Ring paused, their hands on the table, and waited to hear more.

"It is not just a skilled sailor I seek. He must be a shrewd trader, for much depends on this first shipment of mine. And he must be unafraid of the dangers he may encounter along the way; unafraid, and able to fight them off if he must.

"But more than any of this I need a man I can trust. I cannot go with my goods; I must place them in his hands and trust he will bring me full value."

Here Runulv glanced down to the pile of silver he had been gathering up, then looked back to Sidroc.

"I think you are that man, Runulv," he told him. "You saw the extra silver in your winnings, and returned it to me. You are alert, and you are honest."

Runulv's eyes shifted, and a smile broke at the corners of his mouth. "It was a test?" he asked.

Sidroc nodded. "I want you to sail to Frankland for me. One-third of all you yield will be yours."

Runulv gave a whoop of joy, and Gyda turned and embraced me. We were growing friends, and now would be partners as well.

"You will need the best men you can find," Sidroc went on. "The seas are full of my brothers, out seeking treasure, and the likes of Eskil the Svear as well."

He ended by looking at both Runulv and Ring. Ring had no ship of his own, and tho' it was clear he was happy for his brother, his want of having any way to get ahead was also there upon his face.

"Ring will come," Runulv said.

He did not need to be asked twice. Rannveig had once again brought us a jar of her mead, and she went now and poured it out for the men. She stopped a moment after this to tell Tindr what had happened; he had been looking on with curious eyes at the celebrating men. She gave his shoulder a little pat once she explained; a gesture, I thought, that had a touch of consolation in it.

Spring came fully on. Rannveig opened her brew-house, tho' with the still-chilly nights she had need of many braziers to warm the space. Few folk had yet moved back to the trading road from their upland farms, but some who lived on the West side of Gotland sailed along the coast to us, as the few inland tracks would be muddy with the softening soil.

One who did come overland, slowly and surely with a double team of oxen, was Thorfast the stone-shaper. His waggon held the two pairs of millstones Sidroc had ordered, and when he rolled onto the trading road a boy was sent up to Tyrsborg to fetch us. There was a ware-house at the end of the pier, and Sidroc had made arrangement that the heavy stones be stored there until it was time to load them onto Runulv's ship. I wanted to see them too, so we walked down the hill together. The huge rounds were laid singly and side by side, two over the front axle and two over the back, and lashed well down through their socket holes, as Thorfast and his waggon had climbed hills to reach us. He had a few querns in the waggon as well, and when we came up was unloading them to the stall which would sell them for him.

The Hall of Tyr

There is nothing of beauty in a grinding stone, but these gave me great pleasure to look upon. They were fully half of the treasure we would send to Frankland, and would repay us, Sidroc hoped, four-fold. And they were the same fine grained grey-white stone of which the two tall and narrow walls of Tyrsborg were built. For this reason alone I must stretch out my hand and touch the two I could reach as they rested in the waggon bed. Thorfast smiled at me when he saw this; I think he had seen women taking pleasure in receiving their new querns, and as he knew we were setting ourselves up in trading he understood the hopes we had for them, just as a woman hoped for better bread from her new quern.

Ketil came forth from his rope-works, and the man who owned the ware-house, with a helper, and with Thorfast directing their actions they and Sidroc eased the stones one by one down a shallow ramp from the waggon bed to a sort of sledge with peeled logs as rollers for wheels. From there they were pulled through the broad doors of the ware-house, each upon their own sledge.

After they were done Sidroc asked them all to Rannveig's, and stood them I know not how many cups of ale, for it was growing onto dusk when he climbed the hill back to me. He was as glad as I was in them, even more, for he was the one who had thought of having millstones made and sent in the first place.

The next day we had the second part of our goods meant for Frankland, for Holmgeir the amber-worker walked up to Tyrsborg with the basket of promised amber necklaces. About half of them had the silver beads interspersed with those of polished amber, so lovely that it made me proud to have asked for them. Holmgeir liked them too, and I thought it would not be long before he made some himself to lay on his display tables. He brought as well eight small figures he had carved of large chunks of amber. Three were of horses,

247

three were of fish, and two were simple little cups, almost tiny bowls. Sidroc was pleased with all of these ornaments, and I could see how any of them would gladden the heart of those who held them. The tiny cups looked destined to hold rare spices or precious healing unguents. Before we lowered them into the hiding place in the treasure room I held one to the Sun and saw all before me bathed in gold.

Late that afternoon I was out by Tyrsborg's front door. Tindr had brought me some tiny apple trees from Rannveig's upland farm, and had planted them out front for me, along with a small vine of the purple grapes that grew so well on Gotland. To these beginnings of my garden I was adding herbs that Rannveig had dug for me, and was drawing water from the well to sprinkle on them. We had had little rain, but as I lifted my head from the well I saw the skies over the ocean bruised with distant storm clouds. I pulled up the bucket and balanced it on the edge of the well.

Sidroc came out the door behind me, and put the bucket on the ground. He slid his arms around my thickening waist and kissed the back of my neck. We stood looking out at the rolling clouds darkening the horizon.

"Your garden will soon get the water it needs," he said, with a little laugh. Then he let go his hands around me. He dropped something over my head. It was one of the polished amber bead necklaces, one which had the silver spiral-carved beads in it.

I opened my mouth to protest, but he spoke again. "I want you to have this now. We have much to celebrate. This," he said, tightening his hands upon my belly for a moment. "The millstones which came yesterday. The amber which has sat waiting all Winter in the treasure room; and that which came today. All of it. Odin, looking down, surely envies me."

I could do nothing but kiss him. As we stood there the skies grew darker, and the breeze died. A gust of wind blew up. Of a sudden a branch of forked lightning split the purple and blue skies above the sea. The clap of thunder that followed drove me deeper into his arms. It was not just the noise that did so, but recalling our second morning in Tyrsborg, when Sidroc had pressed the twelve pieces of gold into my hand. Odin might envy him his happiness, he had jested, and cast a lightning-bolt at him.

My dun mare came into her heat, ready to be bred. Tindr had watched her carefully, and when one morning she began stretching her neck to whinny, lifting her tail, and passing foamy water he took her from the paddock. Sidroc's stallion was at once alert, sniffing the air after her. Sidroc watched as Tindr led the mare back and forth along the outside rail of the paddock. The stallion snorted and pranced after her with every flick of her dark tail. There could be danger to both horses in mating, and both men wanted to be sure of her readiness. A mare not deeply in her heat could lash out with her rear legs and break the leg of the stallion trying to mount her. A stallion who was rough and bit excessively could frighten the mare and cause her to harm herself in trying to twist away.

They would not breed her here up at Tyrsborg. Tindr told us through his gestures, and through a drawing he made in the ash, that we should take them down to the great standing image of Freyr, Lord of Horses. To do so was to ensure a live foal, and those horses bred within sight of the carved God's wide eyes lived long and hale lives.

I wanted to go too. The dun was my mare, and it seemed fitting that I should be there to witness and ask protection and blessing on her and her hoped-for offspring. So the three of us set off walking together, Tindr holding the halter rope of my mare, Sidroc that of his eager stallion, and me at his side.

But before we left Tindr plunged his hands in water, then scooped up a handful of the soft grey cooking ash from the fire-ring. He squeezed and kneaded it in his hands a moment. He went to my mare, and began singing to her in his own private and peculiar way, a song of honking squeals. He touched her shoulder with that of his own, gently moving alongside her barrel to her flanks. Still resting lightly against her he pressed one finger into the ash paste in the palm of his hand. With three gentle strokes he drew the rune Feoh, V, wealth, for increase, upon her haunch. Feoh, the rune which began the names of Freyr and his sister Freyja, Lord and Lady of all beasts, be they animal or folk, and Lord and Lady of all fertility.

We started down the hill and turned onto the trading road. Folk setting out their wares or working at their benches looked up at us and nodded; other horse-owners who lived near must also bring their breeding animals as we were. My mare side-stepped, her back hooves raising puffs of dust. She kept stretching her neck to whinny, and Tindr walked just at her head, his hand firmly on her halter lead. She lifted her tail almost without ceasing, and tried to turn her head to look over at the stallion in her wake. She called steadily, and he snorted and nickered back.

We reached the end of the trading road and the great standing image of the God. Someone had killed a rooster and left it atop one of the offering poles; a fisherman setting out early, I thought. The green-painted eyes of Freyr looked fixedly across the ruffled white caps on the sea before him. Small waves lapped the pebbled shore, raking back and then slapping forward the shining stones in unbroken rhythm. Tindr led the mare nine times around the wooden image. Of all numbers nine was the sacred one, and if Freyr's gaze could be caught and held Tindr would work to make it so.

The stallion was snorting, prancing in place, stretching his neck towards her each time she neared. Tindr stopped her, and she turned once more to look back over her shoulder at the stallion. She held her dark tail high and well away from her waiting hindquarters, and whinnied sharply. Tindr dropped the lead and stepped back. Sidroc took his hand from the halter and let the stallion approach. He went first to her neck and gave a quick nip to her mane. His upper lip curled back as he sniffed along the length of her body, ending at her haunches. The stallion whinnied sharply, and was ready. He reared up. The mare called back in response, and her back legs buckled slightly as she lowered herself so he might the more easily reach her.

I had seen many animals in the act of mating, watched randy old rams climbing on the woolly backs of ewes, and bulls bellow as they covered their cows, seen whinnying stallions in fields leap upon the backs of their herd mares. At some of these breedings men had been there to lead or guide or protect. The life of any beast was highly valued; they gave food, clothing, and transport to man. I had watched priests bless flocks and try to drive devils from ailing animals. But I had not seen a breeding that was meant also as dedication, as this one was.

The strength of my mare's yearning, the power of the stallion's response, the fact that they had been brought here by Freyr's image to ensure the issue of a foal; these things turned as vital points marking the path in the Circle of Life. All animal life sprang from this simple and natural act, an act as firmly rooted in the drive to live as was the drawing of breath itself. It was the most basic of acts, and one of singular majesty and beauty.

Few but Sidroc yet knew of our coming babe, and this rich secret of our own fruitful coupling made my senses rise. The calling mare, the snorting stallion, my arms bound fast around Sidroc as he lowered his hips to mine; I had known all of this; felt it all; the carved image of Freyr saw and watched and blessed. All desire was my desire, that which teased and inflamed and drove, to peak and end in this melding of female and male. That end was yet a new beginning, the giving and receiving of life-force needful for offspring and for all continuance.

I stood flanked by Sidroc and Tindr and witnessed this, felt without touching either of them their nearness, heard their breathing above the snorts and panting whistle of the joined horses. The great starting eyes of Freyr looked over us, and wordless, I raised my palms to him.

I think my breath was held, not from within but without me, as the stallion stood with arched neck, head tight against the mare's mane. A few thrusts and he shuddered, released his hold, and with a soft squeal fell back and onto all four legs again. Once more and with curled lip he brought his muzzle close to her, filling himself with her scent, that reek which now held his essence as well as hers.

All at Tyrsborg unfolded to the warming Spring. My little apple trees pushed out tight and tiny buds where blossoms showed pink tips, and with them the promise of apples. The barren grape vine was dotted with swelling bumps along its brown curls, which split and opened to broad grey-green leaves. The birches under which our cow cropped the grasses sprouted with their vivid green and pointed leaves. I plucked the tiny leaves and steeped them to drink as a tonic for my coming babe, and for me as well, for I had ever liked the tang of birch broth.

Tindr was busy with his bees. They had given him a great harvest of honey in the Fall, so much so that he could begin new hives. He wove the skeps himself at his work-bench by the stable doorway, splitting and plaiting the straw, sewing it in coils, and then shaping them into domes. Some of these he would set in the crotches of rotted-out trees, and others he would build a low platform for to place at the edges of forest glades. He kept us in as much honey as we could eat, which pleased Sidroc very much, as he ever sought out sweets; and at Rannveig's there were big crocks of the golden stuff.

Sparrow grew as well. I could not say she had blossomed; she was a plain and queer-looking little creature, but as she grew in trust of us all her dark eyes became less guarded and her actions around the hall and yard more at ease. I could not help but like her, small and wiry as she was; she truly looked a human form of the pert little bird whose name she carried. She seemed content as I watched her tending Gunnvor's baking pans at the edge of the cooking ring or standing at Helga's side as they spun together. Both women had become like unto aunts to her, teaching her to care for herself, and tho' she was perhaps not by nature given to much chatter, she learnt Gotlandic Norse quickly and spoke readily when spoken to.

She never told about her past unless she were asked, and I tried not to pain her overmuch with my questions. She did not know the name of the land she was come out of. Eskil told Sidroc he had picked her up at a post near the great river Vistula, but she could have come from anywhere. She thought two Summers had passed since she left her home; she and her parents and one grandfather had lived with her and her siblings, and worked a plot of land belonging to a wealthy farmer. She began to cry when I asked how she came to leave there, and I thought she had been carried off by raiders, and saw perhaps her parents killed during this. I knew at times she suffered from the night-mare, and would wake and climb into Helga's or Gunnvor's alcove in her distress, and that both women had comforted her.

She let Helga and Gunnvor place their hands on her shoulders, but other than this she disliked being touched. Tindr was careful not to startle her; once he came up behind her at the well to help her haul up the bucket and she recoiled so she nearly fell in. Yet I knew she liked Tindr; he showed her how to milk the cow and to give the skogkatts their portion of the milk, two things which pleased her to do.

She had no notion, I thought, of what Free or Slave meant, only being well-treated or ill. When she was older I would make clear to her that she could come and go as she like; tho' it was hard for me to see a day when she might wish to wed and make a life of her own. For now I felt it best for her to feel cared for by Gunnvor and Helga, to have her hands busy at work she was good at, and to know she was safe.

If Sparrow sometimes suffered from the galloping night-mare, the new year freed me from this curse, for as soon as I felt the first wave of my morning-sickness the night-mare left me alone. I no longer felt the alarms of the Idrisid slave ship, or the terrifying sea battles, or the fear of drowning that could haunt my nights even after my happiest days.

But my nights were not always dreamless. Sometimes in dreams I beheld Ceric, saw him at play, and called to him, but he did not hear my calls. In others I was holding the fever-hot body of my little Ninnoc as she whimpered and cried. But the Gods were kind; these dreams were bittersweet, recalling the love I had for these children, so that if I awoke with tears in my eyes I felt blessed none the less.

I dreamt too a glowing and beautiful dream of holding my coming babe. This dream was untainted by any sorrow, and flooded my heart with such pure joy that I clung to it and the hope it gave me.

Chapter the Fifteenth: Ashes

I knew I had been sleeping soundly for Sidroc had both hands upon my shoulders. I heard women's voices, a wailing perhaps, and his voice telling me to awaken. "Shield-maiden," he urged, "there is fire on the trading road. We must all go."

He already had his leggings on and was pulling on his boots. He had left the treasure room door ajar when he had answered the summoning knock. The women I heard were Helga and Gunnvor, talking to Sparrow; and I heard too the door to the kitchen yard open and close in rapid succession. I found a shift and gown and fumbled with my stockings and shoes.

"I am going ahead, with Tindr," Sidroc told me. He looked back over to me before he left the room. "Do not run," he ordered. "Do not get close to the fire. Stay in the women's ranks and do not lift anything heavy."

I nodded, bleary from being jolted awake. I went to the treasure room door and saw Tindr, a bucket in each hand, and watched Sidroc pick up two more. The front door was open and they ran through it and into the night.

Gunnvor had been awakened by cries and by someone pounding on the front door. It was our neighbour Alrik, sounding the alarm. Gunnvor had wakened Tindr, and then come to the treasure room door. While I had been dressing she had been out in the kitchen yard, hunting by torch-light for pails, buckets, and cauldrons; anything which had a handle. Now we four women took one in each hand, and started out the door. We were all of us frightened; fire was a fast and ready consumer of men's homes and livelihoods.

We were no sooner outside than we were greeted by an eerie orange light centred in our view. Billows of greyish-white smoke arose, hanging like a low lying cloud and hiding the darkness which should be the sea. I turned and pulled our door firmly shut. As I turned back the pungent smell of burning tar filled my nostrils; it was so strong I nearly gagged. The tar-maker's shop at the end of the pier must be alight. We hurried down the hill, others of our neighbours joining us, while sleepy-eyed children peered from their doorways.

Rannveig must be already gone to the site; her brew house door swung open and a single burning cresset was set on a table within. As we turned onto the trading road the noise of men shouting filled my ears. Men and boys, and some women too, were running back and forth, looking I thought for more buckets. At least we had a constant source of water in the sea.

Once on the road itself I saw it. And I remembered. The warehouse in which our costly millstones were waiting was next to the tar-maker's. I shook this from my head; they were stone and would suffer no hurt. But from the line of folk snaking out from the tar-maker's and on to the pier I saw that the fire must be quite hot, and likely to spread.

The stench of the burning tar was intense and made me feel almost faint; it gave off black smoke that was choking when it blew our way. Besides the pots of tar he offered to ship-owners and those building houses, he sold lumps of tallow formed from the fat of cattle and sheep, and pottery jars of oil boiled down from walrus and whale blubber. These things would burn hot and fast and they did so now. What had been his shop was only a thin line of upstanding planks, now flaming at their tops like great candles. A bon-fire of flame shot into the air behind them. Tho' the tar-maker's shop was naught but a flaming shell, many men flung buckets into the flames. Across a narrow alley sat the ware-house in which the millstones were stored. Men worked as close to this wall as they could, flinging buckets of water upon the ware-house wall next to the flames. We were caught a moment near them as we tried to make our way through. The heat was such that my eyes, watering from the acrid smoke, dried out and I must blink. We moved back closer to the shoreline. Those nearest the fire were coughing and gasping from the foul grey and black smoke.

A loose line of men stood, swinging filled buckets hand to hand from the mid-point of the pier to where the closest men stood in the road, heaving water at the fire. A line of women and older children stood just behind them, taking up the empty buckets and passing them back along to the men who dropped them into the water from the pier. There were not enough folk yet and the lines had gaps and people must run a few steps. We made our way to the women's rank; to do so we must quickly pass through the line of men. Wooden buckets are heavy empty, and the men who swung them full from hand to hand had sweat glistening on their faces.

The four of us were still together, and I felt glad of it. In the awe-ful glow of the flames, the noise and confusion, I could see no one else I knew, or so it seemed. I took a moment to retie my head wrap. I wore my hair in one thick braid for sleep so we would not get tangled in it. It was still braided, and I coiled up the braid and tucked it in under my head-wrap, tying it at the nape of my neck as the women of Gotland did. My hair was, I thought, my chief beauty and I did not want it to come to any harm.

We passed our empty buckets down the line of women to the men waiting on the pier. These same looped the bucket handles with hooked iron rods and dipped them into the sea. The buckets were hauled up and passed to the men's rank, moving each filled bucket up, man by man.

I looked up and down the rank of men, scanning for Sidroc. I could not see him, nor was he amongst the strongest men who were given the task of hauling the buckets over and over again up onto the pier. More men and women were joining us and the distance we had to reach to carry the buckets grew shorter. The empty buckets, pails and cauldrons we swung were dripping wet and our gowns were soon wet too from the flying droplets. I looked down at Sparrow as she stood between me and Gunnvor. Her eyes and mouth were open as she gaped at the flames on the road, and in her eyes was a fixed stare that did not change even when she must glance down to handle a coming bucket. She may have seen her hut, or even entire village, burn.

On the beach were a group of children a way off, not far from Rannveig's. They had followed their parents down and were standing and milling about, some of them whooping and jumping, others looking on the verge of tears.

"Sparrow," I told her. "Go down to those children and lead them closer to the brew-house and out of trouble."

She ducked her head and left, and we watched as she herded the little ones up and led them to a grouping of big stones, where they sat. She kept her back to us and the fire. Other women looked over to where they had gathered, grateful their children had a watchful eye cast over them.

Several men came running up with long wooden poles in their hands. I could see they meant to topple the standing planks of the tar-maker's shop inwards, so the water they threw might more easily reach the source of the flames. Three men laid hands on each pole, and charged towards the wall, battering it, board by board, in turn. We heard the upright planks crack and shudder over the hissing of the fire. One man fell near the base of the flames and was pulled back, screaming, the back of his tunic alight. He was quickly doused by his fellows. The line of upstanding planks fell in, but the heat it released drove back the line of men throwing water; I could feel the wave of heat increase even where I stood with Gunnvor and Helga, well down the line. Men closest to it grabbed the buckets they had meant for the fire and upended them over their own heads, wetting and cooling themselves so they could work on. Women who stood at the head of the return line ran back, unable to stand the heat anymore, and we all moved forward to make up the lack. All this time we passed the empty buckets steadily down towards the pier. My palms were growing sore and my arms had begun to ache from swinging the pails.

Over the din I heard a great shout, and turned my head to the trading road. Despite the efforts of the water-throwers, the ware-house roof was alight. The wide doubled doors had been opened, and until the smoke grew too thick men had been hauling out anything they could to spare the goods within. Looking up I saw that men were actually upon the steep roof; they must have climbed up on ladders from the other side, for I could see they held buckets, the contents of which they threw on the wooden roof. One man was very tall. Watching him from below I knew it was Sidroc.

Some noise came from my mouth; I thrust the bucket I had at Gunnvor and turned and ran towards the warehouse. Men were everywhere at its base, holding and lifting buckets, heaving water at any part of the warehouse they could reach, yelling encouragement and calling for help. On the other side of the ware-house was Ketil's rope-works. Two ladders were propped up against his outside wall, with a man on every other rung, lifting water. By craning my head I could just make out Ketil himself, standing on his roof, passing an empty pail down. His wife Tola stood at the base of one of the ladders, steadying it. She looked fixedly upward, her face smudged with ash.

I kept on around the back of their rope-works, following the line of bucket-carrying men who now snaked to where the ladders to the ware-house roof stood. Someone grabbed my arm. It was Rannveig.

"They are up there, both of them," she said. She reached up and took an empty bucket dropped into her arms from a man on the ladder. "Go and get women if you can to haul these empties back to the water line."

I took heart from her calm words, and from her firm resolve. She feared for Tindr but the task at hand was to quell the fire. I went back quickly as I could, bringing Gunnvor and Helga and any other women that could be spared. Filled wooden buckets, pails, and iron cauldrons were passed from man to man around from the pier, along the side road, and up the ladders, vanishing from my view onto the steep roof. Empties came down just as quickly, and we women snatched at them and sent them back along the return line. The Sun was beginning to dawn, and the slight breeze that had been blowing died down. At one point I saw Sidroc close to the eaves. His hair was moving in the hot updraught, and I watched as he lifted and dumped a bucket of water over himself to battle the heat.

But the fire was too hot. Water thrown at the heated timbers turned to steam and was lost in the cool dawn air. Dowse the roof as they might, the wall closest to the tar-maker's caught flame, and could not hold. Goods that had been next the wall caught and burned. The oily smell of burning wool mixed with that of wood and tar, telling me the great bundles of sheep-skins I had seen near our millstones were aflame.

Sparks began falling on us from the ware-house roof, shot up in the growing updraught to settle on us below. Something small hit my head; I swatted at it with my hand and came away with a slight burn. I ducked my head over a filled bucket a man held low for me and drenched my head-wrap. The sea water was icy cold.

Men were calling out now, calling back those upon the roof. Then the building itself seemed to jolt. A man on one of the lower rungs of a ladder fell to the ground as the ladder jumped against the eave. We did not know it then, but men had closed the front doors in hope of containing the flames. The fire within leapt upwards in a sort of fire-ball, punching through the thinned roof planks. A massive tongue of flame shot up over our heads from the ruptured gable peak.

We leapt back. The men scrambled down the ladders. Amongst them I saw the ware-house man, and then Sidroc and Tindr as they turned and grasped the ladder ends, half-climbing, half-leaping down to the hard ground and safety. Their faces were blackened by smoke, and rivulets on their darkened cheeks showed where their eyes had watered and run tears. Sidroc's hair was oddly shorter on one side than the other; a spark of burning ash must have caught there and burnt it. One of Tindr's tunic sleeves was missing, and by the way he held his arm, a little out from his body, I knew he had been burned. Sidroc too held his right hand out in front of him and shook it, and I saw how it had reddened. All the men were coughing, hacking, and even retching out the smoke they had been enveloped in.

But they could not stop. Filled buckets kept coming, as did the threat to Ketil and Tola's rope-works. The men took up buckets and once again flung the contents over their bodies. Sidroc looked at me and nodded, nothing more. Then he seized the ladder he had come down. The ware-house man and Tindr took the other two. They must hold them nearly upright in the narrow quarters, and staggered as they carried them.

Ketil was still upon his roof and turned when the three ladders landed against his eaves. Men swarmed up them, some to stand with Ketil and two others already there to receive the lifted buckets, others to take up station on the rungs and lift the heavy swaying vessels up. The hard packed

261

soil under our feet was churned into a skim of mud from the wet, but a thrown bucket of water on the hot wood of the buildings darkened it just for a few moments as it turned to hissing steam.

Rannveig and I stood at the base of the ladders at the rope-works, sending empty buckets down the line. Sidroc and Tindr were above our heads but we could not see them. A rank of men on the ground near us still flung water at the base of the ware-house, tho' we heard a series of crackling crashes which told us the roof was falling in.

The Sun rose over the sea, casting the smoke above us in a golden light. It was not so thick as it had been, and I thought the contents of the tar-maker's must be at last burnt out. The wall of the ware-house closest to Ketil's held; men flung water at it ceaselessly. More folk were come around to where we stood behind the rope-works, telling us that while the ware-house smouldered, the tar-maker's was out. But the ware-house was still so hot that the rope-works needed constant drenching.

Men and women came and took our places in the rank, and Rannveig and Gunnvor and Helga and I stumbled back into the small yard of a maker of leather-goods. His railing fence had been pulled apart to use as prods for the fire, but there were barrels and a bench for us to sink down upon. My arms were aching; I lifted them to splash my face with water and felt how sore they were. My gown was spotted in ash and the hem smeared with mud. I looked to Rannveig, sitting just next me. She had a round brown-edged hole in her gown where a large burning flake must have settled. Our eyes went up to the rope-works roof. A whole line of men stood upon it, flinging water not only upon the roof, but down into the smoking remains of the warehouse. Sidroc and Tindr were amongst them. I feared for Sidroc, and thought Ranveig must have feared even more for her son, who could not hear the shouted commands and warnings, but must use his eyes alone to keep himself safe.

Rannveig's cook Gudfrid came up to her; I had not seen her before, but she was almost as dirty as we. Rannveig squeezed my hand as she rose, and told me to come later to the brew-house. I felt light-headed and almost too tired to speak to Gunnvor and Helga, and they too were quiet. Folk walked before us, some looking in the same daze we felt ourselves in.

At last the men quit the rope-works roof, the threat to it ended. Ketil was the last down, secure that his building had been saved. Tola was still at the base of a ladder and looked as if it were the only thing keeping her on her feet. Ketil put his arm about her, and she burst into tears.

Sidroc and Tindr stood at the foot of building, and Ketil turned to speak to them and the knot of other men who had worked upon the roof with him. Then I saw Sidroc turn and walk back to the remains of the rear wall of the warehouse. He stood a while gazing on it, and then joined Tindr. Together they turned their heads, looking, I knew, for us. I stood up and they came to us.

Their faces were smeared and filthy. I saw again how a hank of Sidroc's hair had burned away. Tindr had his in two braids, and they and his head looked untouched. Both had small holes in their tunics and leggings where burning ash had struck them, and Tindr's right arm, with his sleeve gone, was completely unprotected. Dark stains streaked their clothing and flesh wherever settled ash had mixed with the water they had flung upon themselves. Even their boots, muddy as they were, were scarred by fire. Sidroc lifted the back of his hand to wipe his brow and winced when skin touched skin.

"Let us go to Rannveig's," I told them.

They said nothing, just followed us through the milling crowd and around to the trading road. Once there we stopped. The Sun had risen into the sea, brilliant yellow upon the rapidly deepening blue of the water. Groups of men and women stood before the two destroyed buildings, looking into the smoking timbers, turning to look out to sea or to speak to those who stood nearby. Some folk could not cease coughing, choking up the smoke they had swallowed.

We saw the tar-maker, almost as blacked from the fire as his tar that fuelled it. He had recently come down from his upland farm at which he burnt his pines into tar, and had been setting up his shop for the season. He stood before the ruins of his business, his arms slack, his head lowered.

The ware-house front was not quite gone; the door frame which had held the wide doors still stood, in mocking welcome, tho' the doors themselves had fallen. The ware-house owner stood talking to a small group of men and women. Near them was a tumbled heap of goods, chests and sacks and barrels of things that had been hastily retrieved before the smoke and heat became too great. The ware-house man raised his arms in a hopeless way at the little remaining to them all.

Tindr glanced about, and made for a rain barrel which stood at the corner of a building two shops down the road. It had been ignored or forgotten during the fire, but now we watched as he lowered his right arm up to the armpit into the deep water it held.

"His sleeve caught fire, and he tore it off," Sidroc told us.

Gunnvor and I went to him and gestured he should let us see it. He withdrew the arm, and even with the water dripping from it we saw the masses of tiny blisters which had formed along its length. His brow was furrowed, his mouth pursed, the pain it caused him clear upon his face.

264

"We are going to Rannveig's," decided Gunnvor. She touched her ear and gestured Tindr should follow her. He did not move right away, but looked over to Sidroc, who waved him on.

"We will see you soon," I promised, as they moved off. I knew Sidroc's hand was burned and meant to get him to come with me as soon as I could. As I walked back to where he stood I saw Helga, sorting through the piles of now discarded buckets, pails and cauldrons; even kettles were there, lying upon the ground where they had been dropped when the fire was deemed out. Each wooden bucket was carved with a distinct design upon its rim or body, so if you could recall it you might find your own; but the iron cauldrons were much alike, and unless yours had a dent or mended patch it would be hard to carry back that which you had brought forth.

Two men were standing with Sidroc, and as I came up I saw it was Runulv and Ring. I had glimpsed Ring earlier, he had been one of the men who had scrambled down with Sidroc and Tindr from the ware-house roof before it collapsed, but had not seen Runulv. Both young men were near as filthy as Sidroc, but looked to have suffered no hurt.

Then I recalled that Runulv had already moved his casks of Gotlandic salt into the ware-house, ready to be carried on board when he set sail for us next month. He would sell his salt on his own account in Frankland, or so he had hoped. Looking into the charred and ruined mess that was the ware-house told me that his wooden casks could not have survived. The wood would have burned away, the lead liners that kept the salt safe from all wet would have melted, and the salt itself dissolved into whitish lumps under the steady drenching of the thrown water.

I scarce knew what I would say to him; he had spent good silver for the salt and now had nothing to show for it.

Perhaps he had silver enough to buy more and so make good on his plan. As I was thinking this Runulv's wife Gyda came hurrying. I had seen her in the women's rank but not been able to speak to her. We embraced, smiling a moment at our smudged faces, and went to join the men.

As we came up to the three they turned and walked a short distance away where lay several peeled log poles. These were the poles the men had used to batter the upright planks of the tar-maker's shop down. Near the poles were lengths of unburned wood, some thick, some thin. Sidroc took up a plank in his hands and cast it down into the smouldering ashes that had been the warehouse floor. They did not go through the open and ghostly doorway but at an angle by the narrow alleyway between the ware-house and the tar-maker's. Ring stepped on the plank that Sidroc had cast down, then dropped one he held beyond it. Runulv did the same. In this way they made a plank walk over the hot and smouldering timbers. The ware-house man saw them and came to watch, as did some others. Now the three picked up the peeled log poles, one each, and walked along the plank-way into the ruins of the building. I could see them clearly but with so much rubble about I could not make out anything that was at their feet. I knew it must be very hot within and could only hope the planks would not catch fire until they came out.

They came about to the middle of the ruin, and I heard Sidroc's voice. They pulled the planks closer to where he stood, forming almost a circle. Using the poles in their hands they angled them downwards, lifting off fallen timber, pushing away debris, poking and prodding. I heard one of them holler as they dislodged a fallen roof beam; it must have been white hot beneath it, and the heat scalded him.

I saw Runulv and Sidroc stand opposite each other and brace themselves at their poles as they strained to move something together. Then I heard an oath, loud and angry, from Sidroc. He vanished from my view as he bent over, then stood again, staring fixedly down. He and Runulv and Ring went to work once more, pushing around amongst the charred debris. Another oath followed. I turned to Gyda and we looked at each other.

Now the three men just stood, gazing down at their feet, turning their heads from side to side. Then Sidroc looked up at the sky for a long moment, as he so often did; but this morning he stood looking up through the ruined and missing roof of a destroyed building. His hands were grasping the pole and I could see he heaved a sigh. He brought his eyes back to Runulv and Ring. The three paused together, eyes locking, each to each.

Then they began picking their way out, pushing and steering the plank walkway before them over the tumbled and smoking wreckage. The last few steps they leapt, and lay down the poles they had used. They came to stand near us.

"The millstones," said Sidroc. "Three of them are broken." His voice was hoarse from smoke, and completely flat.

"Broken?" I could not believe it. The thickness of the stone, the great size of them – I began to open my mouth again when Sidroc went on.

"The fire was too hot. The stones got heated, then cracked from the cold water hitting them."

I knew that farmers sometimes built fires around big boulders, then poured water on them to crack the rock and so be able to cart it away. This was what had befallen our precious millstones.

Runulv was looking to Gyda, and just shook his head. She brought her hands to her face, and murmured, "Our salt…"

The Hall of Tyr

We put our arms around each other, and we embraced again. The smell of fire was all about us, on our bodies, in the air, and the hot timbers in the ruins hissed as if mocking our hopes. With so much loss I wanted to get away from the smoking ware-house. I turned my back on it, and raised my hand towards the brew-house. "Come, come to Rannveig's," I coaxed.

The five of us made our way along the road. The Sun was fully up, stretching its arms over the water into a beautiful Spring morning, scorning the destruction we walked away from. Nesting birds swooped and sang, darting into Rannveig's garden as we neared her place. The brew-house awnings were rolled up, and groups of people clustered around the tables inside.

At the first table stood Gunnvor, over a large mortar and pestle. She was pounding the leaves and flowers of violets into butter as a salve to smear on burns. A man who had run several times into the burning ware-house stood next her, holding out his hand; his wrist had an angry red sear upon it. Tindr sat at the end of the table, his bare right arm resting on it, slathered to the shoulder with the greenish paste. He had an ale cup in his left hand, and lifted it to us as we came in, to tell us I think, he was well. I smiled at him and the corners of his mouth lifted. Several other folk, with hands or arms or cheeks dotted with the salve were also at this table, or moving about the room.

Sparrow came in from the split curtains, balancing a platter heaped high with griddled cakes. She set them down on a table so all might help themselves, then disappeared back into the kitchen yard where I knew Gudfrid must be hard at work. Rannveig herself came in next through the curtains, hoisting a pot of steaming broth. She set this at the back table where she kept her pottery ale cups. Already upon this table were two big crocks of ale, and men and women were dipping cups into them and slaking their thirst.

"Do you want ale?" I asked Sidroc, beginning to move towards the back. He nodded as he sat down at Gunnvor's table. I came back with two cups full for him. Gunnvor had finished with the man with the seared wrist. As she turned to look at Sidroc's hand Sparrow popped through the curtains, looking at Gunnvor. It was not hard to read her eyes.

"Gunnvor, go," I told her. "Gudfrid needs you. She and Sparrow cannot cook for all."

"Já, já," she answered, and made her way through the tables to the kitchen yard. She had made up plenty of the butter-violet paste, and I could always pound more.

I sat down next to Sidroc. He had already drunk the first cup of ale, holding it, as Tindr had, in his left hand. His right rested on the table. The linen of his tunic sleeve was dotted with holes where flaming embers had burned through, and I pushed it up to his elbow. His hand and wrist, from knuckles to mid-forearm, was blanketed with the same small blisters that covered Tindr's arm. All the hair on his arm was seared away.

Just to smear the cooling salve on would cause him more pain. I scooped a great gob on my fingertips, wanting nothing but the butter mixture to touch his injured flesh. Even so he flinched as I drew my fingers lightly down the line of burnt flesh.

"I am sorry," I murmured, under my breath.

He nodded and took up the second cup of ale. I knew his voice was hoarse and did not want to ask him to speak, nor did I know what he could say. Like all the men who had fought the fire he must be bone-tired. His hand pained him, and we had lost the millstones, which we had placed great stock in.

I rose and went to the back table and refilled one of Sidroc's ale cups and ladled out a cup of broth for myself. I balanced a couple of the griddle cakes on my splayed fingers and went back. Sidroc shook his head at the griddle cake, but Tindr was glad to eat. I lifted the second to my mouth. I was past my morning-sickness but still craved this sort of wheaten goodness when I arose each day. Tasting it I realised how hungry I was, and how tired I felt. The hot broth was full of savour and I welcomed it.

Rannveig saw us, and came over, stopping first to look again at Tindr's arm. She had a cup of ale in either hand, and set one in front of him. She took a length of linen towelling and ripped it into narrow pieces, and bound the arm from wrist to armpit to hold the salve in place. I could tell from the way Tindr raised his eyes to the roof that it hurt when she did so, but it would allow him to stand and move without the violet leaves dropping off.

She came to us, placing the second cup in front of Sidroc. She peered down at his blistered wrist.

"The millstones are split," he told her. His voice was almost a croak and he need clear his throat. "Three of them."

Rannveig's mouth opened in dismay. A single millstone was of little use; they need be sold and used in pairs, and so perfectly paired were those that Thorfast had made us that he had marked the edges of the stones with daubs of red copper paint to show which was paired with which.

"Can you still sail?" she wanted to know. She was a woman of business, one who looked ahead.

Sidroc shrugged. "I must. We have the amber. But Runulv lost all his salt."

Rannveig looked over to where Runulv, Ring, and Gyda stood with another woman. She was young and comely and I thought she must be Ása, Gyda's cousin and Ring's sweetheart. The downcast faces of all of them said much.

Rannveig shook her head. "Loki," she muttered, naming the Trickster God who sent such calamities to men.

No, I said silently: Odin, who saw Sidroc's happiness and envied him.

She dropped her eyes to Sidroc's blistered hand. "There is linen," she told me, "bind up his arm with it."

As I did so Runulv came to us. He had a cup of ale in his hand and sat down on the bench across from Sidroc. I thought they would want to speak of what they could do next, or perhaps just sit in that silence that men seem to crave when things go wrong. I saw Helga outside the brew-house, struggling with a stacked pile of our buckets. It made me think of Tyrsborg, and the everyday tasks that awaited there.

"The animals," I said aloud. I began to rise. "The cow needs milking, and none have been fed. Helga is here; she and I will go."

"I will not be long," Sidroc said.

Looking at him I thought him wrong; he looked little inclined to move, and if he came back to Tyrsborg and was alone it might only lead to brooding thoughts. He looked over his shoulder toward the table that held the ale. "Let me," I said, and had to smile. I came back with an ewer full of it.

I brought some to Tindr but he began to rise, and I thought he meant to go with me. He was in pain, could not milk the cow easily nor do any of his other chores well, and I wanted him near his mother, and at Sidroc's side.

I shook my head at him. I touched my ear, then my left cheek, and made an upright fist in the air: Tindr stay with Sidroc, and then cupped my hands together to ask Please.

He nodded, and made a little smile.

Helga and I walked up the hill carrying as many of the buckets as we could handle, leaving some at Rannveig's door for later. The wind had risen off the sea, and flakes of cold, black ash wafted in the air as we walked. I was tired and hungry and filthy; I wanted to rinse the smoke from my hair and body and eat and then sleep. I did not expect to see Gunnvor or Sparrow for a while; some of the folk who had gathered at Rannveig's had gone to their own homes, but those who stayed had settled in. All were thirsty and hungry, as Helga and I were. But first we had our beasts to care for.

"I will take the cow, if you please, Mistress," Helga told me when we reached Tyrsborg. A large flake of cold ash drifted above our heads, falling right at the threshold of our front door. I crushed it under my toe, not wanting even this small symbol of the destruction below us to touch our home.

We dropped the buckets by the cook-fire, save the one she would use. As we neared the stable door the two skogkatts rushed at us, tails up, chirping and purring, the yellow and white one from the trees of the woods and the black and white scrambling down from the stable hayloft. As I passed Tindr's work bench I saw a dead mouse, its head bitten off, laid carefully by their empty milk bowl. One cat at least had done its night's work, and here asked for payment. Tired as I felt I could not help but smile as I handed the bowl to Helga.

First I went to the well and drew up water so that it might be heating while we worked. I made several trips to the well as my arms were so tired I could not pull a full bucket. I poked up the fire in the big cooking-ring and set the cauldron over it.

Then I went back to the stable. The skogkatts were at their bowl, already lapping, as Helga went on with the steady pull of her hands as she drew the milk. The cow stood, brown head lowered, eyes half closed, swaying in contentment. I slid open the small doors so that our fowl could get from their stable pens to the enclosure outside, and scattered grain for them, which they flew at, squawking, with beating wings. The horses were outside in their paddock and I took them a fork full of hay, some oats, and added water to their trough. Small as she was my dun mare would not allow the stallion to push her from her hay, but bared her teeth at him and stamped her feet when he tried. She had spirit, and her foal would be one to reckon with.

Helga finished the milking and led the cow to the grassy area in front of Tyrsborg where we often tethered her. There was bread and cheese and butter in the cooking shed and we ate this washed down with deep draughts of the still-warm and creamy milk. Then I just wanted to bathe.

Standing in the big basin in the cooking shed I poured dippersful of warm water over my hair and body. When I finally felt clean I reached for the linen to dry myself. The gown I had worn lay over a barrel. It was the russet gown; the same I had worn when I left Kilton to take ship for Ælfwyn and Four Stones, the gown I had worn later that Summer on St Mary's Day when Sidroc and I were captured. This morning it had seen the destruction of our costly millstones, two of which had not even been paid for. It had been through much, that gown; too much. I would not wear it again, nor did I want to cut it into rags and see it used thusly. When I left the shed I dropped it into the low flames of the cooking fire.

When I awoke I dressed, and made up our bed, shaking out the feather bed and fluffing the down coverlet. I had crawled into it in the same disordered state in which we had left it in the darkness, and now wanted to put to rights as much as was in my power to do so. There was still some smell of smoke about me, caught in my hair or even, I thought, in my nostrils from breathing it in. I combed my hair and stepped into the silent hall. Sidroc was not there. The curtains to Gunnvor's alcove were drawn, telling me she must have returned and was resting, but both Tindr's and Sparrow's were open. Helga pulled back hers and came out, yawning, as I stood there. She shrugged her shoulders at the empty alcoves.

"I am going down to Rannveig's," I told her.

It could not have been far past noon; the Sun stood high above me in a cloudless blue sky. As I neared the brew-house I thought it empty, for tho' the awnings were all rolled up I heard no noise. Then I saw Gyda inside, standing with a man behind one of the tables. Like me she had been home, bathed, and changed. On the table before them lay a man, sprawled upon his back, arms and legs flung wide. It was Runulv, dead drunk, and snoring. The man Gyda stood with might be a brother of hers. They were trying without success to rouse the sleeping Runulv.

At one end of the same table Sidroc sat slumped over on his bench, his head resting on the scarred wood surface of the table. His bandaged hand lay extended before him, and the linen had light reddish stains where it had been splashed with something. Several cups, empty and half-empty, were ranged about the table. Tindr sat nearby and stood up when he saw me. It was clear he had been drinking, and clear too he had stopped well before either Sidroc or Runulv.

Gyda lifted her hands to me in helplessness, and I saw Ring was there too, sitting on the floor, his back against the wall of the brew house, a smile frozen on his face. A third man I did not know lay nearby upon his back on the floor, snoring as loudly as Runulv.

"You would think the ship had burned," Gyda said to me, with a rueful smile.

Rannveig came in from her brewing yard, arms stacked with cups. She put them down and came and joined us as we stood looking over the downed men.

"Did you give them mead?" I wondered aloud.

She made a clucking sound as she shook her head. "Nai, nai; they called for it, but had already too much ale in them. I tried to give them broth. But one of them went home and came back with a big jar of wine."

Wine was stronger than mead, and so much stronger than ale that it would not have taken much to render them senseless on top of what they had been drinking.

The man with Gyda had given up trying to rouse Runulv. He rolled Runulv over, stooped down next to the table and pulled him onto his back. Runulv made a chortling noise; I thought he was about to sing. Gyda and I looked at each other and had to laugh. The man edged sideways through the brew-house door, bent under the weight upon his shoulders.

"Good luck," Gyda smiled at me, nodding her head at Sidroc as she followed her husband out.

Tindr was still standing, a bit unsteadily, and looking sheepishly at us. I could only hope Sidroc could walk supported by us both, and Tindr made a gesture to show me he would lift Sidroc under the arm.

Then Sparrow came in through the split curtains, carrying more cups, which she laid upon the table. She smiled and ducked her head when she saw me. Rannveig waved her over.

"What help she's been; and on her feet all these hours, cooking with Gudfrid and Gunnvor, lifting and carrying ale and cakes, and now with all the cleaning up," Rannveig praised.

Sparrow lowered her head, but anyone could see what this praise meant. Rannveig put her arm about the girl's shoulders, and gave her a kiss on the cheek.

"You come and work with Rannveig anytime you tire of life at the top of the hill," she teased. Then she drew yet another of her glass bead necklaces from around her neck, and dropped this second one over Sparrow's head.

Sparrow cried out O!, as her fingers went to it. I was about to thank Rannveig and then tell Sparrow to go to Tyrsborg to rest when we heard a moan behind us.

Sidroc pushed himself up to sit, and was bracing his hands on the table edge. He squinted over at us.

"Are you ready to come home?" I asked, going to him.

"I am drunk," he said by way of answer.

Chapter the Sixteenth: Tree-gold and Bee-gold

A welcome rain fell the night after the fire, cooling the smouldering ruins. Men hauled out the charred timbers which remained from the ware-house, and the ware-house owner let any take what they like from them, as firewood. The rest was shovelled and scraped down to the low-water mark, a crumbling and blackened mass which once had been bundles of sheepskins, bolts of woollen wadmal, chests of dried stock fish, and barrels of salt. The rising tide would sweep up and carry it away.

I saw this the morning after the fire; I had come down to speak to Rannveig, but instead walked on a little way to where I could see the men working. I did not stand long looking at the ruined buildings. It brought to mind the day Ælfwyn and I first gazed on the blackened remains of Four Stones, and of the burning roof of the hall of Kilton I stood trapped and tethered under when the Danes attacked at Yule. Now another fire had taken the goods of many a Gotlander, and with it high hopes for the coming trading season. We were but two of them.

A drizzle was falling while I stood watching this, and I was holding the hem of a light wool mantle up over my head. The rain had cleared the air of smoke, but a tarry pungency still rose from the little left that marked the tar-maker's shop.

I turned and went back to Rannveig's, shaking my mantle out as I entered. The awnings were down and it was dry inside, and empty, save for she herself. But on the table nearest the door was an assortment of things: A clutch of eggs in a small basket, a sack of grain, a tub of butter. I had come to press some silver into her hand for all Sidroc had drunk yesterday. Now I saw that I was not alone in thanking her for all the food and drink she had provided us.

"Is this –" I began, lifting my hand to the goods on the table, "for yesterday?"

"Já," she said, and made a little gesture with her hands to signify that no payment was needed. As she lifted her hands the keys at her waist jingled gently. "It began even last night."

How good these folk are, I thought, with a justness in all that they do. "Then you will take this," I told her, and began to set my silver down upon the table.

She shook her head. "Nai; I take no silver today for what Sidroc drank. He kept Tindr at his side the whole time of the fire, so I feared less for him." Then she grinned. "And he has paid with his head, I warrant."

I nodded. He had in fact a bad head, as well as a burnt hand.

"But was not my ale that gave it to him, but that wine," she declared, and at which I must smile.

We spoke a while. Tindr was doing well, I told her; I had unwrapped the linen on both the men's burns and replaced them with fresh cloth. The blisters were oozing a clear liquid, and I wrapped the burns up again to keep them from sticking to their tunic sleeves. Tindr's was worse that Sidroc's, as it extended the length of his arm, but it did not appear to pain him overmuch unless it were touched or he flexed his arm. Sidroc said the same of his; as long as he put no pressure on the skin it troubled him little. Helga or Sparrow could milk the cow for Tindr, and his other chores he did with his left hand.

Rannveig told me the tar-maker had left to his upland burning-works, and it was thought he would return to build a new tar shop on one of the side roads. But the ware-house man would begin as soon as his site was cool to build again.

Later that day I returned with Sidroc to the trading road. He had awoken with a head that still ached, but he had eaten, and begun to feel better. I had not seen him drunk before, but it was for good cause. He had fought a losing battle against the fire and placed himself in danger. He had suffered a painful burn, and then found that three of our millstones had split. He had seen Runulv, whom he liked and hoped to enrich, suffer his own disappointing loss. He had eaten nothing to help absorb the ale and stronger wine. And he had paid for a few hours' forgetfulness with an aching head.

The light rain had tapered to a mist. As we stopped before the ware-house we peered though it to the middle of what had been the building. We could not see the millstones, but knew they were there, lying flat and covered with wet ash, the soot masking the fact that three-quarters of their value was lost to us. Sidroc made no move to walk in and look at them again.

"We will pull the one out, then Tindr and I will ride back to Thorfast's," he said, still looking in at the wreckage. His voice was slightly husky from the smoke he had breathed. "I will see if he can bring me a few querns which I can send to Frankland."

He would first have to pay Thorfast for the second set of millstones, plus the extra quarter's worth he had promised him, all for two stones which had been destroyed. If on top of that he bought querns…It would be hard to risk so much silver, but so much more now depended on this first shipment.

As we stood there a couple walked our way – Runulv and Gyda. Ring was with them too, and I could see they talked together. Gyda had a basket on her arm, and I thought she must be headed to Rannveig with some gift for her, just as all the others had done. I was glad to see them, and gave her a kiss. Runulv and Ring had the same smoke-reddened eyes as Sidroc, and the three men looked at each other.

"You got home," Sidroc said to them both.

"And you," returned Runulv, with a grin.

We all now stood, looking at the charred square which had formed the boundaries of the ware-house.

"I will order new millstones, for next year," Sidroc said. "And buy some querns now, for you to take in their stead. Querns from such good stone as Gotland's are always wanted."

It was good to hear him speak thus, to plan anew for us. So I was surprised by his next word.

"Nai," he said of a sudden.

He paused and looked not at Runulv but at his brother. "I will not send querns to Frankland. If I can rent a ship and buy salt, will you go to Dane-mark with it? Go as soon as we can sail? They need salt, and the querns will fetch as much there as at Frankland. A third of all you take in will be yours."

Ring looked stunned.

"And to Frankland?" asked Runulv.

"The amber to Frankland, as we had always planned. But Ring will sail with you as far as Dane-mark, with salt and querns."

The amber filled only two small baskets, as precious as it was. An idea came to me, and I spoke it.

"Honey," I offered. "Honey can go to Frankland too. Tindr has crocks of it; his bees did so well last Summer. I could have jars made up by the potter, and see if the folk of Frankland prize it as much as we."

"Good," said Sidroc, not needing to think more on it. His smile said much.

Ring had still not spoken. He had been ready to sail with his brother, and now was being offered his own ship. I knew he had fished the Baltic with his father, but never sailed so far as Dane-mark, and never to trade.

"Will you?" Sidroc asked again. His thoughts moved on, for he asked next, "Who has a ship I can rent?"

"Orm, an old fisherman, has a good ship," Ring answered. "He does not go out until it truly warms."

"I will speak to him," Sidroc answered.

Runulv and Gyda were both beaming in excitement at Ring.

"So you, Ring, to Dane-mark with salt and querns, and in Orm's ship if he will hire it out," summed up Sidroc. "Runulv, if you can buy more salt yourself, it can go with you or with Ring. Either way it will reach a ready market."

Runulv nodded his assent; Sidroc had told him Eskil's news, that salt was in short supply in Dane-mark.

Ring at last seemed to believe it all, and said, "Já. To Dane-mark with salt and querns."

The ruins behind us meant little at that moment. We gave a low cheer in our new-found hopes.

"And to Frankland, amber and honey," ended Sidroc, looking at Runulv.

"Tree-gold, and bee-gold," I added, to which we all laughed.

That night, as I was re-wrapping the linen about his hand, I asked Sidroc why he suddenly thought of splitting the brothers up and sending two ships.

It took him a moment to answer. I thought perhaps I was hurting him as I wrapped the burn, and stopped in what I did. The skin beneath was inflamed but the blisters no longer oozed. He looked at my hands poised around his and nodded I should go on.

"If one ship is lost, one brother still lives," he told me. He paused another moment. "If one is lost, half the goods we send away will remain, to bring us silver."

Now I had to stop. I had not wanted to think about the dangers of the voyage. I knew Runulv had willingly made trading trips these past three Summers, taking his salt about the Baltic, and was eager to sail for us, and eager to sail so far as Frankland. But in doing so we were sending him. The Gods might summon him; the seas swallow him; or raiders capture him. All who sailed ran those risks, and must accept them. Yet we, and especially Sidroc, would be in some measure answerable if he did not return. An image of lovely Gyda and their little son rose in my brain.

I could not let myself dwell on this, and knew it. I truly wished the success of this trading venture, the safe return of Runulv and Ring, and for Sidroc to be richly repaid for his plans and efforts. This would be the first of many such ventures we attempted, and none might be as important as this. Yet there was new life within me, and having been granted this, my deepest thoughts and hopes had drawn me on to another realm. I knew, even the day of the fire, that the loss of our millstones did not trouble me as much as it would have if Sidroc's babe had not been resting under my heart. There was another I was already living for.

"When I found the stones had split, I cursed Fate," Sidroc went on. "But I had not yet moved the amber there as well. We did not lose that too, it was still safe. Standing there with them I remembered that."

Odin may have thrown a lightning-bolt, but Sidroc would not be deterred. He would note it and go on.

I pressed the tips of his fingers with my own. "They will come back; both of them. With silver for us all."

Tindr was not happy. I knew his arm pained him, and I dressed it as gently as I could. At first I used more of the butter-violet mixture on it, but as it began to heal I smeared the burn with his own honey to sooth and soften the skin. The blistered skin sloughed off, showing the pinkish tissue below was unmarked. The burn was on his bow arm, tho' he did little hunting in Spring, but it was a time he set snares for the large blue hares, and the arm hurt to move it. Sparrow was glad to milk the cow each morning, but Tindr's restlessness was deeper than his forced inaction. So I looked forward to asking him if he wanted to throw in with us and send his honey to Frankland.

I waved him over to the table inside the kitchen shed. I took two small pottery jars from our store and set them down next to the crock of honey that always sat there. I lifted my hands to the empty jars before us, then pointed at the filled crock. I pinched together my thumb and forefinger and moved it around my head, Tindr's sign for his bees. He

smiled at this and nodded. I slipped the tip of my tongue out
to touch my upper lip, and smiled back: Your honey – into
these jars.

I pushed my hand away: Go; and made a wave-like
motion of my hand to signify the sea. I pulled my hand back:
Come. I touched the thick braid of silver I wore at my neck,
then pointed to Tindr: Silver for Tindr.

He frowned slightly, and made a little grunt. I pointed
to the honey, and again gestured the sea, and touched at the
silver at my neck, and then my ear. Silver for Tindr.

He shrugged, but gave his quick shy smile. Then he
nodded his head. Tindr had few wants he could not supply
himself, or with the help of Rannveig; and as the lady of
Tyrsborg it was my duty to feed and clothe him. But he took
pride in the silver pin on his mantle given him by Sidroc, and
perhaps not only as reward for his hunting prowess, but
because the pin itself possessed beauty. Here was a way to
earn silver through the labour of his bees.

I had a plan to sell his golden honey not from large
crocks, but to put it up in sealed small jars. Most honey-
sellers I had seen dipped the sticky goodness out and ladled it
into cups or pots carried by buyers. The apple-cheeked
honey-women from the trading post had shown me
something different, for they had put up their honey in many
different sized jars, making it not only easy to choose but easy
to carry away.

I went that afternoon to one of the potters on the
trading road, and asked her to make up two score jars, all the
same size. The smallness of them would, I hoped, underscore
the goodness of what was within, and make each jar safer and
easier to transport and handle. Tindr could cut wooden lids
for them, and once filled we could use molten beeswax to seal
the jars completely. His honey was so good that I felt certain

that if Runulv opened a jar and gave out samples, almost all who tasted would buy.

As I planned for this Sidroc's words kept sounding in my ears, about the risk of either Runulv or Ring not returning. My thoughts went over and again to Ása, the young woman Ring hoped to wed. He had as yet nothing to support her with; Ring lived at home with his father Botair, and she with her family on their farm. He would have gained some silver by going as part of his brother's crew, but now stood the chance to earn his own by taking salt and querns to Sidroc's homeland. If he did well and could furnish a home for Ása, her people would consent to their hand-fast.

I did not want them to have to wait. I had seen how quickly the fire had changed the hopes and goals of those who had lost goods, and knew firsthand the risks both brothers faced at sea. Life was uncertain, and could be short. I resolved to help Ring and Ása, and in doing so to help us, as well. I told Sidroc of my answer for all this.

Spring was well along, the forest decked in its brightest and freshest greenery, and the tracks that ran through it dry enough for waggon travel. I wanted to go to Rannveig's old farm, with Rannveig and Tindr, and with Runulv and Gyda and Ring and Ása. Ragnfast and Estrid, who lived close nearby, would meet us there. We would bring food and drink and walk beneath the pink and white flowers of the many apple trees.

Rannveig and I went by ox cart, for she sometimes borrowed one from a neighbour when she had need. I did not want to ride my mare, and would have enjoyed the woodland walk, but going with Rannveig meant we could cart the crock of ale and pottery cups, pots of soft cheese and skyr, and smoked deer haunch with ease. And it gave me the pleasure of her company as we moved at a walk at the head of the big brown animal. The cart was too broad for the forest tracks so we went up one of the side roads from the trading road and off through fields from there.

Sidroc and Tindr rode our horses to the farm, not always easy through the narrow tracks, but the trees were not yet fully in leaf. The burns of their arms had healed well, and the singed hair was beginning to grow back through the still slightly reddened skin. I knew Tindr looked forward to this day; he was ever glad to ride out, and we would be seeing his cousin and family too. Sidroc and he were carrying part of our provender, leathern bags stuffed with loaves of bread hung from their saddles. The brothers and Gyda and Ása would walk.

Our ox walked slower than all, for even tho' Rannveig and I made an early start we were the last there. But it was a pleasure to be greeted by all, to see Ragnfast and Estrid after the long Winter, and to be surrounded by their romping children, and Gyda and Runulv's little boy. Sidroc and Tindr had taken the door key and opened the rusted box lock with it, carrying out benches and a table to set in the warm Sun for us. I had not yet seen the inside of the farmhouse, which tho' small and dusty, was snugly dry and had not only six alcoves, but several old but usable tables and benches.

We sat to eat. The apples were indeed in full bloom, their petals dropping pink and white over the lengthening green grass surrounding their gnarled trunks. Little white wind-flowers also dotted the grasses, ranging as far as the neglected fields ran. What was meadow and scrub growth woods was once good farmland, and we must make it so once more.

We passed around the bread and slices of smoked deer, and laughed and talked as the little ones circled round us, whooping as they clambered in the low crotches of the apple trees, stopping to swoop in for a slice of bread or meat offered by their mothers. Estrid's small daughter Alvild was just beginning to stand, and she pumped her plump legs up and down in the tender grass as she clung to her mother's reaching forefingers.

Gyda sat next me. She always wore her two large oval brooches of well-worked silver, one at each shoulder to fasten her gown. Save for the morning of the fire I had never seen her without them. But today she wore paired brooches of cast bronze like onto those that most women of Gotland wore. I could not keep my eyes from resting on her shoulders, and she saw this.

"My brooches," she explained. "They have gone for salt."

So she had sold or traded her fine silver brooches to replace the lost salt. I glanced to where her husband's hand lay upon the table; his silver cuff was not upon his wrist. I took her hand and squeezed it.

"It was my choice," she went on. "Runulv bought them for me from the profit he made trading salt, and to salt they have once again gone."

"And from salt will your silver return," I said, with true feeling.

Her cousin Ása sat on the other side of her, smiling and following with her eyes the antics of Estrid's boy and girl and Gyda's little boy. It was for her this outing was called, tho' she knew it not.

I looked at Sidroc, sitting across the table from me. He nodded and put down the pottery cup which held his ale.

"Friends," he said, with a grin. "We know the most welcome guests listen well at their host's table. Therefore we will now listen to my wife."

All looked at me. I took a breath and stood up, and began.

"Ring and Ása," I said, not able to keep myself from smiling. "All know you wish to join hands." Ása blushed pink, and a flush grew too on Ring's cheek. I rocked back a little on my heels and went on.

"We have this fine farm which Rannveig has sold to us. It is close to town and blessed with apples." Here I smiled again as the slender petals were blowing through the air and landing on us as I spoke. "But we have no one to farm it.

"You cannot hand-fast until you have a fitting place to live. Sidroc and I offer you half-interest in this farm. It will not take much to put the house to rights. We will send the timber for the new barn roof. You can start as soon as you like to clear some space and sow barley and rye. Ring will not be sailing for another month."

I did not know what more to say. Ása had her hand to her lips and Ring looked quickly at his brother Runulv, whose face was nearly as surprised as his.

I had told Rannveig of our plan on our walk, wanting to be sure she approved. To break the silence she called out heartily now.

"Ring, Ása, say já," she prompted. She lifted her arms in encouragement, making her keys jingle where they rested in her lap. "Say já!"

Ása and Ring looked at each other. Ring stood and stepped to her, and took her hand before us.

"Já," they said, almost as one.

Ring and Ása made their hand-fast and drank their bridal-ale a few days later. They bid Sidroc and me and Tindr and Rannveig join the other witnesses at Ása's family farm. We gathered before the front door of the farmhouse, beneath the clear and brilliant light of late afternoon. The young couple wore their best clothes, a green woollen tunic and brown leggings for Ring, and a newly-sewn gown of blue for Ása. She had woven a necklace of violets which lay between her paired shoulder brooches like the loveliest of purple gemstones.

Ring hoped to farm and raise animals, and in his hand he held a hand scythe, the means by which he hoped to provide for Ása in the coming years. Ása, like almost all maids, held a spindle, the sign that would dedicate her hand-craft to the welfare of her husband and children. But she also clutched a dibbler in her hand, the small pointed wooden tool used to open a single hole in the soil to hold a seed. She smiled at me as she took this up; she now would have a good patch of earth to cultivate as well.

They passed the tools of their livelihoods each to each, and joined hands. Ása's aged grandmother wrapped a single woollen thread that her granddaughter had spun around the clasping hands. Ása's father took from round his neck a small bronze Mjollnir, tiny version of Thor's mighty hammer, and dropped this as consecration about his daughter's slender white neck.

"Ring will care for Ása, do his best by her, and harm her not," promised Ring.

"And I, Ása, will give Ring no cause to regret this day," she answered. "The works of my hand I pledge to you and our coming children."

These simple words and age-old acts of exchange bound them as man and wife.

The Hall of Tyr

Botair handed his son a cup of ale, from which Ring drank, and then Ása. We gave a shout of gladness. Now there was the sacrifice to Freyr to make. Ring had chosen a young goat to give as Offering, one of the best of a small number he had been raising up. The goat was tethered, alone, to a sapling tree nearby. When we had arrived Tindr knelt next it and fed it carrots, so that its last meal should be one of sweetness.

We circled round it now. Ring had taken up an axe in one hand, and laid the other on the beast's horned head.

"This goat was given me by Freyr, as all animals are given by Freyr and his sister to feed and clothe us. To Freyr I send it back, asking his blessing upon me and my wife."

He let his hand rest a moment longer on the goat's head, then swung two-handedly with the blunt end of the axe, felling the animal in a blow. A quick stroke of his knife across the corded throat watered the earth with the animal's blood. That bright red fluid seeped into the waiting soil. In it was the young goat's fecundity, its animal drive to rut and breed, its eagerness to eat and thrive; life itself, now returned to a moistened and receptive earth as Freyr's own.

Ása's mother and younger sisters passed quietly between us, handing cups of ale that we might toast the passing of the goat to the endless green fields where wandered Freyr's flock. The body would be lifted to the sky to be eaten of by crows and ravens and any other feathered thing, taking the animal spirit ever closer to Asgard.

Now it was time for the bridal-feast. When Ása came to kiss me, tears stood in my eyes as well.

"Your kindness will never be forgotten," she whispered. "May all your young ones find favour with Freyr."

290

I felt my body course with gratitude that we could, through giving Ring a ship to sail and them the farm, aid them towards a new life of their own.

Runulv had helped them ready our farm house, as had Ása's father and mother, for both families were gladdened at the union. They had been given a small flock of sheep by her parents, twenty of the curly-horned long-haired ewes and two black and white rams, who were set to good use at once pulling at the long grass everywhere about. Ring's father Botair gave them ten hens and a rooster, all young; six grey geese and a quarrelsome gander; and three nannies to add to Ring's growing herd of goats.

The new couple dug and turned over the waiting soil and planted long rows of grains, and poked in the seeds of carrots, parsnips, radish, skirrets, cabbage, and pot greens. It would be enough to feed them this year, with some for we at Tyrsborg, and in the Fall they could expand the ground cleared for grain and vegetables to feed both themselves and us. Ring went to work mending the barn roof, hammering up pens, and fixing the tumbled down outbuildings. The bond between uncle and nephew was always strong amongst Northern folk, and his uncle Ketil came and worked at his side at this, bringing him also much strong hempen rope as a bridal gift.

Sidroc and Tindr rode to the southern tip of Gotland, taking silver and the news to Thorfast the stone-shaper that three of the millstones were broken. They travelled fast and were back in four days. It was the first time we had been parted overnight, but it could not be helped. It was enough to have Sidroc wrap me in his arms when he returned, and then to hear the welcome news that Thorfast would come soon with ten querns which we could send to Frankland. On the way back Tindr had again taken Sidroc to the great ash, and he again left silver threaded in the tree's reaching boughs.

"Twice as much silver," Sidroc told me, "for now we need twice as much help."

Chapter the Seventeenth: The Magic Horn

RUNULV was fast at work readying his ship and picking the men who would form his crew. His ship was a broad-beamed fishing boat, a little larger than most, and, he had told us with a young man's grin, faster than any which fished the Baltic. It had been beached all Winter over past the fish-drying racks at the end of the trading road, where many of the fishing folk stored their craft, and had dried out during the long months out of water. Runulv primed it for sailing by pouring water inside until the straked boards swelled and closed the narrow gaps which had opened. Then he and Sidroc and Ring heaved it down on rollers to the high water mark, raised the mast, fastened the cross-laid linen sail upon it, and used the freshening wind to drive it over the water back to the trading road, and to the pier.

I was at Rannveig's and watched them sail in. We were in her herb garden and she had bent to pluck a handful of new mugwort leaves to flavour her ale. As she straightened up she winced and put her hand on her hip.

"Just a hitch," she said, trying to dismiss it. She had been feeling poorly the last few days, with running pains in her legs, and had just found out that the young woman who helped her serve her ale each evening was shortly to be wed. "It is the Spring winds; I will fare better when Summer comes."

"Let me send Sparrow down to you," I offered. "She can work in the garden or with the washing-up. You need her more than Helga or Gunnvor, and she likes being here with you."

"I will be glad to have her," she agreed. We turned our eyes to Runulv's ship, now edging closer to the long line

293

of the pier. They had dropped the sail down. As they neared Ring leapt from the prow onto the wooden planks of the pier, and Sidroc threw him a line so he might draw the ship close.

"It is like seeing our future sail in," I had to jest, for indeed so much was wrapped up in our hopes for the coming voyage. Rannveig gave a little pat to my expanded waistline.

"Not all good things come by ship," she jested back.

I left her and went down to where the men now stood on the pier, tying up Runulv's ship. When they finished they stood together, eyeing her. Broad-beamed as she was, she was stable, able to carry nets full of herring and cod, or large amounts of cargo. Runulv had told us she was strong as well, for he had been caught in more than one Summer storm and she had stood up ably to the angry waves.

They all nodded to me as I joined them, but seemed lost in thought; and I let my own eyes rest once again on the brown hull before us.

"What," Sidroc asked, "would make her faultless? What one thing is lacking to win your way to our goal?"

Runulv's blue-green eyes went from Sidroc back to his ship.

"I think she could carry more sail: I have always thought so," he decided. "A taller mast, a larger sail. I could get more speed from her, strong as she is, if I had that."

Runulv's ship carried only eight oars, four at the stem and four at the stern, and must depend chiefly on its sail to outrun any raiders in pursuit. I thought Sidroc would agree to almost anything that promised to make the ship faster, and he did now. Runulv was looking back to Sidroc for his answer.

"Then we will put this sail on Orm's ship, which needs it, for Ring to take to Dane-mark," Sidroc said, "and shape a new mast for yours. Can we get a larger sail in time?"

"Já, my father has extra we can start with, and early as it is a few of the traders or fishermen will have cloth I can buy or borrow for coming silver," came the answer.

"We will do it," Sidroc said. Both brothers were pleased at this, but Sidroc's thoughts had moved on.

"For arms –" he went on, and paused.

I had never seen a single man of Gotland with a sword, tho' I knew some must exist, even as family heirlooms, well-wrapped and laying in the bottom of locked chests. Men here had rarely-used spears for defence, and bows for hunting. A few men who traded and thus faced the dangers of the Baltic knew how to use the deadly battle-axe in close quarters. Runulv, we knew, was one of them.

"You may have to fight," Sidroc reminded, simply and quietly.

Runulv had had no problem finding young men who wanted to throw in with him for the journey to Frankland, both for the share of silver they would receive from Runulv's pay, and for the chance to take their own goods, or those of their parents, to trade there. Some fashioned combs from sawn cow horn, or made leathern goods, or collected salt, or had dried fish to sell. One had chunks of amber he had found washed up on the rocky beaches. All would get to see a new and different land. Runulv had his pick of them, and the best of those he did not choose Ring marked to take with him to Dane-mark.

"Each man has a spear and shield," Runulv told him. "All are good bow-men, and all will have axes. And all know the sea and can row hard when needed."

Ring's smaller ship would carry six men besides
himself. His men would also bear spears, and tho' none had
battle-axes, would carry wood axes for fighting in close
quarters if needed. Like the men who would sail with his
brother Runulv, all chosen for Ring's ship were skilled with
bow and arrow.

Sidroc wished to see them for himself, and had the
whole group of them troop up by day to Tyrsborg, fifteen
young men. Over the course of several days he and Tindr
needed to replace the splintered spear targets on the stable
wall twice. I was working at my loom just inside the hall by
the open side door, hearing all, and able to watch as well
when I turned my head to where they practised by the stable.

He had them throw their spears at the targets from a
standstill, and from a run, and then challenged them to
balance on boards which lay upon peeled wood rollers, in
imitation of the pitching of a ship. The men jested and
laughed as they did this, tho' the sweat beaded on their brows
as they hurled their spears over and again in the warm air.
Sidroc jested back at them, but with his practised eye I
wondered how he judged them. None were trained warriors,
none had had need to fight to kill a man, or to keep
themselves alive. They knew the danger that they might be
pursued, might be caught and boarded, but standing or
running in the grassy forecourt of our hall could not make
these dangers real to them.

If they were pursued the best course was to try to
outrun the pursuer, which meant all men rowing and the sail
at its utmost. If this failed and they were to be boarded, a
steady flight of arrows could kill or wound enough of the
raiders to allow them to once again take up oars and escape.
If this did not deter the attack, the men's spears would be
used against an enemy swinging, climbing, or jumping from
ship rail to rail, tho' once thrown they could rarely be
recovered. The final tool they could use to repel a raiding

party would be their axes, in hand-to-hand combat. Raiders like Ulf or Red-beard would have swords, and men like Eskil ring-shirts and iron helmets too. I did not like to look out at these young Gotlanders and think of them meeting any of them.

One of the men, a little bigger and more boisterous than the rest, was given to snickering at Sidroc's words. Gaut was tall, broad-shouldered, with reddish hair and big meaty hands. He had sailed with other men of Gotland to a few of the Baltic trading posts, and now was to sail with Ring to Dane-mark. Like some large men, he was given to trusting his size as a deterrent. Yet he tired easily; I knew from my years amongst warriors at Kilton that such men had not learnt to develop or control their strength. He was also cocky.

"We Gotlanders are the best sailors in the Baltic," he spouted. "We will not get caught. Not with me rowing."

Sidroc had had the men sparring, shields high, practicing aiming blows with their axes when their opponents lowered their shields to take their own swing. Gaut had set his shield down at his feet, and wiped his brow with the back of his tunic sleeve.

Sidroc's eyes narrowed. He fastened them a moment on Gaut, then turned on his heel and walked into Tyrsborg, passing me where I stood at my loom. He went to the treasure room, unlocked the door, and went in. He came back carrying his own shield, and with his sword hanging at his side. Other than throwing spears with the men he had not practised with them, nor worn any weapons but his long jewelled-hilted seax. He stood once more before the gathered men.

"Runulv," he said.

Runulv picked up his own shield, battle-axe in hand, and stepped forward. I thought Sidroc chose him as he was the most skilled in defence, and it was clear Sidroc meant to spar with him.

He addressed all the men, but his words were for Gaut.

"You are going to Dane-mark. Landing there, you will be safe, free to trade, free to leave. On land, our laws will punish any who rob you or kill you, just as if you yourselves had been Danes. But sailing there you will be fair game. My brothers will be out hunting."

Sidroc drew his sword. He just held it a moment poised in his hand, the blade slightly uplifted and catching the glint of the Sun as he moved his wrist.

He turned his eyes back to Runulv. I moved closer to the door. I saw Runulv swallow as he raised his shield, axe-arm drawn back behind and above it.

"Now," said Sidroc.

They stepped towards each other. Sidroc swung and hit the rim of Runulv's shield with a sharp downward blow, making Runulv stagger and step back. Runulv recovered, came forward, and opened his shield slightly so he could aim his own blow, but Sidroc lifted his shield in time and Runulv pulled it back, not wanting the edge of the axe to get caught in the lifted wood. Sidroc turned quickly sideways and thrust again, nearly catching Runulv in his other shoulder, but again Runulv was able to raise his shield in time. He gave a sudden push with it, and if Sidroc had not had his sword ready for another downward blow Runulv might have been able to knock him back and off balance.

"Good," said Sidroc. "Now you, Gaut." Sidroc did not stop in his play with Runulv, kept shifting his shield, taking aim with his sword, as he waited for Gaut to step in and take Runulv's place.

Runulv had a true battle-axe, all steel, long shafted; and Gaut, like the rest of the men who would sail with Ring, a wood-cutting axe with a shorter, wooden shaft. Gaut would now be made to test it against the long sword of a Danish warrior. If he felt unease it did not much show in his red face. He bit his lip and stepped forward as Runulv stepped away.

Gaut raised his shield and stood a moment, still, and waiting. Sidroc swung up, surprising Gaut by almost knocking the shield off his arm from underneath, then sent a ringing blow to the rim on the side. Gaut was moving to shift the shield so he could aim a blow of his own when Sidroc swung the blade down at Gaut's leading ankle, stopping it just before it struck the top of his booted foot. The sword came perilously close and Gaut bounded back a step. It all happened in a moment.

"Now your foot is off," Sidroc told him. "You are sprawled on the deck bleeding to death. Your eyes are darkening. And I have gone on to the next man."

"What – what could I do?" Gaut asked.

"You waited for me; never wait. Hit first. Use your axe as quickly as you can, and anywhere you can. Foot, calf, thigh, head, back. Any unguarded place. You do not have the long reach or the long edge of a sword. You must use power and speed to strike a blow anywhere you can. Knock your man down, then finish him."

I moved back to my loom, but his next words were still clear.

"Always finish him. Many men are killed by turning their backs on one who still has strength to throw a knife."

Runulv had decided that the salt he and Gyda had bartered for with their brooches and wrist cuff would go with his brother Ring to Dane-mark. Eskil the Svear had told Sidroc of the shortage there, and Sidroc would make the most of this knowledge and sell salt of our own to his old home. We had bought our table salt from the trading road, small pottery jars of it at a time. Now we went together to the stall with the green awnings, to buy as many casks of it as Asfrid would part with. She was the widow of a fisherman, with a small house down the coast past the fish drying racks. Large flat rocks, reaching to the lapping sea, lay like stepping stones before her house, and were the source of her salt.

Asfrid collected it herself, ladling dippersful of sea water into shallow rock salt-pans, covering them under threat of rain, raking the growing salt by day and plucking out the largest crystals. Her salt was soft white, pure, and mild, for the Baltic is not a very salty sea, with sharp-angled flakes and many perfectly formed square crystals. For all these reasons it was well prized. I knew Eskil had taken Sidroc's advice and bought his salt from her, and now we would send four small barrels of it across the sea to Dane-mark, two belonging to Runulv and Gyda and two of our own.

She could sell us no more, for fear of not having enough for her regular trade, but we were running short of silver, and could not have bought much more. Of the eight pieces of gold Sidroc had marked to make our start in trading and buy what was needful for our new lives, only two pieces and a quarter remained. One whole piece had gone to Rannveig as part payment for Tyrsborg and her farm; a one-third piece for our horses and their kit; the rest gone to all else we had bought, either for Tyrsborg and the farm, to rent Orm's ship, or to send out trading.

My twelve gold pieces lay safe and sealed in their little jar beneath the floorboards of the treasure room. Knowing they were there eased my own mind, but I knew to Sidroc they did not exist. Despite the setback we had suffered with the loss of our millstones, and the added cost of sending two ships and not one, he would make our way with eight pieces and no more.

The potter came up the hill to Tyrsborg with a cart hauling the forty small jars she had made for Tindr's honey. She had done well, made them as nearly alike as she could, and they had straight sides and a bluish tinge to their glazed faces. I paid her her silver, hoping that whatever Runulv could earn from the honey would make the sum look small. We did not know how to price the honey; Runulv would walk the stalls of wherever he landed and see what was asked, gauge the worth of Tindr's against that which he tried there, and so set a price.

Tindr set to work cutting rounds of wood to top the jars. He had beeswax enough to use to seal the tops to the pottery rims, and Sparrow and I made a fine afternoon of ladling in the golden honey and melting the combed wax in a small but deep cauldron. When the jars were nearly full we took a wooden spoon and ran a bit of molten wax along the top rim, then stuck the wooden top on this until it cooled firm. The finished jars were handsome to look at, and Tindr smiled and nodded when he saw all of them lined up, ready to be packed in straw and set within closed woven baskets for the long trip ahead.

There was something else I would send to Frankland. In the bottom of my work-basket from the Idrisid slave ship sat the two cinnamon sticks, lying by the two little pots of reddened beeswax and the black eye-powder. One of the sticks had come with the work-basket, but the larger one had been given me by the old spice-merchant. He told me it would bring enough to dower the two daughters he foretold me bearing. I could see his bald and shining head now, bobbing above the lustre of his yellow silk robes. He had told me to sell the cinnamon to a Frank.

301

I had not thought to send them this first trading trip; it was not perhaps prudent to send so much of our wealth on one ship. Yet in late Summer I would bring forth a child, and if it were a daughter it would honour the old man's kindness to me to have followed his instruction. And Runulv sailed to Frankland, to the land the spice merchant had directed me to. With the loss of the millstones I felt this was one more risk worth the taking. I brought the fragrant bark curls to my lips and kissed each one, asking Freyja to keep them safe for the sake of my coming girl.

I did not know how to package them, but thought that if I made slender linen pouches, one for each, that would serve, and I did so. I thought of the tiny cups of amber that we were sending, and recalled how I thought they might be destined to hold precious healing unguents. The sticks were used in healing, the priest Eardwulf had told me so, and the same rich man or woman who bought the tiny cups might buy the cinnamon. When I told Runulv this both he and Sidroc listened carefully. Sidroc knew I meant to send the sticks and was glad for it, but what he said now surprised me.

"Do you want none but silver for them?" he asked me.

I did not understand, until he said the rest.

"The spice-merchant said your gain would be large. That means much silver; a gold piece, perhaps. Would you care if Runulv brings you their value in iron?"

Now I understood. Iron always had value, and good iron was highly prized. Above the trading road there was an iron-smith who forged tools, and a weapon-smith who hammered fine blades, carried away each Summer by his brother to Baltic ports. Both smiths were prosperous, but Rannveig had told us the weapon-smith was one of the richest men on Gotland.

302

"If Runulv brings the value of your cinnamon in iron bars, your gain will be the greater. They would buy a great weight's worth of iron. The blade-maker will pay back all your silver, and more, for bars from Frankland."

I looked down at the two narrow linen pouches in my hand. Good iron was as noble as silver or gold, and as any warrior would tell you, far more precious in a fight.

"Then turn these into iron, Runulv," I said with a smile.

Sidroc and I had been at the brew-house one night when Rannveig asked us both to come down to her in the morning, as she had something to show us. Tho' I saw her nearly every day and had many times been inside her house, Sidroc never had. We found her in her brewing yard over one of her crocks, as was usual of a morning. She wiped her hands and nodded to us, and paused a moment before she spoke.

"I have something to sell," she said, looking at Sidroc. "To go on your ship, if you will take it."

We followed her past her herb garden and rows of growing vegetables to the door of her house, which she left open behind us to allow more light. Rannveig knew we were taking pots of Tindr's honey; perhaps she wanted to send along some of her fragrant beeswax tapers; these would fetch a good price in any port.

But she led us past her small trestle table where we might expect to find candles waiting, and drew back the wool curtains to her sleeping alcove. I had never seen inside her alcove, which was large, and surprised me by having all the inner walls lined with hangings of coloured thread-work, much like the cushions of red, blue, and black she had upon her benches. She pulled up the coverlet which hung down from the box bed, to reveal a little door fitted with a small iron lock. She sorted through the bunch of keys at her waist and found the right one. She reached in with one hand, and drew out the end of a narrow wooden box, and kept pulling on it. The box was so long we had to step back to give her room to do so.

She set the box on top of her bed. It was, I think, as long as both my arms open and outstretched; I had never seen such an odd container, long and quite narrow.

The lid was unhinged, and she lifted it off and set in upon the down coverlet. The box was packed with straw, dry and now dusty, but I saw what the straw was protecting.

It was a single animal horn, long and straight, buff in colour, but unlike any I had seen, and I could not imagine what kind of deer or other beast could grow a thing of such length. It was as long as the box that held it.

Sidroc let out a low whistle. "Some fool in Frankland will give you gold for this," he said, and smiled.

Rannveig placed her hands on her hips and grinned at us.

"Where did you get it?" he asked.

Her grin softened. "Dagr," she told us, "was also a good dice player."

So her husband had won it, whatever it was.

"What is it?" I had to know.

"The horn of a narwhale," answered Sidroc. "It is a small whale, but they grow these long horns on their snouts, one only."

Sidroc had told me of whales, and we bought the fatty oil of them for our cressets, but I had never seen one. I tried to picture one with this growing from its head.

"In Frankland they tell tales of a woodland creature, like a horse or a deer, who wears such a horn," he went on. "They are greatly prized for healing, and in other magic."

I reached out to touch it. It was hard and yet grainy, with a spiralling curve that reached the whole length of it. It tapered to a perfect unbroken tip.

"What kind of magic?" I wanted to know.

"Ah – man-magic," he said. "Placed over or under the bed, they give potency to men."

"O," was all I could say.

"What will your price be?" Sidroc asked Rannveig.

She cocked her chin. Her eyes went to Sidroc for help.

He looked again at the horn, lying pale and perfect in the straw.

"Its weight in gold," he offered.

Rannveig made a little gasp. "Will it bring that?"

Sidroc reached in and lifted the horn in both hands. It looked like a spear of magic in his grasp.

"It is not heavy, but heavy enough," he told her.

He made his decision. "Its weight in gold."

She put her hand to her brow. "Whatever it will bring…" she began. Her voice caught and I saw tears brimming in her eyes. "The gold will be for Tindr."

Sidroc and I looked at each other. We had neither of
us met any man who cared less for treasure than Rannveig's
son. Rannveig saw us, brushed her hand under her eyes, and
gave a smile.

"If Tindr is rich, I will not worry about him so much
when I die. If he is rich, then…perhaps folk will see how well
he could care for a wife." She wiped her hands on her apron
front, smoothing it.

She drew a deep breath and let it out before she said
the next. "I cannot leave him to the skogsrå, if it is already
not too late for him."

So she feared the Lady of the Forest had already
claimed her son.

"Gold could help Tindr get a woman of his own," she
ended.

We neither of us said anything, but I nodded to her. I
looked again to the treasure sitting before us. The box the
horn lay in was indeed plain, but sound and undamaged.

"A horn of such magic needs a fitting box to carry it,"
I told them both. "If you will let me take the box to Tyrsborg,
I can use a poker to burn in designs to decorate it. Also I will
line the box with sheepskin, as sword scabbards are lined."

"Já, take it," Rannveig said. "I thank you for that."
The remains of her tears were still glittering in her eyes.

I did not want to have the precious narwhale horn in
my keeping, and we made Rannveig take the horn and wrap it
in linen and return it safe under her bed.

Sidroc and I walked up the hill to Tyrsborg, the empty
box in his arms. I had never seen Rannveig even close to tears
before, and could not forget her hidden distress.

"She truly fears for Tindr," I said to Sidroc. "That he will never wed, and even that he has given himself to the skogsrå." He was silent at my side, but I went on.

"Could you…ask Tindr if he…" My voice trailed off, as I did not know quite how to say it.

He raised his eyebrows at me. "Ask Tindr if he has lain with a wood-spirit," he guessed. "Ah – nai. I cannot do that."

"Besides," he went on after a moment, "to lie with such a lady…she would place the man under a bind-spell of some kind; I do not think he could tell of it if he wanted to."

I saw he thought about this, and after seeing Rannveig's tears it troubled me. One of the old women at Rannveig's brew-house who told tales of the skogsrå held that any man who spent the night in her arms would soon die. The other did not go that far, only warning that he could never again lie with a mortal woman. Both of these women, tho' old, were respected, even revered, for their wisdom; in Angle-land I knew they would be seen as mad crones or even witches.

"Do you think he is in danger?" I spurred myself to ask. "Rannveig told me he has never had a sweetheart; none of the girls will have him. If the Lady of the Forest, or Freyja herself, comes to him, and has taken him to her bower…?"

Now he answered. "He has never had a woman…if there were a whore on the trading road I would take him to her." He shook his head. "Nai, I would not. Tindr must go to his first woman in love, not just lust." We were almost at Tyrsborg. "And if Freyja has taken him to bed, he has had the pleasure I have with you."

I reached out my hand to where one of his held the narwhale horn box. "Thank you for saying that," I said, "all of it."

The new sail for Runulv's ship was pieced together and carried to the pier. Like all the sails of Gotland, it was formed of narrow strips of linen, laid aslant across each other, and sewn only at top and bottom. The sail would billow and fill, but not rip, even in the strongest winds, for some wind could ever escape from its straining curve, and no seams were tried that could split under stress. Gyda had sent half of the linen strips to her family farm, where her mother had dyed the long rolls madder red. Crossed with the white of the undyed linen it made a fine show, with one red square above a white and a white above a red. We were all at the pier the first time it was hoisted. The new mast rose high above our heads, and the big sail filled nearly the length of the deck. I could not help but clap my hands in pleasure in seeing it all. The warehouse in which we had lost our millstones and Runulv and Gyda their salt was behind us, newly built of fresh white timber, smelling of its tree sap. Our remaining millstone was back within, awaiting a mate for next season. But today we knew gladness, and that smoke-filled morning felt far away.

Orm's ship, which Ring would sail to Dane-mark, was rigged with Runulv's old sail, trimmed down to keep the best and strongest parts of the linen. Both ships were now at the pier, and both brothers and their crews busy upon them, replacing oar-ties, checking the steering oar fasteners, caulking any small leaks with gobs of tar. Ketil had made new and strong rope for both ships, and Tola his wife had woven and knotted her stout nettings to capture and hold the goods fast upon the decks.

Fishing boats had been out already, dropping nets in the waters around Gotland, but none of the traders had sailed yet, nor had any arrived from Baltic ports or beyond. It was early, and Sidroc and Runulv counted on this earliness to aid them. Spring weather could be treacherous, and for that fewer sailed so soon. Runulv and Ring would set out in two days, well before any of the other traders from Gotland would sail, and earlier, we all hoped, than most raiders would cast off in search of prey. They would sail together until they found a likely trading post in Dane-mark, and there Runulv would leave his brother, and set out for the longer trip ahead.

Thick and dark rain clouds clotted the sky next morning, and howling wind brought all preparations on board to a halt. Sidroc and Runulv and Ring were down at the ware-house together, going over the goods they had gathered and the provisions and kit they would need. Sidroc was still there when the rain began, falling at once in torrents, soaking everything it touched. I stood inside our opened front door and watched a stream of water surge down the hill. I could just make out the dark forms of Runulv and Ring's ships, bobbing in the churning water at the pier. The rain fell so fast I could not see far out to sea, but only thought with a shiver of what the waves must be like further from land.

I shut the door and went to my loom to work, but could not keep the side door open either for the rain that blew in. But I worked at plain-weave linen, which needed little light. Helga stood not far away, spinning more for me, the slippery flax gathered on the end of her distaff. Sparrow too was spinning, from a length of fluffy wool roving cast over her shoulder. Her small hands were fast and her thread thin and even. The rain drummed upon the pitched roof above our heads, and we heard it falling in great sheets off the eaves, where I knew it was splashing the outside walls of the hall with mud.

It grew brighter within, and the drumming softened until it became a steady drip. I pulled open the door. The sharp yet light smell of rain fallen on green grass wafted in. The side yard of Tyrsborg had the clear and scrubbed look every hard rain gives way to.

I thought to go to the broad oaken front door and pull it open too. As I did so I saw the rolling mass of iron-coloured storm clouds as they raced away from our shore. Everything nearby was dripping and bright in the sudden sunlight. My eyes rested on the tiny apples hanging safe on my six apple saplings. Then I saw movement on the road, Sidroc climbing up to Tyrsborg. Some rain still fell through the air, but I stepped outside to meet him. He raised his arm as he saw me, and I came to the top of the road.

He put his arm around me and we walked to the wellhead before our door. I turned then to look back at the water, and caught my breath. A great rainbow, the span of which I had never before seen, arched across the sky, rooted, it seemed just before us, and reaching far away to lose itself in the briny depths of the Baltic. It was the first I had beheld in Gotland, and coming now seemed a benediction: After the storm comes beauty.

Sidroc gave a little laugh. "Bifröst," he said, naming the rainbow bridge that spans the worlds between Midgard, the Middle Earth on which folk lived, and Asgard, that realm of the Gods. "We shall have good luck."

The storm had swept all clouds away, and work resumed upon the ships. I walked down in the afternoon to watch Runulv and Ring and a few of their men with the lading. Casks of water, boxes of bread, and oiled cloths wrapping roasted sheep's meat and fowl were carried on, along with pots of soft cheese, bags of grains for cooking, and all the cooking kit. The ships would be coasting, stopping each night when they could to beach and sleep on shore, but there might be times when that would not be possible. If nights were clear Runulv planned to sail through them, for he had by far the greater distance to go.

Sidroc had given him the Sun-stone, the same which Ulf had given Sidroc when he took the little boat after the great sea battle. Runulv did not know of these, but Sidroc showed him how to use it, twisting it between the fingers against a cloudy sky until a gleam of the Sun could be caught and fixed upon. Runulv slipped it in the pouch at his belt with his silver to protect it.

Next morning it was time to carry the trading goods aboard. The tide would be full at dawn on the following day, and so at dawn they would be off. The salt and querns were already upon Ring's ship, and Tindr himself brought down, in his wheeled hand cart, the baskets holding his straw-packed honey. The amber, length of red silk, and other small things would be amongst the last to be placed on board.

One great treasure remained after these, and Sidroc called Runulv up to Tyrsborg to collect it. I thought Sidroc wanted to gauge Runulv's reaction to it, to be certain that he was right about its great worth, and for this he would not tell Runulv what he was about to see.

The narwhale horn was in its box upon our long table. I had gone to the trading road and gotten a small jar of the red copper paint, and rubbed it into the raw wood with a scrap of shearling. Then I drew running scroll-work with a thin piece of charcoal all along every side of the box, and on its top as well. I chose the thinnest of Gunnvor's toasting pokers and heated it well in her cook fire, and sitting there by it, pressed the tip of it into the red-stained wood. It had taken me three days to do this all, and on the fourth Tindr rubbed the whole box with his golden beeswax paste. The blackened lines of my running scrolls stood out even against the dark red of the wood, and I was pleased with my efforts.

311

But I was not done. I asked Tindr for a sheepskin, which he brought me, and I cut it and fitted it inside the box, just as the best scabbards are lined with sheepskin to keep the blade from rust. I took a long and narrow length of my whitest linen, and along the edges of it stitched in coloured silk thread designs of green leaves, and red and blue flowers. It was this that I wrapped the horn in, and then set it in the box. The sheepskin Tindr had brought me was from a dark sheep, nearly black, and the white linen with its bright flashes of colour made a fine contrast within its deep curls.

I watched Runulv's eyes widen as we neared the table. The great length of the box, its odd narrow size, and now, I hoped, the beauty of it conveyed that something of great value must be within.

Sidroc was watching him too, and when we came up to it just said in a quiet voice, "Set up your scale."

Runulv unfolded it and hung it from a peg from the wall, the small leathern bag of lead weights on the table and at the ready.

"This is to go to Frankland," Sidroc began. "It is Rannveig's, and she entrusts it to you. Its price is its weight in gold."

He lifted the lid off, and parted the linen cloth.

Runulv did not whistle, as Sidroc had. His widened eyes grew yet rounder, and from his mouth came a swift intake of breath.

"Where – where did she get it?" he asked.

"Her husband Dagr won it at dice, long ago."

Runulv tore his eyes from the horn and looked at Sidroc.

"I have not seen one this long. Or this perfect," he said.

"That is why the price is its weight in gold," Sidroc answered. "You may have to go some way inland, to the keep of a king, or a great lord. Do whatever it takes to get your price."

Runulv nodded. He reached within and carefully brought the horn out. Sidroc held it balanced on the scale bowl while Runulv added one small lead cube after another to the other bowl. When they balanced perfectly Sidroc took the horn and placed it back in its box.

Runulv looked down at the pile of lead in the second bowl.

"Take one sixth-part away," Sidroc told him.

He did so, and Sidroc spoke again. "What you hold in your hand will be your gold for selling it," he told him.

Runulv opened his hand and looked down at the lead cubes resting there. Sidroc had no further need for words.

"I will get her price if it takes me all Summer," Runulv vowed.

Dawn saw all of us clustered at the mouth of the wooden pier. Gyda stood next Runulv, and Ása to Ring, and the eyes of each woman fastened long upon their departing men. Of the other men sailing, only one was wed, and his young wife was there too, along with the mothers and fathers of many of the others. Tindr had come down with us to see the men off, and then we saw Rannveig come out of her still dark brew-house. She came close to where Runulv and Ring stood, each before their ships on opposite sides of the pier, to give them a gift.

"Two casks are waiting, one for each ship, in the brew-house," she told them. "Drink it in health and come back to us."

The men gave a hoot of laughter and thanks, and wasted no time in sending a couple men each to roll the casks down to the waiting ships. Rannveig drew a little closer to Runulv's, and he pointed to where the treasure that was the narwhale horn lay lashed against the side of the stern by his steering-oar. Its long box was swathed in oiled cloth to keep it from all hurt. She nodded her head in satisfaction to see it, but with her eyes I thought she bid it fare-well too, this costly memento of her lost Dagr. Then she turned to see Tindr, helping to pass the ale cask onto Runulv's ship, and her smile broadened.

The men climbed aboard and took up oars to push away from the pier. Sidroc unlooped the line from Runulv's ship, and Tindr from that of Ring's. The lines were coiled and tossed to waiting hands aboard. The tide had just turned from its full, and seemed eager to carry the ships away. The breeze was light, the sky beginning to glow from the lifting Sun.

I stood with the waiting women, all of us calling out our wishes of luck. I had a hand upon my belly, my eyes fixed at Sidroc's back as he watched, arm raised, the ships pull back. We heard orders called out, watched as the sails on each ship were let loose, saw them drop and begin to gently fill with the morning breeze. Someone took my other hand – Ása, who smiled through her tears at me.

Chapter the Eighteenth: Out of the Ashes

ALL fell into a lull for us after the men sailed. Months of planning and work had come to a halt as they hoisted sail and set out. Now our charge was to wait, wait and go about the needful tasks of everyday life. If all went well Ring should return within twelve days or less, but Runulv would be gone far longer.

I felt fit despite my growing girth, prone to some tiredness, but sleep came easily and well to me. The babe seemed to be resting high, and was growing fast. Rannveig told me it was sure to be a son, resting as high as it was; but when I told her of the old spice merchant and his prophecy she listened well. Like all Gotland folk, she had respect for those who had earned great riches, and if they had achieved as well a fair number of years her respect doubled.

When I told her of the spice merchant and his gift of cinnamon it was the first time I had knowingly mentioned anything of our past. Rannveig knew of course that to have crossed the Baltic we would have stopped at trading posts along its shores, but I had never named any of them, nor told her of what had befallen us there. Neither did she, in her mindful way, ever ask. I cared greatly for her and her son, and it was at times a thorn in my side to tell her naught of who I was and whence I came.

One morning, feeling a heaviness in my legs, I sat on a stool near Gunnvor's cook fire in the kitchen yard. At one end of the fire ring the ash was deep and smooth, even powdery, from being raked often when she banked the fire. There was a thin and long iron poker resting on the rim of the surrounding stones, likely the same I had used to mark the narwhale horn box. I took it up idly in my hand, and drew

315

a line in the cool grey ash. The act of doing so, of making a mark upon the flat fine-grained face of the wood ash, recalled to me that it had been more than a year since I had written anything. I had drawn the great knot on the headboard of our new bed that Sidroc had then carved in, and I had burnt in with a poker the running designs on the wooden box that held the narwhale horn. But I had written no message, had no practice in forming each letter that made up that tongue of Angle-land which was mine.

My hand tightened around the poker. Next to the straight line I had drawn I drew a curved shaped: Ic. "I". Me. The speech of Angle-land was part of me. I did not want to forget how to write it.

I bent over the bed of ash, and copied every letter of the alphabet. My hand hesitated at one or two, sending a tiny wave of fear through me that I had lost them, and my hand hovered above my work until I was sure of them and could go on. I wrote it all out a second time, and then a third. The ash was crowded with the tiny furrows of my markings. I took the back of a fry pan and smoothed them away, and began again.

I did not think anyone on Gotland read or wrote in letters such as these. Almost all folk knew the runes, at least some of them, and could mark their tools or favourite treasures with a few of them. There were men and women who had greater knowledge of the runes, and who were called upon to draw or chisel the long inscriptions that wound their way around the great standing stones. But no one I thought could write out the common tongue of the Gotland people using the letters that I had first learnt at the elbow of the Black Prior so many years earlier.

As I sat there Sparrow came over. She watched me from a little distance, seeing the letters arise from the fine ash as I pushed them up with the iron poker tip. Then she squatted down next me. She put her finger in the ash near

316

where I was working, and looked her question to me. I nodded, bidding her go on. If she wanted to copy me, I would try to teach her some of them, how to write her name and other things.

But she was not squatting there to copy me. She drew her forefinger down in a straight line, then lifted it and drew it crosswise through the middle of the first line. She turned her face to me. Her brown eyes were wide open and searching. I looked at what she had drawn for a moment. She drew another, more quickly, with more force. A straight line, with another crossing it in the middle.

"A cross," I said aloud. I had to catch breath. "You are a Christian."

"Já, já," she answered, in her low voice. "Christian."

The way she said it was much softer, in the voice of her homeland, but there was no doubt of her meaning. A Christian.

Perhaps she was indeed of the Franks; it was a Christian land. And we had just sent a ship there. There were no Christians here on Gotland, no one with whom she could profess her faith, receive instruction, pray with. As I had been taken from my heathen hall and placed into a Priory, so she had been taken from her Christian one and placed here in a heathen land.

But even if she were of Frankland, how could we send her back? Her folk might all be dead, her village destroyed or scattered, and she did not seem to know or be able to speak about it. If I had sent her with Runulv and bid him find a priest or nun and turn her over in their care…

I looked at Sparrow's face, still searching my own. To turn her over to another, when she was beginning to find a home here with us seemed a further cruelty. It must be her choice, not mine.

"There are no Christians here, Sparrow," I told her, as gently as I could.

She nodded. "Já," she said again.

"The ship we sent with Runulv is going to a Christian land – Frankland. It might be the land of your home. He could have taken you there and left you with a priest or nun."

She swiftly stood up from where she had been squatting on her haunches. Fear was full upon her face.

"Nai, nai, Mistress. Do not do this to Sparrow. No ship. No ship." She pulled her apron up to her face, but it did not hide the fact that tears were coming.

I reached out to her and touched her arm. "I will not. You are safe, Sparrow. I will not send you. It will be your choice. But Runulv and his men would not hurt you as the others did. It would be a way for you to be amongst Christians, that is all."

She lowered her arms and I tried to smile at her. I almost feared to ask my next question, but ask it I must.

"Do you…say prayers?" I was not certain what her word would be, so I pressed my hands together at my heart.

She nodded her head so hard that a tear on her cheek streaked backward.

"Já, Mistress, each night I say my – prayers. To Jhesu Christus."

Her small brown hand rose to her brow, returned to her breast, then tapped each shoulder as she crossed herself.

I took a breath as I sat there looking at her.

She was devout, believed in her prayers. Knowing this how could I keep her here, in a land where she would be without support in the faith she held.

She pointed at the letters I had traced in the bed of ash.

"Christian, Mistress?"

She must have seen a Testament or prayer-book, or watched a priest or nun work over a quill. She would think all who were lettered to be Christian, and indeed, it was the great gift the Black Monks had given me.

"Nai," I had to tell her. "These are the letters of the tongue of my homeland. But if you are of Frankland they are much the same as a priest would use."

I knew the Gospel stories, could recite many prayers, could, I thought, say the entire Mass beginning to end from having heard it said so many times. I knew tales of Saints from Angle-land and other places. Could I impart them to Sparrow without my own commitment to them, just as I could teach her to stand at a loom, pull back the heddle bar, slide her shuttle between the opened shed, and lay down another line of woollen cloth? Would learning more bring her more comfort, or make her sicken for a home she could never return to?

She knew kindness here on Gotland, tho' she be surrounded by none but heathen folk. They would not care if she worshipped a foreign God; the men here who had been to the larger trading posts along the Baltic had seen signs of other faiths, even met perhaps travelling monks or priests such as Eardwulf, who roamed about in the service of the Church to see how far their teachings had yet spread. But I did not believe there was anyone here other than me who could tell her more.

She squatted down near me again, looking at the lines of letters I had drawn. Her finger rested in the air above the letters I had formed, and then went to the two crosses she had drawn near them. I touched her shoulder and rose. I knew Sidroc was out by the stable, re-stacking the fire wood with Tindr. I must speak to him.

The immense pile of our wood had dwindled over Winter, had shifted and become disordered in parts. They were straightening and stacking, making room to receive newly cut wood for seasoning. Sidroc had his back to me as I went to them but Tindr, who stood atop one of the stacks, nodded at me, causing Sidroc to turn.

"Sparrow is a Christian," I told him.

He blinked, but said nothing at first. He heaved the log in his hands up to Tindr, and turned back to me.

"How do you know?"

"She drew a cross in the ash of the fire pit, two of them. I asked if she were Christian. She knew the word, said já, and even crossed herself as a blessing."

Again he was silent. "What will you do," he asked me. "There is no Sigewif here."

He was right. There was no kind and holy woman to send her to, no priory where she might live and receive instruction. There was no one but me. My face must have shown my trouble, for he then said, "She will have to live without it. Or…practice on her own. No one will care."

He picked up another log, lifted it to Tindr. "You need do nothing," he said, as if to reassure me. "No one will care."

I only nodded and let them get back to work. Sparrow cares, is what I said to myself.

The Hall of Tyr

The next morning Sparrow was sweeping the hall. I came in from the front door where I had been sprinkling my herbs and vines, and in doing so passed by her sleeping alcove. The curtains were open and I stopped as my glance fell there. On the back wall of her alcove above her bed she had taken a piece of charcoal and drawn a cross.

I heard her broom stop and looked over to her.

"It is all right, Mistress?" she asked. She was clutching her broom handle as if she feared punishment.

"Já, já," I told her, in a mild voice. "It is all right."

I went out the side door and to the paddock. Tindr was there, scraping out the soles of the horses' feet with a narrow wooden paddle. He dropped my mare's foot and followed my waving arm. I led him to his stable work bench. There was a thin film of sawdust on one end of the surface, and I drew a cross in it, the upright line longer than the crossing one. I picked up two narrow pieces of wood from the stack by his bench, and lay the pieces over my drawing. We had a small store of drawn iron nails; we could spare one of them to fasten the two pieces in the centre.

Tindr came to me a little later with the cross in his hand. He had smoothed the wood, and cut the pieces to match the lengths I had drawn. The single nail was driven tightly through. I took him to Sparrow's alcove, where he saw the charcoal marking the wall. He nodded and made a little sound. He could not know what it meant; it looked something like the rune Nid, which had the crossing arm running aslant. But he knew Sparrow was from afar, and perhaps thought it was a sign in her own tongue.

I took the cross from him and stepped up upon the platform, placing the cross over that which Sparrow had made. He nodded again, returned to the stable, and came back with hammer and another nail. He drove it at an angle

321

at the top of the cross so that it held fast but could not be
seen.

"A surprise for Sparrow," I told him, placing my hand
over my eyes and then quickly lifting it. He smiled and
nodded.

That afternoon I sat out back in the kitchen yard,
threaded needle in hand. Sidroc and Tindr had built another
table, one easy to carry out into the light and air. It was hard
by the stone end-wall of the hall, and the Sun-warmed stone
made it a pleasant place to sit even when the air was cool, for
here in the back it was away from the wind coming off the
sea. I often used this new table to sew at, as I was now.

As I bent over the tunic I hemmed Sparrow came
from the shadows of the hall and to the door. I saw from her
face that she had found the wooden cross in her alcove.

She ran to me, then stopped before me and took up
my hand where it lay upon the wool. She brought the back of
my hand to her lips and kissed it.

"You are Christian, Mistress?" she asked again. Her
eyes were brimming.

"Nai," I told her once more.

She was now holding my hand in both of her own.
She must have seen folk kiss the hands of priests or nuns, and
knew such a kiss was a Christian sign. I kept looking at her
until she lowered her head.

She had a wooden cross above her bed, but little more.
She had but thirteen or fourteen Summers. She had lost her
family, her homeland, her native tongue. Any meagre
possession which had been hers had been snatched away. Her
maidenhead had been taken from her by violence, and she
had felt the hands of many men upon her small body. This

one thing, her faith, was left to her, pure and undefiled. I would not let her lose that too.

"I am no Christian," I said. She raised her face to mine. "But I have lived amongst them. I know the stories of Jesus Christ – Jhesu Christus – and stories of his Holy Mother. I know stories of saints. I will tell them to you."

For answer she kissed my hand once more, and lay her face down upon my hand. When she lifted it two tears sparkled in my open palm.

At Yule I had made a calendar. The longest night of the year was easy to note, and having found that I vowed not to let the weeks and months slip away from me unknown and unnamed. I drew a circle on the wall of the treasure room; this became the wheel of the year. I put Yule at the bottom, so that Mid-Summer's Day would be at the top. St Cuthbert's Day was that Spring day when day and night were of equal length, as St Matthew's Day served the same in Fall; and for these two days I made marks at one side and the other of my wheel. The cross-quarter days of Candlemas and Hlafmesse I placed between these; Candlemas at early Spring and Hlafmesse at Summer's ripest, as became the day of First Fruits. What I had known as St Martin's Day fell in the month of Blót as kept here on Gotland, which we had called Blodmonath; that month of slaughter and putting up meats and sacrifice and feasting. I marked each Moon when it was at its fullest, and placed this too upon the wheel.

In this way I kept pace with the passing of days, and kept my place in them too. I counted ahead, my fingers walking the small lines I had made for each day. My coming babe should be born at the time of St Mary's Day, that same day when I had ridden away with Sidroc from Four Stones for the last time.

Sparrow wished every day to hear the stories of the Gospels, and came to me with an eager and open face to learn them. She smiled and sometimes gasped when I began a tale she was familiar with, nodding her head in remembrance; and listened hard, her body intent, ear cocked, when what I said was new to her. She knew of wolf-clad John, the wild-man Baptist, and knew of the birth and death of Jesus. She knew too of the great flood, when God in his wrath destroyed all but Noah and his boat, and knew the awe-ful tales of fathers making Offering of their sons and daughters to appease that same God. She knew of Heaven and very much of Hell. But there were many stories she had never heard, and of those she had, I tried to deepen and enlarge for her.

Sidroc knew from the start that I would teach her what I could. He had walked past the fire-ring the day I had learnt Sparrow was Christian and seen the alphabet I had inscribed, looked down at the poked-up ashes and then at me. He knew that writing and the keeping of words in this way was on my mind. He had known from long ago that in my word-hoard were many tales taken from the Bible. I told him Sparrow ought to know them. For answer he nodded. "They are good Sagas," he agreed. "All must know the stories of their own people."

Much of my telling happened past noon while I was at my looms. Morning chores were done, Gunnvor resting before she began the task of making up our supper, and the daylight coming through the open side door at its brightest. It was my favourite time to weave. As in the past Helga and Sparrow would join me, standing nearby or just outside in the Sun with their spindles, or sometimes weaving next me if I had one loom ready warped for linen and the other for wool.

Helga was glad to listen too. She liked the same stories we all did, that of Jesus turning water into wine, or driving

324

the money-lenders out of the holy temple, or raising the dead Lazarus to life.

"Strong magic," she murmured. "true seiðr." Seiðr was the darkest and most mysterious form of magic, that which was needful to do such things as make a dead man live. It was one of Freyja's arts, but Odin was the master of it.

But Sparrow listened with different ears. She was hearing in her new tongue tales which she had heard at home, and in her old. And just as every priest or monk or nun would tell these tales with differences, I too told them in my own way. I did not seek to change any meaning, and tried my best to recall the stories aright, but I had heard them many times myself, first from the Prior and his fellow monks, then from Dunnere, the priest of Kilton, and also from Wilmot, Ælfwyn's priest at Four Stones. I strove to tell them aright, and yet felt I could not harm Sparrow in the hearing should I err, for her belief in them was rooted firmly in her breast. She had been born into them, as had her folk, and she clung to them now.

I knew there was much good in the faith of the Christians. The Prior sought to be merciful to all, preached mercy and forgiveness to all who would hear, and spent much silver in the redemption and freeing of slaves. Christians had the supreme art of pen and parchment, of creating words that stay, and he had willingly taught me this. Yet he could by law take my rightful lands from me as a girl, for as a heathen I had no legal standing. The laws made by Christian kings made me less than a Christian child, and I felt in my heart this was wrong.

I believed that Jesus had lived, and was a man of such wisdom and goodness that others could not let him go on living. I knew he was given a choice to live or to die, and he chose death. But from girlhood I could not understand how that differed from a king or lord or warrior dying to defend that which he loved, his own folk. We thought it their blood-duty to do so. Even less could I understand how those not sworn to protect others with their lives could willingly die to spare them, and not be counted as blest as Jesus. Women, children, old men – folk who had the choice to run or hide – died all the time in Angle-land, and many other places too, to save others from sudden danger.

Kind as the Prior was, he would grow tired of my questioning, and more than once told me I did not understand Original Sin, that darkening cloak which Adam and Eve had cast upon them over an apple. And in truth I never had, and could not now. Like my kinsmen and like Sidroc and like the folk of Gotland, I did not believe in sin. I believed in right and wrong. Those who willingly did wrong would suffer from it. I had done wrong in my life and knew this to be true, for I had suffered from my own acts. Sidroc had killed for treasure alone, and had suffered and did suffer the visit of the night-mare, and felt it to be his due. If we did wrong we must pay the price; no one could pay it but us.

The Christians I had lived with did not feel this way. Any offense, regardless of how great, could be absolved by a priest and through prayer and alms. When Godwin had caught the Dane who had blinded Gyric, he did not tell him who he was, why he was there, and then kill him. He told Hingvar those things, yes; but then he put Hingvar through every torture he could devise, drawing out his death until the man begged for it. Godwin had wounded himself in doing so. He saw it not, but I knew it, and I thought Modwynn and Gyric knew it too. Yet when Godwin returned to Kilton with the proofs of his act all he need do was declare them before Dunnere the priest to be absolved.

No one at Kilton knew how I felt at this, for I could tell no one. Hingvar must be punished for what he did, yes. But Godwin thought he could shrug the savagery of his punishment off like his mantle. He could not.

These thoughts were my own, and I did not let them change what I told to Sparrow. I wished her every comfort from her faith, the last remnant of her home ways.

One day when we were alone I asked her of her prayers. I had not taught her any of those I knew, nor had she asked me to. But she had told me she prayed each night. I knew this was in the speech of her homeland, and knew this was likely the only time these sounds were in her mouth. She closed her eyes and said for me the two prayers she knew, the quick brown hand rising to bless herself before and after each. The first prayer I gauged to be that Jesus had taught his companions upon the hillside. It was the chiefest of all Christian prayers and she said it with the graveness it warranted. The second was a shorter prayer, and she said it with a slight smile on her thin lips.

"Do not forget these prayers, Sparrow," I told her when her hand descended from her brow.

She shook her head to show me she would not, but I went on.

"They are in your own tongue, taught to you by your own people. Now you speak Norse, and soon you may wish to speak to your God in Norse too. But always remember how to say these prayers in your own speech."

I was sitting at the table in the kitchen yard, pulling at the seam I had just sewn to check it. The late afternoon Sun warmed my back, spilling over my work. I think I smiled as I sat there, for the seam I tested was on one of several tiny shifts I was making up. I had worked too at a pile of loin-cloths, building my store of linen for our coming babe.

I heard the running of a small pair of feet and looked up. Geirlaug, one of our neighbour Alrik's children, came pattering up to me. She was slightly breathless from her running, and the wet and sandy marks darkening the hem of her yellow gown told me she had been playing on the beach.

"Rannveig says Ring's ship is coming," she announced. She had only six or so Summers, and by her smile I saw she was proud to have been sent to bring us this news.

I stood and went to the stable door. Sidroc and Tindr were within, up in the hayloft, where they were extending the floor there across more of the rafters. When my mare foaled we would have three horses rather than two, and we hoped to get a second cow. All this meant we needed more space to store fodder and bedding straw.

"Ring's ship is come," I called.

Sidroc took a leap from one piece of new flooring to another and looked down at where I stood with Alrik's little girl.

"Rannveig sent Geirlaug to tell us," I went on.

He was already grasping at the ladder, and nearly sprang down its length. Tindr's head popped up, and Sidroc touched his ear and waved him to come down and with us. Sidroc spent a moment shaking and combing the straw from his hair with his fingers, and brushing the dust from his clothes. His face said much. Ring's ship was back, and safe, and now we would know if all who left returned as well, and with what gain.

The ship was just nearing the pier as we reached it. Folk from along the trading road were already gathered to meet it, a knot of ten or more men and women, kin or friends to those who had sailed. Ketil and Tola were amongst them, come to greet the first of their returning nephews. The sail had been lowered and the men at oars stroked one-sidedly to pull up along the pier. Some of them began calling out their greetings in answer to those who stood awaiting them. Ring was in the back, at the stern, at work tying up his steering-oar, but when he raised his face his grin said much.

The coiled line was thrown and Sidroc hauled it in, the straked sides bumping gently against the edges of the pier planks. Oars were shipped on both sides and the men stood. All four casks of salt were gone, and all ten querns as well, as were the bundles of goods the men had carried along on their own accounts. The decking held nothing but extra oars and the men's supplies.

"Good sailing?" called Sidroc.

"Good sailing," answered Ring. He stepped up upon the ship rail and leapt nimbly to the dock surface. Sidroc took his arm in greeting. Ring stepped back a moment and with another grin lay his hand upon the rounded pouch at his belt.

His crew grabbed their kit, talking and laughing, and came down the gang plank and went to those who stood waiting for them. Some went off with them to their own homes, calling out after Ring, and some came with us to Rannveig's where she stood at the open door to her brew-house.

We sat at the first big table, looking out under the rolled-up awnings at the newly-arrived ship and the sea beyond. Before we sat Ring pulled the leathern pouch and dropped it on the table before Sidroc. He smiled down at it but did not open it. Rannveig handed ale around, and she too stayed to hear. Tindr stood next her, and she signalled to him what was being said.

"Tell me first, and then we will count," Sidroc began. "The sailing went well," he prompted.

"To Dane-mark, já," answered Ring. "Winds were light but in our favour. Runulv's ship was always in hailing distance. We beached four nights together, meeting no one, as we had hoped. The first night we spent on the western coast."

He looked up at Rannveig and smiled. "There we made short work of your good ale," he told her, at which praise she bobbed her head.

"Next day we crossed to Svear-land, spent two days coasting there. The fourth night on Dane-mark, an empty beach. We sailed together, passing a few small farms, until we came to a trading settlement."

"Which one?" Sidroc wanted to know.

"Aros."

Sidroc nodded in recognition.

"Trading had begun; there were folk about. It would do. Runulv left me there, sailed on. We carried the goods off the ship and claimed a strip of land not far from a cloth-seller; he had plenty of trade." Ring glanced down at the unopened pouch.

"The salt – I could have sold twice as much. And the last measures I sold for half again as much as the first measures."

Sidroc was leaning forward in his eagerness at this.

"The querns too sold well, but more slowly. Six I sold to men and women who had heard I had them, and the last four to a merchant for his own trade. These last four I sold four-for-three, as I wanted to get back."

Ring again eyed the pouch. He had carried his scale set in with him, and opened it up on the table now. He nodded his head at the waiting bag.

The Hall of Tyr

"There is almost four pounds of silver there."

I was not alone in making a sound of happy surprise. The pouch did not look that big, but now Sidroc pulled open the drawstring. He upended the contents on the table before him. Amongst them were three thick and long ingots of silver, twice as thick as a man's finger and just as long. Like all ingots they were plain tapered bars of pure metal, but their very size and weight gave them beauty. With them were plain round pieces, of varying lengths, cut from coiled silver rolls, of the thickness of my little finger. A few pieces of broken jewellery nestled by them, parts of belt-buckles and bits of brooches. Landing all around this, rolling and needing to be caught by Sidroc's reaching hands, was a large number of silver coins. They were of all sizes, some more than twice as big as others, and sitting as close as I was I could see they were from many lands. One rolled nearly to me and I caught it up. It was tiny, and inscribed with flowing marks on both sides, marks I could not read. An image flashed into my head, that of the flowing writing on some of the chests and casks aboard the Idrisid ship. These flowing lines could be their script.

I pushed the coin back to the pile. One large coin there caught my eye; it was one of Wessex, for there was the likeness of Ælfred, King. It made me catch my breath to see it. Ælfred, like his father before him, had paid thousands of pounds of silver in tribute to the Danes.

Some of the men had whistled to see so much treasure, and we none of us could take our eyes from it. Sidroc took it all in, saw me push back the tiny coin, saw my eyes widen at the one of Ælfred, heard the murmurs of those gathered around us. He raised his eyes to Ring.

"You have earned your third-share," he said. His grin told how pleased he was.

Ring stood and hung the scale set from a peg on a ceiling beam. Together they massed the silver into the empty scale bowl. Ring placed his square lead weights in the second bowl until they balanced. It was the slightest bit scant of a full four pounds.

It was Sidroc's right to choose first at what he wanted. He chose all three ingots and set them aside. His eyes lifted to me and he nodded; he knew I wished for the large coin of Ælfred. I placed it by his ingots.

Ring was looking at the small coins, and Sidroc saw this.

"These – Ása will like a few of these for her neck," Ring said.

Ása had had her two sisters stay with her in Ring's absence, to help with the farm chores and keep her company. I had walked one day to see her, laden with a basket of Gunnvor's honey cakes, and had a fine afternoon with the three of them. Ring was eager to get back to her, and to bring something to delight her.

"Take them then," said Sidroc. "Make up your share from whatever is here."

Sidroc watched Ring as he scooped handfuls and weighed them out for himself, spilled it out upon the table, and slid what was his back into the pouch. What Sidroc next said surprised him, and me.

"Would you go again?" he asked Ring. "Go now, if I can gather goods to trade?"

Ring's jaw went slack. He straightened up a little from where he sat next to Sidroc.

"Orm will be wanting his ship back," he said in reply.

332

"Silver will buy another trip out. Orm's time can be bought," came Sidroc's answer.

There was a long pause before Ring spoke again.

"But – mine cannot be," he said, with a slight smile. He took a breath, and looked straight at Sidroc. "I have gamed enough to know when I should quit."

Ring was cautious with his silver, and I had seen him drop out of gaming several times when he was being bested.

Sidroc cocked his head at him, and Ring went on. "I have told of the trip out, not of that home."

We had all been looking at Ring, and now we looked as well at those sitting with us who had been on board. Some of them ducked their heads before lifting them again to listen to Ring.

"We spent three days at the trading post. I sold the last four querns cheaply, as the skies were darkening to the West. The wind was lifting and I wanted to be before it. We set off at dawn. But we were too late. Before noon the seas were rolling, big swells tossing us. We made what headway we could, the mast creaking, sail full, and me fighting at the steering-oar. The sky above us turned green, the wind so great we must drop the sail. Rain came at us, almost side-ways, stinging us like nettles. But the sea – the sea was in fury.

"The Midgard Serpent was angry, was thrashing his tail. He sought to swallow us. We shipped oars. Two men joined me at the steering-oar, the rest were bailing. Between the wave-tips and the rain, we filled as fast as we could empty. The Serpent was about to rise up, encircle us, drag us down."

The Hall of Tyr

Ring's eyes moved around the table to the faces of his crew. They all nodded in agreement, the shadow of the fear they had felt still upon their faces. Red-faced Gaut rubbed his nose with the flat of his hand and shook his head recalling it.

"But we are here, safe, and with silver," Ring finished. "And I owe a goat to Njord."

He grinned when he said that, considering such an Offering a bargain for his life and that of his crew. He had called on the God of the Sea, and been answered. But smile or not, I did not think he would want to go out again now, or perhaps ever.

Sidroc dropped his head a moment, but not before I saw the gleam in his dark blue eyes.

He looked again to Ring. "Já," he told him. "Orm will want his ship back." He glanced around the table at the men clutching their cups. "You have done well, all of you."

Ring rose from the table. "If I leave now I will reach the farm before dark," he smiled. Then he made a jest by adding, "Once again I choose Freyr over Njord."

Lovely Ása had been waiting, and now could welcome her new husband home.

Rannveig came to me, and I showed her the coin of Ælfred in my hand. It had his portrait on one side, and a Christian cross on the other; a cross that could also be used to show where the coin could be justly cut into halves or quarters.

She picked it up from my palm and squinted at it, turning it over. The coin was new and the impression sharp and clear. She lay it back down in my hand.

"That will look fine on your neck-chain," she said. She did not ask of what land it was, or why I wanted it.

Perhaps she knew, or guessed, but such was her goodness that she would not ask.

Tindr had been standing next her all this time, watching, his mother signalling to him those parts of Ring's tale which would not be clear from the men's actions or faces. He had not expressed interest in going with either Ring or Runulv, and Rannveig had told me that save for going out in his late father's fishing boat he had never been to sea. Yet I could not help but wonder if he could remain content with us at Tyrsborg, or even on Gotland itself, without making some adventure, as all young men were wont to do.

We three walked up the hill back to Tyrsborg, Tindr ahead of us. Sidroc held the heavy pouch in his hand, and was silent as we climbed. I knew Ring had brought him more silver than he had hoped for, and could guess as well what were his thoughts.

"When Ring said he would not go out again, you thought of going yourself," I ventured.

"It crossed my mind," he said. "Nai," he corrected, turning his head to look at me. "It leapt into my mind."

I said the next in as light a tone as I could, a question almost, despite the concern behind my words.

"But you will not go."

"Nai," he answered. He stopped and turned back to look at the sea. There was Orm's ship, with a few men moving upon it, gathering up their things before heading home. The sea lay sparkling in the setting Sun behind it. We stood together looking until he spoke again.

"I have told you many times you would not take ship again. Something in those words was there for me as well."

I touched his hand in gratitude. Yet I did not want to be that which kept him from more gain. "You are sure?" I asked.

He nodded. "Já." He tapped his chest. "My hamingja – my luck-spirit – tells me. I thought to send two ships instead of one. My hamingja told me that was lucky, and it was. I thought just now to make a second trip, to go myself. My hamingja told me that was unlucky."

"I am glad you listen so well," I said, and smiled in my relief.

He only laughed. "Listening has gotten me much further than talking," he answered.

In the morning Sidroc was awake before me. I slept well every night since I was with child, and now just drowsed by his side. His hand stroking my hair made me raise my head and smile. He was sitting up, his back against the great carved knot in the solid wood backing of our bed. I reached my hand up and touched the blue dragon on his chest. He smiled back.

"Furs and falcons," he told me. His grin told me he had been awake a while, thinking on these things. "Next year we send furs and falcons."

Chapter the Nineteenth: Treasure of All Kind

NOW that he had Ring's silver, Sidroc lost no time in planning ahead for next Summer's trading voyage. Ring would not go out again, but he hoped that when Runulv returned he would want to sail next year back to Frankland. By next Spring Thorfast would have the three great millstones ready, so that two pairs could be carried on Runulv's ship. More amber necklaces would go, and anything else of value we might come across between now and then. But it was indeed furs and falcons that Sidroc wished to spend his time and effort on.

Time he would need, for he would have to capture young falcons and train them himself. He had not forgotten the large goshawk we had seen circling overhead on the way to buy the millstones. He had hoped he could buy one or two trained birds here on Gotland, but none in fact kept them, tho' in the forest clearings or along the beaches a few could be seen gliding high in the warm air, just as we had seen them. They took at least two years to raise up, and so he must begin soon so he might have them to sell in coming years.

To capture a young goshawk meant robbing a nest, one guarded by not one but two fierce and fast birds. Sidroc told me men had been killed in doing this, knocked from cliff faces and from tall trees by beating wings. Other men had lost an eye to the birds' hooked talons. But the hawk must be taken young, hand-fed and gentled by its captor, raised to trust him utterly before it would be strong enough to fly free, strike a bird on the wing or snatch a rabbit from the grass, and bring it back to the waiting wrist of the hunter, there to receive the head of the prey as its reward.

And as Sidroc wished to raise his own, he would need to capture several goshawk chicks, so that he might have male and female and be able to breed them up. This meant the building of a hawk house at the farm, as well as a smaller structure here at Tyrsborg where he could raise the first birds. A hunting bird needed to know different places, and care only for he who wore the special long leathern glove on which he rested; it was he who the bird depended upon for his food.

Sidroc had not captured birds before. The first falcons he had kept at Four Stones were grown hunting birds he had traded for, had bred, and in turn trained their offspring to hunt off the wrist. But if he and Tindr could catch a few goshawk chicks it would save him a vast quantity of silver. It was Spring and the chicks would be on the nest now, so he determined to try.

He went to one of the leather-workers on the trading road, and had him make up two leathern caps of cowhide. These were like onto the leathern helmets that some men wore in battle, those who could not afford a costly iron helmet. The leather was boiled, making it hard almost as stone, and good protection. These he took to the weapon-smith, who fitted each cap with iron eye-pieces at the brow line, to encircle and shield the eyes. He had also two thick leathern tunics made, proof against the sinking talons of an angry goshawk at the shoulder and arm, and sturdy thick gloves. And last he had Tindr carve a wooden hawk with outstretched wings, affixed to a long pole.

Their plan was to ride out and seek the nests of goshawks. Together they would climb the tree or scale the rocky sea-cliff faces where lay the nests. When they neared the nest Sidroc would use the wooden hawk figure to draw the birds away long enough for Tindr to climb past and take a chick. If only one chick was taken, the hawks would not chase them back down, but settle again. Tindr wore a small lidded basket at his waist, lined with straw, and in this would he place the chick for the climb down.

They went out the first day with provisions to overnight, and came back on the second day with nothing. Two days later they went out again, and came back the same day, late, but with a white-downed chick in Tindr's basket. They had ridden along the sea coast and seen birds soaring, and trailed a goshawk to its cliff-side nest. Puncture marks on the wings of the wooden hawk Tindr had carved, and deep scratches on his leathern cap and tunic, told me that the chick had not been surrendered without complaint.

"But Tindr saw there were three other chicks; they will all have food enough to live now their sister is gone," Sidroc told me, as we crowded round the tiny thing. Its pink flesh showed through the fluffy white down, and while it could barely stand, the dark beak was hooked and sharp.

"How do you know it is their sister?" I wanted to know.

"The females are larger than the males, even as chicks," he said, "and Tindr saw this one was much the greater."

Tindr lost no time in fitting up a big wicker basket for one of our hens, and placing her in it with the little goshawk chick for warmth. The hen did not seem startled by such an ungainly chick, but settled over it just as if it were yellow and her own. Feed it she could not, for hen chicks peck at grain and worms almost at once, while hawks need flesh. But Tindr was ready, first with the flesh of one of our own hens, then with that of snared hares or of the mice the skogkatts brought him, dropping a sliver of raw meat into the bright yellow throat as soon as the beak gaped.

Having caught one spurred them to go for others. Tindr left the chick in Sparrow's keeping, and I think she

339

took a sort of delight in checking on the tiny thing, leaving it be if it lay asleep neath the hen, or hastening to Gunnvor for scraps of raw meat if the small hooked beak yawned wide.

They made five trips, and gained four chicks from four different nests in doing so. Each time they returned the wooden hawk carving was more and more punctured, and their caps and tunics more deeply scratched. On the last Sidroc got down from his horse with a turned and swollen ankle. He had been driven down the rotting tree the goshawks had built their nests on, and the last few branches nearest the ground had given way under his weight.

"It is easy to scorn the thief who takes small things," he said later, his foot resting up on a barrel in the stable. Tindr had placed the fourth goshawk chick in with the others, and was ripping meat into narrow shreds to feed the hungry brood. "Yet trained, these chicks will bring us more treasure than could eggs of gold."

The days rolled on. The Moon had waxed and waned since the ships of Runulv and Ring had slipped out of sight of the trading road; two score days had passed. Small apples hung on my little apple trees, and the purple grape vines were covered with clusters of tiny hard grapes. My garden spot was a patch-work of greens with reaching mints, spires of lavender, bunches of parsley, and smoky-grey sage. To pluck a leaf of any of them and roll it in my hands and breathe in the freed scent was a joy to me. I had planted pea-vines as well, so eager was I to taste their fresh sweetness after the dearth of greens in Winter. These clambered wildly about, their pale blossoms giving way to lengthening peapods. Near them ranged two short rows of pot herbs to season and lighten our browis and broths. As I worked in my garden the sea sparkled and glimmered before me, deep blue creased with silver, and I never tired of lifting my head to see it. Song birds and sea birds dipped and called, alighting a moment to take wing again, dark against the bright background. All was alive and awake and growing. The trees in full leaf cast deep and welcome shade from a golden Sun that seemed never out of sight. The days grew so long and light that that same Moon was seen shining in a bright blue sky more often than not. And I grew large.

Mid-Summer's Day was still to come, and my babe would not be due until more than a month after that. At Tyrsborg I was not alone in awaiting young. My mare too was growing in girth, swishing her tail, fat and glossy, as she stood knee high in Gotland's rich green grass. And with our new silver Tindr went and fetched us a second milk cow, and had the first bred up, to keep her in milk. Gunnvor made pots both of soft white cheeses and of tangy skyr. Our fowl had grown in numbers, the speckled hens fluttering about the stable and its yard, and laying well, so we had eggs every day, either seethed in butter or baked up in puddings with our cows' rich milk. Our six geese now numbered twelve, even with those we had fattened and feasted upon, and they ran with beating wings and necks outstretched after the big skogkatts to keep them from chasing after their fuzzy young.

Traders landed their ships every few days at the pier, or brought their smaller ships in aground on the shingle there. Some were ships of Gotlanders from the West or North or South parts of the island, bringing in goods to sell or trade, or stopping here before they made the sail across the Baltic to the large trading posts of the Polanie and Pomerani. Others were ships full of goods from those places, and many more distant lands as well. But the days passed and Runulv's was not amongst them.

Sidroc had reckoned that it would take him fourteen days, with fair winds, to reach Frankland. A warship with many men rowing could make it in less, but that of Runulv was a broader beamed merchant and fishing ship, and with far fewer men. Frankland had a long coast, with many places to land and trade. Sidroc had warned him that he might have to travel far, and even inland, to get the best price for the narwhale horn, and indeed, Runulv would seek to get the best prices for all he carried, as his share came directly from this.

His brother Ring had returned to the farm a far richer man than he had left. He was able to pay men to help him clear more land for sowing grain, to build milking pens for his growing herds of sheep and goats, and uproot some of the oldest apples which could no longer bear fruit. He and Ása worked hard each day, and, I felt certain, with gratitude for the chance to do so together. They had not only a home and half interest in the farm on which it sat, but a good store of silver, all things which a few months ago seemed years out of their grasp. We saw them often, for every few days Ring would come driving the ox and cart he had bought and bring us some produce from the farm.

When five and forty days had gone Sidroc began to look for Runulv. As each day passed we spoke less and less of when he should come, as if the speaking of it might make it never happen. Yet I would see Sidroc stand by the well head in front of Tyrsborg and scan the far horizon. We did not often see Gyda, as the way to their farm was at the other end of the trading road, but when I came upon her at a stall or looking at goods at a workshop we always embraced. She told me how well I looked, and indeed, my small silver mirror told me I was blooming. I wished I could speak the same words to her, but her worry was clear upon her pretty face. Her little boy hung to her hand, yellow curls bobbing; his face looking up at us was so like his absent father's. Gyda touched her own waist.

"We will have another, at Yule," she told me, and managed a smile.

"How happy I am for you, for you both," I said, embracing her again. "This Yule there will be four of you, and you will be splendid in your new brooches of silver."

I said this with as much strength as I could muster, for she needed to hear this, to think ahead to a day when they would be together again, and a new child amongst them. She nodded and smiled again, but bit her lip as well.

I was at my loom when Tindr walked rapidly into the hall. He and Sidroc had left to walk over to the black-smith's forge and order a new hammer, a rasp, and several other things. I did not expect to see either of them back so soon, and the look of glad expectancy on Tindr's face let me know he had good news. He waved me outside and to Tyrsborg's front, and pointed. There, still far at sea, I could see a ship, and if I squinted could make out the red and white squares of its sail.

"Runulv!" I said. The sense of relief I felt made me almost light-headed.

Tindr was grinning, and now raised his hand in the sign for the farm, an action which looked like the biting of an apple, for indeed the farm was known for them. He touched his ear and then pointed to the paddock. Sidroc had sent him to take the horses to the farm, so that Ring and Ása might come as quickly as they could and join in the homecoming. I nodded as he made his way to gather the tack.

I went out back as well, and told Gunnvor, at work on her baking. She smiled and only asked, "Honey-cakes?", guessing that we would wish to have a special meal tonight.

I set off down the hill. The ship had grown clearer, and a small group was already forming to meet it. Runulv and Ring were both well-liked, their father Botair and uncle Ketil amongst the chief men of the area, and interest in both their voyages had been great. Ring had travelled with success to Dane-mark and now Runulv was in view. I could only hope he had half as much luck in his own way as his younger brother had.

Sidroc was standing there in the midst of the gathered folk. Gyda had already been sent for, but like Ring and Ása, was coming from an upland farm. Ketil and Tola were there, but Botair was out fishing in his own boat.

I came and stood by Sidroc and just touched his hand. We were all facing out, watching the rapid approach of Runulv's ship. The sail was still unfurled and full of air, billowing against a smart wind. The red and white interwoven strips of linen held proud and handsome against the dark blue of the water. Some with us began to call out in welcome, and the men called back. Oars were shipped on one side as the ship came about, and then we saw Runulv in the stern at the steering-oar. Sidroc was counting aloud at my side; when he reached nine he turned to me.

"All returned," he said. I knew his eyes were not the only ones who made that anxious count.

Now the sail was dropped and furled, made fast as the ship neared the pier. Sidroc moved closer to the end of it, ready to catch the thrown line. Runulv looked up and grinned, his face Sun-burnt and happy. The prow-man threw the line, and Sidroc hauled, walking along the wooden planking of the pier as we made way. The men were calling to those standing with us, laughing amongst themselves, and gathering up their packs. Runulv finished with his steering-oar, and looped a leathern pack which had been resting at his feet over his shoulder. The gangplank was laid and the men, Sun-browned and wind-blown, streamed over it, heading for those they knew or just waiting for Runulv. He was the last to cross the gangplank, where his uncle Ketil stood to embrace him.

"And to Frankland?" Ketil asked.

"Já, já, to Frankland. And back," grinned Runulv. He scanned the group. "Ring?"

"At the farm," his uncle told him. "All went well for him in Dane-mark. He is coming soon. Gyda too has been sent for."

Runulv nodded in his own relief, then crossed to us. Sidroc took his arm. Runulv had one hand on the leathern bag on his shoulder, and his grin said much.

"Rannveig's," said Sidroc.

Runulv laughed and nodded again. "But I think you first will want to see your cinnamon sticks," he said to me. He took a step nearer to the ship's side and pointed. There by the keel board were a number of black iron bars, as long as my arm and just as thick.

Sidroc whistled. "How many?" he asked.

"Seven," said Runulv.

"Seven bars of Frankish iron," repeated Sidroc. He gave a laugh as he looked from Runulv to me. "Enough to dower a princess."

I had to put my hands to my mouth and laugh in my happiness. I truly did mean to save all the gain from the precious cinnamon for my coming daughters, and now, just as the old spice merchant had promised, I had enough to dower them.

Amidst all the talking and laughing we kept moving towards the brew-house. The awnings had still been rolled down when I passed it, but Rannveig and Sparrow, who was within helping her, had been at work, setting up for the welcoming party. Rannveig met us at the door, a big pottery cup of ale in her hand. She handed it to Runulv.

"Rannveig," he said, bringing it to his lips, "I have missed this. Frankland is a land of wonders, but – their ale. Their ale could never replace yours."

She laughed away this praise. He took a deep draught, then learned in closer to her. "And besides my thirst I bring a pouch of metal for you."

The brightness of her eye showed her gladness in this news, but she herded us all to her tables.

She and Sparrow were busy around us, and the first round had been downed before Runulv began his tale.

"We left Ring and sailed almost straight into a storm," he began.

"We heard of it," Ketil said. "It caught Ring, and he nearly went down."

Runulv shook his head.

"You sailed into it," Sidroc said.

"Já. Due West. It was strong, but my ship stronger. The new mast, new sail; we were tested. We furled as soon as we could, made all fast, and rode it out. Leaving as early in the season as we did was a risk, but one it was good to take. No one else was out and after us, or if they were, the storm took them.

"We sailed without seeing any but a few small fishing boats. To go so far as Dane-mark and then on…" He gave his head a little shake of wonder.

346

"The night skies were clear after the storm and twice we sailed right through them. Other times we beached where we could, waiting until owl-light to make certain no one was near. If we saw no fires, we felt safe enough to land.

"We kept on. After twelve days we saw a farmhouse or two near the shore; fishing folk. We beached, went to speak to them, but their speech was so strange to us we must sign. They told us a trading town was two days away, so we hauled back, and set West again. Sure enough, we found the town, a few ships already there, but not many folk. We went on, always West, tracing the coast.

"At the next post we sold some of the honey, a few necklaces, and some of the goods the men had brought. But there was no trader or rich folk to whom I wanted to show the cinnamon, silk, or Rannveig's box to."

At this many around the table who had not been aboard Runulv's ship looked to Rannveig. None knew but Runulv and Sidroc and I of the great treasure she had sent.

"So we went on. The next post was twice as large, many streets, ships from lands I had never heard of. Some folk spoke the same strange tongue, but some spoke Norse or close enough. Not that trading needs speech; the scale does that for you," he ended, taking another draught of ale.

"I had a few offers for the silk, but only pieces of it. I did not want to cut it if I did not have to."

I had unfolded the length of red silk, and knew it was more than enough to make two gowns. Yet I thought Runulv wise to keep it whole, lest some great lord or lady wish for it thus.

"The amber necklaces sold quickly and well there, and all the rest of the honey. The honey I offered tastes of, and it sold itself."

Some sitting facing us lifted their heads towards the road outside, and we turned too to look behind us. As if he had been summoned by these words, Tindr was there, on my dun mare. Next him was Ring on the stallion, with Ása sitting behind him, her arms around her husband's waist.

They came in, and after Ring and Ása embraced Runulv, joined us. Rannveig signed to her son that the honey had done well for him. Tindr stood by her, grinning, and waiting to see what his share might be.

Runulv looked over at Sidroc. "Folk told me that the king was at one of his halls, a five day's sail, and up a great river. I had the amber carvings, a few necklaces, the silk, the cinnamon, Rannveig's box…all things that needed a rich man to buy. Where there is a king there are other rich men. We made ready to sail.

"We found the river mouth, wide and easy to sail. Small villages on either side, much good farmland, much timber and unsettled places too. The river was broad, broader than any I have seen. We kept on."

He put his cup down. "We came at last to an island in the river. Spanning the river was a bridge of wood and stone, far greater in length than any I had seen. But the island – it was covered in buildings. All stone."

"Paris," said Sidroc.

"Já, Paris," answered Runulv. "You have seen it?"

Sidroc shook his head. "I have heard tell of it. It is rich, beyond counting." He smiled a little to himself, and then looked to Runulv. "You did well to make it your business to go there."

"What I saw there… the roads inside were crowded with stalls and merchant-goods. Cloth, woven in ways I had never seen. Silver and gold ornaments the Gods would covet. Stalls selling wine, so sweet and strong one cup made you feel drunk. Folk stopped us on the way to see what we had brought to sell, many folk talking at once and calling for others to come. The red silk I sold to men, dressed in long gowns, like women's. They took me to a stone building, which had a table. It was me and Thorir and Jorund, just enough of us to carry the goods and make show of it; the rest I had stay with the ship in case of danger."

Thorir and Jorund sat with us at table, grinning with pride that they had been chosen to enter the deepest part of the stone city.

"The linen on the table was pure white and fine and thin, had been woven by the best weavers. On the table were two candleholders of silver, so tall that one would need a stick to reach the candle to light it. Also upon the table was more silver, even larger and standing upright, a thick upright of silver with another crossing it in the middle."

He drew a simple cross with his finger upon the table top. I lifted my eyes and Sidroc's own met mine.

"The building was a temple, a hof, for the men knelt before the table and bowed their heads. Another man, also in a gown, came forth. He wore a gold ring on his hand, and was their chief, and to him I showed the silk. He was greatly pleased by it. I showed him the cinnamon, and this he wanted too, and bought one piece. He bought also one of the tiny amber cups."

Runulv looked to me and smiled as he said this, recalling how I had told him I thought they might sell together.

"He sent me to the king's hall. I still had the rest of the amber carvings, a few necklaces, the second stick of cinnamon, and Rannveig's long box."

Again everyone looked to Rannveig, but her gaze was fixed on Runulv's face.

"Their king is named Charles. He is short, fat, no warrior to my eyes. But he was eager to look at my goods. He wore fur of ermines on his mantle, a gold-hilted knife, thick twist of gold around his neck, from which hung a golden disk with a man's head on it, a single piece of gold larger than any I have seen. Pretty women were with him, and a few of his men, as well dressed nearly as was he.

"He wanted all I showed him. I began with the necklaces, as the women were there. They all wanted them; he bought every necklace and I could see by his smile he would make them earn them. Those with silver beads I could ask twice as much for as the plain.

"The cinnamon he knew at once, just as the chief in the temple had. He wanted it, and then I showed him the little cup of amber, the amber carvings of fish and horses. These pleased him; he clapped his hands and called for a man to bring a chest of silver.

"All this time he had been looking at Jorund, who still held Rannveig's box in his arms. The box was covered with the oiled cloth, so he could not see even the wood. I had him pay me my price for all else before I would show him what was in it."

Runulv wiped his mouth with his hand, and we all leaned closer in to him.

"We set the box on a table, and I drew off the cloth. The king stood a moment and looked at the red box, the burnings, the size of it. He came to it, waved one of his men to lift the top.

"But I would not let him. I made a show of stepping in, lifting it myself for him, as if none but the king should grow near it. I took off the lid, parted the sheepskin. He stepped closer. I touched the linen wrapping, made it fall open. He looked in.

"His head moved, he said something. His hands went to it. I lifted it for him, slowly, from the box, held it out for him and all to see.

"He did not speak; he was dumb. But his eyes said all. Finally he reached out and laid hand on it, felt it was real. His men came forward too. He would not let them touch it. I just held it up for them to see, then passed it to his fat hands.

"My scale was still hanging there; I had already taken the silver for the other things. I had a piece of gold I had traded for, and put that now in one of my scale bowls, and gestured to him that was the price: The horn's weight in gold.

Those at the table were restless in their eagerness. "Horn?" several asked. "Which horn?"

"Rannveig gave me a narwhale horn to sell; the longest and best I had ever seen," Runulv told them.

Ketil recalled it. "The one Dagr won, long ago," he said, looking to Rannveig, who nodded back.

"The king could not take his eyes from that which he held," Runulv went on. "He had seen one before, at least heard of them, kept running his hand over it. He kept it in hand and held it himself as we weighed it, one of his men laying gold piece after gold piece in the other bowl."

Runulv's leathern bag had been before him all this time, and now he drew out a series of pouches, large and small, rounded and lumpy. I was watching Rannveig's face, and thought she might begin to weep. She turned to her son, and signed to him that two of the pouches that lay there were for them.

Runulv plucked one of the pouches up, pulled open the drawstrings, and gently upended the contents on the table.

We all gasped at the sight of so many gold coins. They were small, a little smaller than my own, but there were many of them, dazzlingly bright and yellow. Runulv looked up at Rannveig, and she smiled through her tears at him. He reached in his belt.

"All this is yours," he told her. "I have taken my sixth part away." He opened his hand to show us the gold which lay there.

She looked now to Sidroc. "Take your part away, without you I would have none of this," she told him.

But he shook his head. "I take none of it. It was Runulv did the work, and did it well. It was Tyr and Freyja who brought us here; make Offering to them for me if you must."

"I thank you both," she said. Her voice was trembling. "Dagr always provided well for us and does so now." She lifted her head, calmed herself with a breath. "This gold shall be Tindr's, his and his wife's," she told all.

A murmur went round the room. I knew that by morning all would know of Rannveig's new-found wealth, and that Tindr and his future wife should have it.

Gyda came in; she was breathless from walking fast, and had her sister and her little boy with her. Runulv leapt up and embraced her. More folk arrived too, family of some of the men who had gone with Runulv, and more ale was called for. We stayed a little longer, but Runulv need tend to his ship, and then would be eager to get home with Gyda. He turned back to us.

"This is the honey silver," he told us, fingering a small pouch. "You did right to jar it up small as you did. Next year we will take twice as much, if Tindr's bees agree."

I did not think Runulv could have said anything to make Sidroc as glad as the words Next Year. He grinned as he said it, making it clear he meant to go again for us.

"This is the amber." He pulled open the pouch, which was also small, and we saw why. He had changed some of the silver for gold, for there were several half and quarter pieces of gold coins there, along with silver coins and hack-silver.

"The silk," he went on. This was the smallest pouch of all, and he emptied it into his palm. Six pieces of gold lay there. They were full coins, again a bit smaller than mine, but sharp and new. A tiny nick in the side of each showed where they had been tried and found to be pure and not plated. I did not like to think of Eskil the Svear, but through him we had brought Sparrow to safety, and through the length of silk Sidroc had won from him we now had far more gold. The red silk which had travelled so far would now be worn by churchmen in Paris.

"And the cinnamon lies in iron bars at my keel," he ended. "We will unload it before I go to the farm and take it to the warehouse."

Tindr had been looking on and now I gestured him closer. I made the sign for his bees – finger and thumb pinched together and hovering about my head – and placed the honey silver pouch in his hand. He sat down on the bench next me and pulled it open. Silver tumbled out when he overturned it, small coins darting so that Tindr must flatten them with his quick hand. There was also hack-silver, short bits of silver coils, and two silver finger rings. Both were of two thick silver wires, twisted together to encircle the finger. Both were whole and unblemished, and both lovely to behold. He picked up one and threaded it on his finger; it was too small. But when he moved it to his little finger he found it fitted perfectly. The other he held to me. They looked a pair to me and I did not like to split them up, so I smiled and gestured he should keep both rings. He spread his hands over the silver, telling me to take our share. We had determined that half would be Tindr's, and that we and Runulv would share the other half. But now Runulv said to us, "Just as you would take none of Rannveig's gold, I will take none of Tindr's honey silver. It was easy to sell, made us look good to the Franks. You bought the jars and did the work; you and he should share it."

I thanked him for his kindness, for now we could add Runulv's quarter share to Tindr's. Runulv set up his scales from the ceiling rafter, and we had a fine time measuring out and dividing such bounty. Nearly all stayed to watch, for who would not wish to see such quantities of silver and of gold be handled, weighed, and shared out? Tindr ended up looking well pleased with one thick silver ring on each of his little fingers, and a small pouch more from his honey, and as we walked back to Tyrsborg together he kept looking at the twisted silver glinting on his hands, and weighing the little bag by bouncing it up and down in his palm. But I did not think he understood what his mother had told us all about the narwhale horn gold. I knew Rannveig would take care in accepting any girl for her son, and only hoped she was right in thinking that the prospect of such riches might win over any doubting parents.

After we had supped Sidroc and I still sat at the broad table. He brought forth the various pouches and we once again opened them, turning the silver and gold over in our hands, sorting through the coins, plucking out a few sound pieces of jewellery. Then he stopped and just looked up at the dimness of the ceiling beams.

"We have been here less than one year," he recounted. "We have this hall, and folk to fill it. We have a babe to come, and soon. We sit before a pile of silver and gold, all ours, and the promise of much more from the goshawks. Surely the Gods love us."

Chapter the Twentieth: The Summoning

THE goshawk chicks had grown so quickly that soon, and for her own safety, Tindr must take the hen from their wicker cage. Their white down had been overgrown with feathers, and handsomely, in rippled shades of silver grey and brown, with some chicks darker than others. Their hard and glossy eyes were as golden as were their yellow feet. They stretched their short wings and beat them up and down, and soon were chasing the skogkatts across the stable floor. Tindr fed them shreds of raw flesh from his own hand, and already had them resting upon his gloved wrist as he did so. The black talons were deeply hooked and sharp as razors, and I did not fault the big skogkatts for fleeing when the young goshawks reared up and showed them to them.

Summer rose, was at its height, the Sun seemingly still in the blue sky far above us, the nights so short that sleeping was hard for all. Fishing boats went out and returned with bulging nets of silvery herring and cod, and the work of flaying and drying the fish was at the full. Folk drove ox carts to the trading road from their upcountry farms with baskets of rye and barley and oats. Calves and lambs were weaned. The Moon waxed and waned again, the coming days no less bright but the Sun not reaching so high above us. The dawn came later, and the heat of Summer was at its peak. The apples reddened and grew large both at Tyrsborg and the farm.

I was making ready for my coming babe. I had counted over and again, and felt the time would be at St Mary's Day. Yet I was so large that I thought the child eager to come early, and was surprised when it did not.

"Is a boy you have there, a fine big one, like his father," Rannveig told me again.

She had promised to be with me when the child came, and we had Gunnvor and Helga to help as well. But the midwife all revered was an old woman named Ingirun. She was one of the wise women who told stories at the brew-house, and was well-regarded by all mothering women, both for her herb-craft, and her knowledge of the birthing rites. She was rich from it, and many silver chains hung from her wrinkled neck from grateful mothers. Around her waist was strung so many brass and iron keys that I wondered how any could own so many chests.

Birth was a time of danger for all women, and as it neared I knew Sidroc feared for me. My back ached and I could neither sit nor stand long without discomfort, but I tried ever to be light in my speech and actions. I wanted this child, longed for it with a fierce yearning, and recalled always Sidroc's joy when I told him of it. And I had borne three children alive, knew my body was strong and able.

The first pang woke me in the dark. I pulled myself from bed and just stood, holding to the wooden footboard. Grey light filled the high window, but the room itself was still in deep shadow. I watched Sidroc as he slept, lying on his back, and listened to his breathing. I gave thanks to all the Gods that be to have been brought to this morning, to stand there, gazing upon the man I loved, our child stirring within me and eager to join us in our lives.

I lifted my face at this, and felt the sudden dampness between my legs, and then a rush of water. A sound escaped my lips. Sidroc awoke and looked at me.

Sparrow went for Rannveig, and Rannveig sent word to Ingirun. Helga picked up all the deerskins from the floor, and my precious carpet, and lay down the clean birthing straw. Gunnvor cooked the morning meal, made me broth, brought in hot water to make compresses for my back and belly. I thought the child might come quick, and indeed, almost the first words the old midwife asked when she came into the treasure room were "This is not your first?"

Rannveig was already walking with me when Ingirun asked this, and was not, I think, surprised by my answer.

"Nai," I told her. "I have borne three babes, all alive."

Ingirun nodded, and Rannveig too. I felt of a sudden ashamed that I had not told Rannveig this; there was much I had not said to her, much she had been left to guess at. Her arm was about me now as we walked the narrow confines of the room. The pangs were coming in well-spaced waves, and walking helped to ease my back as my belly tightened.

Ingirun had a basket with her, set closely with small jars. She put it down upon a chest top and looked about the room, nodding at the preparation which had been made. We had asked our neighbour Alrik to build us a cradle, and he had made a handsome one, and there it sat waiting by the side of our bed. Linens had been brought by Helga, a jug of ale and hot broth too. Her eyes fell on all this and more before they fixed on me. Ingirun was a short woman, thin and wiry, with near-white hair caught up and tied in her head-wrap. Her hands were stained from her herb craft or from dying, but the fingers, tho' small and wrinkled, looked strong and capable. Her many keys lay in knots at her waist, strung from a corded sash, and were drawn so tightly together that unlike Rannveig's far fewer they barely made a sound.

She stooped over her basket, pulled from it a charred stick, and with it drew runes on the outside and inside of her left hand, and then holding it in her left, did the same with her right. They were smaller runes than what Tindr drew to ask Freyja to release a deer for him, but I saw the meaning was the same, asking a Goddess to be open-handed, and for her own hands to be in service to the end she sought.

She then placed herself in the centre of the room, and walked to all four corners, counting her steps and looking at her feet as she did so. When she was done she came and stood a long pace before me.

"Let us loose this child," she said to me.

She looked up at the ceiling beams and lifted her small hands. "Unbind, unbind, unbind this woman, Mother Frigg. Let loose this coming child, unbind it out of the darkness and into the world."

Rannveig walked me closer to her, and Ingirun's hands rested briefly at my temples, then reached round and pulled my thick braid over my shoulder.

"I unbind her hair! I unbind all that holds her!" she cried. Her fingers pulled swiftly down the length of my hair, loosening the braid, letting it fall freely about my shoulders and breast. "Frigg, great mother, wife of Odin, see that she is unbound!"

A pang struck me so that I cried aloud, and Ingirun's eyes brightened. I wore naught but my shift, but she stepped to the wall where hung one of my sashes. She looped it about my belly, tied it in front, and spoke again.

"I loosen this woman, I unbind this child, all knots are nothing to great Frigg." Again her fingers went to work, pulling apart the knot she had just tied. She let the sash drop upon the straw.

"Frigg and Freyja! Guardians and guides to waiting women, to babes and beasts awaiting their turn in Midgard, loosen this woman, unbind this child!"

A pang came, hot and hard, so that I cried aloud and with strength. My knees buckled a moment, yet I knew I was not ready to kneel. Ingirun bent down, pulled up my shift and took a peek, then laid both hands on my trembling belly.

"Not yet, not ready, but soon, soon," she said.

She walked at my other shoulder then, she and Rannveig each with an arm about my waist, and each time I groaned or cried out they praised my efforts and called on Frigg and Freyja. Helga came and went, told me Sidroc was in the kitchen yard, chopping wood with Tindr, at which news Ingirun gave a little grunt of approval, as if this was but another form of unbinding or opening. They gave me broth to drink and laid wet linen, wrung from the hottest of water, across my belly. The tightening of my belly felt like the babe could not be long in coming, and I cried out with them in asking the Goddesses for release.

"Come, come, little one," I said aloud as well, speaking to my coming daughter. "Come here to my arms."

I was kneeling now, my back against a mound of cushions, Rannveig holding my shoulders as I shuddered with each pang. Ingirun pulled back from where she squatted between my legs. Her hands went to the massed keys at her waist, unknotted the cord. The narrow fingers touched one key, pulled it from its tie, and this she dropped to the floor.

"I unlock this child! I free this child!" she cried out. One by one she fingered the keys, then dropped them, proclaiming with each the same words.

I watched the withered fingers hold and then release every brass and iron key, heard over my own panting and groans the tinkle of its drop as it hit the wooden floor or struck against its fellows.

Then came a clenching so great I knew it was my babe, and I arched my back and could do nothing but push. I knew I screamed, not through pain alone, but of a gathering of all the strength I had left. Rannveig was crying out encouragement, her hand upon my brow, and Ingirun holding my knees and chanting the names of the Goddesses.

I felt a turn, a twist, a final burning stretch, and then release as the dark head of my babe appeared. Ingirun caught it up, wet and filmy, and raised it before me.

"Your daughter!" Rannveig cried, and kissed my brow. I fell back and clasped the tiny girl on my trembling belly. It made a piping cry, the red mouth opening.

Ingirun took her shears from her basket and snipped the cord. Rannveig rose and reached for linen to swathe the babe. I began to lift my head to look at her when I shuddered again. I had had after-pangs before, but this was greater, so great that I clenched my hands and Rannveig took my girl from off my belly. Then the pang was gone, and I reached my hand again for my girl, but then came a second pang, as great as that which had brought her into the light.

"Another – another is coming," Ingirun told us.

I could not answer, just took breath and gathered my strength to push again. It took two more pangs, but then, and without any pain at all, I felt a shrug of release. Ingirun's withered face creased into a broad smile as she held the dripping babe.

"A boy," she said, and laid it on my belly. I placed my hand on the tiny slick back, unable to do more than weep in my relief and happiness. Rannveig brought the girl to me, and laid them side by side. The boy whimpered, then cried out lustily.

I looked to Rannveig. In Angle-land some held that twinned children were unlucky, as folk thought Cain and Abel had been twinned. I scanned her face to see what she thought. There was naught there but gladness for me.

361

Ingirun too looked pleased, but the rites did not end with the birth of the babes. "Words must be spoken," she told me, "words of thanks to Frigg and to Freyja, words of blessing and thanks to me."

She said the next slowly, with me repeating after her, heartfelt in what I said.

"May the holy beings Frigg and Freyja and all other Gods help you, even as you have saved me from danger."

I had indeed felt protected. Lying there, my little ones light against my breast, I gave thanks for an easy and safe birth.

"Sidroc," I said.

Rannveig nodded and rose, went to the door. I thought he might be just outside and he was. His hair was so tousled that I smiled, knowing he had run his hand through it a hundred times or more as he waited. He strode over to where I still lay against the cushions, and squatted down at my side. I had one hand each upon the tiny backs of our babes, and I smiled up at him. It took him a moment to see that there were two, then his eyes opened wide, and his finger went to first one dark head, and then the other.

"A girl, and a boy," I told him. "The spice-merchant was right, and Rannveig too."

Rannveig had brought a hen with her when she had walked up to Tyrsborg, a hen that she would kill in thanksgiving for my being delivered safely of my child. I knew this was what the grand-mother of a new babe did here on Gotland, and was greatly moved when she told me she did it for me. But she smiled when she added she had had to return to the brew-house kitchen yard for a second hen, for no one had expected two babes to give thanks for.

We were all surprised. But both babes were perfect, tho' a little small, and the fact that a boy and girl had been given to us at one time made them truly a doubled blessing. Ingirun and Rannveig washed the babes and swaddled them. They lifted me and I went to our waiting bed. I had my gift ready for the midwife, a necklace strung with some of the tiny silver coins Ring had brought back, and was glad now it was of such richness. I reached and took the necklace from the shelf by my bedside, and placed it in her hands. She slipped it on her neck with a bow, and began gathering up her dropped keys, humming to herself as she did.

The household came in, Tindr and Gunnvor and Helga and little Sparrow, all with happy faces. Sidroc sat in the chair by the bed, and Rannveig brought first one and then the other babe to him.

"This is my daughter," he said, taking hold of the tiny bundle and setting her upon his knee. He passed the babe to Ingirun at his side.

"And this is my son," he said, touching the swaddled babe to his knee.

In this way he acknowledged before witnesses his duty to our children. All came forward to greet the newcomers to Tyrsborg, Gunnvor beaming and taking up each babe in turn, Helga and Tindr and Sparrow smiling shyly at the scrunched pink faces. I ate broth and bread and then I slept, a babe tucked up under each arm, until their piping cries told me they were hungered too.

I had milk enough for both, and both ate willingly and well. That night I kept them in bed with us, as I did not like to give them up so soon to the waiting cradle. Sidroc lay on his side and stroked their little brows as they rested between us.

"The boy," he said. "I will name him Yrling."

"Já," I whispered back.

It was his uncle Yrling who had brought Sidroc to Angle-land, who had made the Peace with Ælfsige that had brought Ælfwyn, and thus me, to Four Stones; Yrling who had been killed by Godwin over Gyric's maiming, and left Ælfwyn a widow; Yrling who Sidroc knew would be waiting for him in the Halls of the Slain.

"Já, Yrling," I said again. I smiled at them both; the babe's eyes were closed, and his father's finger as it traced the line of his tiny nose looked so large.

"And the girl?" Sidroc asked.

I looked down at the rosy face, eyes shut, the daughter which had been promised to me, now here, sweet and warm, between her father and I, and resting too with her brother. I had not a name ready as I did not wish to suffer the disappointment of holding her so clearly in my mind before I knew she was truly here and safe.

Now she was, alive and real next to my breast. Breathing in her milky sweetness I could not help but think of my Welsh mother. She had been nameless to me, and perhaps to all of Mercia; mayhap even my father. Her name had been her own, perhaps all that had been left her, and if she would not share it I could not fault her. Yet now that this girl lay next my breast, so far from the land in which my own lost and nameless mother had first held me, I felt a great need to give her a Welsh name. I spoke from some half-forgotten memory.

"Eirian, I shall call her," I said, touching her face, "for she shall be bright and beautiful."

"Eirian," Sidroc repeated. "It is of your mother's people?"

I nodded. "Já, it is of the Welsh."

I slept that night a deep and dreamless sleep, a sleep of rich content and completion. The babes, having suckled well, and wearied from their journey to the world, slept too. It was near dawn when first the cries of one and then the other woke me.

Rannveig came every morning to see us. Gunnvor and Helga and Sparrow did all needful for me and the babes; the washing and drying of linens alone was a large task. But Rannveig came just to sit with me. It gave her pleasure to hold each babe and see the growth and change from day to day. Even swaddled she could tell them apart as well as I; Yrling had the bigger head, and of a different shape. And Yrling was ever the hungrier of the two, wanting to eat more and longer. Sometimes I had one at the breast while she held and dandled the second, or she would help me lay both babes so that they might feed together. Alrik had built us a second cradle, but while Rannveig was near neither babe would lie within one. I knew she feared having no grand-children to call her own, and to act almost as grand-mother to these was a help and comfort to us both.

One morning while she held Yrling she asked a question. We had been silent as Eirian took her milk, but now, looking at us, she spoke.

"Your three babes," she said. "Do they yet live?" Her voice was low, her query gentle.

I could not do otherwise than tell the truth. "The last born, my daughter, was taken by fever, when she was teething."

She only nodded, but held Yrling a little closer to her.

"Já," she said. "Tindr had two sisters, the prettiest maids on Gotland, of four and six Summers. The fever took them both, and almost Tindr too. He was spared to us, but it was days before we knew his hearing was taken, along with his pretty sisters." She looked a little past me, into the darkness of those days. "Dagr spent much time out on his boat that year; the quiet house was too much for him."

Her eyes met mine, and we needed no word nor sign between us.

"The other two?" she wanted to know.

"Two boys I had before my daughter," I answered. "Both live. But they are in –"

"Do not tell me," she broke in. "It matters not; I know you came from afar. And I know Sidroc does not want this known." She paused a moment before going on. "There is good reason you must be parted from them."

I could only nod, tho' I hoped she read my gratitude to her in my eyes.

"A man like Sidroc…such a man…he will have enemies," she finished.

The Moon waxed and waned; the days, tho' warm and bright, grew shorter. I took the babes outside and laid them in baskets on the table where I sewed or spun. If they slept I worked as well at nålbinding, building up stockings in quick loops about my thumb, for like spinning it was easy work to set down and take up again. I stood little at my looms, for it seemed I could do no more than lay a line or two of wool or linen before one or the other of the babes would cry, face reddening, asking for my breast. But I ate as heartily as they did, Gunnvor making rich milk puddings or eggs for me each day. I was tired by day and grateful to sleep when the babes did. I walked out when I could and took pleasure in each flitting hour.

The young goshawks were flying, flapping from Sidroc's or Tindr's wrist to the top of the stable roof, or to the peak of the little hawk-house they and Alrik had built. They took their food from the hand, avidly, their sharp beaks tearing at what was offered, and now were learning to wear the small light leathern hood and leathern ties on their strong feathered legs. All had rippled brown and white breasts, but their backs and wings were unique to each, one being mostly brown, another silver grey, the other two an admixture. Their bright eyes, hard and yellow, watched small birds fly overhead, and they sometimes opened their wings as if they would spring after them, but as yet had not the strength to pursue prey.

Sidroc was pleased with their growth; soon he and Tindr would ride with them to the farm and begin training them in open country. And he had a plan how we might buy many furs from the northern trader who supplied Ragnfast's cousin with the furs which had kept us warm in Winter. This trader, a man from the far North, a place of walrus and giant deer, would sail to Gotland before the cold fell, and come to Tyrsborg with his goods. So these waning days of Summer, full as they were, brimmed with plans for the next trading season too.

One night as we lay in bed, the babes asleep in their cradles by my side, I turned to Sidroc and just snuggled next him, my face in his neck, my arm across his chest. His arm came round me, pressing me closer to him. The room was dim and the hall was still, tho' a nightbird sang out in the depths of the spruce trees. I lay there, relishing the quiet and his nearness, breathing in his scent, feeling the strength of his arm around me and the hardness of his chest against my own full breasts. But he began to shift and move away. I tried to hold on to him, but he took my hand and lifted it off his chest.

"Shield-maiden," he whispered. His own hand came to my hair and lay there. "I cannot have you so near."

I began to lift my head when he spoke again.

"I want you too much."

We had not coupled since the birth of the babes, these two tiny strangers who were the fullest expression of our love, our desire, our new life together. He had shown tenderness and good humour in our changed estate, lying in the dark with one babe on his chest as I had one at my breast, had complained not of our shortened nights nor my need to sleep at times during the day. I rose on my elbow and looked at him.

"And I – I want you," I answered back.

I thought my body healed, and knew I wished for that deepest closeness. His arm closed over me again, pressing me against his chest, then he lifted my face so he might kiss me. To know he desired me and fought back that desire out of love for me inflamed my own passion for him. I kissed him, deeply, fully, rising up so that my milk-heavy breasts brushed his chest.

The gentleness of his hands upon me, his fingertips just tracing the lines of my body, his mouth caressing my lips and face as he drew me nearer and beneath him; this sweetness and concern for me swelled my heart and flushed my skin with warmth and ardour. Our mouths, our bodies met slowly; yielding, giving, accepting, his eyes watching mine. Joined in embrace, my hands about his neck, I looked up at his face, looked up at him in the dusk as he bent to kiss my eyelids now closing in pleasure.

Chapter the Twenty-first: Joys, and Sorrow

The Year 884

THE wheel of the year had turned twice since our babes were born. Eirian was slender-limbed, as tall as her brother, with dark chestnut curls and her father's dark blue eyes. Yrling was sturdy, his hair lighter than his sister's, a true chestnut-gold like my own, with blue-green eyes and already a few freckles on his snub nose. Both were happy, romping children, never apart like most who were twinned; much spoiled by Gunnvor and Helga, played with by Sparrow when she was with us, and prized by Tindr, who took pains to guide the little hands to the reaching neck of my mare's black colt, or show them how to slip under a hen and see if she had left us an egg.

Sparrow had grown, her thin body rounding slightly, and gained some in height, tho' she stayed much like her namesake in quickness and brownness. She still said her prayers every day, and tho' I had told her all I knew twice over, still looked forward to hearing stories from the Gospels. She came with us as part of the household when we made Offering in the month of Blót, watching quietly, and not, I think, judging us the worse for what she witnessed, for I thought no one had told her heathens were evil. Nor did I think she told anyone of the faith she privately held. To Helga and Gunnvor they were Saga-tales from afar, and if Sparrow had ever spoken to Rannveig about Jhesu Christus I did not hear of it.

Sparrow now spent some of her time down the hill at Rannveig's. She had ever paid close attention to Gunnvor when she cooked, and at Rannveig's was a help to Gudfrid in the kitchen yard. But Rannveig had discovered that Sparrow had a talent for brewing, a sense and feel for the sloshing mash wort, a nose that could trace any hint of sourness arising from the big pottery crocks, a tongue that knew how much of Tindr's sweet honey should be dribbled in to make the golden liquid foam. Rannveig took pleasure in teaching her, and pride in Sparrow's interest and growing skill.

What Sparrow did not like was the brew-house itself. She helped at table only if Rannveig had no other woman at hand. On one such night, a man deep in his cups grabbed for Sparrow's rump as she passed him. She turned on him, pottery jug in hand, and struck him across the head with it, breaking the jug and knocking him from his bench.

"And a good customer too, Eirik the cooper," Rannveig told me as she recounted it next morning. She shook her head. "But it was coming to him for snatching at her. She almost could not help it, was white as snow after, then burst into tears. All I could do was get him to his feet, scold him roundly, and send him on his way."

Sparrow did not tell me of this when she came back to Tyrsborg, nor did I ask. I had been teaching her to write out the alphabet, and each day if we found time we would do some work with it. At first we just drew a poker or stick in flattened ashes, but then I asked Tindr to make me a shallow wooden box so I might have a wax tablet. I filled it with melted yellow beeswax from his hives, and we used slender wooden sticks as our stylus.

She could write out 'Jhesu', which she asked me to show her, and then I thought to teach her her own name. 'Sparrow', I wrote out in the soft wax. She watched me with interest, and sounded out each letter as she traced it.

I gave a short laugh. "Sparrow," I told her, "this name is not a Christian name. Your people would not be pleased with such a name."

371

She nodded and bit her lip, her small chin rounding slightly. "My real name...it does not feel like me." She lifted her head to the trees nearby, from which sparrows cheeped. "I want to be a bird, who can fly from danger."

I let my eyes rise with hers to where the unseen birds hopped, safe in the thick boughs of the spruces.

"I cannot teach you much more about Jhesu, Sparrow. There are lands, Christian lands such as Frankland, which might be your home, and Angle-land, which lays across the water from it, to which you could go. There are priests and nuns there, monks and lay-sisters. You could be amongst Christians, worship Jhesu amongst friends."

She had heard Runulv speak of the priests in Frankland, and recalled my spurned offer to send her there. I had told her, as well, that I had once met a holy woman, a great Abbess, who kept a convent full of women, and men too, who had given themselves up to God and good works. She looked at me now, the green flecks in her brown eyes glittering, and I saw she listened.

"You can bake and brew, are a hard worker; you would be welcome to live with such sisters. Perhaps you would even become a nun. I would pay to send you, and give you also silver as your dowry."

Her mouth twisted at this word. "Dowry? I will not wed," she told me.

"Nor will you need to. The silver is called that, but nuns – they are wed to Jhesu alone. You would live amongst them like sisters – quiet sisters – and have your own small room to sleep in; no man will trouble you. The dower-silver is a gift to make sure you are cared for in old age. Also if you leave the convent, they will return the silver to you, by law they must."

She was looking down and not at me. "To go I must get on a ship," she said.

"Já," I answered. I did not think any other, save her, shared my fear of taking ship. "You must sail there. There is danger, always, at sea. But you would not suffer what you suffered before. I would send you with men who would care for and protect you."

For answer she looked down again, then lifted her stylus to the wax and once again began tracing out her name.

We had sent three ships with trading goods in the past two Summers. Runulv went the first year to Dane-mark, and then onward, back to Frankland, carrying salt, amber beads, two pairs of great millstones, and bundles of furs. The furs we had bought from the same trader Ragnfast's friend Gautvid had himself bought from the past few seasons, a man with white-yellow hair and blue-white eyes like Tindr's. Gautvid and the fur trader came up the hill seated on a waggon drawn by two horses, for Gautvid could afford horses through all his fur selling; but later Gautvid told us that the waggon this man travelled in in his home land were pulled by giant deer.

Osku was the man's name. He was from far to the North, and Gautvid called these folk Skridfinn, or striding Finns, for the distances they travelled; but Osku called his own folk the Sámi. He wore no linen nor wool, was clad entirely in the soft skins of beasts, both tunic and his leggings. At the neck of his leathern tunic was stitched thread-work in brilliant red and blue, and the cuffs also were so adorned. His boots looked of the warmest, with the fur still on them, and on the outside, like onto the boarskin boots Tindr made for himself. Tindr stood with us to greet them as they came, and he could not take his eyes from the man, for he looked almost a wild animal, tho' his blue-white eyes were gentle as Tindr's.

Osku knew a little of our speech, but unlike all traders I had ever seen carried no scales. He traded not for silver, but for goods, and Gautvid had told us he would want bags of grain, lengths of woollens, and balls of woollen thread. We had these things in abundance for him. But first we offered them food and drink: Rannveig's ale, loaves and cheeses, and honey-cakes too. He relished all we fed him, and ate his honey-cakes slowly and carefully, licking his fingers when he was done.

The furs he brought us were of the best, that of white foxes such as adorned my mantle-hood, and narrow dark brown pelts of thick and surpassing softness called mink, and the big glossy skins of the water-living seals. Sidroc traded for every one he could afford, and when all the goods we had amassed in exchange now lay in the waggon bed, had another thought.

"Honey," he said aloud. He turned to Tindr, made the pinched-fingers sign for his bees and their honey. Tindr nodded and went to the kitchen yard, coming back with a big jar of it. He took it to Osku, who looked within. Sidroc made a gesture that he should dip his finger, and taste. The Sámi trader did.

His grin was wide when he pulled his finger from his mouth. He took the jar from Tindr, set it in the waggon, and pulled out a seal skin, then another. He held them out to Tindr, who took them.

Sidroc looked well pleased. "One is yours, Tindr," he told him, pointing to the skin and touching his ear, "and one mine," and here he put his finger to the scar on his face. The sealskins were so large that a man could wrap himself up in one. I held the one Tindr passed to Sidroc and it was soft and supple under the fingers as well.

Osku and Gautvid bid us fare-well then, with promise to come again the next year, which they did. Tindr took his sealskin to his mother, who fashioned it into a warm and waterproof tunic for him, so that he looked a kin to Osku the Sámi when he wore it. That which the honey had brought Sidroc was set aside to go to Frankland. The pile of furs was more than I think even Sidroc had imagined being able to send, and Runulv, when he saw them, could not hide the gleam in his eye at the thought of taking such things to the island city of Paris.

Runulv again sailed early in that second Spring season, again dodged storms, but with Njord's favour went unpursued to and from Frankland. He returned with not a leathern satchel of silver and gold, but a small chest full of it. The millstones he had sold without trouble and at twice what we had paid for them, and the furs had won him, and us, much. Gyda had not only splendid silver brooches pinning her gown, but two pairs of them, each different; and had as well a second little boy, as winning as her first.

This year two ships sailed for us, Runulv, and once again his brother Ring, and therein lay the only deep sorrow to have visited our circle, for Ring would not have gone otherwise.

When Ring returned from his salt-selling to Dane-mark, he and Ása settled down on the farm, working hard to extend the rows of grains, hills of vegetables and greens, and breed up their sheep and goats. They were blessed with happiness, and we saw them often, lovely Ása taking pleasure in little Eirian and Yrling, and then telling me of her own babe to come next Summer.

When her time grew near, her mother and the midwife Ingirun went to the farm. I sent Sparrow next morning with a basket of honey-cakes and a jar of Rannveig's mead, a gift to celebrate the new child. I was in the kitchen yard when Sparrow came back, her hair dishevelled, breathless from running and her own tears.

Gunnvor was standing over her baking, and Helga next me as she spun. Sparrow ran to us, spreading her empty hands.

"Ása – Ása is dead," she sobbed out. "The child too; they could not bring it out of her."

We all cried aloud, looking in each other's faces in our shocked grief.

"The child too," Gunnvor managed to ask, at which Sparrow nodded rapidly.

"They could not bring it forth; Ingirun has rent her hair, Ása's mother weeps and cannot stop."

Little Yrling was standing, learning to walk, and was at my feet, pulling his way along the bench I had been sitting on. His sister sat up in the grass, pulling green shoots and stuffing them in her pink mouth. She stopped now and looked up at me. I bent down and placed my hands on both their backs, safe and here.

"Ring?" I asked Sparrow. I thought of Ása's young husband, hearing his wife's screams, hearing them end in silence.

"I did not see him," she told us. "Runulv and Gyda had been sent for; I do not know more."

The next day we gathered on the trading road, awaiting the waggon that would bear its tender cargo to the burial ground. All from the trading road were there, and many from outlying farms, for Ása and Ring's families were large and well liked. Sidroc and I waited with the rest, Tindr and Rannveig too joining us. I had Eirian in my arms, and Sparrow held Yrling. Almost none spoke as we watched the cart come across a field and then onto one of the side paths leading to the trading road. A single ox pulled the light load. As it passed I saw Ása, laying on a cloth of snowy linen, her white brow smooth, her yellow hair carefully combed and resting on her shoulders. A sheet of linen was drawn up as if she slept, drawn up and over her still-swollen belly that held her child that never knew breath nor light of day.

Ring walked behind, with Runulv at one shoulder, and Ása's parents at the other. Ring's face was stricken; only by sheer force of will do I think he kept his feet. Then came Botair, and Gyda, and Ketil and Tola, and Ása's sisters. We joined them and made our slow way along the road, the sea gleaming dully under a scudded and clouded sky.

At the burning place the waggon was stopped. The wood had been laid and sprinkled with oil. Ása's body was drawn out with the board she lay upon, and set upon the firewood. Those things that had ridden with her now were taken up by those who loved her. Ring placed a silver necklace over her breast, his face near as white as her own. He lay a hand scythe at her right hand, the same I thought they once had passed from hand to hand.

Her mother set a pair of shears, a comb of horn, a spindle charged with wool, a smoothing board of whalebone by her daughter's side. Her sisters brought jars and pots, sealed and open, and as their tears fell ranged them about her. Her father took his bronze Thor's hammer amulet from over his head and touched it to his daughter's brow and feet, then dropped it back around his neck. Flower heads were strewn about her, falling on the smooth linen and about her face. One violet petal landed on her blanched cheek, calling to mind the necklace of violets she had woven on her hand-fast day.

The fire was lit. It rose quickly, the oiled firewood flashing into flame, hungry to carry two so blameless away.

The women wailed. My tears rained down; Eirian's hair grew wet as I hid my face over her curling head. I felt Sidroc's hand on my back, saw him watch with narrowed eyes the smoke cover what the flames consumed. His eye went to Ring, standing with lifted eyes before the byre.

"They will meet again," Sidroc told me. "They will meet again."

Ring stayed on at the farm. I feared he would leave, but I think it gave him comfort to remain in a place which Ása had loved, and hoped to live long with him. But even a small farm cannot be managed alone, and for a while his father Botair came and lived with him and worked the farm. In the deep snows of Winter Ring walked to Tyrsborg and told Sidroc he wished to sail again, to Dane-mark or any other place. Come Spring he and his brother set off together, Ring to Dane-mark with fine grained Gotland salt, and Runulv on to Frankland with furs. This time Runulv took a goshawk in its wicker cage with him, a large silver female which Sidroc and Tindr had deemed ready to show.

Ring came back before him, better for the journey, and richer as well. To leave and come back had been a tonic to him, that, and the turning of the year. We were all heartened when he asked Ása's sister Astrid to wife. He was young and must go forward with his life. They had each loved Ása and this shared love proved a balm to their grieving. As soon as his brother returned they would hand-fast.

Runulv came home with tales of Frankish wealth, with bags of silver and of gold, and huge jars of Frankish wine. The fat king of the Franks had not been at his Paris hall, but Runulv had found ready buyers amongst the lords and ladies in residence there, and laughed at how those who had recalled him rushed to meet him and be first to claim the right to see what he bore. The furs and amber necklaces he sold within two days, and at good profit.

The goshawk had been bought by a rich lord, but not before he must contend with another lord for the privilege of carrying so majestic a bird on his wrist. The silver female was well-trained, calm on the wrist, and lightning fast in the air. She had brought down a blackbird and seized a rabbit from the riverside grassland in rapid order, so that the men nearly came to blows over who should have her. Runulv only solved the quarrel by having them roll dice to see who would pay another tenth over the last offered price.

"The brown male – he will be ready next year, will he not?" Runulv asked, with a grin. "I have a ready buyer for him if he is."

Chapter the Twenty-second: The Reckoning

THREE months had passed since Runulv and Ring had returned. It was a fair late Summer's morning, a day which made me pause in my tasks to savour the clearness of the blue sky and softness of the air. Sidroc had left early, headed by foot through the woodland path leading to our upland farm. He had wanted to stop at Ketil's farm first, but would be back, he told me, before the dusk of owl-light. Helga was busy with her spinning, and I with some sewing, while Eirian and Yrling tumbled about our feet in play. I had taken my work out into the kitchen yard behind Tyrsborg, where the light was strong and where I was near both Helga and Gunnvor as she worked at her baking. Sparrow was down with Rannveig at the brewing yard.

The children just then were running in and out of the open hall door along the long side; I could hear their pattering feet and whoops of laughter. I sat at the table placed by the narrow stone end of the hall, happy to hear the laughter of the little ones, and happy in the little shift I was sewing for Eirian. A breeze was blowing, and made the leaves in the trees before me rustle gently. Then – I do not know why – I raised my head from my work. A boy stood a few feet from me; he must have stepped out from around the corner of the hall past the kitchen fire pit.

It was Ceric. I had seen him in dreams; seen snatches of him in other children here in Gotland; but now he was here, standing before me, the roundness of his little boy's face lengthening into that of a young man, for he had now twelve Summers. Buckled at his waist was his father's seax, no longer seeming far too long for him.

His eyes were wide and round but other than that I could not read his expression.

"Ceric," I gasped, and came around the end of the table, my arms reaching for him. "Ceric."

He took a little bound to me now, and into my arms, and let me smother his face and head with my kisses as I clutched at him. "Mother," he whispered, and smiled at me. A tear was on his cheek, and I kissed it away. He had grown so that his head was level with my chin, and as I hugged him I saw first Gunnvor and then Helga stop in their work as they turned, with puzzled looks, towards us.

From over Ceric's head I saw another boy, dark-haired, as lean and tall as a sapling. "Hrald," I called, reaching my hand out to him, and the uncertainty dropped from his face and he too came to me, and I hugged and kissed them both. My heart was so full that I could scarcely order my thoughts; my mind was in a tumult to see not only Ceric but Hrald too. Was somehow Ælfwyn here as well?

I opened my lips to question them, and raised my eyes to where I thought they had come from. No woman stepped forth from around the stone end of the hall. Instead came two men, and the red-gold hair of one, now paling with age, told me this was Godwin. The other man with him was the young horse-thegn, Worr. They must have watched Sidroc leave, and been waiting to find us unguarded.

They were dressed for travel, in simple clothing, well-made but with no show; but both bore the weapons that marked them as warriors, for besides the long seaxes strapped across their bellies they both carried leathern baldrics on their chests bearing their fine swords. Worr carried also a round wooden shield slung upon on his back.

Godwin took a step closer to me, and something like a smile broke the line of his fixed mouth. I felt a horror in seeing him, and know I clutched harder at the boys in my arms.

"My Lady Ceridwen," he said, and these words, so unnatural, struck terror within me. "We are here to take you home."

I shrank back, and began to cry out to Helga and Gunnvor, but Godwin did not let a moment pass.

"Get the serving women and lock them inside," he ordered Worr. Worr laid down his shield and hastened to the table at which Gunnvor, open-mouthed, stood with flour up to her elbows. He grasped her by the arm, and with his other waved to Helga, but she did not move.

Godwin glanced around for just a moment, then said to me, "Get your things together so we can go. There is a ship waiting for us." His eyes were glittering, and the fine lines around them deepened as he stared at me.

My mouth opened in disbelief. "Go? I am not going with you. I am staying here, with my husband and children."

"Your children? What about Ceric, and Edwin? Or have you forgotten they are yours, as you have forgotten so much? Hurry. Get your things."

"I am not going, Godwin."

Just then Yrling and Eirian ran around to us from the long side of the hall, where they had been prattling in their play. They were now quiet, and their eyes were round from alarm at our loud voices. Godwin glanced at them.

"You are going with me if I have to pull you by the hair through town like the whore you are!"

Ceric made a sound, and his uncle pointed at him. "You two, stand over by the shield and stay alert. We are leaving soon."

Both boys were of a sudden ashen-faced, and Hrald, just ten, scanned the yard, his blue eyes flitting from outbuilding to outbuilding. Godwin would have told him he would see his father, and now he was being told he would not. I did not want to let the boys go from me, but they obeyed, and went and stood near the lowered shield.

Eirian began to whimper and pull at my skirts, and little Yrling too clutched at Helga, who now stood next me. "Lock them up inside with the serving women," Godwin told Worr.

"No!" I cried, and took a stride towards him. But Godwin grasped my wrist, and now wrung it with such force that I dropped to my knees, yelping in pain.

"Take them," Godwin commanded, and Worr herded the little ones and Helga within. Her eyes were starting in her pale face as she lifted the bawling Yrling in her arms.

"Godwin, you are mad," I told him, as he gripped me. He was bending over me, eyes flaring in anger, and I thought my arm would break from the force he used. I wanted to scream, in pain and in fear both, but I tried to steady my voice and reach him with my words. "You do not know what you are doing. You have no claim on me. Leave now, and Sidroc will not learn of your visit."

"I will leave, but it will be with what I came all this way for – you."

"I am not going."

He yanked me to my feet, but released me, and I stood, holding my wrist in my other hand. I felt at that moment a panic that I had not felt in years. Sidroc would be at Ketil's farm by now, or nearing it. Sparrow was down at Rannveig's and we might not see her until next day. No one would climb the hill to Tyrsborg unless they were coming to see us. We were all in the kitchen yard, hidden behind the hall itself, where none from a nearby croft could hear or see us. My back was to the trees and I stood nursing my wrist and looking at the stone face of the home I cherished.

I saw a movement from the door of the stable. I had not seen Tindr since we had broken our fast in the hall, was not in fact certain if he had gone with Sidroc or not; but now I saw he had been working in the back of the stable, for he peered out, a rake in his hand. He had no way to understand our voices, but he took in the scene at a glance. I lifted my aching wrist to my face and tapped my left cheek.

He nodded, and slipped again into the shadows of the stable. There were windows, and another door too, and I must believe that he would find Sidroc quickly at either Ketil's or our farm.

I turned back to Godwin. Worr had returned and looked with uneasy eyes between us, and the boys too stood frozen in their fear.

Godwin's eyes flicked about the space, from the stone wall of the hall, to the kitchen sheds, to the stable, to the trees behind me. I could not tell what he was gauging. I tried to master my fear.

"Godwin, I am not going with you. You have brought Ceric to me and for this I am grateful. It is up to him if he wishes to stay here, and up to Hrald, too. But I am not returning to Kilton.

"My life is here now. I am Sidroc's wife –"

"He has a wife – your 'friend,' Ælfwyn. Or are you now so heathen that it does not trouble you to think of that?"

"What of you?" I answered in my anger. "You too have a wife, who you so easily forget. If I had returned to Kilton, I would have been forced to take Ceric and go to Sceaftesburh and wed a man I do not love. Yes, forced, because all the good of Kilton – Edwin and Edgyth and Modwynn – was already lost to me, because of your lust for me. You would give me no peace. I will not keep paying endlessly for my mistake!"

To say these things before my frightened son, before the puzzled Hrald, before the true and good Worr, was to shame and accuse both of us. Yet I would say and do anything to keep us from utter disaster.

"Leave now," I pleaded, and then said that which I feared was not true. "Sidroc will be back soon."

He did not move, and I spoke the warning I truly believed. "He will kill you, Godwin. I do not want your blood on his hands."

"I am taking you back," Godwin answered. He again grasped my wrist, but I broke from him.

I turned to Worr. His brow was furrowed, but he met my gaze.

"Do not let him take me away, Worr," I begged, and raised my hands in supplication. His troubled blue eyes went from me to Godwin, and then back, and I saw he listened. "You were the pledged man of Gyric. You served him well, and for years. No man spent as much time with him as you did, nor knew him as well. I beseech you, by the love you bore for him, and by the love you know he bore for me, not to let Godwin take me. I will be in danger, great danger, if he does."

I could not speak my fear before the boys, but Worr was a man, and he read it in my face and voice. He opened his mouth as if he would answer me, but before he could speak Godwin broke in.

"You speak of danger? You live in sin with your captor, tempting Hell-fire, and see danger in my taking you back to your rightful home at Kilton?" His eyes were fixed on me, not seeming to see Worr and the boys before us. He kept staring at my face, as if I were the answer to all that had befallen before. Then he began a shrill recounting.

"I have come a long way for you, left those who need me to bring you back. I have lost too much to the Danes; I am not losing you, not a second time. Half my life I have fought them. Huge sums of silver I have paid them, as did my father Godwulf before me. We have lost many good men. Gyric was blinded by a Dane. I lost my shield-arm to a Dane trying to kill me and destroy my hall. Wulfstan, Godwulf's best warrior, was crippled by this thief who has stolen you." He ended with a vehement demand. "Or do you forget all this?"

He knew I would not give answer. He took breath, seemed of a sudden to calm himself. He raised his hand to the hall and all around it. "Why would you stay? You are of Angle-land; a woman of Mercia who found a home in Wessex. These are not your kind."

"No; I am more, or less than that, as you might have it," I told him. "I am half-Welsh, and have their wildness in me. These folk here in Gotland are nearer to me than you can ever know. I worship as they do, to the Gods of my old kinsmen – and yours. I am here because Fate gave us this place to live, and make our lives in, and I am grateful for it. And it is here that I will die."

"No. This one thing I can recover, and I am taking you back."

I looked again to Worr, and saw that he was moved by my plight; yet being the sworn man of Godwin kept him from acting for me. It would take a dire act by Godwin for Worr to break his pledge to him. I had no weapon near me, not even a kitchen knife or poker with which I could defend my right to stay.

As my eyes searched about for answers I heard pounding footsteps coming up behind me from the trees. I turned to see Sidroc as he stopped himself at the edge of the woods.

He drew breath and looked at all of us where we stood. Sweat was beaded on his brow from his run, and shone when the sudden sunlight hit it. He drew another deep breath. I was closest to him, and a little behind me stood Godwin, and then Worr, who had moved back to Godwin's side when Sidroc appeared. It was me his eyes came back to.

"He has not harmed you?" was the first thing he said, but I could not trust my voice and only shook my head No.

Now he saw Hrald and Ceric, and spoke to his son in his own tongue.

"Hrald. I am glad to see you," he said. Hrald looked as if he might run to his father, but Sidroc put his hand up to stay him, and the boy stood stock still next to my own.

He looked at Godwin and the thegn who stood with him. He spent a long moment taking them in. Sidroc had no weapons other than his seax; his sword and all else was in the treasure room.

Within the hall Yrling and Eirian began to cry. Sidroc looked his question to me. "Godwin locked them in the treasure room with Helga and Gunnvor. They are only scared," I assured him.

The Hall of Tyr

Sidroc now took a step closer to Godwin.

"How did you find me?" he asked, and then answered himself. "It was the Saxon."

Godwin smiled. "Yes. Aldhelm was his name."

"Was."

"He is dead. I paid him his silver and cast him from my hall. Then I found he had stolen one of my horses. Worr tracked him, and killed him."

Sidroc's eyes glanced for a moment to Worr, then back to Godwin. "But you had what you wanted," Sidroc told him. "And your silver back." He paused a moment. "Whatever he told you was a lie."

Godwin snorted. "He did not lie about where I might find you."

"We could have been anywhere on the Baltic coast. How did you know to come here, to Gotland?"

"Silver goes a long way. I paid many men," Godwin answered. "When a man has luck at trading his name gets known. Word came at last."

As I looked to Godwin I saw that Tindr was now standing behind him, at the edge of the kitchen yard, just where the trees began. His bow was in his hand and an arrow at the ready, drawn for Godwin's back. It was a boar-arrow he held poised between his fingers, its steel point twice as long as that he used for deer; it would go nearly clear through the body of a man. My eyes went to Sidroc, and watched as he took this in, and watched too as he lifted his hand and gestured to Tindr to lower his bow.

"My man has an arrow pointed at your back, but I make him put it down," explained Sidroc.

Godwin turned his head sharply and saw Tindr drop the bow, arrow still cocked, to his knee.

Sidroc spoke again. "And now that you are here you think you will take my wife from me. But in this you are wrong."

"She is not your wife, only your whore. And you are an outlaw, and a thief."

Sidroc's eyes flared, but tho' his jaw clenched, his voice remained steady.

"No," he said. "She is my wife. But she did not become such until we arrived here, and it was of her own free will."

Godwin scoffed, but Sidroc went on. "I will forget you said that of her. Let her and my children come unharmed to me, and you will walk free."

Godwin gave his head a violent shake. "I am taking her to Wessex."

"You can have any woman," Sidroc said. "It is your pride that drove you here."

Without answering, Godwin took a step closer to him. It was two warriors with swords to one, who had only a seax. If Godwin drew his sword Worr would follow, and draw his. With only his seax Sidroc had no chance of a fair fight. I turned my head to see if Tindr would raise his bow again, but he did not; his eyes awaited a signal from Sidroc.

Godwin lifted his hand, but to wave Worr forward with him. Worr did not move.

Godwin spoke, looking only at Sidroc. His voice was low and carried a kind of deadly force I had rarely heard. "She is of Kilton, my brother's widow, and she is coming back where she belongs."

Sidroc looked up into the sky and drew breath before he answered.

"Kilton, they say every man is haunted by one mistake. Yours is that you did not kill me years ago, when you could. And that is the mistake that will send you to your death, for I am about to kill you.

"I know you cannot hold a shield," he went on. "You decide how we will fight. Your choice."

I could bear no more, and my throat opened in a scream. "No!"

I turned in desperation to Godwin.

"If you kill him, Godwin, I will kill myself," I swore. "But not before I have tried to kill you too."

"It is your shame that makes you say that," he challenged. "Come home with me to Kilton and all you have done will be forgiven."

"You will not take even my body back!" I shrieked at him. "'Forgiven' – I do not need your forgiveness."

He raised his hand, beckoning, as if he thought I would take it. His voice held not an offer, but a command. "Come back where you belong."

All my fury was in my answer. "I will die before I let you take me from my husband and my home!"

Ceric broke from where he stood with Hrald and ran, drawn seax in hand, to stand between me and Godwin.

"You will not hurt her, uncle," he warned.

Godwin looked at him, his amazement full upon his face. "Do you defy me, you who will be my pledged man?" He took a step nearer to us, and I saw Ceric's hand tremble, both I think in anger and in fear. I reached for my son, but Godwin swung his right arm against Ceric's upraised hand, and knocked the seax to the ground. In doing so the edge of the hilt caught Ceric across his mouth, and a small seam of blood opened from his split lip.

Sidroc had seen enough. He stepped forward and spoke.

"Kilton, draw your knife, and face me. You" – he pointed at Worr – "and you, Tindr," and here he gestured with crossed wrists to him, "will witness only. We will fight to the death. Do not interfere.

"Is that your choice, Kilton? Knife? In in the past I have thought about killing you, and thought knives would be the fairest choice." His voice was so calm that I could not bear the contrast to his deadly words.

Some sound escaped my strangled throat, and Sidroc looked to me. "I am sorry for what you must see, shield-maiden," he said softly. He almost smiled; the scar on his cheek just lifted. I could do no more than fix my eyes on him, and he nodded at me.

Godwin's hand went to his sword belt, pulled at the buckle, and then shrugged off the baldric that held his sword. Worr took the baldric and stepped away.

I looked at both men as they faced each other. Godwin had nearly forty years, three more than Sidroc, but looked as battle-hard and powerful as ever. Sidroc was much the taller, but Godwin broader through the chest and shoulders. And sounding in my head were words both Gyric and the warrior-monk Cadmar had told me, how Godwin was the smartest fighter they had ever seen, quick to spot any weakness and exploit it.

Sidroc moved in closer to Godwin, but waited for Godwin to draw his seax before he drew his own.

Godwin looked at the gleaming seax and spat out, "Even your weapon is stolen from us!"

This charge ignited Sidroc, and he lunged at Godwin with a yell. It took me a moment to see that Sidroc had caught Godwin on that very first thrust, for tho' Godwin leapt back, a rivulet of blood appeared on his right forearm. Godwin barely glanced at it, then returned his gaze to Sidroc.

Godwin kept his left hand holding his belt; he could not extend it for balance as Sidroc could. Sidroc saw this, and placed his own left hand at his belt. "I give myself no advantage," he said.

The men began moving in a circle, seaxes foremost, and they stepped, eyes locked, around an invisible centre-point. The rest of us were rooted to the ground, and I had my arms tightly around Ceric's shoulders. Neither Worr nor Tindr could stop them, they were honour-bound. My begging, and Sidroc's offer to let Godwin go peacefully had been futile. Now one of them would die.

Without taking his eyes from those of Sidroc, Godwin spoke. "She was my woman before she was yours."

Sidroc did not flinch. "You cannot taunt me to recklessness. I know every warriors' trick. I have used them myself. She has made her choice."

He paused a moment and cocked his head. "Or maybe I will speak," he went on. He just glanced at me, then brought his gaze back to Godwin. "She chooses me over you. My bed to yours."

Godwin gave a howl and with an oath lunged forward with his seax, but missed. Again they locked eyes and resumed their circling.

My silent tears were nearly blinding me, but from the tail of my eye I saw Worr move, and I looked to him. He was staring at Godwin, his disbelief and dismay clear upon his face.

Of a sudden Godwin stormed at Sidroc. Again the blade missed home, but Godwin hooked his knife arm in under Sidroc's. They locked at the elbow as the men pushed against each other, strength against strength, their seaxes quivering at face level. One gave ground, and then the other, equally matched until Sidroc was able to throw himself off balance enough to lift his left foot and kick Godwin in the knee. This broke their hold, and Sidroc leapt sideways, free. Godwin again charged, but Sidroc once again stepped to the side and Godwin overran him.

As he did so Sidroc's seax caught Godwin high in the left shoulder, just the point at which long ago a Danish spear had pinned him to the wall of Kilton's treasure room. Godwin's left arm flailed open, blood running down the length of it, and swiftly dropping from his fingertips. He gnashed his teeth as Sidroc closed on him, the gleaming point of Sidroc's blade aiming for his chest. But Godwin himself lunged, and as Sidroc spun to avoid his extended seax Godwin swung his hand low, catching Sidroc in the right thigh. The blade ripped up from the knee in a long straight line. Sidroc staggered and dropped to his left knee. Godwin turned on him and flung his seax like a throwing knife at his head. The scream rising in my chest was locked in my throat, and I stood mute in my horror and fear.

But Sidroc pitched forward to the ground, and the thrown seax hit the ground off to one side, raising a wisp of dust. Godwin rushed to him, but Sidroc gripped his ankle and cast him down head-over-heels onto the hard earth. Godwin lay sprawled on his back, his seax an arms-length from his reaching right hand. But Sidroc had gained his feet, tho' blood poured from his right thigh. With a bound he drove his left foot on top of Godwin's right wrist, and bore down with all his weight.

Godwin howled as his wrist snapped, and his back arched as he tried to lift himself. But now Sidroc, boot still planted on Godwin's wrist, leaned over him, and placed the tip of his seax at Godwin's throat. Sidroc was panting, but Godwin was beyond sound. His golden-green eyes were staring up at Sidroc.

Sidroc took a long moment to look into those eyes.

Then he screamed "Yaa!"and thrust the seax blade into Godwin's throat, just above the hollow. Godwin's head jerked back and a sucking gasp escaped his opened mouth. Sidroc did not pull the blade, but kept driving it forward so that his arm shuddered with the effort behind it. Blood was now come into Godwin's mouth, and the blood of the wound he had given Sidroc rained down from Sidroc's leg upon Godwin's battered body.

Still Sidroc did not draw his blade from Godwin's throat. He looked long at Godwin's opened eyes as he bent over him. When he at last pulled back his seax he spoke.

"You are the last," he muttered as he stared into those lifeless eyes; but only I knew of what he spoke.

Worr came and dropped on his knees by Godwin's head, where the coppery hair lay clotted with blood and dust. The two boys were crying, unabashed, at the carnage before them, and Hrald ran to his father and threw his arms about his waist.

Sidroc had stepped from the body and dropped to his left knee, his injured right leg rigidly straight before him. I snatched at the linen I had been cutting for our little daughter's shift, and pressed it over the gash. Sidroc's right hand still gripped his seax, and Tindr was now at my side, trying to peel open Sidroc's clenched fingers so he might take it from him. Tindr grunted and Sidroc released his hold. I looked up at Hrald, reached for and took his hand.

"Hrald, hold this linen against your father's leg. Press hard. Use both hands."

I saw Ceric bending near Worr. "Ceric, come with me, I need your help."

I flew into the hall, Ceric at my heels. I could hear the cries of Eirian and Yrling. Together Ceric and I heaved away the heavy chest that blocked the treasure room door. Gunnvor opened the door, and Helga came out, holding Eirian in her arms and with Yrling clinging to her skirts.

"Helga, stay in the hall with the children. Do not let them see what is in the yard. Gunnvor, bring me the Simples chest, and all the linen you can gather."

We had a small store of choice Frankish wine, kept in pottery vessels in a chest in the kitchen passage. My fingers fumbled as I searched for the key at my waist, but I found it, seized one of the jugs, and tore at the waxed stopper. I ran back to the yard. Tindr and Hrald had moved the table at which I had been sewing so that it now rested against the stone wall of the hall. Sidroc sat upon the table, his back against the stone. I saw that Tindr had strapped his belt around the top of Sidroc's thigh to stem the bleeding. The linen both Sidroc and Hrald pressed to the leg was now coloured so that no one could have known a few moments ago it was snowy white.

I put my arm around Hrald and quickly kissed his cheek. "You have done well, Hrald. Go wash your hands and come back to us." The wound was still pumping blood, and I tightened the belt at the top of the leg. I took up the length of the linen I had been cutting and pressed this larger piece over the gash. "Ceric, go to the treasure room. Bring bedding or blankets, anything I can use to lift his leg."

Ceric ran and came back with cushions and rolls of blankets, and I propped Sidroc's leg up upon them. I pressed hard against the fresh linen I held to the wound.

I looked at Sidroc's pale face. His eyes were squeezed shut in pain, and I feared, loss of blood. I lifted the linen under my hand and saw the wound had begun to slow its bleeding.

A noise behind me made me turn to see Worr and Tindr hoist the body of Godwin and carry it to the stable. Worr was at the head, holding him at the shoulders, and Godwin's arms trailed down from his body, fingers almost touching the hard and dry earth. Both arms were red with blood, and I shook my head to turn my gaze away.

Gunnvor had come with a basin of water and linen of all lengths, and Ceric was just behind her with the small Simples chest.

I took up the jug and with a shaking hand poured a quantity of the wine into a cup. The wine was quite strong and we always drank it watered, but now I poured it whole into the cup. I pressed my lips to Sidroc's brow and spoke to him for the first time. "My love. Drink this wine."

His eyes opened, and his hand came up and took the cup from me, and he drank.

"Drink it all," I said. "I am going to stitch your wound."

The Hall of Tyr

My work basket from the Idrisid women sat there at the end of the table, and I still had much of the strong silk thread left. I shook my hands in the air to feel them again, then chose my largest steel needle and threaded it up with a long piece of red silk thread. Sidroc was watching me now as I pulled off the linen dressing and with my sharp bird-shaped shears cut the wool legging open.

"The cut is very straight," I told him. "It did not cut across the muscles, but straight up; you will have no limp."

He looked down at the ugly gash and nodded.

I took the jug in my hand and poured the red wine over the wound, the thin wine mixing with the brighter red of Sidroc's blood and seeping into the blankets below his thigh.

I pinched the flesh together between my fingers, and pierced it with the sharp needle. I began sewing the gash up, climbing up its length as I did, like lacing, from one side to the next. I began at the knee, where the leg was narrower, and then climbed to the broader part of the thigh.

Sidroc made no sound; I do not think he could feel where I pierced his skin over the greater pain of the gash, and I thought the loss of blood too, and the strong wine I had forced on him, made him light-headed. I kept my eyes set upon my work, not allowing myself to think of what I truly did; of whose flesh I was piercing. The wound was much longer than my hand; as long I think, as Sidroc's hand.

When I was done I unbuckled the bloodied leather that had stemmed the worst of the bleeding. I opened the Simples chest. I kept always a pot of Tindr's clearest honey there, to sooth burns and help heal cuts. I dipped my fingers into the pot and smeared the thick golden liquid across the stitched wound. I crumbled earthgall over all to help staunch the blood.

Gunnvor had been tearing linen into long and narrow lengths for me, and now I bound the leg firmly from knee to upper thigh with the white linen. Before she left us she gestured to the cup Sidroc had set down, that I should drink; and I took it up myself now, and filled my mouth with the strong and deep flavour of the wine that lay at the bottom like a glistening ruby.

I drew a long breath and sat upon the bench before Sidroc. I took his hand and just looked up at the paleness of his face.

"He did not touch you," he asked. It was the first time he had spoken since he had delivered the killing thrust.

"Nai, nai," I assured him, hearing the torment in his question. I swallowed hard. "Worr was with us the whole time; I was never alone with him. Worr would not have let him – hurt me. He grabbed my wrist, only, to try to take me away."

But he could not let go his fear. "Nothing more," he asked.

"I swear to you, my love, he did nothing more than hold my wrist."

Godwin had done us both so much harm that to hear him fear for me in this way was almost more than I could bear. "Worr was with me, and the boys too. They will tell you. I am unharmed. Please believe me."

He nodded and answered, "I believe you."

I lowered my head on his hand and pressed my lips to it.

"Do not touch his body," Sidroc said next. His voice was so low that I knew he spoke of my preparing Godwin for burial. I lifted my face to him, recalling how I had helped

Modwynn wash the beloved body of her husband Godwulf, and how she had in turn help me wash that of Gyric. To wash the body of one you have loved is an act above all others, and after all that had passed between the three of us, one I could not perform for Godwin. Yet his battered and bloody body lay in the stable, and he had neither loving mother nor wife here to render this final service.

"I will not," I promised. "I will ask Rannveig; Rannveig will help," was all I could say.

I dreaded to look towards the stable but forced myself to do so. Worr was sitting on a bench just outside the opened doors, his shoulders slumped, hands clasped between his opened knees. I knew that what he stared at was Godwin's body.

"Sidroc, I must speak to Worr. Please tell me that I may."

He nodded his head, and I raised his hand and kissed it in reply. I poured a deep cup of the red wine and stood up. Hrald had been bravely standing at the end of the table all this time, and I motioned him over to his father. Sidroc reached out his hand and laid it on his son's shoulder, and Hrald leaned forward. I saw them speak.

I went to where Worr sat, and turned my back on the stable door, blocking his view and making him look up at me.

"Worr," I said, and reached towards him with the cup. "Drink this wine; you have need of it."

He looked dully up at me, and did not move.

"Godwin of Kilton lies dead on a pile of straw," he said.

"Then drink to him, who was your lord in life," I answered. After a moment he extended his arm and took the cup from me.

"Drink," I told him, and he put the cup to his mouth and took a long draught.

He passed the cup to me, and I too lifted it. I drink to the man you could have been, Godwin, I said within my heart.

I looked at Worr, friendless in a strange land, a thegn no older than myself and twice made lordless. He had been a boyhood friend to Gyric, had loved and served him, had fought shield to shield with him. Even after Gyric's blinding they had ridden to war side by side, when my own king Burgred fled. And I had known Worr well. It was Worr who spent long days with Gyric at Kilton, making easier the burden of his blindness; Worr who had been entrusted with taking Gyric out on long and fast rides; had swum with him in the swirling sea waters beneath the hall, had sailed the small boat with him. Worr had sat in the pleasure garden with us, laughed with us, played with Ceric when he was a toddler and then taught him how to ride. After Gyric's death Worr had served his older brother. Now both Gyric and Godwin were dead, and Kilton was left lordless.

He turned his face to me, but took a long moment before he spoke.

"Is it true, what my Lord Godwin said?" he wanted to know.

In his faithful service to us all he deserved to ask the question, and I would not make myself unworthy in my answer.

"For four nights, yes," is what I said.

His eyelids lowered over his reddened eyes, and his next question was scarce above a whisper.

"While my Lord Gyric still lived?"

I could not flinch from the truth when a man lay dead before me because of it.

"Yes. Gyric knew, and allowed it."

His face looking up at mine was so full of hurt that my heart twisted within my breast.

"I do not ask you to excuse in me what I can never excuse in myself," was all I could tell him. I sat down on the bench next him.

He sat silently, and then turned to look in my face. "Godwin would not relent," he said.

I held his gaze, and then nodded and said, "He would not relent. And neither Gyric nor I were strong enough to resist his desire for me."

Worr looked back through the stable doors at the body lying on the bloodied straw. I made bold to take his hand.

"Worr, forgive him. Forgive us. Godwin was – mad. He never loved me, but he loved his brother, and Gyric's blinding made Godwin go mad."

He squeezed my hand, and I felt a sudden freeing within, as if I had been deeply understood by one from whom I had not thought to expect it.

A fly buzzed over our heads and made for the stable, recalling me to the dreadful task at hand. The Sagas tell of great battles, of valiant warriors, of blood and sword-play; but they do not tell of what comes after, that men and women must then walk amongst the wounded and bind their wounds, and prepare the dying for their death, and the dead for burial or the funeral pyre. All this is also the truth of war. I drew a deep breath before I went on.

"There is a kind woman here, a friend to me, and she will wash Godwin's body. There is no consecrated ground in which we can bury him; there are no Christians here. But we cannot burn him as befits a heathen war-chief; Godwin did believe in Christ. There is a burial ground at the edge of town, and I think we can bury him there."

He nodded to all this, but did not speak. "I will return soon. Drink," I told him, and left.

Chapter the Twenty-third: Aftermath

I started down the hill, walking as fast as my racing heart was beating. Despite the warmth of the day my teeth were chattering in my head. I wanted to run but could hardly feel my feet, and I did not wish to draw the notice of any of our neighbours on the way there. When I reached the brew-house the awnings were rolled shut as I knew they would be at that hour. Rannveig was not within, and I crossed through the space and into her little yard, where she stood over one of her great pots. She was alone, and turned to me and stopped in her stirring. I felt cold all over and knew I trembled.

"Sidroc has killed a man, up at Tyrsborg. Someone he knew in the past. It was an old enmity. But the dead man is a nobleman of Angle-land. Please Rannveig, can you wash his body; we must bury him here."

She looked me up and down and her mouth opened. "Two men and two boys landed at dawn," is how she answered. "I saw them walk up to Tyrsborg early."

"Já, it was one of those men. The boys are our sons, come from Angle-land."

She was already pulling off her brewing apron. "Go, go back to Tyrsborg. I will come with what is needed as soon as I may."

Hrald was still standing by his father when I returned, and now I took linen and basin and washed the dirt and blood from Sidroc's hands and face. I poured more of the strong wine for him, which he drank without urging. I knew the pain from such a wound would be great, and that now the leg would begin to stiffen. He spoke almost not at all, but he could breathe without effort, and no new blood stained the outer layers of the linen I had bound the gash with. I sat by his side as we watched and waited.

Rannveig came walking up the hill, with a man who led a small cart pulled by a single ox. Tindr and Worr lifted Godwin's body and set it upon the high work bench within the stable. I brought Rannveig linen and water. I did not stay and watch her at her pitiful task, but left and went back to where Sidroc lay, his back against the stone wall of Tyrsborg, watching it all. I could just see Rannveig and Tindr in the shadows within as they moved about the body. Worr sat outside, upon the bench before the stable door, his arm around Ceric as if he were an older brother.

Rannveig came out from the stable and looked to me, telling me she was done. Worr and Tindr lifted the body, now tightly wrapped in a plain linen shroud, and hoisted it upon the flat boards of the small ox cart. Tindr brought an oiled tarpaulin and cast it over the body. I stood up and spoke to Sidroc.

"Tindr and Worr are going now to bury him," I said. "I think Ceric will wish to stay here." I feared to say the next, but steeled myself and went on. "For Worr's sake I would like to go with them; for Worr's sake alone." He did not turn his head from me as I had feared, but he lowered his eyes a moment.

"I will not go if you do not wish it," I told him, and meant it truly. To leave Sidroc in pain from the wound Godwin had driven so I could be there at his burial seemed almost akin to a betrayal of him I loved, and who had killed to protect us. Yet pity for Worr, now alone and with the body of his dead lord spurred me on; and when I thought of those who would grieve for Godwin back at Kilton I could not in

404

decency's name excuse my absence as he was lowered into the ground.

"Do what you must do," he said.

"Thank you, my love," I said, and touched my lips to his. "I will be back as soon as I can."

I crossed to where Ceric sat, and bent down to him. "Worr and I are going to bury your uncle now," I told him. "You may come with us or stay here."

He looked up at me, his eyes bright with tears, and shook his head. "He tried to hurt you," he said. "Why did he want to hurt you?"

I placed my hand on his brow and whispered, "We will speak of it later. Please stay with Hrald, who fears for his father. We will be back soon."

I began to walk to the little cart when Gunnvor stopped me. She handed me my Summer mantle, and I pulled the hood up over my head, thankful for the softness of the light wool and the chance to shield my face. We rolled down the hill, Tindr at the oxen's head with the driver, and me and Worr walking behind. It was past midday and the town was busy, but no one stayed us as we rolled through to the end of the store-houses and past the fish-drying racks.

We neared the place of burial. To my gratitude Rannveig had sent men ahead to begin the digging, and we rolled on to where they worked, a growing mound of soil behind them. Worr had said nothing on our walk, and now he looked about at the round-topped stones lying here and there upon the green grass. Some of them were plain, but many were marked with runes, telling who lay below. I stood alone as Tindr and Worr finished digging. The two men who had begun the grave climbed back in it, and Worr and Tindr pulled the shrouded body from the cart and lowered it to them. They climbed out, and without a word the four men began shovelling and pushing the stony dark earth in over Godwin's body. When the grave was filled the two who had helped turned and nodded at Tindr, and left us.

Tindr went and stood at the oxen's head with the drover, but Worr stopped at the edge of the disturbed earth, and then fell on his knees in prayer.

For many reasons I could not join him, there on that soft and welcoming earth; but stood back and bowed my head and covered my face with my hands. I wept, but not for Godwin. I wept for Edgyth and Modwynn, and little Edwin; and for Ceric and Worr too; my tears were all for them.

I left Worr at the brew house, and climbed the hill alone with Tindr. Worr would stay with Rannveig until we knew if the boys wished to return with him. Now that they were here the thought of losing them again made me feel faint, and I drove the thought from my mind as we neared Tyrsborg. I smelled our supper that Gunnvor was busy with before I turned the corner into the kitchen yard. She looked at us from over her work, gesturing that all was well. Both Hrald and Ceric sat by Sidroc. His eyes were closed and I knew he drowsed as he lay there. I spoke to the boys a moment and went into the quiet hall. Helga arose from outside the alcove where Eirian and Yrling slept. She had fed them and they were asleep. I leaned in and kissed their faces before I turned to the work at hand.

I went to the door of the treasure room. Chests were flung open, our bed had been rifled, and cushions and clothing strewn about, all in the search for linen and dressings. I walked about with Helga, placing fresh linens on the bed, ordering and folding that which had been scattered.

When I came out to the kitchen yard Gunnvor was at Sidroc's head, and he was drinking the warm broth she had brought him. Gunnvor brought food for the boys and us, but when I asked Sidroc if he could eat, he shook his head. I gave him as much broth and wine as he would take, the first to warm him and give him strength, the second to help ease his way to sleep, for only by rest would he heal. Then we must get him to bed in the treasure room.

I cast about in my mind how we might do this, when Tindr stepped from the stable. In his hands he held a stout hay rake, from which he had sawn off the tines. He stood before us and placed the blunt end of it in his armpit, like a crutch, and pointed to Sidroc. Sidroc pushed himself from the table and eased his good left foot onto the ground, and then took the crutch under his left arm. With Tindr holding him at the waist for balance we slowly travelled the few strides inside the hall, and then to the waiting treasure room.

He lay back, eyes closed, on our bed. I took his clothing off, able to wipe the splashed blood from his legs and the grime from the rest of him. I pulled off my own clothing and lay down next to where he lay, eyes closed but still, I could tell, awake. It would be another hour before the sun set, but the day felt it had lasted a week. I held him, my arm over his chest, until he slipped into sleep, and then I too fell into a deep and mercifully dreamless sleep.

I awoke in the dark, sensing that he too was awake. I lay on my back next him, and just moved my shoulder so that he knew he was not alone in his wakefulness. He lifted the hand that lay between us and placed it on my belly, and then slipped it down my thigh between my legs. He let it rest there and I listened to his quiet breathing. I turned, opening to him. He pushed himself up on one elbow, but groaned and lowered himself down upon his back.

"I cannot move," he said.

"You will not need to move," I whispered. "Lie back, and let me give to you."

I hung over him, letting my breasts brush his chest as my lips kissed his face and mouth. I caressed and teased him with my hands, until he groaned again, one of desire and not pain. I swung my leg over him and lowered my hips to his. His hands gripped my waist as he drove me down slowly upon him.

We were wordless in our love-making; what we had been through that day was beyond words. His need for me was a man's desire for the woman he loved, and the pleasure and comfort he will find in satisfying that desire. But in that darkness I knew that far greater was his need to reassert his claim upon my body. Injured tho' he was, my surrender to him was complete.

Day was fully upon us when I awoke again. Sun streamed into the high window onto the floor beside our bed. It fell on the gown I had been wearing yesterday, and I saw the brown streaks of Sidroc's blood where it had dried upon the light blue wool. He was sleeping deeply. I touched his cheek and felt he had no fever. I kissed his lips and slipped out of bed.

In the hall I found Ceric and Hrald, sitting at the table finishing their food. I could hear the little ones outside in the yard, already at play, and Sparrow's voice above their own. I sat down on the bench by the two boys, and tousled both their hair. Hrald's blue eyes looked at me from his thin and solemn face.

"Your father is sleeping," I told him. "He is a strong man, and will heal well, with no limp when he walks. He will wake soon, and then you may see him."

I had no such glad news for my own Ceric, and just placed my arm about his shoulders. Yrling peeped in from the kitchen yard door and gave a little yell and came scampering to me, Eirian at his heels. I hugged them and lifted them both in turn and kissed their round and still sticky faces. Helga was just behind them, spindle in hand, and she came to me. I took her hand in silent thanks for how well she had served us since the last sunrise.

Then Gunnvor came in, carrying warm bread and butter, and I ate with gratitude, with my children and Sidroc's son around me.

When I had finished I stepped into the bright sunshine of the kitchen yard. It was a morning like the day just past, with a brilliant sun lifting in a cloudless blue sky. The yard too looked unchanged. Tindr had raked and swept the hard ground upon which the men had fought and bled until no trace remained. He had gathered up Godwin's torn and blood-spattered clothing and burned it with the bloodied straw his body had rested on.

As I was standing there Tindr stepped forward from the shadow of the stable. Even if he could have heard my words there was no way I could express my thanks to him. He had swiftly and quietly brought Sidroc back. He had carried Godwin's body with respect to the stable and helped his mother wash it. And he had earlier stood at the edge of the trees, bow raised in his arms, ready to send an arrow through a man's back if need be. I could not pretend to know what this last had meant to him, that he would kill his fellow man, and do such a thing for us.

I looked at him and touched my heart a long moment, then turned my hand to him. He answered by opening both his hands to all around him, then touching his ear. Then he lightly touched his own heart and turned his hand to me.

I took this to mean that we had given him all this, given him a home at Tyrsborg, and that we had his thanks, and his loyalty, unto death. Our eyes met for a long moment as we nodded to each other.

I knew Worr was waiting down at Rannveig's, and knew too that the boys must decide if they wished to remain with us or return with him. I knew I must somehow write letters to send with Worr, one to Ælfwyn and one to Modwynn and Edgyth. Worr was a friend to me; I could trust him to say those things which a short letter could not.

But first I returned to the treasure room. Sidroc was awake, sitting up against the back of the bed, his leg propped up on the cushions beneath his knee. His eyes were closed but he opened them when I shut the door. I tried to smile, and kept from asking any foolish question; his face alone told me he was in pain. Instead I sat down on the bed.

"Could you eat?" I asked. "You must try, for the strength it will give you."

He nodded. "I can eat," he said. "It was the battle-sickness. It is over now."

He had not spoken of this before, and told me of it.

"How you feel after you have fought and killed, whether you get hurt or not. The taste of iron in your mouth. The belly tight and churning. That deep weariness after."

I nodded, thinking of how ill I had felt when I had gone to Rannveig for help. And he was the one who had fought and killed, and had lost blood.

I placed my hand over his. As I extended it he saw the five dark bruises on my right wrist, five ovals where Godwin's strong fingers had pressed into my flesh. He looked at them, and then spoke.

"Tindr came running, using his whistle to call me. He gestured that men with swords were with you at Tyrsborg. I knew it was Kilton. What I could not know is if he had already raped you."

I closed my eyes and leaned my head into his shoulder. I did not doubt that Godwin, gone mad from old hurts, and driven by his rage and possessiveness, would have treated me thus.

"I am sorry for what you had to do," I told him.

Sudden defiance was in his answer. "I am not."

After what he had said over Godwin's body I knew this was not true, but I said nothing.

He lowered his voice and went on. "It is just that I got cut."

He paused a moment and conceded, "Two warriors cannot fight with knives as we did – to the death – and not both get cut."

His voice hardened once again. "He would have killed me if he could, and taken you and raped you. Do not think he would not have killed that thegn of his, too, if he thought he had to. He would have. And it was he who killed Yrling. I have not forgotten that." He stopped himself. "What matters now is that he is dead, and you are unharmed."

I tried again. "You are in pain. I am sorry for that."

"I have bled before. But it was for treasure. This was for you, and our children."

I nodded. "The boys saw ghastly things. And it feels my fault," I said. "What you had to do. Your wound..."

"Nai. In only one small thing do you bear any blame, and the greater blame is mine. I should have killed the Saxon. I did not, for I was trying to win you. You had stopped me once from killing him.

"But," he went on, and now he almost smiled, "I should have had more faith in you, that you would grow to want me regardless."

He looked again at my bruised wrist. He laid his own hand over the wrist, and gently closed his fingers upon it, and drew my palm to his lips, and kissed it.

"It is over now," he ended. "You are truly free."

The leg was painfully stiff and Sidroc knew he should try to move and thus ease the swelling that now reached down to his ankle. Using his crutch he moved through the hall and stood looking out into the kitchen yard. Gunnvor was at her work as on any day, and raised her head to us in greeting. Sidroc spent a moment staring into the hard and dusty ground, and then we slowly moved around the long side of the hall to the front door. The sea lay sparkling before us, and Sidroc hobbled to the bench that sat near my little fruit trees. Their ripening apples and plums were just beginning to make the boughs heavy enough to sag. We sat together in the warm sunshine in grateful silence. Then Eirian and Yrling came tumbling out the front door after us, laughing as they chased each other, trying to be the first to be picked up by their father, and we opened our arms to them.

In late afternoon a small group of men, and a few women too, trooped up the hill to Tyrsborg. These were the chief men of the place, come to hear what had caused the death of the stranger now buried at the edge of town. A few of them, like Ketil, knew us well, and had been feast-guests many times at our hall. Botair, Runulv and Ring's father, was also there, as was the weapon-smith who had bought our Frankish iron. Rannveig walked amongst them, for she had been part of it; and also two other women, who, like Rannveig, were respected and well-to-do traders. Worr walked also with this group. As he stood at the back as the men questioned Sidroc, his steady blue eyes met mine.

Sidroc told of an old conflict, that the stranger from Angle-land had killed his uncle, that I had once been wed to the dead man's brother, and that now he had come here to collect me. He would not leave peacefully, and words were spoken. Did you fear for your home, the men wanted to know; did you fear for your wife, they asked. Yes, said Sidroc. Worr and Tindr were questioned, and nodded that the fight was a fair one. Rannveig told of the wounds, all driven from the front.

The chief man amongst them had been eyeing Sidroc's bandaged leg, seeing that he too had suffered. Sidroc had built much good will since we had come here; was respected and known. The group turned and spoke together. In Wessex Godwin was a powerful lord, and his killing could mean war; but here he was little more than a man trying to steal another man's wife. No damage had been done to anyone's property, none hurt except the parties involved. With good wishes towards the folk of Tyrsborg they left.

Ceric and Hrald were with us, Hrald sitting at his father's feet, and Ceric standing by my side. I whispered to Ceric what was being spoken, what questions asked. He watched all, and saw I think, that it was not far from the Hallmoot that met at Kilton twice each year, when men and women spoke their grievances and judgements were made. When the group walked, satisfied in the justice of the thing, down the hill, his eyes followed.

When Worr walked up the hill he brought with him the boys' small travel packs. When the group had gone Ceric and Hrald shouldered their packs and took them within the hall. But a few moments later Hrald came back to where Sidroc and I sat. He had something in his hands, and looked uncertainly from my face to his father's. It was me he stopped before.

"My mother's letter," he told me, "and her love."

In his hands was a plump pouch, sewn of undyed linen. I drew breath as Hrald gave it me, my eyes already watering at the way he had been told to deliver it.

I looked to Sidroc. His eyes held steady. I glanced down at the pouch. It had been sewn shut to protect what was within.

"I thank you, Hrald," I told him. Ceric was just behind him, and over in the paddock I saw Tindr combing out the stallion's mane. "Tindr will be glad to have you help him with the horses," I told them.

I sat back down next to Sidroc, watching the boys as they trotted off. Yrling lifted his head from where he was playing in the dirt by the stable door, and pattered after them.

"I will get my shears," I said, almost to myself. I left the linen on the bench and fetched them, and sitting back down used their sharp bird-shaped points to snip through the fine stitching.

I did not know if I could read Ælfwyn's letter while I sat next Sidroc, but knew that there was nowhere else where I could feel more loved. And Hrald's greeting to me from his mother gave me courage.

It was a thick roll of parchment, and more than one piece. Separating them I saw one was blank. Ælfwyn had rightly guessed that I might be in a place where parchment would be hard to come by, and sent along a second piece for my reply. Inside the second was a tiny pottery vessel, sealed by a wood plug and wax: Ink.

I tucked the blank piece back into the pouch, and unfurled the message before me. Each letter was small and well-formed, the ink black and sharp, her quill well cut. Over the years she had spent time and effort perfecting her hand. I read to myself, slowly and with care. My throat caught at the very first words.

MY DEAREST CERIDWEN

If you hold this letter I know you live, and that Hrald and Ceric are safe and with you. For this I offer my great thanks to God.

Godwin of Kilton has been searching for you since you were taken. Folk of Lindisse saw the red-sailed ship, and the next Spring a thegn of Wessex came to Kilton and told Godwin you had been taken as slaves, then freed by Danes. Godwin wrote me that he would seek you out with men and with silver, and urged me to do the same. I did not.

There is peace in Lindisse. Asberg and Jari hold Four Stones in Hrald's name, and with Guthrum's consent. I am Lady of Four Stones still, but spend much time at Oundle, from whence I write you now, blest to be so close to my mother, and to Sigewif, good Mother of us all. Hrald will rule in his own right when he is ready. I have told him that his father cannot return, the danger is too great.

The Hall of Tyr

At this last Mid-Summer's Godwin wrote again. His spies had learnt where you were, and he would set off after you. He stopped at Four Stones. To my shock he had Ceric with him, a lure for you. Hrald at once wished to go as well. I could not gainsay it, despite the peril to them both. Sending Hrald was a way for him to see his father again, and by sending him I knew you would know the regard I hold for you both, even should this letter be lost or destroyed by Godwin on the way. He has not been pleased by my coolness towards finding you. I am proud that Hrald kept the letter well, and secretly.

God's Providence allowed you to be spared from the greatest of dangers. He has a divine plan for us all, and we live it now, despite outward appearance. I can say nothing against a man who ever held me in regard, and who I think saved my life when I myself no longer wished to live. He restored my lost mother and sisters to me. His riches have allowed me to do God's work in Lindisse, and he gave them unstintingly. That he has ever loved you and been bound to you I need not speak. I know you would not stay with him without returning that love.

If Hrald should want to stop with you a year, he may. He has longed for his father and seeing him will heal that longing. Godwin intends to bring Ceric back, just as he intends to bring you back. I fear Godwin and pray God you are safe. I know you will find a way to send to me. This parchment will I hope serve you well.

I would I could say more; Hrald will tell you what a child can. His sisters thrive, and my own sister Eanflad, through the benison of Holy St Mary, speaks again and is of us.

You will ever be a true sister to me, as true as my own flesh and blood. We have shared too much for it to be otherwise.

The Hall of Tyr

Tell Sidroc I release him, with my thanks.

YOUR LOVING ÆLFWYN

Burginde sends you her kiss

I raised the back of my hand to my face to brush the tears welling in my eyes. Sidroc had been looking out at the sea, and now as I lowered the parchment brought his gaze back to me. I began to read it again, aloud.

When I finished we sat in shared silence. Her great goodness did not surprise me. Her gentleness and wisdom did. I brought the smooth parchment to my lips and kissed her name.

"The ease this brings me –" I began to tell Sidroc. My voice was no more than a whisper, and now in danger of cracking into tears. I laid the letter in my lap. His hand came to mine.

"Hrald and Ceric," I went on. I again brushed away tears, but I was smiling at him as I did. "Would you have them stay the year with us? We will ask them, and then I will write my letter."

"As soon as I can ride I will take them to Ragnfast's, and get them horses," he said as answer.

Chapter the Twenty-fourth: Letters, and Leave-taking

SPARROW saw me over at the goose pen, trailing a big gander with a drooping wing feather. I gave it a yank and it slipped out, long and grey, with a broad white open tube at the body end. I climbed out with it, and looked at her. She had returned from Rannveig's sometime last night, and had no doubt heard all that could be told.

"I will write a letter, Sparrow," I told her, "a real letter, ink on parchment. Two of them."

"You will let me see, Mistress?"

I nodded. "They are going to a Christian land, Angle-land. They will start tomorrow on their way, carried by a friend of mine. He is a warrior, a Christian warrior. He says prayers every day to Jhesu Christus. If you wish he will take you to Angle-land, to the holy woman Sigewif I told you of. He will protect you and not harm you. His speech will not be clear to you, but you will soon learn it.

"If you go, you will be close to my dearest friend, the great Lady Ælfwyn of Lindisse. It is to her I write one of my letters. The dark haired boy, Hrald, is her son; she sends him to us to foster for one year. Lady Ælfwyn has built the convent and church where Sigewif is Abbess, and her own mother is there now, professed as a nun. If you go you will have her protection and care, as well as that of Abbess Sigewif. Sigewif will teach you many new prayers, also how to write as you will see me do now, with a feather and dark liquid."

"I would pray with the other women," she wondered aloud.

"Já, and men too, men who have left the world and are under the orders of Abbess Sigewif. You will work in the gardens, or brewing and baking, and pray many times each day, and sing too with them. They will be as a family to you."

She swallowed, her eyebrows lifting over her brown eyes. She drew a deep breath and rocked slightly from side to side.

"Angle-land is a rich and green land, with broad rivers. Much wheat grows there. Great forests too. Only," I felt I should tell her, and must smile as I did, "it rains much.

"But you must decide now. The warrior, whose name is Worr, is leaving at dawn on the tide."

Her lips parted.

"He will care well for you, as if you were already a nun," I promised.

Her chin dropped, her eyes scanned the ground we stood upon. Then she lifted her hand to her brow, crossed herself.

"I thank you, Mistress," she consented.

I took her wrist. "It will be best for you, Sparrow," I said. "Come, come with me."

We went into the hall and I told her to get needle and thread from my work-basket. I went into the treasure room, pulled back my carpet, pried open the floor boards and drew out a jar. I took a whole gold coin and went back to where she waited by her alcove.

"Sew this in your mantle," I told her, pressing the piece in her hand. Her eyes widened and she said, "O".

"You will give it to Abbess Sigewif when you are brought before her. It is your dower-fee. She will keep it for you, to care for you always, and if you wish to leave, she will give it back."

"Gold, Mistress?" was all she could say.

I only nodded. "Please to tell Sigewif that the Lady Ceridwen sends her greetings, and that she is ever recalled warmly by her."

She took my hand and once again kissed it.

"Go to Gunnvor and Helga and tell them you are going; ask Gunnvor to make a food basket for you for tomorrow. I will call you when I write my letters so you may watch."

I then went out to the paddock. Tindr had put a halter on the black colt, and Hrald was leading him. Yrling was on the bare back of my dun mare, Tindr holding him there, while Ceric led her about. Yrling was crowing with laughter, and Ceric was trying to tell him to hold on to the dark mane.

"Ceric, Hrald," I called. "Please to come just now; we must speak to you."

Both boys came, tho' slowly, and Tindr lifted Yrling down and set him outside the paddock gates.

"Hrald, go please to your father. He has something important to ask you. Ceric, come with me." I held out my hand and gestured he should follow. Hrald walked off across the stable yard back to where his father waited at Tyrsborg's front door. Ceric I led inside. Both Helga and Gunnvor were in the kitchen yard with Eirian, and the hall was ours.

We sat down on a bench at the big table. The afternoon Sun was streaming through the window, the opened doors, and the smoke vent in the gable. Little motes of dust rose and danced in the strong shafts of light falling through the front door.

I put my arm about Ceric's waist a moment and just squeezed him. "My boy," I said, lowering my lips to his copper curls.

I leaned back a little and put my hands on the table before me. As I did I saw him look at the dark bruises where Godwin had wrenched my wrist. His own hand lifted for a moment. I recalled my first day at Kilton, when Godwin had taken off his heavy bracelet of red gold and placed it on my wrist as reward for bringing back his brother. I thought too of all the years Godwin would close his fingers about that same wrist, first in affection and then in desire. I pulled the sleeve of my gown a little lower down.

I turned on the bench to him, and he looked at me steadily as I spoke.

"Ceric, Worr must leave tomorrow; the ship you came on can no longer be delayed. It is your choice to go with him back to Wessex, or to stay here with us. If it were up to me, I would ask you to stay with me a year, because I have missed you so and want you with me. But please listen to what I will tell you, and then take the night to decide.

"You and your uncle and Worr came a great distance to find me. Once here, you saw terrible things, things none of us will ever forget. You saw your uncle try to take me from a place I do not wish to leave, and then you saw him die. You heard and saw things I wished you had not."

Ceric had seen men fight, many times, both in practice and in mortal combat. He knew that insults were thrown as well as blows, and that men would goad each other with words as well as with spear or sword.

"I know you feel anger towards your uncle. I beg you not to hate him. He was wrong in trying to take me when I did not wish to go. Your uncle had many cares and duties. He cared strongly about them. He was – protective about things he cared for. He felt that I should come back to Kilton, and I did not wish to. He felt – protective about me. You know as well he could become angry, and let his anger overrule his wisdom. He saw I had children with Sidroc and called me names…He was angry with me.

"Let me tell you now what I could not tell you three years ago. When I left you at Four Stones with Hrald and his family I knew that when I returned to Kilton I would have to wed a man at Sceaftesburh, Lady Modwynn's girlhood home. You and I would be leaving Kilton to go and live there. It was not my wish to do this, but I felt it was my duty. You have already heard what happened; Sidroc and I were captured by slavers. We were only saved by Danes who attacked the ship we were on.

"I think you remember your father well, even tho' he has been dead five years. I want you to know how much I loved him, and how much he loved you. Because of his maiming, it was hard for him to take any real pleasure in his life, but he took it in you.

"When he died his last words to me were 'Live'. He wanted me to go on living, even when I wished I had died myself. But I did live. And I am glad for it. I want to go on living here with Sidroc, and little Yrling and Eirian, and with you, if you will stay a year. I think Hrald will stay too, which will give us all joy.

"I know you watched Sidroc kill your uncle. But he did this to protect me; and as you have heard now, Godwin had killed Sidroc's uncle years ago. Despite what you had to see him do, Sidroc has ever been kind to me. When we were captured together he worked ceaselessly to keep me safe, and risked his own life many times to free us both. The danger we were in was great. We were twice attacked at sea, were caught in a storm in a small boat and almost sunk, and other things you will learn of.

"Through it Sidroc thought only of keeping me safe. I know he was wed in the eyes of the Church to Lady Ælfwyn, and she is my dearest friend. She wrote in the letter Hrald brought me that she releases him, and wishes us well. I consider myself to be his wife, and I am proud of the great esteem he bears for me. I love him. We have been blessed with those two little ones, and I hope for more. My life is here with him, and them. I will never see Kilton again, yet I am content. I will love and honour your lady grandmother and aunt, and little brother, to the end of my days; but my life is here.

"You are of Kilton, of the line of Godwulf, and tho' I hope you will stay with me for a year, Kilton is your home. You know Godwin's heir is his son, Edwin, your little brother. Until he is of age men like Worr and Cadmar will guide and guard Kilton. When you are a man you will be a great help to him as he rules."

I could think of nothing more to say. Ceric had lowered his eyes a few times as I had spoken, and cast them down again now.

"I want to stay," he said.

"Do not make your mind up so soon; think on it –"

"I want to stay," he said again, with a nod of his head.

"Our life is simpler here," I warned him. "It will not be just weapon-play and hunting; you will have to help chop wood and care for the animals."

"I want to stay."

"We will not be able to send you back until next Summer if you change your mind."

"I want to stay."

I hugged him with that fierceness that a mother has for her child.

Hrald came running to find Ceric a little later; both would stay with us the year. I embraced them both, smiling to myself with the knowledge that as they grew such embraces would be awkward for them. "Go off to Tindr and the horses," I told them, and they turned on their heels and sped back outside.

Now I must write my letters. I did not have time to rule the parchment or to plan out what I would say. I must gather my thoughts a moment, and begin. First I called Sparrow to me. The single sheet was large enough to cut and this I did first, with my shears. I lay one half on the table before me, and weighed it down with a stone cresset at the top corners to keep it flat. I pressed the goose feather on the bench and took the sharpest knife Gunnvor had and made my five cuts. I poured the vial of ink into a little bowl, dipped the cut quill tip into it, and began.

MY DEAREST ÆLFWYN

Your letter brought me more comfort than I can say. I do not say more than you can know, for your heart is truly boundless. Know that your Hrald carried your letter safely and secretly all the journey, and had proved his courage to us all on his first day here. As you grant he remains with us for the year. We will send him back to you on our own swift trading ship next Summer.

Ceric also remains with us, and he too shall return on that same ship.

Know, my sweetest Lady, that Godwin of Kilton is dead, killed in single combat by Sidroc. His horse-thegn Worr bears this letter to you and witnessed all; he shall tell you of it.

Worr has also brought a young woman of our household, a Christian, to the foundation at Oundle. I have commended her to Sigewif, and hope you too will aid and help Sparrow as you can.

Sidroc and I were indeed guided through great peril and danger. The home we have found here shall be our last. We have twinned children, boy and girl, now of two Summers, Yrling and Eirian. Now that Ceric is here the only joy I lack is of your face, but I bear that ever in my heart.

I rejoice that you and your mother are well, Lindisse at peace, and that Eanflad's silence has been broken. May you receive every solace and succour from all who surround you, just as you have ever been the source of comfort to so many.

Hrald shall be cared for as my own, indeed I cannot look at him without seeing the faces of the two I love most on this Earth. He shall bear another letter when you see him next, and have much to tell you.

My final thanks for your foresight in sending me parchment and ink. The sheep here are the finest, and would make you proud. I shall have parchment drawn and so take up the quill again, but today beg your pardon for my ungainly hand. Your own, who once drew a crossed mark in wax as your sign, is now as fine as Sigewif's.

I lay my hand on my heart and send you love from

YOUR CERIDWEN

425

I feel Burginde's kiss and send one of my own

I leant back on the bench and rolled my shoulders, and shook out my cramped hand. Sparrow had watched every stroke I made, tho' she could read it not. I looked to her now.

"The Abbess Sigewif will soon have you doing this, working on scraps of parchment, holding a quill as I do now."

She bit her lip, but smiled.

"Get some linen from the chest in the passageway; we must make pouches for these. You can stitch as I write out the second."

I wanted to keep that pouch which Ælfwyn had made, and felt I could not work on this second, far harder letter, with her watching so closely.

I shook my hands out and flattened the second sheet of parchment. I scarce knew where to begin, but begin I must. The quill nib had spread and I cut it afresh. It scratched across the smooth face of the sheet I held.

TO MY DEAR LADIES MODWYNN AND
EDGYTH OF KILTON

I know you receive and read this letter in bitterest grief. No words of mine can aid or comfort a loss so great, to you, to Edwin, or all of Kilton. Indeed, if you destroy my letter unread you should be blameless.

Worr has told you all he saw, also perhaps that the chief folk of this place, men and women of age and wisdom, heard an accounting of the quarrel, and have deemed the fight a fair one. Your loss is none the less for that, this I know.

At his request my beloved boy Ceric will remain this year with us, and return to you next Summer. He is here with

Hrald, the son of the Lady Ælfwyn; she sent him so they might be together. My lady Modwynn, who was ever so kind and just to me, I ask that the treasure which your dear lord Godwulf left in his will to me be divided, two thirds to Ceric, and one third to Edwin, and that any other of my goods be given as you see fit.

My dear lady Edgyth, on his return I know you will continue to raise Ceric as your own, just as Edwin is blest with the best of mothers. I trust such worthies as Cadmar and Worr will guide and guard them both.

I would beg more of you both: To understand that I was fully prepared to do my duty to the family of Kilton at the time of our capture; that Sidroc of Lindisse treated me with the greatest respect and restraint over the course of many weeks of perilous danger; that being convinced of the difficulty of return to Wessex, I allowed a heart which had felt dead inside my breast since the death of Gyric to bloom, and love again, and to love a man who had in return loved me for ten years. He is my husband.

No thanks I could convey in this letter or standing before you are adequate to the kindnesses I have known at your hands. To have become the seeming cause of bitter sorrow to you would break my heart if I did not also bear the memory of your joy in Gyric's return. I beg you to cling to the good we have shared, to care for Ceric, and try to forgive

YOUR LOVING CERIDWEN

My words felt feeble; but they were from my heart, and I must hope they would be enough. Together Sparrow and I stitched the narrow linen tubes shut. I marked one with the letter Ash, Æ, so that Worr could know which was for Ælfwyn, taking a strand of blue silk and working it into the sewn end of it.

427

The Hall of Tyr

I walked through the hall and out the broad oak door. Sidroc was alone, head tipped slightly back, looking with lowered eyes out to the sea shimmering under a dropping Sun.

I sat next him. "My letters are written. And Sparrow wishes to go with Worr. I will ask him to take her to Oundle."

He nodded his head. I knew he was in pain from his wound. "Ceric and I will go now and say goodbye to him; his ship leaves on the tide at dawn. When I come back I hope you will take wine, and rest."

He surprised me by saying, "Send Tindr to bring him here."

When Tindr returned, Sidroc was still seated on the bench near the front door. Ceric and Hrald and I stood nearby. Worr came walking towards us, and I was most aware that I would likely never again see him. He was a link to my old life at Kilton, to Gyric and yes, to Godwin, too; to Ceric as a child and to my other son, Edwin, who would, if the Fates be willing, one day rule Kilton.

I did not understand why Sidroc wanted Worr to come to Tyrsborg; he had not said one word to him from the moment he had found Godwin here, and had, I felt, an anger so great towards him that he had not even looked at him. Yet I recalled when I had seen Sidroc and Worr ride together, talking, as they approached Kilton after Guthrum had put his hand to the treaty of peace; and how later that day the two had drunk and jested together in the great hall.

Now Worr stood before us, and the two men eyed each other without speaking. Sidroc raised his hand, and Tindr came forth to Worr, holding in his extended hands something covered with a piece of plain linen. Sidroc took his crutch in his hand and pulled himself to his feet. He gestured Worr to the linen, and Worr lifted it.

There in Tindr's arms lay Godwin's fine seax and sword. These were now forfeit to Sidroc as battle-gain; all warriors claimed the weapons of the men they killed. It was always the greater part of any plunder taken.

Tindr extended his arms to Worr, as if he should take them. The thegn looked to Sidroc.

"He has a son," is how Sidroc answered. That was all he said.

I caught my breath at his open-handedness. A son that was also mine.

Worr lowered his head in gratitude, then took the offered weapons.

Sidroc turned and walked with Hrald into the hall, leaving us alone to make our fare-wells. He and Ceric spent a few minutes speaking. Worr wrapped his arms about him and then rumpled Ceric's curls and sent him away. Ceric turned, and by his glinting eye I knew he had need to be alone. He went within the hall where Hrald had gone with Sidroc.

I gave him my letters. I looked over to Sparrow, who waited by the side door.

"Worr, please to do me a great service. On the way to Four Stones will you take this young woman to Oundle. She is a Christian, a slave we redeemed; I think she is of Frankland, but she has little memory of it. She is devout and wishes to go as a nun. Please take her to Sigewif the Abbess."

He looked over, eyebrows raised, to where she watched, twisting her hands as she awaited us.

"She has gold to give Sigewif, and I will give you silver for her passage and care on the way."

"I need no silver," he said, looking back to me. "I have that of my Lord Godwin's; it is much. I will take her," he ended.

"I thank you, Worr. I thank you truly. For all."

I looked to Sparrow and nodded that all was well. She put her hands to her face and made a bow to us. "She will be ready at dawn, and come to Rannveig's," I told him.

I felt it hard to speak to him, standing there holding the weapons, and almost within sight of the place where Godwin had died. Yet I did not want to part so soon, and said, "I will walk back with you."

We walked down the hill and passed the brew-house, and then stood looking out at the empty pier. We sat down on a bench together. The late sun was making the ripples in the paling water sparkle, and we both gazed upon it without speaking for some little time.

"Worr," I asked him at last, "do you recall the day I came to Kilton? It was long ago; I had not yet sixteen Summers."

"As I did," he said. "Yes, no one at Kilton will ever forget." His eyes travelled out across the blue waters. "It was – thirteen Summers back."

I looked into my empty hands lying in my lap. "I was received with such honour. Now I feel that I have brought almost nothing but grief to Kilton."

He turned his head to me quickly, and spoke.

"You brought Gyric home alive. That was a miracle to us." The way he searched my face told me he was surprised I

430

had forgotten this. "Then you and he gave the hall sons, so that the line of Godwulf would continue. There would be no heir for Godwin if you had not given him your boy. What you and Gyric did assured Kilton it would continue. It was the greatest of gifts."

I nodded, but turned my eyes back to the sea, unable to look at him. With Godwin's death no one at Kilton would ever learn that he himself was Edwin's father; and that the precious gift that Gyric and I had made had been rooted in such anguished sorrow.

"And I carry this," Worr went on, dropping his eyes to the weapons upon his lap. "For these to be returned to Kilton – it is much. It will have great worth to the hall of Godwulf. These are weapons from father to son; I was there when Godwulf gave them. One day Edwin, Lord of Kilton, will use them with pride."

I lowered my eyes to the seax and sword-bearing baldric. Tindr had carefully cleaned and polished them, but I could not look at them. He who had wielded them was dead; and knowing whose blood they had shed made me feel of a sudden sick. I took a breath and looked away.

I knew I should be starting back, but had one more thing to say. To do so I must face him.

"Worr, when you return to Kilton and speak to Modwynn and Edgyth, I...I know you will say nothing which will bring shame to Gyric, or to Godwin."

He looked steadily at me. "I will tell the truth: My Lord Godwin came to find you, believing that you were being held against your will. But you desired to remain. There was a fair fight, witnessed by me, and Godwin was killed. I will also say that I found you well, and happy in your new life."

431

"Then you will be telling the truth, indeed." I had to smile at him, my heart brim-full at the firmness with which he said this, and the goodness from whence his words sprung.

I stood up. "For being what you have always been to Ceric you have my endless thanks. You will see him next Summer; we will send the boys to Lindisse, and Lady Ælfwyn will send him with an escort by sea to Kilton."

For answer he only said, "He is a fine boy. So like his father."

This prompted me to ask, "Worr, have you still no wife?"

His smile broadened into a grin. "I wed on my return. To Wilfgyfu, the daughter of the bailiff of Defenas."

"I recall her from Yule-tide feasts," I said with a smile. "Roses in her cheeks, and nut-brown hair. Your babes will be pretty indeed. I wish you every joy."

Again I took his hand. "Fare you well, Worr. Kilton is the better for your faithfulness to it."

I walked the hill back to Tyrsborg. The Sun had vanished behind the trees, and that hour of owl-light nearly come on. I could smell the supper Gunnvor cooked for us as I neared the hall, the savour of newly-baked loaves. I went in the front door and saw the curtains already drawn at the alcove where Eirian and Yrling slept. I peeked in. They were both asleep, the little mouths slightly opened from their soft sighing breaths. Yrling's feet were off the box bed and I lifted him and lay him next his sister; his hand rose and without opening his eyes he patted my face. I kissed them both and drew the curtains shut. As I stood I heard Sidroc's voice coming from the treasure room. The door was open and I could hear the piping tones of Hrald and Ceric as they spoke in answer; he must be showing them something we had stored there, or perhaps my plush weaving, my prized carpet.

I went out the back passage to the kitchen yard. The skies were darkening, but the cook fire, and that of several rush torches struck into the earth, shed a warm and flickering light on all. Helga and Gunnvor were standing near one with Sparrow, a knot of women smiling and crying at the same time, saying early fare-wells and also seeing to the coming meal. Tindr came out of the stable where he had just shut the geese and hens up for the night, and looked to them.

He cocked his head, not knowing why they wept and embraced. Sparrow saw him and walked to him as I neared. I stood next her as she touched her chest, then made the waving motion that told she would go by sea. Tindr looked at her, following her motions, his puzzled face wearing his confusion. He tapped his temple, the sign for What, or Why.

She turned to me. We could not hope to make him understand that she left to seek out those who followed her faith.

I looked up at Tyrsborg's steeply pitched roof. Sparrow sought a true home, and that is what I signed to Tindr. I pointed to Sparrow, put my hand at my brow as if looking for something, then pressed the fingertips of both hands together, the sign for Tyrsborg, our home.

Now Tindr understood. She sought to return to her home. It was close enough in meaning, and true enough in spirit.

He placed one hand in the other, making his first symbol for Sparrow, that of a small bird in the nest. Then the hand lifted from the other, leapt for the sky. She would leave the nest.

She smiled at him, and nodded. Then she touched her hand to her heart, turned the hand to Tindr in thanks, Tindr who had brought her food and drink in the forest, who had won her trust enough to lead her back to us. He made his shy smile and touched his own heart in return.

She looked now to me. "When I see Rannveig in the morning, I will give back her gifts to me," she said, fingering the two glass bead necklaces around her throat. "She will remember me by them, and I want her to remember me."

"We none of us will forget you, Sparrow, and always wish you well."

A movement in the open doorway to the hall caught my eye. Sidroc stood there, his arm propped up by the crutch. Hrald was on his other side, his arm about his father's waist, and Ceric just behind. Ceric lifted his eyes to me. I looked at his face, in which I saw my own and that of Gyric. I looked at Hrald, face craned up at his father's, and saw that of Ælfwyn and of Sidroc.

I went to them. They made their way to the table at which I had been sitting yesterday morning at my sewing, the table that Sidroc had later lain and bled upon. The table had been scrubbed with sand, the new wood of which it was built made even newer. The three of them sat on the bench there now, Sidroc, Hrald, and then Ceric. His hurt leg he held straight before him, and he let the crutch rest against the bench edge on his other side.

"We have goshawks," he was telling them. He looked at Hrald. "They are bigger than the falcons at Four Stones, can take big hares, and birds of every size. Tindr and I captured them as chicks and are breeding them. They are at our farm, where we train them. We will go soon to see them."

"And I will fly them?" Hrald asked.

"You will fly them, both of you," Sidroc promised. "And feed them too, whether they bring you back a bird or not. They are young and do not always make a strike."

"And will we hunt?" Ceric wanted to know.

"You will hunt. There are few folk here; the hunting is good. There are red deer, and many boar. Tindr hunts with his bow," he went on, looking across to where Tindr moved in the dusk of the stable opening, "and fills our larder every Fall. He brings us deer, and even boar which he takes with his bow. He is as good, I think, as the men of Angle-land with it, and they are famed everywhere as bowmen. He weaves snares, and keeps us in rabbits too; he will show you how.

"And I will teach you both to fight. Fight so that you will not get cut." His mouth twisted into a grin as he looked down at his leg. "But once a man is five and twenty he should gain his riches by trade. So I will teach you what I know about that, too. How to choose the best stuffs to send, whether amber or furs, find the purest salt, hire men you can trust to take your goods for you to sell."

Years ago in the pear orchard outside Kilton's walls I had promised Sidroc that one day I would send Ceric to him to foster, to teach him just the things he vowed to teach the boys now. That day had come, yearned for and yet unbidden. I stood before the three of them, and their eyes lifted to me. Sidroc smiled and pushed the crutch a little way off, gesturing for me to sit down by his side.

Ceridwen wife to Sidroc of Gotland

The Wheel of the Year

Candlemas - 2 February

St Gregory's Day - 12 March

St Cuthbert's Day – The Spring Equinox, about 21 March

High Summer or Mid-Summer Day- 24 June

St Peter and Paul - 29 June

Hlafmesse (Lammas)- 1 August

St Mary's Day -15 August

St Matthews' Day – The Fall Equinox, about 21 September

All Saints -1 November

The month of Blót – November

Martinmas (St Martin's) -11 November

Yuletide - 25 December to Twelfthnight - 6 January

Anglo-Saxon Place Names, with Modern Equivalents

Æscesdun = Ashdown
Æthelinga = Athelney
Basingas = Basing
Caeginesham = Keynsham
Cippenham = Chippenham
Cirenceaster = Cirencester
Defenas = Devon
Englafeld = Englefield
Ethandun = Edington
Exanceaster = Exeter
Glastunburh = Glastonbury
Hamtunscir = Hampshire
Hreopedun = Repton
Jorvik (Danish name for Eoforwic) = York
Legaceaster = Chester
Limenemutha = Lymington in Hampshire
Lindisse = Lindsey
Lundenwic = London
Meredune = Marton
Sceaftesburh = Shaftesbury
Snotingaham = Nottingham
Sumorsaet = Somerset
Swanawic = Swanage
Wedmor = Wedmore
Witanceaster (where the Witan, the King's advisors, met) = Winchester
Frankland = France
Haithabu = Hedeby

Land of the Svear = Sweden
Aros = Aarhus, Denmark

Glossary of Terms

brewster: the female form of brewer (and, interestingly enough, the female form of baker is baxter...so many common names are rooted in professions and trades...)

blästjärna :"blue stars"; Siberian squill, an early bright blue spring flowering bulb

browis: a cereal-based stew, often made with fowl or pork

ceorl: ("churl") a freeman ranking directly below a thegn, able to bear arms, own property, and improve his rank

cooper: a maker of casks and barrels

cottar: free agricultural worker, in later eras, a peasant

cresset: stone, bronze, or iron lamp fitted with a wick that burnt oil

ealdorman: a nobleman with jurisdiction over given lands; the rank was generally appointed by the King and not necessarily inherited from generation to generation. The modern derivative *alderman* in no way conveys the esteem and power of the Anglo-Saxon term.

frumenty: cereal-based main dish pudding, boiled with milk. A version flavoured with currents, raisins and spices was ritually served on Martinmas (November 11th) to ploughmen.

fulltrúi: the Norse deity patron that one felt called to dedicate oneself to

fylgja: a Norse guardian spirit, always female, unique to each family hamingja: the Norse "luck-spirit" which each person is born with

hvit fagningsblóma: white wood anemones; "hvit" is white in Old Gutnish, the form of Old Norse spoken on Gotland, "fagning" is the preparation of the meadows in Spring, and "bloma", of course, is bloom

nålbinding: a form of early knitting or crochet, using one's thumb and threaded needle to form interlocking loops

raukar: the striking sea- and wind-formed limestone towers on the coast of Gotland; the one on the cover of *The Hall of Tyr* is at Fårö, Gotland

seax: the angle-bladed dagger which gave its name to the Saxons; all freemen carried one.

scop: ("shope") a poet, saga-teller, or bard, responsible not only for entertainment but seen as a collective cultural historian. A talented scop would be greatly valued by his lord and receive land, gold and silver jewellery, costly clothing and other riches as his reward.

skep: a bee hive formed of coils of plaited straw, built up into a conical shape

skirrets: a sweet root vegetable similar to carrots, but cream-coloured, and having several fingers on each plant

skogkatt: "forest cat"; the ancestor of the modern Norwegian Forest Cat, known for its large size, climbing ability, and thick and water-shedding coat skogsrå : "Lady of the Forest"; a womanly wood spirit who protected woodland animals, and yet guided hunters she favoured

Sun-stone: a piece of calcite crystal

thegn: ("thane") a freeborn warrior-retainer of a lord; thegns were housed, fed and armed in exchange for complete fidelity to their sworn lord. Booty won in battle by a thegn was generally offered to their lord, and in return the lord was expected to bestow handsome gifts of arms, horses, arm-rings, and so on to his best champions.

trev: a settlement of a few huts, smaller than a village

tun: a large cask or barrel used for ale

wadmal: the Norse name for the coarse and durable woven woollen fabric that was a chief export in the Viking age

wergild: Literally, man-gold; the amount of money each man's life was valued at. The Laws of Æthelbert, a 7th century King of Kent, for example, valued the life of a nobleman at 300 shillings (equivalent to 300 oxen), and a ceorl was valued at 100 shillings. By Ælfred's time (reigned 871-899) a nobleman was held at 1200 shillings and a ceorl at 200.

verjuice: "green juice"; an acidic juice from unripe grapes or crabapples, much used as we would vinegar

vintargekko: the yellow-flowered Winter aconite

Witan: Literally, wise men; a council of ealdorman, other high-ranking lords, and bishops; their responsibilities included choosing the King from amongst their numbers.

withy: a willow or willow wand; withy-man: a figure woven from such wands

The Hall of Tyr

I would like to thank Thomas Gahm of Gotland for his generous help with Old Gutnish, the dialect of Old Norse spoken on Gotland during the Viking Age.

To the three pair of eyes that first read this novel I offer my great thanks. First Readers Tom Blair, Jennifer Joyce, and Judy Moseley, your comments and encouragement place me in your debt.

About the Author

Octavia Randolph has long been fascinated with the development, dominance, and decline of the Anglo-Saxon peoples. The path of her research has included disciplines as varied as the study of Anglo-Saxon and Norse runes, and learning to spin with a drop spindle. Her interests have led to extensive on-site research in England, Denmark, Sweden, and Gotland. In addition to the Circle Saga, she is the author of the novella *The Tale of Melkorka*, taken from the Icelandic Sagas; the novella *Ride*, a retelling of the story of Lady Godiva, first published in Narrative Magazine; and *Light, Descending*, a biographical novel about the great John Ruskin. She has been awarded Artistic Fellowships at the Ingmar Bergman Estate on Fårö, Gotland; MacDowell Colony; Ledig House International; and Byrdcliffe.

She answers all fan mail and loves to stay in touch with her readers. Join her mailing list and read more on Anglo-Saxon and Viking life at www.octavia.net.

27103298R00264

Printed in Great Britain
by Amazon